C.S. QUINN

DARK STARS

THOMAS & MERCER

Published by Thomas & Mercer, Seattle

www.apub.com

Amazon, the Amazon logo, and Thomas & Mercer are trademarks of Amazon.com, Inc., or its affiliates.

ISBN-13: 9781503942110
ISBN-10: 1503942112

Cover design by Lisa Horton

Printed in the United States of America

DARK STARS

ALSO BY C.S. QUINN

THE THIEF TAKER SERIES

The Thief Taker

Fire Catcher

Death Magic

DARK STARS

London, October 1666, ONE month after the Great Fire

London is a city of burned-out buildings and smoking ash. In the smouldering backstreets, astrologists predict the future and alchemists conjure wonders. Traitors' heads line London Bridge, where witches sell potions and gamesters turn cards. The murky Thames washes ashore a daily tide of smuggler gangs and pirates.

England has traded her republic for a monarch of the blood. But London's wealth lies in sea trade, and with Dutch ships setting their sights on England, royal blood has become a dangerous currency.

Prologue

The old sailor leaned forward, his face glowing in lantern light.

'I tell you,' he said. 'It's the same murders all over again.' He adjusted his position slightly on the tarred plank deck. 'Nineteen years ago,' he continued, 'at Deptford. A young girl washed up. Her skin was missing, and her eyes were poached like a griddled fish. I'll never forget it,' he concluded. 'She'd been carved with constellations and such.'

'But why does he strike again now?' A young sailor leaned forward into the circle of lamplight, outsized canvas shirt gaping at his skinny chest.

'The arrangement of the stars, Sam,' said the old sailor, pointing to the night sky, 'is the same. All Hallows' Eve approaches. Halloween. The dead will rise.' The elder man paused for effect. 'The astrologers say there'll be an eclipse.'

There was a general hush as they all considered this. They all knew the power of eclipses.

The old sailor rubbed his rough chin, looking at Sam's rapt expression. 'You were press-ganged from Deptford?'

'Last week,' Sam replied. 'On my thirteenth birthday. Everyone there wonders about the murders,' he added. 'You seamen know more than landlubbers.'

Sam didn't want to admit that he stayed up late with the grizzled deckhands because the sounds of the huge ship at night gave him bad dreams and he missed his mother.

The old sailor took in Sam's boyish face and gave a slight nod of pity. He adjusted the lantern flame – the only light permitted after dark. The ship was a floating castle of tarred decks, waxed ropes and oiled sail. If the timber monolith caught aflame, the surface of the water was a long way down, and few could swim anyway.

'Think you the murderer seeks to fulfil the prophecy?' asked Sam. 'To find the All-Seeing Eye?'

A little shudder went around the circle. Every sailor had heard the tale of the mythic Eye.

For a moment the only sound was of the rum tankard gulped, passed and gulped again. The old tar took his turn, sucking his teeth noisily as he tipped back the bitter spirits.

He wiped his mouth. 'All I know is they were dark times before,' he said. 'Brother against brother. Civil war. When the old King knew he was beaten, he summoned a powerful sorcerer. A man who had travelled to the four corners of the earth, who had studied with the ancient scholars and learned the secrets of the gods themselves.' The sailor paused to let this sink in. 'The sorcerer laboured for the King in the depths of the palace. And strange things began happening on the river. Bodies washed up. Then after many months the sorcerer made the King a gift. An eye that gave the gift of Sight.' The sailor tapped his forehead. 'The power to predict the future.'

There was an intake of breath amongst the sailors. The rum tankard had paused in its passing now.

'Had I not seen its power for myself,' continued the sailor, 'I would not have thought such a thing possible. But I was aboard when the Eye discovered an enemy ship hidden at sea.'

'What happened to the Eye?' asked Sam, transfixed.

The old sailor smiled. 'The King ran mad and betrayed the sorcerer. Lost his head to Cromwell, and the Eye vanished. Though legend tells it this year it will be found, to rule or destroy the world.'

'The power of kings is restored,' pointed out another sailor. 'Cromwell is dead. Charles II is back on the throne. Our own mighty ship is named after his Queen Catherine.' He patted the deck affectionately.

Sam blinked. He wrinkled his nose. Was he imagining it, or did the air feel thicker? A waft of rank air rolled suddenly over them. Sam was sure of it now. Something was wrong.

'Do you smell that?' he said. 'I swear I caught a whiff of brimstone.' He eyed the dark deck fearfully, imagining ghosts and ghouls at sea.

Drink-addled sailors scratched their heads and sniffed the air. The smell was growing thicker. A few stood uncertainly. It was sharp, cloying. A stench to make your head hurt.

Then a cloud of smoke rolled lazily over the deck.

The sailors froze, rum tankard halfway through passing.

'Where does the smoke come from?' asked one, his voice tight.

Shouts rang out from below. The sailors were uncertain now. Panic rippled through them. An elaborately carved cabin door flew open. Their captain emerged, wig askew, his gold-frogged coat unbuttoned.

'Does a candle burn uncovered?' he demanded, peering towards the little clutch of men. 'There is smoke!'

One of the sailors was pointing out to sea. Stretched across the inky blackness was a mass of glowing embers, making strange lines and shapes on the waves.

Sam was on his feet. The sharp stench was burning his eyes, making it hard to think.

The older sailor grabbed him by the arm. 'It's a hellburner,' he said, steadying them both against the swell.

Pure fear tunnelled through the younger sailor. He'd heard of fireships. They were terrible weapons that the Dutch sent to destroy their enemy – flaming vessels that crashed into their targets and set all alight.

'The hellburner means to hook on to our rigging!' shouted the old sailor. 'We must turn about.'

Sam could make out the shape of the fireship now. A flaming monster coming fast out of the dark with an enormous metal hook jutting from her prow.

The ear-splitting sound of breaking wood erupted all around. The fireship's curved hook thrust aboard with enough force to split the wooden side of the deck.

The captain, standing nearest the water, took the full brunt to his side. The arc of metal tore through his ribcage, leaving a gaping hole. He raised his hand, drenched in scarlet blood, then staggered back and collapsed.

The fireship's hooked prow tunnelled relentlessly forward, tangling tight in their mass of rigging. Blinding smoke billowed inwards.

Sheer terror hit the deck. Sailors were pouring out from their hammocks, sleep-slack faces trying to understand the horror on deck. Half-dressed men were screaming for water butts and vinegar to douse the fire.

'What should we do?' managed Sam, coughing deep to his stomach.

'We must cut our ship free, or we'll all burn to death.'

The old sailor guided them blindly towards the rigging. Sam could make out part of the great hook, caught deep in the mesh of webbed rope. It was thick with sailors sawing at the tough rigging.

The air crackled. Then a demonic roar sent a plume of red flames racing upwards and an explosion hit. The force threw Sam backwards. He felt a blow to his midriff and saw a dismembered torso had knocked him to the deck.

Sam felt rough hands pulling him up. Their waxed-canvas sails were aflame now. The tarred deck was spotted in green fire. Attempts to dislodge their attacker were abandoned as the crew ran for their lives.

'She'll burn through in moments,' gasped the old sailor, drawing Sam to the side of the ship. 'Do you swim?'

Sam shook his head, noticing the old man had a great bloody gash from hairline to chin. Torrents of screaming men were hurling themselves into the dark waters.

'The Devil and the deep blue sea,' said the old sailor, looking down.

Sam swallowed. Tears filled his eyes.

'You've family back in Deptford?' asked the old sailor.

He nodded.

'You'll see them on the other side,' comforted the old man. 'Don't look down.'

Below them the cold water was scattered with drowning sailors.

Sam could feel the white heat of the burning ship behind him. There was a juddering beneath their feet.

'The munitions will catch soon,' said the old sailor. He squeezed the younger man's arm. 'I won't let you go, boy.'

Flames dived down below deck, exploding barrels of gunpowder and oil, throwing the huge vessel from side to side. The body of her dead captain slid across the deck, smashing into the masthead.

Sam closed his eyes and jumped, holding tight to the old sailor. They hit the water together, just as the munitions deck blew out the side of the ship.

The *Queen Catherine* lurched, her anchors tearing from the seabed. Then the weight pulled her back and she began to sink fast.

As the ocean drew him down, Sam saw a shower of gold leaf fall softly around. The ship's gilding was flaking away, raining down on to the drowning men. Sam cast around for the old sailor but could only see dying men. He fixed his gaze on the prow, with its bright bust of Queen Catherine. The ship tilted up and began to descend, the figurehead's red mouth smiling.

Sam gulped cold water and felt himself sinking. He watched black ocean close over the Queen's dark hair, saw her flames circle and die. Then the current pulled the last strength from his legs and he sunk down with her.

Chapter 1

Charlie took a seat in the chophouse, the smell of grilled meat filling the air. He assessed his surroundings. Men sat at tables, talking, reading, chewing meat, swigging beer and punch. With his back to the narrow window, Charlie could almost forget he was in a debtors' prison.

A woman in a low-cut dress bearing two large jugs arrived at his side.

'Ale or punch?' she demanded.

'Ale,' said Charlie. He'd noticed a telltale mineral tidemark on the punch jug where lead had been added to disguise rancid wine.

'Coin or tab?' she asked as Charlie held out his tankard to be filled. He could tell she was sizing him up. Charlie's battered long gentleman's coat had weathered plague and fire in the last few years. Several tiny buttons running down the expensive brown leather were missing, and the large cuffs were scuffed. He made an unlikely visitor to the aristocratic section of a debtors' prison. Charlie looked more like a visitor to the commoners' side, where starving debtors begged for scraps.

'Coin,' said Charlie firmly, pushing money into her hand. 'I'm a thief taker. Here on business.' He was nervous of being confused with the incarcerated debtors, who ran weekly tabs.

The woman leant back for a moment, considering him. 'I didn't think many thief takers still did business,' she said, 'since Charlie Tuesday is so famed for catching villains.'

'I am Charlie Tuesday.'

The woman's eyes widened. She scrutinised Charlie's face, taking in the kink where his nose had been broken and the slight scar to his upper lip. Her eyes skimmed Charlie's dark blond hair, then dropped to his patched breeches, hidden to the knee beneath the coat, and his toughened bare feet.

'Always wondered what you looked like,' she said finally, clearly expecting him to have been better dressed. 'You are handsome I suppose, in your own way. Is it true you solve crimes for poor folk?'

'When I can afford to,' said Charlie gruffly. Unlike most thief takers, he undertook cases for food and favours if he felt the victims deserving. And the petty criminals he caught often mysteriously escaped the noose once property was returned.

'Finding out villains for a profit must be a hard business,' decided the woman. Her eyes settled on the key at his neck. 'I heard you saved that woman from hanging. And your key can open any lock in the city.'

Charlie lifted the double-sided key. 'I've saved many women from hanging,' he said, 'but this is only a trinket. Something I was orphaned with.'

His eyes settled on the astrology almanacs scattered around the room. They made predictions for the coming months based on the stars.

Charlie pointed to the printed booklets held by several prisoners. He'd been wondering about them since he arrived.

'They follow the astrologers' prophecies here?' he asked.

'Oh yes,' the woman nodded. 'It's a revelation, isn't it? Ishmael Boney killing them poor folk what washed up at Dead Man's Curve. His almanacs are fought over.'

'He's been found guilty?' Charlie was surprised.

'Vanished,' said the woman with some satisfaction. 'After the bodies were dragged from Dead Man's Curve, all marked like constellations in the heavens. But we all know it was him, don't we? The markings on those poor dead girls were drawn in his almanac.

'It's a shame,' opined the woman. 'Ishmael was a phenomenon before he turned dark. The Moorish astrologer seemed to know all,' she said reverently. 'My brother consulted him on whether to marry, and he and his wife have barely a cross word. Except for that business with the baker's girl and the sacking,' she reflected.

As the woman sashayed away, Charlie eyed the other customers, assuring himself his man was not yet here. Most of the men eating and drinking Charlie judged to be prisoners, though he could identify the odd lawyer or devoted wife.

There was a flash of red and Charlie breathed a sigh of relief to see Lily. She was perennially unreliable, and like Charlie, Lily had a phobia of London prisons – though hers came from experience, whilst his was born of caution. Charlie prided himself on having never been caught.

Heads turned as Lily passed the tables. Her toffee-coloured skin, dark eyes and jangle of talismans at neck and fingers marked her out as a gypsy. But this wasn't the main reason men looked.

Charlie noticed with amusement the expressions of confusion as Lily seated herself next to him. He could see people wondering how a mere thief taker – albeit London's best – had secured the company of a girl who looked like one of King Charles's mistresses. Whilst Charlie had enough luck with women to know he wasn't bad-looking, he was nothing to Lily's captivating beauty. Unbeknown to everyone in the prison, she was a spy for King Charles. But her allegiances were mainly to herself, and Charlie doubted her loyalty went much beyond pay.

They'd had a brief liaison the last time they'd worked together, but Lily seemed to have forgotten all about it. Now Charlie wasn't sure if they were colleagues, relying on one another's talents to seek treasure, or something more. He wasn't even sure what to hope for.

'The debtors' prison is not so terrible,' Lily remarked, settling her red skirts next to Charlie.

He hid a smile. Lily's gypsy upbringing made her a formidable knife thrower. And she'd sat in a way that suggested she'd concealed the blades beneath her dress from the prison guard.

'This is the nobles' side,' said Charlie. 'Most only wait for family to bail them out. You should see the common part,' he added darkly.

Charlie noticed a familiar pamphlet tucked in Lily's belt. 'Not you too,' he said, eyeing the horoscope almanac.

'It's the only thing Londoners talk of,' said Lily, ignoring his tone. 'The city's most famed astrologer turns to murder. Do you think Boney did it?'

'Most likely a rival astrologer,' said Charlie. 'People wouldn't think Ishmael guilty if he wasn't Moorish. If you were a murderer, why would you publish pictures of your victim's mutilations? Take the ale,' he added as the woman approached with the jugs.

Lily pointed for beer, watching as the woman filled her tankard. 'Right to the top,' she said as the beer stopped a fraction from the rim of her cup.

The woman gave an ill-natured grunt and splashed more beer. Lily passed her coins.

'My money is as clean as yours,' she said sharply as the woman examined the pennies, glaring pointedly at Lily's gypsy talismans.

'You brought the ring?' asked Charlie as the woman retreated.

Lily nodded. She waved a small hand, causing charms and gold bracelets to jangle at her wrist. Amidst the cheap rings decorating her fingers a ruby sparkled.

'You have yours?' she asked.

Charlie nodded, patting the top of his long buttoned coat.

'We should be careful who sees us here,' said Lily, casting her dark eyes around the prison.

'Because you stole your ring?' Charlie sometimes couldn't help but bait Lily on her dubious ethics.

'I retrieved it on behalf of the Crown,' said Lily defensively.

'You pickpocketed it from a drunk man after convincing him you were a prostitute.'

'I'm a spy,' said Lily with a dismissive wave of her ringed fingers. 'Such means are necessary in the King's service. Besides,' she added, lowering her voice, 'just because you found your ring in your dead mother's possessions means nothing. She might have thieved it for all you know.'

Charlie couldn't dispute the truth of this. His mother had been murdered when he was a small boy, and he barely remembered her. He and Lily had unearthed a bundle of Sally Oakley's possessions from the household where she had worked as a maid – mostly meagre servant things, along with a mysteriously expensive ruby ring.

'You're certain your spymaster won't miss the ring he sent you to steal?' Charlie countered.

Lily made an exasperated noise. 'Do you want to uncover the treasure or don't you?'

'We don't even know if there is treasure,' Charlie pointed out reasonably.

'I have a feeling for such things,' said Lily. 'These rings unlock something important. Your thief taker mind cannot help but wonder what.'

Charlie had to concede it was a tantalising mystery. Two months ago, during the Great Fire, Lily had been dispatched as a royal spy to retrieve a matching ring to his mother's.

'I do wonder,' admitted Charlie. 'My brother and I were orphaned with no family. Perhaps there is more to our past than we realised. But,' he added, his brown eyes on hers, 'I also suspect you're making a greater violation of your spying obligations than you pretend.'

Until she'd met Charlie, Lily had never lost a card game. It had taken him a while to see any tell in her expression. And the glimmer in Lily's face now told Charlie he'd hit the mark.

'What does it matter?' she said, batting her long eyelashes and moving a little closer. 'You need me.' She held up her ringed finger. 'You need both rings to solve the mystery. And I'm the only woman in this city you can't charm this clue from.'

Lily brought her face almost to his and laid a seductive hand on his chest. Then she drew back, holding up Charlie's ring, pickpocketed from his coat.

'Yet I can take your ring,' she concluded, 'anytime I choose.'

Charlie smiled. 'You need me too,' he pointed out. 'I know how London's underbelly works. And I keep a close network of friends who owe me favours. You leave only betrayed men and angry women in your wake. And what makes you think,' he added, 'I can't take your ring when I choose?'

Charlie held up Lily's ring, slid from her hand whilst she'd been delving in his coat. Lily gave an annoyed gasp and stared at her empty finger.

'You forget I'm a better pickpocket than you,' he grinned.

Lily made to snatch her ring back. Charlie drew it away and put his hand out. She pushed his ring begrudgingly back in his palm, and he dropped hers back on the table. Lily pushed it on to her finger.

'I hope your jewellery man is as good as you say,' said Lily, leaning down to sip from her overfull tankard. She eyed a plate of griddled meat as it passed. 'Is he here yet?'

Charlie was about to shake his head. Then the door opened and a tall silver-haired man entered the debtors' prison chophouse. He had a magnifying lens mounted above his left eye that gave him the appearance of a friendly Cyclops.

'There,' said Charlie, pointing.

'He's a prisoner?' said Lily uncertainly, taking in the man's strange hotchpotch of fashionable clothing.

'Riley was gaoled as a debtor after the war, when the jewel trade turned sour,' explained Charlie. 'He began valuing and selling on jewels for other prisoners. Now he stays by choice. If anyone will know the history of two old rings, it's him.'

Lily nodded, her expression evaluating.

Charlie stood. 'Riley!'

'Charlie Tuesday,' said Riley, drawing closer and enclosing Charlie's hands in his large ringed fingers.

Before Charlie could reply Riley signalled to the waiting woman.

'Add a splash of the other,' Riley said with a wink as the woman filled his tankard from the punch jug, leaning low to expose another inch of deep cleavage. She produced a glass bottle of plum-hued liquid from her skirts and added a generous slug.

Riley turned to his visitors. 'What do you think of my new coat?' he asked, turning the red velvet sleeves for Charlie to inspect. 'I won it from a debtor,' he explained, seeing Lily's gaze travel over his mis-matched clothes. He adjusted his overtight striped silk breeches, which exposed six inches of hairy unstockinged thigh.

'Shall we eat?' asked Riley. 'The mutton is excellent.'

Charlie nodded the weary approval of a man who wasn't particu-larly hungry but would be footing the bill. Dishes were ordered and the woman bustled away.

Riley settled back comfortably, bringing out a long white clay pipe and packing it with leaf tobacco. He adjusted the magnifying lens strung around his forehead like a third eye, reached for a candle and lit his pipe.

'Back for another jewel thief?' Riley asked, puffing contentedly.

Charlie shook his head and reached into his coat.

'Something else,' he said, bringing out the ruby ring. 'Wondered if you might take a look at it.'

Riley eyed the jewel in Charlie's hand and sent up a cloud of pipe smoke.

'Times are hard,' he said. 'I'd need to ask for something for the information.'

7

Riley held his hands up at Charlie's expression. 'I know you've done me a few good turns . . .' he began, toying with his magnifying lens.

'I saved your wife from Newgate,' said Charlie indignantly.

'All the same, charity has to end somewhere,' said Riley, business-like. He took a deep draw on his pipe. 'And she's not my wife any more,' he added, blowing out a stream of smoke regretfully.

Charlie hesitated. Riley was the best. They both knew it.

Two steaming plates of griddled chops, a haunch of mutton and a dish of pickled carrots were dropped unceremoniously in front of them.

Riley's eyes widened hungrily. He slid a plate closer and began eating. Lily took out her knife, stabbed the nearest chop and gnawed at the edge. After a moment Charlie cut himself some meat and chewed. It was good. He was hungrier than he realised – a side effect of growing up in a London orphan house.

'What price did you have in mind?' Charlie asked Riley, cutting another mouthful of pork chop.

'My usual price for a valuation is a shilling,' said Riley between swallows of mutton shoulder.

'By my reckoning,' said Charlie, 'I've sent five shillings of new business your way this year.' He met Riley's eyes. 'You're the best jewellery man,' he concluded, 'but not everyone knows it.'

Riley took in Charlie's expression. 'Show it to me then,' he grumbled, defeated. 'But if anyone asks, you paid a shilling.'

Charlie slid him the ring. Riley's eyes dropped to the jewellery. He picked it up and looked at it for a long time.

'Where did you get it?' he said finally.

Charlie hesitated. 'It was my mother's,' he said. 'I found it amongst some old things of hers.'

'Where exactly were these things?'

Riley's fingers were clutching the ring tight. Charlie had a sudden compulsion to grab it back.

'She was a . . . servant in a household,' said Charlie cautiously. 'She left a bundle with the master of the house. They were lost for a long time. Then the master died and her things came to me.'

Charlie didn't add that Master Blackstone had murdered his mother. That the key at his neck unlocked a chest of dangerous papers. Papers he and Lily had managed to discover during the Great Fire.

Riley brought down the magnifying lens, leaving a red ring on his forehead. The glass made his left eye loom huge. He turned the ring carefully, examining the stone. His finger slid around the edge of the ring casing.

'Had you noticed this?' he asked. 'This marking?'

He tapped a familiar symbol. Two wavy lines to represent water.

Charlie glanced and nodded. 'It's an astrological symbol,' he said. 'For Aquarius.'

Riley nodded his confirmation. 'Common enough to mark a sun sign on jewellery,' he said. His face crinkled. 'Perhaps your father was a sailor?'

'My father died at sea when I was a baby,' said Charlie. 'He could have been a sailor. I don't remember.'

As an orphan, Charlie had scant details of his family. He had no memory of ever meeting his father and barely recollected his mother.

Riley peered deep into the ruby. 'Peculiar,' he muttered. 'Most peculiar.'

After a moment he set the ring on the table. Charlie picked it up.

'It's a very unusual item,' said Riley. 'I've only ever seen one other like it.'

Charlie and Lily waited patiently.

'I can't be certain,' continued Riley, 'but to my best understanding it's a Royalist codebreaker ring. But it's very strange you should come to me with it now.'

'Why?' asked Charlie.

'Because the last time I saw one of these rings . . .' Riley paused. 'At that time bodies marked with constellations had washed up at Deptford,' he continued. 'Exactly nineteen years ago.'

9

Chapter 2

The Earl of Amesbury's thick military cloak fanned behind him as he strode down to the dungeon. The naval fort was old and dilapidated, and the general's well-worn leather boots crossed cracks in the stone floor.

'How does His Majesty?' asked the naval officer nervously.

Men of rank rarely knew how to take Amesbury. He'd switched sides twice during the Civil War and should have been condemned as a traitor. But his excellence in military strategy made him too valuable to execute.

'The King is lovesick,' said Amesbury bluntly. 'He is chasing a fifteen-year-old lady-in-waiting when he should be looking to naval business.'

Amesbury was approaching fifty, his thick, dark hair greying and his tall frame now large rather than muscular. But he retained the stature and self-assurance of a man who had never lost a battle on sea or land. He'd worn the same boiled-leather military clothes and thick sash of office for as long as anyone could remember.

'You're sure it's him?' Amesbury demanded. 'Janus? The fireship pilot who sunk the *Queen Catherine*?'

'He's confessed his name is Janus,' said the naval officer. 'But he doesn't speak English.'

'Doesn't or won't?'

The naval officer frowned. 'He only says two words of English. Your name, and something we don't understand. We think he's saying "the Eye".'

'He requests me by name?' asked Amesbury.

The officer nodded. 'Other than that, he's told us nothing. Not even after I showed him the instruments.'

'I used to speak good Dutch,' said Amesbury. 'Perhaps it will suffice. How were our losses at sea?'

'Bad,' admitted the officer, glancing back at Amesbury's bear-like bulk. 'They attacked in the dead of night.'

'Not much defence could have been made,' grunted Amesbury. 'Not once a fireship is so close. It took some skill to launch at night.' Amesbury assessed the crumbling corridors of the old naval fort. 'Better we take Janus to a more secure place,' he added, slapping his hand on a rotting door. 'Repairs should have been made here. The fort is as loose as Barbara Castlemaine's wedding vows.' Amesbury shook his head. 'Plague and fire have bankrupted us. The Dutch mean a full-scale invasion – and soon. Those Dutch hellburners,' he swore quietly, 'will be the end of us.'

'Fireships have no place in honourable warfare,' agreed the naval officer loyally. 'They're a Devil's trick.'

Amesbury raised an eyebrow. 'Warfare isn't an honourable business,' he said. 'We'd use fireships if we could. But the Dutch have the best pilot. Janus,' he added, smiling, 'named from the two-faced Roman god. It makes him sound mythical.'

They'd reached the door of the fort strongroom. The naval man inserted a thick key and turned the rusty lock with difficulty. He stepped back to let Amesbury go first.

The old general quelled a start of surprise. The mention of the Eye had filled him with strange memories and secret fears. He didn't know who might come asking, nineteen years later. But he wasn't expecting the man who sat in front of him.

Chapter 3

In the debtors' prison a song had started up. The chophouse was awash with spilled punch and cheers.

Amongst the chaos, Charlie and Lily were hanging on Riley's every word.

'The last time I saw a ring like this,' the old jeweller was explaining, 'was during the Civil War. People were all talk of the dead girls washing up at Deptford tide, just like now.'

'So where did you see this ring?' asked Charlie.

'It was just a picture I saw,' said Riley. 'A kind of joke that went around the jewellers. We thought them too intricate, too difficult to be made.' He hesitated. 'The rumour was the King's astrologer made the rings. A man named Thorne.'

'What happened to Thorne?' asked Charlie.

'He was executed,' said Riley. 'By the old King.'

Riley gestured for the ring again and turned it wonderingly. 'What you have here is a codebreaker ring,' he explained. 'They're valuable.' He looked hard into the depths of the ruby.

Riley's eyes met the thief taker's, assessing the other man for a reaction. Instinctively Charlie's card-sharping skills set his face impassive.

'It was your mother's?' added Riley. 'You're sure?'

'Why do you ask?'

'Because I've never known these rings to be given to women,' said Riley. 'They were made during the war for elite Royalist spies.'

'How is it used to break codes?' asked Charlie.

Riley shook his head. 'I don't know.' He hesitated. 'And all the cryptographers from that time were executed by Cromwell.'

'Not all,' said Charlie. 'There's the Cipher.'

Riley's laugh sounded the futility of this observation.

'Who's the Cipher?' Lily looked to Charlie.

'Best codebreaker in England,' said Charlie. 'The only one who lived past Cromwell. His genius for codes kept him alive. But those high up keep him closely guarded. The Cipher's whereabouts is the best kept secret in London.'

'Clever as a fox and just as deadly,' interjected Riley. 'They say he's a ghost who can vanish at will. Lives in a Temple of Death.'

'I do know the rings come as a set,' added Riley helpfully, watching Lily's disappointed face. 'They were designed to be used together, in case a spy is discovered and his ring falls into the wrong hands. No single ring can break the code.'

A second ruby ring clattered on to the table. Lily had taken off her ring. Riley looked at her in surprise.

'We also have this one,' she explained.

The way Riley picked up the second ring told Charlie they were extremely valuable. And perhaps not just for the jewels inside.

'The same,' he breathed after a moment. 'Old stone. They don't turn gems like this any more. Not for a long time.' His eyes flicked up to Charlie. 'This one is engraved with the sign for Leo. The royal sign,' he added. 'A lion.'

Riley began turning the ring delicately, touching different parts on the inside band.

'Why are these rings so hard to make?' asked Charlie.

13

Riley held the two rings together. 'To make something so small, so intricate,' he said.

The woman arrived at the table. 'Shall I take the leavings?' she asked, eyeing the leftover scraps of meat. They'd all stopped eating.

'The leftovers will be sent to the poor side?' asked Charlie, whose thoughts had lingered on the starving common debtors since entering the prison.

The woman gave a bored nod and began clearing. Charlie met her eye.

'Truly?' he asked, knowing how corrupt the Marshalsea prison was. Judge Walters had recently taken it over. His gruesome convictions had earned him the nickname 'the Bloody Judge', and his lack of charity to the poor was legendary.

Her expression changed and she leaned closer. 'If you really mean them to have it,' she said, lowering her voice, 'best you take it yourself. Judge Walters pays no mind to the commoners. Things go missing,' she added, 'on the way to the poor side.'

Charlie took out his handkerchief to wrap the scraps of food.

Riley gave a low gasp of excitement. He'd sprung a catch on the side of the ring. Charlie and Lily watched in amazement. A tiny hook now stuck from the side of the jewellery.

'Well hidden. Lovely workings,' said Riley in acknowledgement of their amazement. He picked up the first ring. 'They fit together.'

Riley examined Charlie's ring and sprung a second hidden catch. Then before their eyes he pushed the two rings together. They fitted seamlessly with a click, the two rubies set next to one another.

'Beautiful,' breathed Riley. 'Such craftsmanship.'

Lily took the conjoined rings into her own small hands. She turned them this way and that.

'They're not complete,' she said.

Charlie looked up at Riley, disappointment growing fast after the sudden hope. 'It's not just two you need?'

Riley shook his head. 'I think four,' he said, taking the conjoined rings back. 'Two more would fit here and here. The rubies would make the shape of a cross,' he concluded, 'and the gold bands would hang underneath.'

Riley took a pull on his pipe. 'Do you have a code for the rings to solve?' he asked. 'Any papers or letters found with the ring?'

Charlie shook his head. His mother's bundle had held only simple maid's possessions.

'There was a . . . a kind of story,' continued Riley carefully, reading the despondency in their expressions, 'told amongst jewellery men shortly after the war. I don't know how much truth is in it,' he added, sucking his pipe. 'But it was said a set of special rubies were set as codebreakers after the old King was beheaded. The rumour was they unlocked something old. Something powerful.'

'Treasure?' suggested Lily hopefully.

'The stories were different. Some said treasure. Some said a weapon. But mostly people said they led to an All-Seeing Eye.' Riley gave an uneasy laugh. 'You hear sailor's tales about it mostly. This year's eclipse is said to be when the Eye will be revealed.'

Lily's hand dropped thoughtfully to her almanac.

'Of course,' added Riley, adjusting his magnifying lens, 'I assumed the Eye was just a story. But that was before I'd seen these rings.'

Chapter 4

'I told you,' said Lily jubilantly as they left the close air of the debtors' prison. 'I told you the rings uncovered something important.' They walked out on to The Borough. Along St Oleff's Street prostitutes lounged against mouldering buildings, lifting their skirts when a likely prospect passed.

Clustered on every corner were astrological almanac sellers, shouting their wares. With All Hallows' Eve days away, stargazing and prophecy had risen to fever pitch in London. Stalls had been hastily erected to sell talismans and lucky charms to protect against a forecast eclipse.

'Who would have thought the rings fitted together?' continued Lily, buoyed into unusual cheer by the discovery. She reached into her red silk dress to take out the ring.

Charlie stopped her, eyeing a nearby coach house heaving with degenerate drinkers.

'Not here,' he said. 'If you take out a ruby this side of the river, we're liable to end up floating in the Thames.'

Charlie's eyes settled on a grating in the wall, from which emaciated debtor hands waved. 'It might just be a story,' he added, deliberately casual as he took out the parcel of scraps from the chophouse. He didn't want to admit it to Lily, but Charlie had the stirrings of excitement he always had before a big mystery began to open.

He began passing food, settling larger pieces on the smallest hands.

Lily thought for a moment. 'Riley said the rings were very fine,' she said. 'Could we discover more from other jewellery makers? Surely Thorne would have had to buy tools and jewels from someone.'

'Cromwell's reign wasn't a time for fine jewellery,' said Charlie. 'The best men fled to Europe or changed profession. We were lucky Riley lasted here.'

'Do you think the rings have something to do with the bodies at Deptford?' asked Lily.

'They both bear astrological symbols,' said Charlie, remembering what he'd heard about the murders.

'Let's go over what we know,' he decided. 'My ring,' he continued, 'was amongst my dead mother's possessions. Riley told us the rings weren't given to women. So most likely it belonged to my father.'

Lily nodded at the logic of this. 'Your father was killed at sea,' she reasoned, 'but if he knew something of all this, he must have been an important man. You could have some great fortune awaiting you. Lands.'

'I've no interest in great fortune,' said Charlie. 'Only to know if I've any family living. The ring was with my mother's belongings. Perhaps it's some clue to my family story.'

A sudden pain seared through him. His brother, Rowan, had now been missing for a year and a half. Charlie had never given up hope, but some days were more difficult than others. He'd always suspected his older brother knew more about their mysterious past than he let on. They'd been orphaned together after their mother's murder, with only Charlie's key as a clue to their past.

'You still hope to find your brother?' Lily's face bore pity for his misplaced optimism.

'You don't know Rowan,' said Charlie. 'He's irresponsible and inconsiderate. But he's good deep down. He could easily be hiding from a bad debt with a long-lost relative.'

'Why would your brother know of a relative that you don't?'

Charlie's forehead creased. He rubbed the scar on his lip.

'He was older than me when we were orphaned,' Charlie explained. 'I think Rowan might remember things . . . perhaps dark things he wants to forget about. He didn't speak for a year in the orphan home. But perhaps he's overcome some demons and it's led him to some part of our past I don't know about.'

'I thought your brother was always in some kind of trouble,' said Lily.

'He is,' agreed Charlie. 'But Rowan and I look out for one another. Always have.'

Lily maintained the tactful silence of someone for whom the other's false belief is to their advantage.

'He might be dead of plague,' admitted Charlie finally. 'Dead in some commoner's grave. He might not.'

Lily looked away with an expression that Charlie was all too familiar with. Everyone knew what it meant to vanish during plague time. Charlie was the only person in London who chose to believe Rowan was still alive.

'The bodies at Deptford,' Charlie decided. 'You could be right. There might be something in that.'

'But they already know who the killer is,' said Lily. 'Ishmael Boney.'

'London's most revered astrologer incriminates himself in his own almanac?' said Charlie. 'It seems a foolish act for such a famously clever man.'

'Not if he's turned to dark ways,' said Lily. 'Perhaps he's in league with the Devil. Taken leave of his senses.'

'Maybe,' said Charlie. 'But Ishmael has become phenomenally successful since his predictions on fire and plague. If I were selling a thousand almanacs a month, I'd have no cause for dark arts. I think it's worth a visit to Dead Man's Curve.'

He hesitated. Something had caught his attention. A face in the teeming streets of Southwark was paying them just a little too much notice.

'What is it?' Lily whispered.

'Maybe nothing,' said Charlie. 'I have a bad feeling someone is following us.'

'Someone overheard us?' suggested Lily. 'In the Marshalsea?'

'Perhaps,' said Charlie. 'The prison is stuffed to the gills with pirates and smugglers. The Bloody Judge keeps spies inside. And he doesn't like me.'

Lily rolled her eyes. 'You've made an enemy of the most brutal judge in the city?'

'We don't share the same views on what should be a hanging offence,' said Charlie.

'Maybe someone there saw us showing Riley the rings,' said Lily.

Charlie caught something in her tone. 'Or some other reason,' he said, looking carefully at her face. 'You're hiding something. I know treasure isn't your only interest, so try again.'

Lily looked away, twisting the ring on her finger. 'Very well,' she conceded. 'The Bloody Judge is looking for the Eye. He was the drunk man I stole the ring from him.' She glared a challenge at Charlie.

'So we likely have the Bloody Judge on our tail?' Charlie surmised, not hiding his outrage. 'You've made me a wanted man.'

He let out a deep sigh of frustration. Nothing with Lily was ever straightforward.

'We'll switch back on London Bridge,' he said, 'and lose them in the crowds. Then we'll walk back to Dead Man's Curve. And on the way,' he concluded with a threatening glare, 'you'd better tell me the whole truth about how you came by your ring.'

Chapter 5

In the old fort, Amesbury regarded his prisoner. The man seemed to be dressed in a sort of disguise, with a black handkerchief pulled over the bottom half of his face and tricorn hat brought so low, his eyes were in complete shadow.

He reminded Amesbury of an English highwayman, with high leather boots and long dark cloak, and his demeanour, considering his circumstances, seemed impressively calm.

'Take off his mask,' said Amesbury.

The officer stepped forward to remove the mask, but the prisoner held up a gloved hand.

'If you want to know the Dutch plans,' he said, 'I stay masked.'

Amesbury hesitated, translating the Dutch.

'I'll decide when I hear what you have to say,' he agreed begrudgingly, speaking slowly as the Dutch language came back to him. 'You are Janus?' he affirmed. 'The fireship pilot who flamed the *Queen Catherine*?'

The man gave the smallest of nods. 'You are the Earl of Amesbury,' he confirmed. 'The turncoat?'

Amesbury smiled at the description and nodded.

'Then I must speak with you alone,' said Janus.

Amesbury considered the request. Then he signalled the officer should leave. As his colleague departed, Amesbury removed a flask of wine from his coat, filled a tankard for Janus and passed it across. Janus took the cup with a nod of thanks. Amesbury swigged from the flask cradled in his enormous hands.

'In the last few months you've destroyed some of our finest ships,' he said. 'You got a flaming ship attacked in the dark. Reports from our men say you're the best fireship pilot they've ever seen.'

The prisoner acknowledged the compliment with a slight smile.

'So my first question,' said Amesbury carefully, 'is how much to make you work for us?'

Janus's mask rose slightly with his eyebrows beneath it. 'You offer me money to fight for the English?'

Amesbury nodded.

Janus considered. 'You don't have enough,' he said finally.

Amesbury swigged from the flask. The strong wine was helping his Dutch speaking skills.

'What makes you think that?' he replied.

'King Charles doesn't have enough money to pay his sailors,' said Janus. 'I should know. Enough of your men defect to Dutch ranks for pay.'

Amesbury acknowledged the truth of this.

'Money would be found,' he said shortly.

Janus sat back. 'And what if I don't want money?' he said. 'What if I want something else?'

'Jewels?' suggested Amesbury warily. 'Gold?' He thought he knew what was coming.

Janus shook his head. 'I want a ruby ring,' he said.

In the gloom of the small prison cell, Amesbury hoped his surprise didn't show. If Janus knew about the rings . . . Was it possible he was looking for the Eye?

But Thorne was dead. The rings had been lost long ago. Amesbury remembered the last time he'd seen the astrologer, walking to his death.

Thorne's thick dark hair had waved in the breeze as he approached the executioner's block. He tucked it behind his ears in a nervous gesture, but his face gave no sign of fear. His expression suggested he was working through a complicated calculation in his mind. Thorne was tall and slight. His long limbs had a scarecrow quality that was softened by his expensive appearance but never quite dispelled. The silk stockings were bunched and awkward, his shoe buckles slightly askew and snowy lace collar too large for his neck.

Thorne was always moving, Amesbury noticed, drumming his fingers, pulling at his large cuffs. As though his genius couldn't be contained in a normal body. Even taking his last steps, Thorne's wiry frame pulsed with pensive energy. But his great mind was soon to be stilled forever.

What a great loss, *Amesbury thought.* What a great, great loss.

He realised with a start that Janus was looking at him keenly.

Janus smiled. 'I've been told the rings lead to the Eye,' he said.

Amesbury shrugged his great shoulders. 'Only stories. Each of the four ring bearers is long dead,' he lied. 'The rings are most likely melted down, the jewels traded. The Eye is lost.'

'Then you can't give me what I want,' said Janus, his jaw tightening.

Amesbury gave a weary sigh. 'You're our captive,' he said bluntly. 'Your choices are few. Let me outline them for you. Join us for gold, or be hanged as the enemy.'

Janus looked amused. 'I always heard of you as a clever man,' he said. 'Do you really think the Dutch will let me fall into your clutches so easily?'

As he spoke, he drummed a quick little tattoo on the wall of the cell with the ring on his index finger.

'And do you think,' Janus continued, 'I am your prisoner by chance?'

It only took a split second for Amesbury to realise he would react too slowly. The cell door was flung aside, and facing him were two men dressed in Dutch clothes. Each held a heavy flintlock gun pointed squarely into the cell.

Janus stood and straightened his cloak, still holding the tankard of wine.

'It was a great pleasure,' he said with a short bow. 'I'll be sure your enemy knows you as a general of honour.'

'It's not what my countrymen know me as,' retorted Amesbury gruffly.

Janus and the men exited the cell, closing Amesbury in behind them. The general heard the door being bolted from outside. Sighing, he picked up the remainder of the wine and thoughtfully awaited rescue.

Janus knows of the Eye . . .

The more he considered it, the more he thought Janus's eyes above the mask had been familiar. Had he met him before? Long ago? Before the war? His fingers tightened around his cup. He'd underestimated his opponent. And it might cost England dear.

Chapter 6

The way to the deserted palace was overgrown with thorns and creepers.

Betty followed Janus through the broken door. She thought he was a kind man. He'd set her free from the Marshalsea prison and given her wine.

She hiccupped, staggered, then righted herself. As they emerged into the ransacked chamber, Betty stopped and stared. It was a palace. A forgotten palace. The room was large and grand, with what had once been a tiled floor. The remains of an imposing staircase stood wrecked and broken. Windows were shattered, gilt ripped from the walls and beams torn away for firewood.

There was a flapping sound up ahead, and Betty scratched her scabbed arms nervously.

'What's that noise?' she asked.

'Only crows,' said Janus. 'They've made parts of it their home.'

They moved further inside, through to an adjoining room, equally grand, but now with signs of occupancy. Smoking embers, a palette bed.

'You live here?' she said after a moment. 'It must have once been magnificent.'

'I was once apprenticed near here,' said Janus. 'The King wants to rebuild but has no funds.'

Two large black crows were tussling over a sinewy scrap of bone. Betty noticed a blanket strung across a far corner, concealing something. She hoped wine. Then her eyes settled hungrily on a small barrel sat by the plain sleeping arrangements.

Betty stared at it. Her wine-induced stupor was beginning to slip away. She didn't like this room so much. It smelled like a butcher's shop.

'I didn't realise fine folk were apprenticed,' Betty said, her eyes never leaving the barrel.

'My master was a great man,' said Janus. 'I loved him deeply,' he added, his eyes burning with a fierce animal intensity. 'Feared him too.'

He saw the direction of Betty's gaze and fetched wine. She held out her tankard and watched delightedly as he filled it.

'Masters can be cruel,' she agreed, drinking deeply. 'My brother was apprenticed to a carpenter. Came home with bleeding hands.'

'Thorne kept me confined in the dark,' said Janus, nursing his tankard thoughtfully. 'Punished me for the slightest transgression. But he taught me the power of the stars. I thought him a god.' He smiled slightly. 'Hard, merciless and all-powerful.'

Something flickered deep in his eyes, like a long-forgotten pain.

'Why did you free me from the prison?' she asked.

She was looking at the bed.

'I heard in the Marshalsea,' he said, 'about a commoner named Charlie Oakley.' Janus looked into the tankard. 'He is searching for something,' he continued. 'Something rightfully due to me, as a noble.'

'He must not find it?' deduced Betty.

Janus nodded slowly. 'His father, Tobias Oakley, was a traitor,' he added. 'All these years I was uncertain. Now I know. He left secrets to his son.'

Despite the heady effect of the wine, Betty found herself flinching at the hatred in Janus's face.

'You want me to kill this man?' she suggested. 'As I did the others? That's why you set me free.'

'I want you to help me uncover a lost object,' said Janus. His eyes sought the curtain in the corner, and Betty felt a swirl of unease in the pit of her stomach. 'An Eye,' he continued, touching his forehead. 'The Sight. A power to see as angels see.'

'Sorcery?' suggested Betty uncertainly.

'Some would call it that.' Janus drank thoughtfully. 'De Ryker will use the Eye to defeat the English.'

Betty blinked uncertainly. Had she heard him right?

'The Dutch pirate?' she asked.

Janus's hand was inside his coat now. He was drawing out a copper-handled knife.

'He is no pirate,' said Janus. 'If you saw De Ryker on deck, his tanned face surveying the sea, salt-stiffened captain's coat barely rippling in the strong breeze . . . You would understand his power,' he concluded.

'You talk treason,' she said, appalled.

Betty tried to move to standing, but Janus grabbed her wrist tightly and forced her back down.

'Let me go! You hurt me!' She twisted to free herself from his bruising grip.

The angry movement startled the tussling crows. One flapped upwards in an ungainly circle. It veered across the room and blundered into the mouldering curtain hanging in the corner.

Janus was on his feet as the ragged cloth fell.

Betty's whole body flashed cold with terror. The . . . *thing* behind the curtain. Arranged at its feet . . . Had they once been children?

Suddenly there was cold metal at her throat. She swallowed, feeling the blade pressed firmly. Janus was behind her, holding her tightly.

'You meet my master sooner than I intended,' he said.

Betty's eyes filled with panicked tears. Janus twisted her face, forcing her to look at the Thing.

It glared out, teeth bared savagely. What scared her most was the small boy, dangling upturned by an ankle in the Thing's terrible grip. The child's face was stricken in anguish, mouth poised in a silent scream.

'If you mean to kill me,' she managed, panting the words in her terror, 'why deliver me from the noose? I was condemned.'

'I mean to keep you from hell,' said Janus. His face was close to hers. 'The Romans believed,' he continued, 'that everyone's soul crossed the River Styx. Their crimes were tried. But redemption was always possible.'

Janus's free hand was drawing something out of his pocket. As his fingers emerged in front of her, Betty's eyes locked on the shining object.

'A silver coin,' continued Janus, 'is all you need to pay your way.'

He held the blade tighter at her neck, and Betty stood numbly as he pushed the coin between her lips.

'You are to be offered to the Thames,' he explained, an icy surety in his voice. 'You will not suffer. And your body will show me what I seek.'

Chapter 7

The approach to Dead Man's Curve was a solitary patch of water east of Deptford Docks. In contrast to the shipyard, it had only a few low buildings and was slick with ancient mud.

'Judge Walters has great investment in the slave trade,' Lily was explaining. 'I couldn't see a man like that find the Eye.'

'Why should you care about his slave business?'

'Gypsies,' said Lily quietly. 'Gypsies are enslaved and shipped abroad.'

'But that is no longer legal,' said Charlie. 'The new King made a law—'

'Which the Judge breaks for profit,' interrupted Lily. 'Though I can't make anyone believe me. I've heard Judge Walters's plans,' added Lily. 'He thinks the Eye will allow him to grow his slave business ten-fold. But if the Eye can find ships at sea,' she concluded, 'I could use it to prove the Judge's crime. Find his slave ships of gypsies and bring him to account.'

There was something deep in Lily's eyes when she talked about bringing the Judge to justice. A childlike terror. Charlie remembered her mother had been drowned for the crime of being a gypsy. Most probably by a man like the Judge.

Lily's eyes were burning. 'So now do you see?' she said. 'Do you see why the Judge cannot get to the Eye? If it's as powerful as the legends say . . .'

Charlie had a sudden image of a frightened little gypsy girl watching her mother die. He felt a lump rise in his throat.

'You should have told me your reason,' he said.

'It makes no difference,' she said stiffly. 'You have your own reasons for seeking out the Eye. Why should mine concern you?'

'That was why you bought the almanac,' said Charlie, realisation growing. 'You thought all along that the rings were linked to the eclipse.'

'Not for certain,' said Lily defensively. 'I heard things in Deptford taverns. Sailor stories.'

'Deptford taverns don't allow gypsies.'

'I've made a friend of a landlord's daughter.'

Charlie let his face signal his suspicion. 'I didn't realise you had friends. Don't tell me you're finally learning London ways?'

Lily dug her toe in the dirt in a curiously childish gesture. 'The Judge is not to be trusted. I'm sure of it. I tried to find Ishmael Boney, but he'd vanished.'

'You should have told me the truth,' said Charlie. 'The Judge is dangerous.'

'You wanted to discover your past,' she countered. 'Find your brother. You're known to the Bloody Judge in any case. I've hardly harmed your reputation.' Lily glanced behind her. 'And we've lost whoever was on our tail.' She paused. 'I've never been to this part of the river. Why is it so empty?'

She was looking at the scant bankside dwellings, now noticeably thinner on the ground.

'We near Dead Man's Curve,' explained Charlie. 'It's the part of the Thames where bodies collect. They drift downstream from the city. Mostly suicides,' he added, 'but you get murders too. The current swells on the curve and beaches them on the mud.'

'Only bodies collect?' said Lily. 'Surely anything going downstream would gather there.'

'Mudlarks get anything else,' said Charlie, pointing to the teenaged boys trawling the banks. 'There's not a stick of wood or a splinter of metal gets past them. They have anything of value before it passes the Tower, but they won't touch corpses.'

'They must have made a fine business after the fire,' observed Lily. 'Half the city was thrown into the river to be doused.'

'Many things sunk besides,' said Charlie, 'as people tried to escape with their goods by water. I imagine Father Thames has been generous these past few months.'

The river was thick with ships making their way to Custom House to pay tax before entering London.

'Captains fear a Dutch invasion,' observed Charlie, noting the ships piled with metal and timber, spices and tobacco. 'They come to sell their wares fast.'

'Or an apocalypse,' said Lily. 'All the astrologers say it comes.'

'Do you believe it?'

Lily thought for a moment. 'I think the same as everybody else,' she decided. 'The stars were put there by God for us to understand something of our future. But astrologers have not yet mastered the science.'

'And what do you hope your future holds?' It was the first time Charlie had come close to asking Lily about their relationship. Were they just treasure hunters together, or something more?

In answer she pointed to a large ship sailing out of London. Charlie followed her gaze.

'With the Eye,' Lily concluded, 'I'll buy my own ship and crew and find new lands. And I'll sink any slaving ships I see,' she added with a grim look in her eye.

This surprised Charlie. He'd always thought Lily meant to return to the country some day.

'I thought you had family,' he said, 'north of London.'

'The best of my childhood camp were killed, the men hunted and the women drowned,' said Lily. 'The rest are long gone. I learned what I needed. Horses, knives. Winning at cards and spying. I've no reason to chase sad memories.'

She looked at Charlie as if she'd like to suggest he do the same.

'You can't swim,' he pointed out.

Charlie was one of the few to discern her terror of drowning.

'Most sailors can't,' countered Lily. 'I sailed down the Thames once, almost to the great wide ocean. There's a freedom to the sea,' she concluded. 'There are no laws there and a whole world to discover. A woman is not a gypsy or a whore or a wife or a spinster but herself just as she pleases.'

They walked in silence along the shoreline. It was a sad contrast to the wealth afloat on the river. Slowly, a few feet at a time, the grim sight of Dead Man's Curve came into view.

Chapter 8

The child's skull was staring. For a terrible moment Janus was back there, in Thorne's cold workshop. He had woken from a dream of boys screaming and knew his turn was to come.

Then Janus came back to himself. He was in the forgotten palace. In the room he'd made for himself, with Thorne's old things.

There was a groan from the other side of the room. The woman. Janus had forgotten about her. She lay in the corner of her wooden cage, eyes growing glassy as her throat pumped out the last of her lifeblood.

'It won't be long now,' he promised, moving nearer to the dying woman. 'A painless end. I kept my word.'

In her death throes the woman had managed to retreat to the far corner of her cage and was lying on her side, arms wrapped tight around shuddering legs. Janus remembered adopting the same posture himself as De Ryker chose the next prisoner to meet a brutal end. He tried to recall an emotion from the experience and found he couldn't.

'You'll cross the river,' added Janus, 'and meet with Him.'

He motioned to his god, Saturn, cold and terrible in the corner of the palace room. The woman had choked in terror as Janus had drawn the blanket back, revealing the deity and his sacrifices.

Janus couldn't explain why he'd brought the god and human remains back here. Why he recreated the terrors of his boyhood. It was like a wound he couldn't help prodding.

He turned away from the woman and addressed Saturn's merciless gaze. She blinked now. Was she seeing a terrified child suspended from the god's hand?

'As a boy I dreamt of you,' he said, addressing the statue. 'I saw your knife cutting my throat. Felt myself sink into the dark waters of the river.'

Saturn's savagely bared teeth made no reply.

'You were my god,' continued Janus. 'How could you have let them take you away from me?'

They were questions he'd once screamed over and over in his head. But as Janus stared into the stony face he felt nothing. The realisation should have pleased him. Instead he was filled with a painful, unidentifiable feeling.

'Charlie Oakley,' he tried, 'will suffer for his father's betrayal.'

This time something seemed to stir. Then a sudden guttural rattle alerted him to his victim. She'd breathed her last now. In a few hours he would consign her to the Thames.

Janus's gaze switched to the little palette bed he'd made for himself, and he knew suddenly he couldn't sleep in it.

His current dwelling was eerie and sinister. It reminded him of the dark place. The room of his nightmares. Janus remembered every last detail of Thorne's room. He could see the huge black cogs, smell the stench of blood. And the children. Especially the children. Tiny bones haunted his dreams.

A twist of shame stirred in the pit of his stomach. He moved to the wooden cage and opened the door. The dead woman's blood had soaked the floor beneath her enclosure. It ran into her hair as Janus dragged her limp body free, painting a waving stain on the palace tiles. Soon he would carve her. But for now he needed to think.

Ignoring the coiling disgust in his gut, Janus crawled into the bloody cage and wrapped his arms tightly around his knees.

Chapter 9

Dappling the bank of Dead Man's Curve were a few sad wooden huts. They were made of rotting driftwood, bottom halves splashed with mud from the tides. All appeared empty of life, with no fires burning.

'Where are all the people?' asked Lily as they approached.

'The only people who live here are deathlarks,' said Charlie. 'People who drag out the bodies for a few pence. They work at night,' he added. 'Sleep during the day.'

They were nearing the huts, and Charlie pointed to one set slightly further back than the others.

'I've paid Norris for information a few times,' he said, heading towards it. 'He's older than the others. Doesn't work when the tide is so far out.'

Charlie approached the dark hut and knocked on a half-rotted door. From inside a stream of hacking coughs went up and a wheezing grumble. For a moment it seemed as though the occupant would not emerge. And then they heard footsteps, and the flimsy door creaked back.

Norris was a bent little man with only a tiny wisp of hair left on his mottled head and two black teeth wobbling in his ancient mouth. He wore an old sack tied at the waist with string and a pair of handmade wooden clogs strapped to his twisted feet with rags. On seeing Charlie, he acknowledged the familiar face with an incline of his head and a grunt. His eyes lingered on Lily's red silk dress, dark hair and gypsy charms ranged around her slim throat.

Reaching inside his coat, Charlie brought forth a roll of string and passed it to Norris. The old man took it, unfurled it and tested the strength.

'Good,' he said, pleased. 'No mould.'

'We've come to know of the bodies with astrological markings,' said Charlie.

Norris nodded. 'We have one still,' he said. 'Waiting for a church to claim her.'

Norris was racked by a sudden fit of wheezing coughing. Charlie moved to thump him on the back.

'River air,' explained Charlie to Lily as Norris's coughing abated.

The old man turned, beckoning them to the shoreline, where a few decaying boats lay upturned.

'We puts 'em under here,' explained Norris, nodding to the dilapidated boats.

He moved towards the furthest boat and, showing surprising strength for an old man, heaved it from the slick riverbed, righted it and fell to another fit of heavy coughing.

Lily inhaled sharply, taking a few sliding steps backwards in the mud. Underneath the boat was a bloated body.

'She came by only last night,' explained Norris.

The naked corpse lay prone in the mud. The limbs lolled obscenely, exposing a dark patch of pubic hair travelling down the inner thighs. Her eyes were bleached to a ghoulish translucence, the corneas opaque.

Thick black hair was tangled with weeds, giving the staring head a hideous Medusa appearance.

'Why is she that colour?' asked Lily eventually. 'She looks . . . burned.'

The corpse's remaining skin had a charred appearance, contrasting horrifically with the bloated, bulging eyes.

''S the water that does it,' said Norris, gazing philosophically at the body. 'Turns the skin brown and black. The eyes too,' he added, pointing. 'They all look like that.'

The girl's wounds seemed to eye them darkly. Her throat was cut completely open. All over the naked flesh were cruel knife marks. Astrological symbols had been slashed and cut in a kind of frenzy. In some places the blade had gashed deep lines to make the shape of constellations and planetary symbols. On other parts of the dead body, thick patches of skin had been removed completely.

Norris sucked his teeth. 'We're closer to the old ways out here,' he said. 'Us river folk speak of a dark god,' he said, 'who drags people into the deep waters. Drowns 'em, marks 'em for his own.' The old man cast a glance at the river. 'Long ago, Londoners made sacrifices to Father Thames to appease his thirst for blood.'

Norris looked up at the dun-coloured sky. 'The stars are foul over London, so they say. An eclipse comes. Perhaps old things return.'

'What do you think?' asked Charlie.

Norris rubbed his bearded chin. 'I think astrologers' dark ways have predicted knowledge mortal men should not be entitled to. It's troubled the dark nature of the river. Same as all those years ago.'

'You remember the bodies from then?' asked Charlie, surprised.

Norris nodded slowly. 'I remember them alright. Clear as that one lying there. The markings were just the same.'

He moved forward and picked up a stick from the mud. Then he moved a chunk of muddy hair from the corpse's face.

'An eye,' he said, 'made in the same place.'

Lily and Charlie stared. There, carved on to the girl's forehead, was an eye. The murderer had cut through to the white skull, depicting rays of light spanning out and a triangle enclosing the shape.

'I've seen that image before,' said Lily, her voice tight. 'Gypsies use it to ward off evil.'

'I recognise it too,' said Charlie. 'You see it in old churches. The Eye of Providence, watching over us.' He raked a hand through his dark blond hair. 'It can't be a coincidence,' he said, 'Riley speaking of an All-Seeing Eye, and this symbol.'

Lily nodded. 'But if the Eye is good,' she said, 'why is it carved into the body of a dead girl?'

Chapter 10

King Charles II was reclined in his private apartments, wine goblet clutched in his long, ringed fingers. His usual expanse of deep rugs had been rolled away to make room for a small stage. Three musicians stood in readiness to play the score.

Amesbury seated himself next to the King on a carved teak chair. He shuffled back to avoid brushing King Charles's large black curling wig. They made a strange contrast, the King in his black silk suit and snowy-white shirt, the battle-hardened general in a military jerkin and thick thigh-high boots.

Amesbury reflected that he was probably the closest thing the King had to a real friend. His eyes drifted to a succession of paintings depicting the King's famous mistress Barbara Castlemaine and their children. There were none of Queen Catherine. Charles doted on his children and had given them all titles and lands despite their illegitimacy.

'Your Majesty,' Amesbury begun, clearing his throat, 'we have some trouble in Deptford.'

'Oh?' The King held his hand up for an extra wine goblet.

'Janus escaped,' said Amesbury, taking the proffered cup.

A servant splashed Burgundy. Amesbury nodded his thanks and drank.

The King raised his heavy eyebrows, the long nose furrowing into his dark deep-set eyes.

'Not like you,' he said after a moment, 'to fail.'

Amesbury bowed his head in acknowledgement of the compliment.

'Janus asked about the rings,' he added. 'I think he is looking for the Eye.'

'The Eye?' The King seemed to be searching his memory.

The attempt was interrupted by a short fanfare from the musicians. Servants were covering the windows with thick red velvet curtains.

King Charles turned away from Amesbury and gestured to the stage. 'Lady Castlemaine has a surprise for me,' the King explained.

'Surely,' said Amesbury, who had often borne witness to Lady Castlemaine's shocking behaviour, 'she has no surprises left.'

'Never underestimate her,' said Charles, tapping his large nose. 'She notices my interest in the new lady-in-waiting.'

Her and everyone else, thought Amesbury privately. The King's love for fifteen-year-old Frances Stewart had become the talk of the court.

A servant arrived, bending his knee to offer the King a plate of meat, fruit and cheeses. Charles took the plate with a gracious nod of thanks and plucked up food with his fingertips.

'I treasure Lady Castlemaine,' sighed Charles. 'I adore our children. There was a time I wanted to make her Queen.'

Amesbury kept a tactful silence. Rumours of Lady Castlemaine's faithlessness had become ridiculous.

'All summer Frances has resisted my attempts to make her happy,' confided Charles, chewing meat, 'but she is starting to yield. Only yesterday . . .'

He stopped mid-sentence as the stage curtains rolled back, revealing a candlelit bed. Lady Castlemaine stood next to it wearing an open white man's shirt showing almost all of her naked chest. Her legs were clad in tight breeches, revealing a scandalous portion of bare lower leg and the tantalising outline of her curving thighs. A cloud of auburn hair framed her beautiful features, the large violet eyes set in calculated seduction. In her hand was a large wooden phallus, graphically carved in intimate detail.

The King gave a short applause. One of the musicians' mouths dropped clean open.

Amesbury tried unsuccessfully not to imagine where Lady Castlemaine might have bought such a lifelike object.

'It's been some time since we saw a wedding,' announced Lady Castlemaine, shaking out her shining hair and fixing her lovely eyes on the King. 'But,' she continued with an arch smile, 'for a wedding you need a virgin bride. And as Your Majesty well knows, virgins are difficult to find in court.'

Charles laughed and gestured for his wine goblet to be refilled.

'But there is *one* little virgin,' continued Lady Castlemaine as the King drank, 'who is famed.' She paused for dramatic effect. 'La Belle Stewart.'

Charles's eyes widened as Frances Stewart tripped on to the stage, her face soft with drink. Amesbury sat a little upright. How had Lady Castlemaine done it? Frances was renowned for her modesty, and she was play-acting half naked.

The King moved forward in his large chair. Frances had been dressed as Venus, Goddess of Love, in a flowing white toga that was practically transparent. Her hair was decorated with roses and tiny apples to represent the goddess.

The poor girl never stood a chance, thought Amesbury grimly. *She'll be ruined without even knowing Lady Castlemaine plotted her downfall.*

As Queen Catherine's prettiest lady-in-waiting, Frances appeared younger than her fifteen years. Her chubby frame was girlish, her fresh blue eyes not yet hardened in courtly manners. As they watched,

Lady Castlemaine wrapped a seductive hand around Frances's nubile waist, plucked an apple from the younger girl's hair and took a suggestive bite.

The King sat a little straighter, his eyes roaming the illicit glimpses of Frances's young body through the shifting fabric. Frances stumbled slightly, giggling childishly, her little dark curls bouncing around her face.

'I shall be the lucky groom,' continued Lady Castlemaine, holding her dildo aloft theatrically. 'The priest shall perform the ceremony.'

A man in priest's robes walked on to the stage and began the process of marrying Lady Castlemaine and Frances.

The King watched, transfixed.

'The Dutch are well positioned to invade,' said Amesbury. 'De Ryker is the best admiral Holland has ever known. Little stands in their way. If Janus finds the Eye, they could be unstoppable.'

Charles frowned at the mention of De Ryker. The admiral was famed for his ruthlessness and skill at sea.

Lady Castlemaine was slipping a ring on to Frances's finger and leaned forward to give her a lingering kiss. 'The wedding night!' announced Lady Castlemaine. 'The bridal bed!'

Stagehands were quickly assembling a stack of thick eiderdowns and cushions behind them. Lady Castlemaine led Frances slowly to the bed.

Charles swigged deliberately from his wine goblet as though his mouth was dry.

'My virgin bride has much to learn,' continued Lady Castlemaine with a wink, twirling the wooden sex toy, 'but I will teach her everything.'

She began loosening Frances's dress. The younger girl allowed herself to be manoeuvred under the covers.

The King tried to focus on Amesbury. He felt an important issue was evading him.

'So Janus knew of the codebreaker rings,' confirmed the King. 'I thought them lost.'

'I know of one still in London,' said Amesbury. 'It's owned by Judge Walters. He came by it a few months ago from a pirate in his custody, according to my informant in the Marshalsea.'

'The others?' The King was watching the stage.

'I believe the Cipher had a ring,' said Amesbury. 'Where it is now, no one knows. Thorne likely had one. There was talk one ring was given to a royal.'

His eyes flicked to the King.

'Who is Judge Walters?' Charles was trying to match the name to a face.

'He used to sail in your navy,' said Amesbury helpfully. 'Now he runs the prison at Marshalsea. Drowns pirates,' he concluded.

Charles's dark brows lifted in memory.

On stage Lady Castlemaine was working to free Frances's toga. She threw it triumphantly over the side of the stage. Frances, now naked beneath the sheets, pulled the bedcovers high and giggled.

'You think Janus is killing girls to find the Eye?' asked the King.

'It's possible,' said Amesbury. 'Identical killings took place while Thorne was your father's astrologer. There was something familiar about him. I don't believe he is Dutch. Perhaps a seafaring noble with a reason to be bitter towards his King.'

The King gave a short laugh. 'You name half my court,' he said. 'Including my own brother.'

'What of Buckingham?' asked Amesbury carefully. 'You banished him two years ago. He is a great sailor.'

The King's eyes automatically moved to the empty spot on the wall, where a picture once hung. His eyes softened in adoration as they took in his painted children. But the portrait of Lady Castlemaine's sixth child was noticeably absent. She'd been born two years ago, when rumours about Buckingham and Lady Castlemaine were at their height.

'I don't doubt Buckingham's loyalty to England,' said Charles, 'but I don't wish to speak of him.' The King's dark eyes tracked back towards the stage, their expression brooding. He lowered his mouth to drink.

Lady Castlemaine was taking Frances's face in her hands. She kissed her full on the lips. Then she raised the large wooden dildo. The King swallowed.

'Since I am ill-equipped,' Lady Castlemaine announced, 'a widow's comforter must play the part.'

Her bewitching gaze swept the stage, gauging her audience. Frances lay prone.

'The delights of the flesh,' Lady Castlemaine announced to the King with a wag of her finger, 'may only be enjoyed in wedlock. Frances must retire to her own chambers.'

Barbara exited the bed. On cue the curtain was untied, shielding her young bedfellow in a thick swathe of velvet.

The King's face registered disappointment.

'But if His Majesty joins me in my apartments,' continued Barbara, 'I shall play the willing bride.'

The King sat watching the stage for a long moment. Behind him servants moved like a well-oiled machine, letting in daylight, rearranging the rugs. He tried to focus. The room seemed warm and liquid. He got unsteadily to his feet. Something was nagging at him. He needed to make a decision about the Dutch threat. But Lady Castlemaine's apartments seemed much more inviting, even without Frances. Then from beneath the fug an idea took form.

'We shall go to Deptford,' decided Charles, thinking aloud. 'Judge Walters is at Execution Dock today. We shall secure his ring and be sure the Eye cannot be found.'

Amesbury felt relief wash over him. He'd been trying to persuade the King to take the Dutch threat seriously for months.

'Frances will accompany me in the carriage,' continued the King, 'and see aboard our magnificent *Royal Charles*. We'll show her why she need never fear Dutch invasion.'

Amesbury resisted the urge to put his head in his hands. The King's true motive was embarrassingly clear. He wanted a pretext to get Frances alone in the royal carriage and impress her with his Naval Majesty.

What Charles had likely forgotten was that the Great Fire had decimated royal funds, leaving Deptford Docks on a bleak skeleton crew. The King would be mortified. And when Lady Castlemaine discovered Frances had been toured at the Royal Dockyard, the King's most volatile mistress would be furious.

Chapter 11

Charlie and Lily were ankle-deep in the mud at Dead Man's Curve. The body was staring up at them.

'The bodies from nineteen years ago,' said Charlie. 'They were just like this one?'

Norris nodded. 'I was just a boy. But you don't forget such things. People blamed the old King. He and his crow of a Queen had fled to Greenwich Palace, just over the way.' Norris scratched his testicles reflectively.

'The murderer carved star signs?' Charlie suggested, turning to Lily.

'I think it's a map of the heavens,' said Lily. 'See how it's arranged? Like a star chart in an almanac.'

Charlie examined the shapes. Most prominent was a large pentagram.

'Devil worship?' suggested Lily.

'I don't know,' said Charlie, frowning.

'Perhaps the girl's birth chart?' suggested Lily.

Charlie shook his head. 'Look at the hands,' he said, pointing to the fingers. 'There's the marks of an old prison brand on the thumb. She's a convicted thief. Folk as poor as her don't often know when they were born. I only know my nativity because . . .'

Charlie stopped. It suddenly occurred to him he had no idea how he knew his birthdate. Only that he did. Had his mother told him? Charlie remembered hardly anything before the orphanage. Sometimes scraps came to him in dreams. Dark images he'd rather forget.

'Perhaps the charts show the time of her death,' Charlie theorised, trying to shake off the uneasy feeling that always surrounded shrouded memories of his past.

He noticed something else. A flash of silver where the mouth now gaped slightly.

Charlie took a stick from the bank. He knelt and carefully opened the dead girl's mouth. There was a coin inside.

'What are you doing!' cried Lily in horror as a squirming shrimp writhed free of the dead tongue.

'It's a silver coin,' said Charlie, pulling it free. 'A shilling.' He turned it. 'Minted near St Ursula's Church,' he said. 'That's a sailor's place, downriver. They buy coin there after landing at Custom House.'

'So the killer is a sailor?'

'Could be,' said Charlie. 'But it's a busy part of the city. Could have been a local from Deptford.'

He thought for a moment. 'Didn't Ishmael Boney live in Deptford?' he asked Norris.

The old man gave a snort of annoyance. 'He did, but he's long fled,' he said. 'If we could find Ishmael Boney, we'd have justice. Us poor river folk could get on with our business, without Deptford folk cursing us, and the King's men poking their noses,' he added bitterly. 'No,' he concluded, 'Ishmael has disappeared to whatever close and dark hole he came from, and we'll not find him now.'

Charlie logged this. Then he tossed the silver coin to Norris, who caught it gratefully, pocketing it in one swift movement.

Charlie moved forward and gently turned the body. It rolled wetly in the mud, exposing the naked back.

They all stared. The mud-dappled skin bore yet more patterns. On to the girl's back had been carved a crude image. Four rudimentary angels fluttered around a cross.

'Why are you staring?' asked Lily, taking in Charlie's haunted expression.

'That picture,' said Charlie. 'I see it every day. On a tapestry. A tapestry stitched by my mother.'

Chapter 12

Lily and Charlie were walking fast back to Covent Garden.

'In my mother's lost bundle,' Charlie was explaining, 'there wasn't just a ring. She'd stitched a sampler. Angels around a cross. I never thought it anything more than a maid's seamstress work.' He called the tapestry to mind. 'Four angels with different heads,' he said, 'just like on the back of the dead girl.'

'You think there could be a hidden code in the sampler?' asked Lily excitedly.

'It's possible.'

A man holding a rooster was passing a lively coach house, on his way to a cockfight. Automatically Charlie assessed the scar-mangled bird's chances and noticed its head drooping to one side. Then sharp instincts caught an impression of something amiss by the coach house. A figure standing upright and alert – not nearly drunk enough for the company he kept. But before Charlie could properly take him in, the man twisted away and vanished into the thick crowd. The impression Charlie was left with was the man had been tall, smoking a Dutch pipe. Charlie was suddenly certain it was the same man who'd followed them from the Marshalsea prison.

'Come on,' he said uneasily to Lily. 'My room isn't far.'

They crossed London Bridge and passed through the bizarre hotch-potch of London's Great Fire aftermath. Rebuilding had happened in spurts, and pockets of the city boasted smart new buildings of white stone.

They passed by Cornhill, where the Royal Exchange was being rebuilt in earnest. Large white arches were already taking shape, and well-dressed architects and planners watched from the Olde Mitre Tavern, sipping warm ale.

On Cheapside traders took a more hands-on approach, peddling stoically from temporary stalls erected in the ruins of their former shops. Towards Fleet Street the expanse of black ash was punctuated by posts nailed into the ground. String perimeters plotted the shape of a new house, shop, tavern or church. Thick huddles of Londoners queued out-side temporary shacks, erected to resolve the constant boundary disputes.

They entered the unburned west of the city, now heaving with extra occupants. Charlie led Lily through a sawdust-strewn butcher's shop to his lodgings. The butcher looked up, knife in hand, and nodded a greeting.

'If you pass by Southwark today, don't bet on the cockerels,' advised Charlie as they passed. 'One of the fighters is doped. Things could turn ugly.'

'I'll save my pennies,' agreed the butcher amiably. 'I've already got money on us winning the war with the Dutch this year.'

The butcher gave a last lingering look at Lily as they mounted the stairs to Charlie's small room, then went back to his carving.

'You remember my rooms?' Charlie asked, eyeing Lily as he pushed open the badly hung door with effort.

Since he'd met Lily, it had never really been clear what their involve-ment was. They'd discovered a long-lost chest together, retrieved papers that threatened England, narrowly escaped the Great Fire and spent the days after scarcely leaving Charlie's bed. But then Lily had vanished, only to return touting the ruby ring, a new mystery to solve and an apparent amnesia for their prior intimacy.

'I never noticed your mother's sampler,' was Lily's only observation as they entered.

The stitched cloth was displayed over the straw mattress. The threads were still bright and depicted a thick red cross, surrounded by four angels. Beneath was written:

When the sun goes down, you shall return your pledge to Him.

Charlie nodded. They both stood and looked at it.

'When the sun goes down, you shall return your pledge to Him?' read Lily.

'It's common enough to make a tapestry with a Bible quote,' said Charlie.

They looked at the angels, flying around a squat red cross.

'The cross could represent the shape of the joined rings,' suggested Lily. 'It's stubbier than a usual Christian cross.'

Charlie was looking at the angels. Instead of serene human features, these angels had animal heads. A fierce lion and snorting bull glared out. One was a strange-looking bird, and the last was a man glaring a challenge.

Lily was scrutinising each angel.

'They're cherubim,' Charlie explained. 'Warrior angels, closest to God. You see them in churches.'

'Four cherubims,' he added. 'Four rings.'

He called to mind the symbols marked on the rings.

'Leo could be the lion,' he said. 'Aquarius the man. That leaves a bull and a bird.'

'Taurus for the bull,' said Lily. 'I don't know for the bird.'

They both thought for a moment.

Charlie had a sudden idea. 'Do you have your almanac? Perhaps it could tell us something we're missing.'

Lily reached inside her waistband and drew out the almanac. It was a large booklet of twenty or so sewn pages. The front cover bore the title *The Starry Messenger* and was illustrated with moons and suns.

Lily flipped open the pamphlet and began leafing through. She turned a page, and both of them froze. The forecast was titled 'All Hallows' Eve, 1666'. Beneath was a triangular star chart, peppered with symbols. The picture accompanying the symbolic prediction was of a familiar four angels.

'It's the same,' breathed Lily. 'Angels with animal heads.'

'No wonder Ishmael Boney was accused,' said Charlie.

'The picture is about a specific lunar event,' said Lily, reading the writing. 'The impending eclipse on All Hallows' Eve.'

'Two days from now,' said Charlie. 'What else does it say?'

'Saturn will overcome Jupiter,' said Lily. 'The moon will be turned to blood. A great power will be revealed and herald the end of time.'

They looked at one another.

'Saturn is bad,' said Lily uncertainly. 'Jupiter is good. But angels are in the Bible. What has that to do with astrology?'

And my mother? thought Charlie privately. He had only fragmented memories of Sally Oakley before she'd been murdered keeping him and his brother safe. He'd only later discovered his father, Tobias Oakley, had died at sea.

'We need to find Ishmael Boney,' said Charlie.

He unhooked the sampler, rolled it and put it thoughtfully in his coat. The fabric was light and took up surprisingly little space.

'But Ishmael has vanished,' said Lily. 'Gone into hiding.'

'I'm a thief taker,' said Charlie. 'I have a talent for finding hidden people. And if you want to track a man in London, the first thing you should consider is who might be paying him.' Charlie tapped the front of Lily's almanac, where the name of a printing house was prominently displayed.

'We're going to visit Ishmael's publisher.'

Chapter 13

King Charles steered Frances carefully over the cobbled pavements of Deptford Dockyard. It was cold, but a double intoxication of wine and women was keeping him comfortably warm. Frances Stewart was divested of her scanty toga and wearing a yellow silk dress fitted to her youthful frame. With pearls dangling from her ears and ornamenting her shining brown hair, she looked like she was playing dress up in an older woman's clothes.

Charles and Frances had made successive toasts in the carriage, and his heart sang with love for her. Several yellow ribbons in her brown hair had come loose, and her dress hung slightly unlaced at the back.

Charles squinted. Where were all the ships?

The enormous dockyards were virtually empty. The large mast pond and long rope-walk employed only a handful of men. Then he spied Amesbury's pet monkey, a lucky plunder from his seafaring days, cannoning back and forth on the cobbles. The general had ridden ahead to summon Judge Walters and arrange a royal welcome.

'Your Majesty.' Amesbury wore only a grey cloak to ward off the autumn chill.

His monkey bounded back to its master and slipped a sly hand into his hanging pocket. It freed a few grapes before Amesbury batted it away.

Frances smiled hazily and managed a curtsy. Her eyes were warily fixed on the monkey, decimating the grapes with sharp teeth a few feet away.

'Where are our grand ships?' asked Charles.

'We've been forced to mothball most of the navy,' said Amesbury. 'It's upriver at Chatham. After the fire we haven't the funds to sail it.'

Amesbury stepped forward to offer the King and Frances wine. Frances stared at the contents before taking a tight sip.

She's going to throw up, thought Amesbury, thinking Frances's youth exacerbated the King's ageing appearance.

'What of the dock workers?' pressed Charles, sipping wine. 'The shipbuilders?'

'Many are too afraid to work, Your Majesty.' Amesbury held out a large hand in explanation. 'The murders at Dead Man's Curve. They fear ghosts and spirits. Seafarers are superstitious, and the shipbuilders are already on reduced pay. And with All Hallows' Eve approaching . . .'

'The eclipse,' said Charles, nodding.

The King glanced at Frances. She was swaying slightly as she stood and appeared not to have noticed the sad state of the Royal Docks. Charles held her protectively.

Frances mumbled something unintelligible.

'Of course,' said Charles. 'Frances requires the pot,' he announced to the assembled men.

Amesbury quickly assessed who seemed the dock worker least likely to molest the drunken Frances and summoned him with a click of his calloused fingers.

'Take this lady to the naval offices,' he said. 'There's a fire there and a chamber pot she can use.'

'You see how good-natured she is?' said the King, sighing as she left. 'I would do anything for her, Amesbury.'

Amesbury said nothing. Charles's capacity for love was one of his most endearing qualities, but also the most incompatible with kingship.

Another man stepped forward. Charles narrowed his eyes, trying to keep focus. Inappropriately, the man's dockside nickname reared up through the haze of Madeira wine.

The Bloody Judge.

Judge Walters stood poised like a carrion crow in his judicial robes. His former life as a naval officer had divested him of an eye and several fingers. But he'd supplemented the loss with a leather eyepatch studded with a pearl cross, and a merciless zeal for penal law. His hatred of pirates earned him his nickname.

'Your Majesty.' The Judge gave the briefest of bows.

He wore black from neck to toe, with the exception of a round white collar that reminded the King uncomfortably of Cromwell. Charles was rather afraid of Walters. The pearly cross seemed to watch you even when the man himself wasn't.

'You summoned me?' asked the Judge.

Charles nodded. Amesbury stepped forward.

'My naval intelligence informs me you came by a ruby ring,' he said.

The Judge looked surprised. 'I did come by such a ring,' he said. 'I cut it from the hand of a pirate. He captured it during a sea raid and was convinced it led to some great treasure. But he couldn't divulge the location. Even under my strongest means.'

Something unpleasant glimmered in the Judge's face at this last revelation.

'The only thing I could get from him,' he added, 'was that he thought the ring had once belonged to royalty, because it was marked with the sign of Leo. And there was some kind of prophecy. A treasure would be revealed this year. On All Hallows' Eve.'

'Where is the ring now?' demanded Amesbury.

The Judge's face drew rigid in fury. 'It was stolen from me,' he said tightly, 'by a gypsy girl. I am taking steps to have it returned and the thief punished. Am I right in thinking,' continued the Judge, his good eye trained on the King, 'that there were four ring bearers? The astrologer Ishmael Boney could perhaps tell us more.'

There was a false note of concern to his voice.

'Ishmael is under royal protection,' said the King. He had grown noticeably pale.

'What do you mean by it, man?' interjected Amesbury, his booming battlefield voice ringing around the docks. 'Think you this your courtroom and His Majesty a witness?'

The Judge gave one of his imperceptible bows. He pulled his black robes tighter against the chill and righted his white collar.

'Forgive me, I mean no impertinence,' he said formally, his eyepatch twitching. 'Only that if this crime is frightening the dockers' – his single eye flickered to the King, then to the near-empty dockyard – 'I am moved to help solve it.'

'If you want to end the fearfulness of Deptford folk,' added Amesbury, addressing the Judge, 'you might try not drowning pirates on their doorstep.' He waved his hand in a tired kind of way. 'We have more pressing matters. If the Dutch search for the Eye, they could be planning a sea invasion.'

'Your new penal policies have become quite the spectacle, so I'm told.' King Charles was speaking to Judge Walters. For the first time his love-struck flush had been replaced by something more steely.

'Terror is the only language a pirate understands,' said the Judge. 'We chain miscreants to the dock whilst the tide rises. After a spell dangling from a short noose,' he added with a malevolent grin. 'Large crowds frequent the bankside inns to see the pirate's last dance. The next drowning is this afternoon. If Your Majesty should like—'

'Mercy,' interrupted the King, 'is a noble thing.' His eyes veered automatically to a swinging gibbet further downriver. Even from this distance he could see the slumped corpse inside, the dead mouth gaping in remembered pain. 'Perhaps you should pay more mind to more conventional executions. This next drowning will be the last.'

The Judge made the King a short bow. 'As Your Majesty wishes,' he said silkily. 'I shall make it my priority to discover the gypsy villain who stole my ring,' he concluded, 'and bring her to justice.'

Chapter 14

Charlie and Lily stared up at the printing house, sticking up like a single brick tooth on the razed remains of Fleet Street. Fire had blazed up the road, burning down the older wooden-jettied buildings. Black caverns were etched deep into the ground where cellars had fallen in. A stench of smoke still hung on the air.

'Fleet Street still smokes,' said Lily sadly, 'weeks after the fire is out.'

She was looking at the men working to shovel deep ash and throw water on any remaining smoulder. Elsewhere people who'd once owned taverns and shops on the street were trying to mark out their old territories. A table had been erected with a solicitor appointed to resolve disputes of land, and angry voices flared around it.

'Old Macock is the oldest printer in London,' said Charlie. 'He makes most of his money from astrological almanacs and has been printing them for over thirty years.'

'He must be a clever businessman,' said Lily, assessing the expensive brick building.

Charlie nodded. 'Sharp as a whip and rich enough to build a brick print house with its own fire engine.'

They knocked on the smart wooden door, inscribed 'Macock and Son, Esteemed Printers est. 1630'. The sound of a pounding print press echoed from within. A heady smell of linseed and resin greeted them as they moved through the doorway.

Inside was light and airy, with several large wooden print presses illuminated by hexagonal glass windows. A handful of men turned presses, mixed ink, chiselled at print plates and papers. There were piles of completed manuscripts stacked all around.

'Mostly almanacs by different astrologers,' said Lily, moving uninvited towards the piles and scanning the titles. '"*Christian Astrology in 1666*",' she read. '"*Will She Marry? – A Maid's Astrological Wedding Predictions*", "*Musings on the Latest Terrible Eclipse*".'

A thick-armed man with his linen shirtsleeves rolled up made towards them.

'What's your business?' he asked, eyeing Lily suspiciously.

Lily lifted the jangle of charms at her neck. 'Gypsy curses,' she said.

'We're here to see the owner,' interjected Charlie quickly as the man drew back, crossing himself. 'John Macock.'

The man pointed an arm towards a large printing press but continued to back away. 'John!' he bellowed, keeping his eyes on Lily. 'People here for you!'

A young man emerged from behind a clattering printing press, wiping ink-stained fingertips on a small handkerchief. His elaborate black curls spoke of nightly curling papers and painstaking application of bear grease.

'John Macock,' he announced loudly, 'at your service.'

He was wearing a flamboyant scarlet jerkin, a collar of gold Venetian lace and his leather shoes had been polished to within an inch of their lives.

The man threw out a hand, from which a brash garnet ring twinkled. 'Have you some print business?' he asked, taking in Charlie and then Lily. 'Some legal documents?' he hazarded, sizing them both up.

'You're John Macock?' said Charlie, confused, shaking the proffered hand.

'The younger,' confirmed the man, pumping his arm enthusiastically. 'The elder died last year. Plague. Lucky he did. The Great Fire would have broken his heart. But have no fear' – Macock surveyed his print shop – 'I'm to make some changes,' he said proudly. 'Out with the old. We're to fit the latest presses from Germany. That's if any of us survive the eclipse,' he added with a laugh that sounded a little loud to be genuine.

'I'm a thief taker,' said Charlie, retrieving his crushed fingers. 'My name is Charlie Tuesday.'

Macock's glossy-curled head tilted, assessing. 'Charlie Tuesday,' he ruminated. 'I've heard all about you. "The People's Thief Taker",' he added, fanning his hands in an imaginary book title. 'The man who solves crimes for rich and poor. Wealthy ladies would love to read about you,' he added with a wink. 'They'd beat a path to your bed. Is this your wife?' he added, realising Lily's presence might call for greater tact.

'She's—' began Charlie.

'An associate,' said Lily firmly. 'We have business together.'

'I would have said a friend,' muttered Charlie.

Lily only shrugged her little shoulders.

'A good business associate is always a friend,' said Macock, beaming broadly at Lily. 'And a pretty friend the best kind of all.'

Lily gave him the siren smile she reserved for men she wanted something from.

'Charlie Tuesday,' repeated Macock. 'Tell me you're here to commit your stories to print. I could give you very good distribution. Make you a lot of money.'

'Reading and writing isn't my strong point,' admitted Charlie.

'Something to consider in any case,' said Macock, thumping his shoulder. 'If you do, you must come to me.' His youthful face darkened.

'Don't go to that crook William Taylor. He stole Milton from under my nose.'

'If I ever come to publish,' promised Charlie, 'I'll come to you. But for now I need your help.'

'In which case,' said Macock delightedly, 'what can I do for you?'

'You print Ishmael Boney's almanacs?' asked Charlie.

'We did,' said Macock easily. 'We print all the astrological almanacs. No longer Ishmael's, of course. Not since such high-feeling flares. Not good for our reputation.'

'Do you think Ishmael was wrongly accused of the Deptford murders?' asked Charlie, noting Macock's choice of words.

Macock thought for a moment. 'I couldn't say,' he admitted. 'I only met Ishmael once. Mainly he did business with my father.'

'You don't know where he is now?'

'I don't,' said Macock. 'My father likely knew his address, but that died with him. And I will not search too deeply. We owe Ishmael substantial royalties,' he said, winking. 'Though I'm sad things turned out as they did,' he concluded with feeling. 'Ishmael made us a lot of money.'

'How did he strike you as a person when you met him?' asked Charlie.

'As I say, I only met him once.' Macock frowned. 'I'd expected him to look more exotic,' he added sadly. 'Ishmael's skin is not so dark as his Moorish kinsmen's, and he dresses as an Englishman. If not for his frizzled hair, you might mistake him for a Spaniard.' Macock seemed very sad at this, as though Ishmael had shirked his astrologer's duty to appear foreign and magical.

'What did he speak of?' prompted Charlie.

'I'm afraid I don't recollect much of what Ishmael said,' replied Macock. 'I'd been out the previous night, celebrating our recent sea victory against the Dutch,' he added. 'Too much ale.'

'So this would have been less than a month ago,' said Charlie, logging the occasion. 'October the first?'

'I suppose it would,' agreed Macock.

'What about Ishmael's manner?' asked Charlie. 'Anything notable there?'

'Now that I do remember,' said Macock, 'Ishmael was excitable. Frightened even. He kept looking at the door as though he expected someone to break it down.'

'But Ishmael gave you his latest almanac to publish,' confirmed Charlie.

'He did.' Macock toyed with a luxuriant curl. 'We took some ale. I believe I asked about his predictions for our printing house, but he wasn't forthcoming.' His forehead crinkled in memory. 'I do remember Ishmael said this latest almanac was the most important he'd published. That it would guide a worthy man to his destiny. Or perhaps it was his birthright. I forget.'

'Did you not think that an unusual remark?' asked Charlie.

'Not at all,' said Macock. 'Most of our authors are rather strange. Particularly astrologers. You should meet Isaac Newton.'

Charlie drew out the ruby ring, taking a chance that a man like Macock would have an eye for jewellery.

'What about this?' he asked, flashing the gem. 'Have you seen the like before? Perhaps Ishmael was wearing something like it.'

Macock hesitated, staring at the ring. 'No,' he said finally. 'I've never seen a ring like that before.'

Charlie thought for a moment. His mind turned to the mountain of astrological almanacs ready for distribution.

'Did Ishmael leave any other unpublished material?' suggested Charlie. 'Anything you've not been able to print because of the recent' – he searched for the word – 'unrest?'

Macock thought for a moment. 'No, not exactly,' he said. 'I think he did leave us some papers. Many authors use us in that way, to hold their letters and such.'

'Do you still have them?' asked Charlie.

Macock shook his head. 'I don't think so,' he said. 'I'm afraid when Ishmael disappeared I filed his documents with my father's old things. I've just started the process of pulping.'

Chapter 15

Lady Castlemaine lay back on the bed. 'Tell me where you've been,' she said. 'The whole court wonders.'

Buckingham eyed her. Then he reached a hand to the front of her dress, torn where he had ripped it. He'd only just washed clean from his visit to Deptford, and the memories still sickened him. But Barbara Castlemaine had the kind of beauty that was mercifully distracting. The large violet eyes below soaring eyebrows had a permanent seductive cast.

'Surely Charles told you the reason for my banishment.' He toyed with the frayed ribbons.

Buckingham raised his dark eyebrows. His handsome face had grown rugged at sea, giving his white teeth a wolfish quality. The hard muscular body had yearned for Barbara. But Buckingham sensed things had changed in his absence.

He wondered if Barbara was fishing for information. Did she know something about his nightly visits to Deptford and his dark past? He didn't think it possible.

'He has too many distractions,' said Barbara ruefully, 'to tell me everything.' But she couldn't quite hide the discomfort on her face.

'Anyone in particular?' Buckingham was suddenly interested.

'A lady, named Frances Stewart, a cousin of yours. Perhaps you could distract her?'

'I've never met Frances.' He pulled her towards him. 'Is she pretty?'

'The court talks of nothing but her beauty. And her purity,' she added bitterly. 'There was a time when Charles valued skill.'

'Frances Stewart is taking attention from the King,' Buckingham guessed. He sounded amused.

'Your cousin is a child,' said Barbara. 'He'll tire of her the moment he has her. The poor girl will be ruined.'

'You're all heart.'

'She's an easy conquest for you,' suggested Barbara. 'Young. Virginal.'

'Get me back in court,' he said, keeping his tone casual, 'and I'll consider it.'

Barbara thought about this. Her gaze drifted round the unadorned room, so unlike the places Buckingham was used to. The room bore a small fireplace, low, cosy ceilings, a large trunk in which travellers could lock away their valuables and a writing desk. The adjoining room held the rest of his travelling possessions. Chests and trunks loaded with his fine clothes and riches.

It was a plain dwelling for an aristocrat. Barbara could only guess at Buckingham's humiliation.

'You must miss court,' she said.

'Yes,' he replied.

There was a bitterness in his voice. Barbara felt her body tense. She'd forgotten how quickly Buckingham could turn.

He moved his body to shadow hers. Buckingham wasn't as large as Charles, but his muscled frame reminded her of a snake ready to strike.

'Perhaps I should take my revenge on you,' Buckingham suggested, letting his fingers circle her neck.

'You'd be gutted for treason,' said Barbara, and she realised she was fighting to keep her voice calm. Had he been like this before? She couldn't remember.

Buckingham let his fingers tighten just a fraction, and Barbara felt a wave of real fear. In this moment, she realised, she just wanted to be with Charles.

Catching her expression, Buckingham laughed and rolled back on the bed.

'You're losing your touch,' he grinned. 'The old Barbara would have flown at me like a wildcat.' His expression changed suddenly. 'Tell me why you're really here,' he said, 'if you've not come for the old passion.'

Barbara kissed him deeply. 'Tell me your crime,' she whispered, letting her fingernails rake his back. 'What did you do?'

Buckingham smiled, his mouth lingering on hers. 'I used astrology,' he murmured, unable to resist the urge to shock her, 'to predict the hour of the King's birth.'

Barbara sat back. 'That is all?'

He nodded. 'It is a sensitivity of his,' said Buckingham, 'as I discovered. The law says it to be treason,' he added. 'The old King made it so. If you know a man's exact nativity, you might make his birth chart. Predict his weakest times. Even his death.'

'And where did you go,' asked Barbara, 'during your long banishment?'

'I was at sea,' he said.

'The sea is a big place. There was talk you met with the Dutch. I might be tempted to think you up to some treason.' She eyed him meaningfully. 'Some piracy then?' she murmured.

'Perhaps.' He ran a hand over her breasts, partially exposed where he had hastily pulled open the top of her dress. 'Should you like that?' he whispered. 'To be ravished by a pirate?' He let his hands slide downwards, pulling aside the torn dress. 'A man who hadn't had a woman in months?' he suggested. 'Who would show you no mercy?'

She smiled, taking hold of his wrist. 'First,' she said, 'he should need to prove his worth with jewels and plunder. Then,' she continued, her violet eyes flashing, 'even a pirate might be shocked by me.'

Buckingham felt himself falling into their promise. Barbara would do anything, he knew, for the right price. But her price was an ever-changing game of cat and mouse. He loved and hated the game in equal measure.

'Be a little careful,' he said. 'One day I will tire of your games, and you'll be sorry for it.'

She sat up a little. 'Show me your sailing amounted to something.'

Buckingham slid from the simple bed. 'As you wish,' he said with a grin, striding from the room.

Barbara lay back, watching him move into the adjacent room, white shirt skirting his tanned legs. When he was out of sight, she darted soundlessly from the bed to his Chinese writing desk. She pulled open the first drawer.

Her eyes widened in surprise.

Inside the drawer was an almanac she vaguely recognised. It had been written by an astrologer named Ishmael and had been sold all over London. On top of the astrological work was a lock of muddy hair. It was strangely dirty, as though it had been in a river.

Barbara lifted the hair, and her eyes widened further. The memento was caked in old blood.

Chapter 16

The clatter of the printing presses echoed around the bright room.

'We've many old books and unpublished almanacs with my father's old things,' explained Macock. 'I started sending them to pulp weeks ago. I'm making space at the back of the printing house for more presses.' Macock caught Charlie's and Lily's disappointed expressions.

'It's a large task. I haven't yet destroyed all,' he said. 'Perhaps something of Ishmael's still remains.'

Macock turned on his highly polished heel and gestured they follow him towards the back of the print house.

'It's a dreadful shame about Ishmael,' he opined as they walked behind. 'His predictions were phenomenal.'

'Better than other astrologers'?' asked Charlie.

'You live in London,' said Macock. 'You must've heard of Boney's great predictions. Plague, then fire.'

Charlie rubbed the scar on his lip as he and Lily followed Macock through a small door.

'I've lived in London long enough to know astrologers come and go,' said Charlie as they entered a narrow corridor beyond. 'To my mind, Ishmael could have had a lucky streak. A man like you,' he concluded, 'would know the real truth.'

Macock seemed to grow a few inches.

'You know how it is,' he said conspiratorially. 'An astrologer predicts a few things right, and everyone overlooks inaccuracies in their excitement.'

'Yet that's not what Londoners believe,' said Charlie.

Macock threw up his hands. 'Who am I to protest?' he said with another exaggerated wink. 'It's made us printers rich. Do you know last year Londoners bought one almanac for every twenty citizens?'

Charlie shook his head.

Macock nodded. 'Everyone wants to know the future,' he said. 'Wars, famines. The King himself consults with astrologers.'

He opened another small door, into a room stuffed to the rafters with books and manuscripts. Shelves were crammed to bursting. Towards the front an ominously empty area yawned.

Macock plunged into the milieu of paperwork and began lifting and dropping books and papers. Dust rose up.

He searched amongst the papers for a tense few moments, then turned with a regretful expression.

'I'm sorry,' he said. 'The papers aren't here. They must have been destroyed.'

Charlie tried not to let the disappointment lower his spirits. He switched his attention to the mounds of papers and manuscripts. Perhaps there was another chance to gain information on Ishmael Boney's work.

'Do you have any almanacs from the time of the Civil War?' he asked. 'Nineteen years ago.'

Macock made an apologetic expression. 'The old man would have known,' he said, 'but it's too long before my time. Father kept all kinds of nonsense,' he added, shaking his head. 'He hoarded printed materials at the cost of progress.' He swept a hand around the printed chaos. 'Father started with some kind of ordering system,' said Macock. 'But it isn't by date. I think it's by author. Do you have a name of an astrologer from back then?'

'Thorne,' said Charlie. 'Try Thorne.'

Macock pulled forth a sheaf of documents, blew away the dust and coughed. Then he glanced back up at the chaotic shelves.

'Thorne you say?' He began flipping through the papers. Several fluttered to the floor.

Charlie waited patiently. Lily twisted her dress.

'Thorne,' muttered Macock. He was staring at a large sheaf of papers in his hand. 'Well, this is very strange,' he said. There was a pause. 'It seems as though Thorne *did* attempt to publish some material with us,' he continued. 'Some mathematical works. And an essay – "How the Roman Gods Became the Planets".'

'So Thorne believed in Roman gods?' suggested Charlie.

'Many astrologers are interested in how the planets got their names,' said Macock, 'but people began to believe in all kinds of things during the Civil War.' He gestured towards the ageing documents. 'You only have to leaf through these to see it. Fairies and druids, old ways and dark gods. Of course,' he added quickly, 'we couldn't publish such things now.'

'Do you have a copy of Thorne's publication?' asked Lily hopefully.

Macock shook his head slowly. 'That's the strange thing,' he said. 'It says here that Thorne's work was recalled before it was published.'

'What do you mean, recalled?' asked Charlie.

'Burned,' said Macock. 'By order of the Crown. All Thorne's papers were taken and burned.'

Chapter 17

At Deptford Docks, Amesbury and King Charles were looking uncertainly at Judge Walters. Behind them lay an enormous hull of an upturned man-of-war. She'd been docked and tilted with the aid of a towering crane, and a few skinny men were clambering over the hull, scraping tall clusters of barnacles and forests of seaweed from her underside.

The Judge slid a finger beneath his pearly eyepatch and rubbed at the skin. King Charles found himself watching the pearly cross lift and lower, mesmerised.

'Did anyone other than Thorne see this mysterious Eye?' the Judge pondered aloud. 'I thought the astrologer and the Cipher were great friends,' he suggested.

Amesbury looked at the Judge, wondering where he'd got his information.

'They were held together,' he said shortly, 'the best codebreakers in England. There was talk that the Cipher had been given a ring. But it was never found, and I don't believe the Cipher ever saw the Eye.'

'I thought the Cipher escaped,' said the King, visibly plumbing his memory.

'Tried to,' agreed Amesbury. 'We recaptured the Cipher and found a way to make the situation permanent.'

'How?'

'We found a way,' said Amesbury shortly. He sighed. 'I never saw the Eye myself. All I know is it must be small for Thorne to hide it. And likely an invention of great cleverness.'

'The stories tell it that Thorne's Eye somehow discerned the enemy's position at sea. His small ship attacked and was victorious against all odds.'

'They were *nearly* victorious,' corrected Amesbury. 'The *Naseby* survived under great duress and limped back to land. But there is no doubt Thorne's Eye gave some mysteriously powerful advantage.'

'How could you know so much about it?' accused the Judge.

'I captained the ship that was attacked,' smiled Amesbury. 'I've pondered for many years how Thorne knew our position.'

'Thorne had the Eye of Lucifer,' said the Judge. 'The Devil's own sight.'

Amesbury considered. 'I am a simple man. I think the answer less mystical.'

'Then what else could have located your ship?' demanded the Judge.

'Thorne was no sailor; he was a cryptographer,' said Amesbury.

'I heard of him as an astrologer and sorcerer,' countered the Judge.

'Thorne didn't believe in magic,' said Amesbury. 'But he believed in . . . illusion.' The general frowned, remembering. 'Looking here when you should be looking there,' he murmured, calling to mind Thorne's words. 'Most likely his Eye is a codebreaker of some kind,' concluded Amesbury. 'Though how he might have accessed information from our shipping log I have no idea. All I do know is if De Ryker comes to have the Eye,' added Amesbury, 'things must go badly for England. I hear you've met with the Dutch admiral personally,' he added, glancing at the Judge. 'So you know his ruthlessness.'

Something in the Judge's face twitched. 'I met the Dutch pirate off the coast of Gibraltar,' said the Judge. 'De Ryker's ship entered against ours in a skirmish. We looked to win; then De Ryker scuttled his own ship.'

'Why should he sink his own ship?' The King looked intrigued.

Judge Walters smiled. 'Most sailors can't swim,' he explained. 'De Ryker had given his crew one option. Win our ship or sink with their own and drown.'

'That is monstrous!' opined King Charles. 'He would sacrifice his crew for victory? I would never expect such barbary from the Dutch.'

Judge Walters's smile twisted slightly. 'His plan succeeded,' he said. 'De Ryker's men attacked us with new gusto, boarded and took our ship. I barely escaped with my life.'

'So you see,' said Amesbury, 'what kind of man we're up against. He may be closer to finding the Eye than we realise. Our navy is in no position to defend us. You know my advice. Negotiate with the Dutch. Give them back some colonies. It's our only hope.'

The King tapped his nose. 'Have no fear, Amesbury,' he said. 'My brother James has a solution to win us the war. A new science that will fill English coffers so deep, we shall have no need of negotiation.'

The King pointed to the beleaguered docks. Amesbury turned to see a magnificent ship turning gracefully into the harbour. It was a palace afloat, its vast carved sides gilded in gold and the three-storey officers' quarters twinkling with a hundred glass windows.

'The *Royal Charles*,' beamed the King. 'My brother is at the helm.'

Frances's yellow dress had appeared on the horizon. She was making an unsteady path towards them. Amesbury wondered if she'd already vomited or if that part was to come. He reflected on discovering an aspect of youth he didn't miss.

'We shall wait for Frances,' said the King, 'so she might see. We need not fear the Dutch. Aboard the *Royal Charles* my brother has the means to win us the war.'

Chapter 18

The room at the back of the printing house seemed suddenly claustrophobic. Charlie felt the weight of dusty tomes and old papers close around him.

'Thorne's works were burned,' he confirmed.

Macock nodded. 'He didn't write many,' he added. 'A few with academic titles. But they were all recalled and burned twenty years or so ago.'

'By who?' asked Lily. 'Who has that authority?'

Macock was frowning. 'I remember Father complaining about royal guards taking papers. He was very bitter about the loss of profit.' Macock's face twisted in thought. 'It was around the time of the Civil War. It must have been, because Father was furious about the cost of coloured inks, and we don't make handmade finishes like that now.' Macock's lips were moving as he tried to remember. He flipped some papers. 'Father might have recorded some details about Thorne before the publication was cancelled,' he said. 'Where to send payments. It would be here.' Macock's ringed hand landed on a thick pile of manuscripts. But as he pulled them out, a shower of paper confetti fluttered free.

'Mice,' he said, brushing away droppings. 'They love the taste of linseed. Perhaps something still remains.'

He plucked out a slim document. It was latticed with holes. As he turned the pages, it quickly became clear what was left was unreadable. Macock flipped a page and then another. He turned the papers sideways hopefully. Then he paused and smoothed out a portion of paper. Charlie made out a blot of ugly black ink.

'It's been crossed over,' said Macock, touching a section where previous writing had been scored over again and again. Above the blotted part were five neat words.

'Temple of Death,' said Macock, frowning. 'The forest.' Then his face lifted in understanding. 'Codebreaking!' he announced. 'Thorne became a royal cryptographer. I'm sure that was it. The Crown was concerned his books might reveal state secrets. Tricks to decoding. So they removed them from our print works.'

'They have that authority?' asked Lily.

'I think back then the King did as he pleased,' said Macock. 'But if a man becomes a cryptographer it is a very serious business. I imagine we'd be bound to hand over any material that might compromise a royal codebreaker even now.'

'Your father wrote that Thorne was in a Temple of Death?' said Charlie. 'That's his writing?'

'It must have been his joke,' said Macock. 'He could have fits of humour. The Temple of Death is where the Cipher resides, is it not? He must have only meant Thorne had become a cryptographer.'

Lily turned to Charlie, puzzlement rippling her pretty features. 'The Temple of Death. It's a real place? In a forest? Surely not.'

Charlie was thinking. 'It would be a clever way to hide something,' he said. 'Tell the truth in such a way that no one believes it. A temple of death. It's a fantasy, isn't it? What fool would genuinely look for such a place? It's just the kind of subterfuge a spy master would invent.' He thought for a moment. 'London is surrounded by woods. Perhaps they

75

built some prison or holding place for cryptographers they couldn't risk escaping. Then gave it a frightening name and let rumours do the rest.'

'That's a lot of potential places,' murmured Lily.

Charlie nodded, thinking of the Thames's wooded south bank, the thick and robber-infested forests from King's Cross to Hampstead Heath. Trees ran from the Tower of London to the new brickworks near Aldgate.

'Too many to search,' said Charlie.

Squirrelling the problem aside, he turned his attention to the issue at hand.

'You're sure everything was burned?' asked Charlie. 'All Thorne's works?'

Macock nodded. 'If the Crown ordered it, my father would have complied. He was a stickler for rules. But at a guess I'd say Thorne's ideas impressed my father enough to try a short print run. Quite a feat. My father was a difficult man to please,' he concluded with an expression that hinted of personal experience.

Charlie looked thoughtful. 'So we have Thorne, the King's astrologer,' he said. 'A codebreaker. But he also published a work on the old Roman gods.'

'Surely no king would employ a pagan as a codebreaker,' said Lily.

'There's one man still alive who would know for sure,' he added. 'The Cipher. It seems they were likely held together during the war.'

'You'll not find the Cipher,' opined Macock. 'He's kept safer than all the gold in the Tower of London.'

'We must find Ishmael Boney then,' said Lily. 'Surely he must have left clues.'

Macock spread his hands with the defeatist air of a man who had already mentally spent Ishmael's royalty payment.

'Gone without a trace,' he opined unsentimentally.

'Even hidden men have their weaknesses,' said Charlie. 'You say Ishmael Boney made a lot of money selling almanacs this year.' He looked at Macock, who nodded in agreement. 'Which means he would have been looking for places to spend it,' continued Charlie.

'Such as?' asked Lily.

'If Ishmael Boney is flesh and blood, perhaps an expensive brothel. Mother Mitchell might know something,' he decided.

'The old madam?' Lily wrinkled her nose. 'You'll need a fat purse of gold to make her talk.'

'I grew up in her household,' said Charlie with a grin. 'She's a soft spot for me. Although,' he added, 'she'll probably still want payment.'

Chapter 19

Barbara Castlemaine was staring into Buckingham's writing desk. The tavern sounds echoed up from the floor below. She looked to check Buckingham was safely in the adjoining room and that she couldn't be seen.

Lying atop a stack of letters was a lock of girl's hair, tied with muddy ribbon. Lady Castlemaine lifted it out and blinked in surprise.

The hair was deeply matted, as though it had been submerged in a dirty river. It was old, brittle with age. And was that . . . ? She thought there was blood as well as mud caking the tresses.

She put it down, puzzled. Did Buckingham secretly pine for some long-lost love? Perhaps a girl killed in the Civil War? Lady Castlemaine knew of no such a liaison.

Her eyes dropped to the papers. Astrological, she thought, not understanding the symbols. Something tugged at her mind. She thought there'd been some news of girls drowned recently.

She began rifling the other contents of the drawer. Papers. Letters. She scanned them. Love letters from various women. All names she knew or had guessed. Nothing of interest.

She leafed through more handwritten letters, her large violet eyes flicking over signatures. One was signed 'Sally Oakley'. Lady Castlemaine remembered her vaguely. She'd been part of the pack of those hoping to reinstate the King back in Holland.

Another bore a man called Thorne's name. Lady Castlemaine frowned at this. She'd heard of the astrologer. He'd been executed by the old King. She had a sudden memory from her girlhood. It had been . . . in one of the grand houses, she thought. Before the war. She and her mother had accidentally chanced upon Thorne in the gardens, crumpled in two, his thin body heaving in guttural sobs. He might have been eighteen then, she thought.

'Why is he crying?' she'd asked as her mother had drawn her quickly away.

'They burned his friend today,' said her mother, fanning herself with theatrical vigour. The way she said 'friend' implied something unpleasant.

Her mother leaned closer, fan still pumping. 'It was a great scandal,' she confided. 'The family paid a large amount of money to save Thorne from trial.' She paused for dramatic effect. 'Sodomy,' she breathed. 'Their fine name will never be recovered. The church refuses Thorne entry.'

Barbara's eyes fluttered in horror.

The woman nodded slowly. 'They say he keeps to his room,' she added. 'Inventing things. Weapons. He was always clever, but I think it's turned to bad. He reads books on Roman gods over and over.'

Barbara's eyes crinkled in confusion. 'Roman gods?'

Her mother studied her face. 'You're too young to know about such things,' she decided. 'The Romans had a taste for his kind. Thorne's kind.'

Barbara felt a blush rise up. She didn't fully understand but was too embarrassed to ask. It was a full five years before her mother gave the answers.

Her eyes landed on the matted lock of hair again, and this time she had an uneasy feeling. It seemed to her the blood was more obvious now. If it was a lover's hair, would it not have been washed and brushed clean?

Lady Castlemaine replaced the bloody hair, along with the letters. Then she tugged at the second drawer. Locked. Why would Buckingham leave his love letters, worth a fortune to a blackmailer, unlocked, but lock something else away?

She turned, her eyes settling on Buckingham's discarded breeches, slung in the corner of the room. His purse lay nearby. Could the key be inside?

Suddenly she felt strong fingers tighten around her neck. She threw up her hands instinctively, but the pressure was too great. She felt herself dragged, choking, across the room.

Buckingham threw her on the bed.

'You,' he accused, settling his weight on top of her, 'have been looking where you shouldn't.'

Lady Castlemaine was trying to disguise her shock.

'I am entitled,' she said, 'to know whom you write to. A woman must know who her lover is in love with.'

For a moment she thought she'd pitched the tone wrong. That he suspected her. Then his face shifted and he laughed.

'I like you jealous,' he said. 'It suits you.' He moved back on to the bed, taking her hand. Buckingham laid down the letter.

'You must not go looking again,' he said.

She shook her head.

'You'd be unwise to test me,' he added. 'I'm a different man from the one you knew.'

'Different?' She caught something in his tone.

'A story for another time.' He leaned closer and kissed her neck. 'Open your hand.'

She obeyed. In his hand, she now saw, was a small velvet purse.

He opened it and tipped the contents into her little white palm. She gasped as seven large creamy pearls rolled out.

'They are perfect,' she breathed, her large eyes on him. 'Perfect.' She closed her fingers tightly on the gems.

'Pirate treasure,' he said. 'Will you keep your word?'

He pushed her back into the bed, and the pearls clattered one by one to the dusty wooden floor.

Chapter 20

Charlie's welcome at Mother Mitchell's grand town house was not a warm one. The elderly madam was clearly drunk. This, combined with the loud noises echoing from the house, made Charlie think he'd visited in the midst of some kind of party. Lily, a previous employee of the old madam, had opted to wait a tactful distance from the door, but Mother Mitchell's keen eyes spotted her loitering near the fashionable brick houses further down the street.

'She owes me money,' growled Mother Mitchell, directing a squinty death stare towards Lily. 'Better she waits further away,' she added, balling her fists. 'Or I might just forget my kind heart and have her killed.'

Catching the furious brothel keeper's expression, Lily slipped down a side street, looking not the least concerned at the annoyance she'd engendered.

Charlie followed Mother Mitchell hurriedly inside the house before things turned ugly. The old madam had once been beautiful, but now worked determinedly to contrast herself against her young harem. Hard, greying ringlets, unplucked eyebrows and a prominent moustache framed her handsome features. A habit of pipe smoking had thickened her voice. The once famed figure had swelled to formidable bosom and hips, all clad in enough silk and ribbons to leave no doubt as to her authority and income.

'Lily Boswell is trouble, Charlie,' rumbled Mother Mitchell as she waddled along her sumptuously clad corridors. 'Didn't I warn you? Ran from my house with one of my best payers. In a rented dress,' she fumed, this last insult obviously hurting the worst. 'You had Maria before,' continued Mother Mitchell. 'Why couldn't you keep her? I like her. She's stable. Good for you.'

'She wanted things I couldn't give her,' said Charlie. He'd never admitted to anyone how deeply Maria had broken his heart. His unresolved past had stood between them, paralysing his ability to commit. Charlie had stupidly imagined she'd wait.

Mother Mitchell waved a dismissive hand. 'So you say,' she said, obviously unconvinced. 'You could still win her back. You were the only man she loved. I could see it in her. Loyal. Not like that gutter girl.'

'Maria is married now,' said Charlie, cutting her off before she could launch another attack on Lily. 'So I hear.'

'Not yet,' countered Mother Mitchell. 'Still a few days.'

'How on earth,' asked Charlie, baffled, 'would you know that?'

Mother Mitchell opened her mouth, then shut it again. 'I good as raised you here within these walls,' she concluded darkly. 'I brought you up better than to fall for a thief with a pretty face.'

She took out a long silver pipe from her hanging pocket, packed tobacco, lit it using a candle from a nearby gold candelabra and drew.

'Still taking on crimes for poor folk?' she asked, puffing.

'When they need my help.'

She gave a grunt that sounded like disapproval, but Charlie knew better. For all her talk of gold and profit, Mother Mitchell secretly liked that he caught felons for Londoners less fortunate. Though she enjoyed less that Charlie let some petty criminals escape hanging.

'Be sure you take enough gold from nobles too,' she remarked. 'Any word from Rowan?' she added, puffing out a stream of smoke.

Charlie hesitated. The pause told Mother Mitchell all she needed to know.

'Try and forget,' she advised with uncharacteristic gentleness. 'He may show up yet, but worrying won't bring him faster. You know your brother.'

Charlie nodded. Ever since they were boys, Rowan had caused him grief. He suspected his older brother knew far more than he let on about their early childhood before their mother died. But Rowan had never quite forgiven Charlie for being orphaned with a key whilst he got nothing.

'What was he selling when you saw him last?' asked Mother Mitchell. 'Fake black powder?'

'Plague protectorates,' said Charlie.

'A better trade,' surmised Mother Mitchell. She paused to hack phlegm from deep in her lungs. 'Men buying black powder are dangerous,' she added, 'but those sold a poor plague protectorate will not return to make trouble.'

There was a shriek, and a half-dressed girl flew through a door, giggling breathlessly. She ran clutching her skirts high to reveal bare white legs, pursued by a laughing young man in silk breeches and an open shirt. The man tackled the girl around the waist, and they both fell drunkenly on to the thick red rug of the hallway. The girl smiled enticingly and they kissed.

Mother Mitchell eyed them for a moment, clearly making some cost calculation.

'What are you here for?' she asked, frowning at the canoodling couple.

'Ishmael Boney,' said Charlie. 'He's missing and I need to talk to him.'

'You thought Ishmael would come here?' she supplied. 'Rich man that he is nowadays.'

Charlie nodded.

Mother Mitchell considered for a moment, then beckoned he should follow her. He expected her to lead him away from the loud revelry of the party room. But instead she beckoned him towards a large walnut-panelled door. Charlie raised his eyebrows.

'You're taking me into the party room?'

Mother Mitchell nodded, puffing on her pipe.

She really must be drunk, thought Charlie as she twisted the handle of the huge door. Mother Mitchell never let anyone have for free what could be paid for.

The door opened and noise rolled forth. A heavily painted girl was sat on the lap of a bewigged man, both murdering 'Greensleeves' on a gilded harpsichord. Girls in various states of undress were every-where. Men were lounging on cushions, drinking from gold cups, eat-ing sweets.

The stench of rancid grapes hit Charlie like a slap. In the centre of the room stood a faux-Grecian fountain, through which cheap red wine gushed. One youth was bent backwards, crimson liquid splashing over his nose and open mouth. Two friends were cheering him on.

'Finest burgundy,' said Mother Mitchell smoothly, noticing Charlie's expression and nodding to the flow of low-quality wine.

Charlie, who remembered watering down Mother Mitchell's cheap smuggled imports with vinegar, smiled to himself.

She placed her smoking pipe on a table, filled herself a glass and took a wincing sip.

'Good stuff,' she said. 'Lively. How do you like my new Celestial Room?' she added, pointing out the sun constellations writ large over every wall.

'As always,' said Charlie, taking in the gaudy star murals, 'your house is the latest fashion.'

Two men danced past them to the enthusiastic shouts of the onlookers.

'I give my customers what they want,' said Mother Mitchell proudly. 'Almanacs are all London talks of. My girls spend all their money on them.'

'Is this why you brought me here?' asked Charlie. 'Did Ishmael Boney help you design this room?'

Mother Mitchell shook her head. 'Ishmael Boney has never been here,' she said. 'Though I've extended invitations. Mr Boney is interested in something more specialist than I provide.'

'What?'

She shrugged. 'If I knew, I'd offer it. Ishmael Boney would be a great attraction at my house. All the fine lords talk of him. He's a great favourite with the King,' she added.

Charlie logged this.

'Then why bring me to this room?' he asked, confused.

She winked. 'I can't help you with Ishmael Boney,' she said, 'but there's a girl in here knows a little of astrology. Maybe she can help you.'

Charlie sighed inwardly. A street girl with a penchant for the zodiac could hardly compare to a famous astrologer.

'She's over there,' added Mother Mitchell, 'on the stage.'

Charlie turned to see a modest stage with a velvet pelmet stood in one corner. Acting on it were seven girls, each costumed as a star god or goddess. A chubby Saturn had a purple cape drawn low over her face and carried a scythe. She was throwing a red cloth over the silver-painted face of a moon goddess in diaphanous white robes.

'Nobles love the almanacs,' explained Mother Mitchell. 'We act it out for them, make it an entertainment. Though I'll lose a pretty penny with this coming eclipse,' she added, smoothing the expensive silk of her dress. 'The men will play good husbands and my girls will fall to hysterics.'

Charlie was automatically looking for Venus, who was usually depicted naked, holding an apple. He identified Mars in her short leather skirt and Roman helmet, then the sun, gold crowned and glorious in a low-cut yellow dress. His eyes lingered on her features. It was a face he'd once loved.

The symmetrical blue eyes, blonde hair and straight nose. Suddenly Charlie realised why Mother Mitchell had allowed him in her hallowed Celestial Room.

The sun goddess was Maria.

Chapter 21

Charlie made to look away a split second too late. Maria's blue eyes landed on his and widened in alarm. A slow blush crept over her face. Then she stepped down from the stage and strode towards him, moving upright through the drunken people. Charlie shot an accusing look at Mother Mitchell.

'Maria knows about astrology,' said the portly madam innocently. 'She helped me design this room. And it's time you young people talked,' she added.

Charlie was about to tell Mother Mitchell exactly what he thought of her suggestion when a sudden eruption of shouts sounded from the other side of the room. A blonde woman threw her glass of wine at a chubby girl in a jet-black horsehair wig. Furious, the raven-haired victim grabbed a chunk of the girl's blonde hair and began wheeling her around. Men began shouting encouragingly.

Mother Mitchell hurried away to intervene, her silken bulk cutting a path through the drunk girls and leaving Charlie alone with the scantily clad Maria.

'What are you doing here?' Maria demanded, tugging self-consciously at her low-cut dress.

'I could ask you the same question,' said Charlie. He was suddenly furious with her. 'You should have told me,' he said angrily, 'if you needed money. I would have done anything, Maria. All you needed do was ask. You didn't need to come here.'

'It's not what you think,' she hissed, glancing about to check no one was watching them. 'I'm just part of the display. I don't . . . I never take my clothes off,' she added.

'You don't need to,' said Charlie. 'That dress is tight enough to show everything.'

He saw the hurt on her face and regretted the remark.

'It's no business of yours,' snapped Maria, 'what I do or what I wear.'

He felt an urge to wrap her in his coat, to carry her away.

'Does your fiancé know?' he asked. It was a low blow and he knew it.

Maria flinched. Her face darkened. 'Don't use your thief taker tricks with me,' she hissed, flushing. 'You've no right. Not after what you did.'

'*You* left *me*!' Charlie's voice rose without his meaning it to. A few aristocrats turned, wondering why the sun goddess was arguing with a commoner.

'What choice did you give me?' Maria accused. 'You *weren't there*. All you cared about was your family secrets and your no-good brother.'

She stopped abruptly, biting her lip. Guilt flooded her features.

'I heard about Rowan,' she mumbled. 'I'm sorry.'

'Nothing to be sorry about,' Charlie said evenly. 'Rowan vanishes all the time, plague or no. He'll come back owing money, and I'll bail him out again.'

Pity glowed in Maria's eyes. It was worse than the anger, Charlie thought.

'Why are you here?' she asked softly. 'Did you come for me?'

'No.' He admitted it too quickly and wondered how she always did this to him. Maria somehow made him honest when he shouldn't be. 'I didn't know you were here,' he added. He wanted to tell her that if he'd have known, he would have stopped her working for Mother Mitchell. But he didn't want her angry again.

'Mother Mitchell thinks you can help me with some information,' he admitted, 'about astrology.'

Maria hesitated, taking him in. Charlie saw something flash in her face. Something she was trying to hide. Maria missed him, he realised.

'Come on,' she said. 'We'll go somewhere quieter. These men love a drama. They're so bored spending their money.'

Her eyes ranged the room and landed on Mother Mitchell, who was now physically restraining three drunk girls from attacking one another. The old madam was trying to separate the girls without damaging their dresses and didn't notice them slip away.

'You have some new mystery?' asked Maria, closing the dressing room door behind them. 'Something to do with astrology?'

The room was small and stank of thick perfume. It had once been the Palace of Venus room, Charlie remembered. His eyes found the old statue.

'Yes. The beer is still in the marble Venus?' asked Charlie.

She nodded.

Charlie took out his tankard, filled it from a tap strategically placed on Venus's nipple and dutifully laid small change at the base. This particular statue held cheap small beer for the girls, whilst their high-paying clients drank fine wines. But nothing in Mother Mitchell's house was ever free, even for friends.

Drinking the beer, Charlie outlined everything he knew, watching Maria's disappointment grow.

'You're still chasing that mystery,' she said sadly. 'Charlie, perhaps some things can't be solved.'

She was talking about Rowan, he realised.

'It was never about that,' Charlie retorted angrily. He stopped himself, knowing he was on the brink of starting the same argument.

'You want to find out who you are?' she interjected. 'I'll tell you who you are. You're Charlie Tuesday. Everyone in London knows you or owes you a favour. Particularly the women,' she added with a wry smile. 'You're clever and quick and unreliable and impossible. When you get a mystery under your skin, you can't let it go. But I believe you're good-hearted underneath it all. What else do you need to know?' She glared at him.

'Right at this moment?' Charlie grinned at her. 'I need to know something about the stars.'

She looked defeated and charmed all at once.

'You'll never be happy,' she said, 'if you keep this mystery hanging over you.'

'So help me solve it,' Charlie said. He took her arm. 'I know you're interested too. And I think you might know enough about astrology to help me. Because whenever you set your mind to something you do it properly.'

She hid a smile.

He told her about the rings. About his mother's bundle, the angels and finally the corpse at Dead Man's Curve.

'What about the astrology on the body?' asked Charlie. 'Do you understand anything of it?'

Maria shook her head. 'I only know a little,' she said. 'Maybe no more than you. There are seven planets,' she continued, 'the sun, the moon, Saturn, Jupiter, Mars, Neptune and Venus. The planets move around constellations of stars – the twelve signs of the zodiac. Dependent on where the planets are in relation to the constellations, astrologers predict future events.'

She noticed the disappointment on Charlie's face.

'Show me the almanac,' she suggested.

He took it out and flicked through until he found the right page.

'The cherubims were taken from old astrology,' she said. 'It's quite well known. The four seasons that surround the sun became the four angels closest to God. The cherubim heads still mark it,' she added. 'Aquarius, Taurus, Leo and Scorpio – spring, summer, autumn and winter.'

Charlie looked at the angels' faces. What he'd assumed to be a bird was a scorpion.

'Much of Christianity and astrology is mixed,' added Maria. 'It was how they tempted pagans to believe in Jesus. The festivals – Christmas, Easter – they mark equinoxes. Changes in the stars and the seasons.'

'Four rings,' Charlie was thinking out loud. 'Four people. Each given a ring to solve a code. So the cherubim could match their star signs,' he decided, 'but they could also represent something else.'

'What of the date?' he said. 'All Hallows' Eve.'

'Yes.' Maria nodded. 'According to the astrologers, that is the darkest time of all. There's a lunar eclipse,' she said slowly. 'At midnight. The moon will turn to blood.'

Charlie nodded, remembering the same words in Ishmael's almanac.

'The moon into blood,' repeated Maria. 'It's from the Bible. Every churchgoer has heard it. The sun will be turned to darkness and the moon to blood,' she intoned in the static voice of someone repeating by rote. 'Armageddon,' she concluded.

'The end of time,' said Charlie. 'That's what Ishmael meant. The end is nigh.'

Maria nodded. 'The astrologers are all in a frenzy. They think the All Hallows' eclipse heralds a kind of apocalypse.'

'A kind of apocalypse?'

'No one can quite agree on what terrible event will take place,' said Maria. 'Some think the whole world will end. Others say when the clocks strike twelve, London will fall. And others say a great discovery will destroy the world or be lost forever.'

Chapter 22

Janus's boat bobbed on the water. She was a small ship and old. Not large enough to make any deep-sea venture, but fitted with sails and easy enough for one man to work.

In the hull the dark shape lay under its blanket. Was it Janus's imagination, or was the river calling to it? He could feel the tides tugging at the underside of his boat, adding dead weight, calling for their offering to be returned.

Janus looked at the covered shape. Then he dropped the sails, jumped easily down and unveiled his offering, ready to begin work.

First he weighed the corpse, hitching it to the mast with a rudimentary pulley and approximating the mass, as Thorne had taught him. Then he took a calculation of the height and breadth – factors likely to impact on the woman's journey along the Thames.

After logging the position of the moon and the high tide, Janus was ready to begin his work. Carefully he pulled away the blanket and drew out his knife.

The copper-handled blade twisted in his grip. Waterlogged skin gave way easily, and dark liquid flowed from the wound. He moved the rag, wiped, cut again, then grasped the edge of severed flesh and pulled. The corpse's blood leaked under his fingernails. His breathing was ragged, he noticed, his upper lip beaded with sweat. A neat triangle of skin came away in his hand, cold and wet. Dark blood ran in rivulets down the corpse's neck.

Janus's mind was flipped back nineteen years, to the day of the execution.

Thorne, walking silently up the steps to his end. Janus had watched from the crowd, his every muscle tensed. Had Thorne really betrayed him? He couldn't believe it. And yet here Thorne was, moving calmly to the executioner's block, his secret ready to die with him. But there was still time. His master was not yet dead.

Janus's eyes scanned the crowd. Then he saw him. Tobias Oakley. Hot hatred swirled in his belly. Then a flash of fear. What was his rival doing here? Had Oakley convinced Thorne to betray him?

The astrologer was on his knees now. Janus saw the condemned man shake his head, and cold disbelief shot through him.

Thorne had declined to say any last words.

Janus's eyes filled with tears of fury and betrayal. His fists were clenched in tight balls.

The Eye. You said it was mine!

His eyes switched again to Tobias Oakley. The sailor's face was pale, lips murmuring a prayer.

Janus wanted to shout to him that Thorne wouldn't want his prayers. Then he saw Thorne make a slight movement. The astrologer touched his mouth, as if in benediction.

The crowd screamed and taunted, thinking Thorne was making a Catholic gesture to save his soul. But Janus knew better.

Thorne has slipped a silver coin into his mouth, the Roman token of passage to the underworld. His soul will cross the River Styx, *thought Janus,* to Saturn, the dark god.

Suddenly Janus knew. The coin was a sign. Something he knew only Janus would understand. He leaned forward, straining to hear against the noise of the crowd. The executioner raised his axe. Thorne's face was calm, almost serene.

The axe fell. And Janus's heart seemed to split in two.

Thorne, his greatest love and deepest fear, was gone.

As the blood gushed over the wooden scaffold, Janus felt his hopes leak away with it. Then the mouth of the corpse had dropped open. The silver coin had fallen free. With blood streaming from the neck, Janus was the only one to see it drop. And no one had noticed a little boy run through the crowd and scoop it up from the bloody mud.

Not even Tobias Oakley.

It was only when Janus later examined the coin that he realised it was meaningless. He'd been right to suspect Tobias. Oakley had stolen almost everything from Janus. Even Thorne's trust.

Suddenly back on the river, Janus realised the woman's dead eyes were staring up at him accusingly. He drove down his self-loathing.

Embrace your dark stars.

If Thorne would not leave him his birthright, then Janus would take it for himself.

And destroy Charlie Oakley.

Tobias Oakley's son had no noble blood, no learning. He knew nothing of the stars. Janus looked at the body, carved with his calculations. Only he and Thorne knew what they really meant. Every other ignorant Londoner would mistake them for astrological predictions.

Janus made a quick assessment of the Thames.

The river was full of boats going about their daily trade. But no one would notice another Londoner dumping his detritus into the water.

He dragged the body on to the deck, leaving a slick bloody trail behind. Then he slipped a silver coin in her mouth.

'Go to the deep waters,' he murmured as he heaved her up, 'into His embrace.'

Janus let the body fall with a heavy splash into the water. As the tide took the dead girl, she left a trail of scarlet in her wake.

Janus drew out a leather tankard in a toast, splashed red wine, drank, then bowed his head to Saturn and watched. The dead body had begun her inexorable journey towards Dead Man's Curve.

Chapter 23

The dressing room at Mother Mitchell's house suddenly seemed close and stifling. Maria was toying with the edge of her tight-fitting dress.

'Lunar eclipses are always bad omens,' she continued, 'but this is a total eclipse. The moon will be in complete shadow. And it happens on All Hallows' Eve, when the dead walk the earth.'

'Do you think the stars have such power?' asked Charlie.

'I don't know,' said Maria, 'but all the astrologers agree this is a year of revelation. Of great change, good or bad. Mostly bad,' she added.

'How?'

'When the planets align with the constellations of the zodiac,' she said, 'they mean things.'

'Such as?'

'Each planet is a god,' said Maria. 'An ancient Roman god. Some think the planets each have their own personality, their own whims. They must be appeased to prevent bad luck. Each demands an offering to bring in the next term.'

'What kind of offering?'

'Well,' said Maria slowly, 'Venus is the Goddess of Love and Fertility. When she ascends, we offer apples, rose oils, candles. She traditionally comes at Halloween for Libra. This year Saturn is in Gemini, the sign for London.'

'What does Saturn want?'

She swallowed. 'Saturn is the God of Death,' she said. 'He comes in winter and walks with a harvest scythe. Saturn demands the greatest of sacrifices to make the sun rise again.'

'Blood sacrifice?' guessed Charlie.

'Human sacrifice,' nodded Maria. 'Specifically he demands children. It's where our notion of Satan the Devil comes from,' she added. 'Saturn, the Roman death god, became Satan, the Christian force of evil.'

'What about the All-Seeing Eye?' asked Charlie. 'Does that have any connection with Saturn?'

Maria thought for a moment. 'In the Bible there's a story of Lucifer and a lost eye,' she said. 'When the Devil was cast from heaven, an emerald fell from his crown. It's sometimes represented as an eye with rays of light emitting. The Eye of Heaven. But you'd have to ask an astrologer if there's a connection to the stars.'

'It sounds like Devil worshipping,' said Charlie, remembering the five-pointed star carved into the body of the dead girl. 'Pentagrams, symbols of Lucifer, human sacrifice.'

She gestured with her thumb to the room they'd just come from. 'The nobles here are all talk of a Dutch fireship pilot named Janus in London. They have it he is searching for the Eye. Means to destroy London.'

Charlie digested this. The name sounded familiar somehow. He had a strong image of a dark figure, burning with hatred.

'Do they think him dangerous?' he asked.

'Very,' said Maria. 'Janus is suspected an English noble. Someone very high-born.' She eyed Charlie. 'You should be careful,' she said. 'He sounds like a powerful enemy. A man who will stop at nothing.'

Chapter 24

The men were sweating, heads pounding. Reeking fumes swirled in the close confines of the ship. The hull had been gutted, and a flammable mixture of pitch, pine resin and pork fat painted on the wood floor.

De Ryker's one good eye watched his men as they worked to build a snaking path of metal guttering. His deeply sun-lined face was folded in concentration.

'Very good,' he said approvingly. 'Janus's plans are excellent.' He tapped the high metal gutter. 'Once we fill this with flammable things, it will take fire fore and aft in moments.'

'You're certain we should venture such an expensive ship?' managed his first mate, Cornelius, a beanpole-thin man who was reeling from the stench of sulphur and pitch.

De Ryker turned to his first mate, who shrank back a little. The admiral cut an imposing figure, tall in his long captain's coat, with well-worn black leather boots, a grey shirt open at the neck and a thick crucifix hanging down to chest level. A thick brown belt crossed his torso, fastened with four loaded pistols. His long greying hair was tied across with a green handkerchief and topped with a battered black hat.

He was the only one of the crew who didn't seem to suffer from the headaches and fainting fits that troubled the fireship sailors.

'You still don't trust Janus?' asked De Ryker.

'He was a prisoner of war,' frowned Cornelius. He didn't voice what most of the crew thought. That Janus was cursed. The fireship pilot's ascent to De Ryker's side had been fast enough to justify mutterings of sorcery.

'Janus and I have an accord,' said De Ryker. 'I know his weaknesses. He is clever, but not so clever as he thinks.'

The admiral noticed two men rolling a huge barrel below deck. He moved to help position it.

'Another of Janus's inventions,' he told Cornelius as he rolled up his sleeves. The admiral's muscular forearms were etched in rudimentary black-inked tattoos – planetary symbols and constellations for luck in navigation. 'Pork fat mixed with dry brush and pine resin,' continued De Ryker proudly. 'With the right fuse it will blow like a cannon.'

'We'd better pray it hits its target,' said Cornelius pointedly. 'The price of pine resin has skyrocketed. The purser calculates the total cost of flammables runs to thousands. And the use of such a fine ship—'

De Ryker patted the wooden side of the boat. 'A fireship must be fast,' he said. 'We are not like the English. We need not fear she will miss her target. We have the best pilot on the seven seas.'

Cornelius had to grudgingly agree with this. Aboard a fireship, Janus was a phenomenon. He was clever as a snake and twice as fast. He'd burned targets others wouldn't have attempted and escaped with his life against impossible odds.

'The English will not expect such boldness,' agreed Cornelius, 'as to attack the Thames.'

'No navy has ever assailed the Thames,' said De Ryker. 'She is a slippery mistress. We shall be the first, Cornelius.' De Ryker smiled. 'Do not forget,' he added, 'Janus is bringing us the Eye.' He looked out into the dark deck of the ship. 'The English have made atrocities on our people,' he said. 'We will teach them the price of their horrors.' He looked proudly at their latest fireship. 'Our night attack on the *Queen Catherine* showed the English our might,' he said with a smile. 'Now we will show them what we're truly capable of. Our latest fireship is the fleetest and deadliest yet. She will take fire straight into the heart of their fleet. We'll blow the heart from their navy.'

Chapter 25

Charlie found Lily lounging against a wall near to Mother Mitchell's house.

'I'd heard the Dutch fireship pilot is searching for the Eye,' she pondered as Charlie explained what he had learned. 'He seems to have links with the Marshalsea prison. Perhaps he and the Judge are both involved in the Deptford murders.'

'You think the Judge is helping this fireship pilot?' surmised Charlie.

'Perhaps. The Judge disappeared at sea for the last two years. Plenty of time to turn traitor. We should be alert in any case. What else did you discover?'

Charlie told her.

'So our rings match the Aquarius and Leo cherubim,' she said when he told her what he'd discovered. 'Which leaves Scorpio and Taurus still to find. And you think the Eye is an emerald. We're hunting a jewel?'

'Could be,' said Charlie. 'Could be something else.'

Lily considered. 'A jewel cannot locate ships at sea,' she said. 'Perhaps it has some other value – for bribery or buying arms.'

'Did you keep watch for our Dutch-pipe-smoking friend?' Charlie asked. 'The man who followed us from the Marshalsea prison?'

'We must have lost him,' said Lily. 'I doubled back when you went into Mother Mitchell's house, and there was no sign of him.'

'Good,' said Charlie. The man's presence had made him distinctly uneasy. He had a bad feeling Judge Walters knew what they were looking for.

'I've been thinking,' said Lily. 'Shouldn't we be looking for the Cipher? He was the codebreaker at the time the rings were made. Maybe he even made them. You're the best thief taker in London,' she added coaxingly. 'Surely you could find him?'

Charlie shook his head. 'The Cipher is more of a legend than a man. There are whispers about him. That he's a ghost. He's run mad. Anyone who searches for him ends up dead. Besides, it would take me weeks to track him, and we only have days until Halloween. I've a feeling,' he added, 'All Hallows' Eve is tied up in finding the Eye. After that our chance might be lost.' He didn't add that Maria predicted London might also fall.

'If only we knew where Ishmael Boney was,' she said.

'There are a few possibilities,' said Charlie, turning over what he knew. 'Ishmael Boney never visited Mother Mitchell's. Which is strange for a wealthy man.'

'Particular tastes?' suggested Lily.

'That's what Mother Mitchell suggested,' said Charlie. 'Though she makes it her business to cater to every unusual whim.'

'I'm well aware of it,' said Lily archly. 'I worked for her, remember?'

'Mother Mitchell also said Ishmael was a favourite with the King. So there's another place he could be.'

'Which is?'

'I think,' said Charlie slowly, 'we should look for Ishmael Boney in the Maze of Lost Souls.'

Chapter 26

The astrologer was looking nervously at Janus.

'I've seen your chart before,' he said finally.

Janus remembered the astrologer's grimy room. The larger, meandering building housed a variety of murky trades. One rickety door led to a woman manufacturing sheep-gut contraceptives. The apothecary across the dark hallway sold abortion potions, and his rank green fumes crept under every doorway.

'Years ago,' agreed Janus, his eyes drifting over the familiar desk. There were charts, papers and a heavy metal globe depicting the stars in the heavens. 'You told me my destiny was set,' added Janus. 'The stars decreed an evil in my soul that couldn't be remedied.'

It was strange repeating the words now. Janus remembered his terror. The realisation that long after escaping Thorne's dark room of horrors, his life would be one of death and fear.

But he wasn't scared now.

'I'd never seen a chart with so much Saturn,' agreed the astrologer. He was wall-eyed and tiny – only just able to see over his own large table by a raised chair. His voice shook as he spoke. 'I was certain it was some mistake.'

Janus remembered the astrologer all those years ago flipping through papers, his fingers tracing at a chart.

'Saturn,' the astrologer had mumbled. 'And Saturn again. A deadly man,' he'd said more to himself than Janus. 'You're certain your birth-date is correct?'

When Janus had nodded, the astrologer reverted to his books, verifying, dipping his feather pen into ink and making notes.

'It is very bad,' he concluded, 'a very unlucky chart.'

The fortune teller was looking at Janus intently now, though his crossed eyes made it difficult to read his expression.

'You told me before that something very bad happened in your past,' he said. 'Someone misused you badly when you were a boy. You saw things no child should see.'

The way the astrologer said it reminded Janus of him. Thorne. So sure of his own cleverness. So unable to understand the feelings of others.

Janus was suddenly glad of his disguise. The handkerchief mask and low hat. He didn't like people to see his face when he was reminded of the Bad Thing.

'I don't come for my fortune,' said Janus. 'I want you to make a chart.'

He took a slip of paper from his coat and handed it over.

The astrologer hesitated. 'Charlie Oakley?'

'He's a thief taker.'

'You know a great deal about him,' said the astrologer. 'The hour of his birth. His family connections.'

'I knew his father well,' said Janus. 'A lowly sailor named Tobias Oakley,' he added disapprovingly.

The astrologer hesitated. 'I cannot help you,' he said. 'Your old master was an evil man. A traitor.'

Janus felt suddenly uncertain. Did the fortune teller know who he truly was? A sick feeling bloomed. He'd been so careful to keep his identity secret.

'Thorne was a god,' said Janus. 'You could never understand the things necessary to such a powerful man.'

'Thorne hurt you?' the astrologer suggested quietly. 'Hurt other children?'

Janus hesitated. It had been hard to know what truly happened. Only that Thorne was a dark creator, to whom painful sacrifices must be made.

'Thorne protected me,' said Janus. But he was suddenly uncertain. Anger at the astrologer flooded through him.

'I cannot aid a man of Saturn so near to the eclipse . . .' the astrologer began.

Black rage bloomed in Janus's heart. Suddenly he was standing up and the large table had been upended. The astrologer lay on the floor, a stunned expression on his face. Then Janus had the heavy globe in his hand, his fist striking again and again.

Thorne's face was floating before his eyes, mocking him.

You promised me you'd leave me the means to find it. You promised me.

Janus looked down to see that the astrologer's eyes had glazed. His own hand was slick with blood. He let the metal globe fall.

Despair rippled through him.

The astrologer is right. You are evil to the core.

The dead man's eyes seemed to confirm the voice in his head.

Janus righted himself. He took a breath.

Embrace your dark stars.

It was the lesson De Ryker had taught him over and over again.

Chapter 27

'You don't have to be so cryptic,' complained Lily as they headed back through the ash-strewn streets towards Whitehall. 'Can't you just tell me where Ishmael Boney is?'

'I did tell you,' said Charlie. 'The Maze of Lost Souls. It's part of the Palace of Whitehall. A place where all the hidden people go. The ones under the King's protection at least,' he added. 'The others go to London Bridge or the bottom of the Thames.'

'I've never heard of it,' said Lily with a slight smile. 'Do no spies hide there?'

'Spies bad enough to need the Maze's protection tend to die first.'

The smile slid from her face.

Charlie's eyes were darting from building to building. He froze.

'We're still being followed,' he muttered. 'The man with the Dutch pipe.'

Lily glanced back nervously. 'I don't see anyone,' she said.

'It's the same man as was behind us at the debtors' prison,' said Charlie. He sniffed the air. 'Smell that? That's wet tobacco. Dutch. You don't get much of that in London. He's close by.'

They'd stopped walking, and Charlie had the sense of their pursuer sliding away into the shadows, avoiding being seen.

'Do you think he knows something about the rings?' asked Lily.

'Can't see any other reason for him to have our tail.' Charlie thought back to the Marshalsea. He hadn't noticed anyone listening to their conversation. But perhaps some inmate had overheard something. There were dangerous people locked away. People who knew people.

'Can we lose him in the Maze?' suggested Lily.

'He might know something important,' said Charlie. 'If he's Dutch, or working for Judge Walters, there must be a reason.'

He was watching her face closely. Every time Judge Walters was mentioned, he noticed, Lily seemed to flinch. She noticed Charlie looking and turned away, feigning interest in seeking out their stalker.

'Judge Walters,' said Charlie. 'What haven't you told me?'

'There's nothing to tell,' said Lily. 'He's an evil man.' She was turning the ruby ring on her finger distractedly.

'An evil man who has likely set a mercenary on our tail,' said Charlie. 'Lily, if there's something more, you must tell me.'

Lily bit her lip. 'I told you. He enslaves gypsies.'

Charlie had a sudden glimpse of something in her face.

'What else?' he demanded.

'I didn't tell you the whole of my intelligence,' she admitted.

'So tell me.'

Lily took a breath. 'The Judge went to sea and came back with a ruby ring,' she said. 'He's deeply involved with the Eye, I'm sure of it.'

'And?'

'Things filter back, from smugglers, pirates,' said Lily carefully. 'Your name was mentioned.'

'*My* name?' Charlie blurted, shocked.

'Janus seems to have a personal grudge against you,' said Lily. 'Or perhaps your family. It's not entirely clear. There is talk he could be an old apprentice of Thorne's.'

'You're certain?' said Charlie, his voice thick with disbelief.

'It's only whispers,' said Lily. 'Nothing firm. It might not be true. I didn't want to concern you unduly.'

Thoughts were spiralling in Charlie's head. A Dutch fireship pilot knew something of his family. What? And why was the name Janus attached to a cold feeling of dread? Charlie had a half memory – more of a feeling – of someone who hated him. Someone he'd feared as a boy.

Charlie considered for a moment. 'If you think the Judge is more than he seems,' he said, 'then it might be in our interest to talk with whoever he's put on our tail. This Dutch-pipe smoker could know something of the Eye or the rings.'

'What do you suggest?' asked Lily sarcastically. 'We call out and ask him to help us?'

'We might be able to trap him,' said Charlie. 'Discover what he knows.'

'He could be dangerous,' said Lily.

'Almost certainly,' said Charlie, 'but he could know something important.'

Chapter 28

Frances Stewart allowed the King to lead her up the gangplank of the *Royal Charles*. Her yellow dress trailed on wet wood, and her little brown curls hung dishevelled around her pretty face.

'It is more beautiful than I ever imagined,' she gushed, staring up at the enormous ship. 'A golden city afloat.'

The gilded ship towered above them, its grand back section tiered in multiple-windowed storeys. Her curving sides bore two layers of cannons, and the poker-straight mast rose a hundred feet into the air.

'We've improved it since Cromwell's time,' said the King, waving a hand towards the towering tiers of the mighty ship. 'The carved crests alone took fifty men a year to complete.'

They reached the elaborately carved balustrade and moved on to the deck. Frances lurched slightly, then righted herself, clutching her stomach.

The ship was a tight network of rigging, with highly decorated doors leading to the officers' quarters at the back. Gold-painted wood rose up to depict England's lion, towering high over the water.

Charles pointed up to the deck. 'And there is the Duke of York! See how well he captains the ship.'

The King's brother leapt down from behind the tiller and bounded to meet them.

'Pleased to be back aboard the *Royal Charles*, James?' smiled Charles, noting his brother's energy.

The brothers embraced. They had once looked very alike, with their full noses and hooded eyes. But the strain of kingship had aged Charles, tempering his impetuousness with wisdom. In contrast, James was looking more like his father every day and had the same restless, irritable energy. He kissed Frances's hand, allowing his eyes to linger.

'She's a lucky ship,' agreed James. His eyes lighted on Amesbury moving easily across the swaying deck, adjusting his wide sash.

'Amesbury!' called James. 'Remember our first time aboard?' He took an affectionate look at the deck. 'The *Royal Charles* brought the King and I back from Holland,' he explained to Frances, 'to return Charles to his throne. She'd been Cromwell's. We renamed her there and then. Toasted her with wine.' James grinned at the memory. 'You must let me back at sea, Charles,' he said. 'I cannot stand dull court life.'

The King's smile faltered. 'Show us your new discovery,' he said.

James nodded. 'In the captain's cabin,' he promised, 'the new dawn in science awaits. Follow me.'

'It takes two thousand trees to build a ship this size,' explained Charles proudly, leading Frances across the deck. 'All English timber. For the mast a man must hunt a whole forest to find the tree tall and straight enough . . .' He hesitated, catching Frances's face. She was leaning heavily on his arm. 'Should you like to disembark?' asked Charles kindly. 'The harbour waters are rougher than I expected. I used to get seasick myself.'

Frances shook her head, but her eyes were glassy, fixed longingly on the unmoving dockyard.

Amesbury felt a wave of sympathy for whoever cleaned the King's carriage. The poor girl was bound to lose her guts on the journey back.

James led them into the captain's cabin. Through a glass-windowed door was a large office, sumptuously decorated in rugs, carved wood and bookshelves lined with expensively bound tomes. Rolled charts filled another richly carpentered walnut-wood shelf, whilst elaborate tools of navigation were neatly laid on the desk. A gold-plated compass was arranged with a jewelled spyglass and a magnificent globe.

In the office was a neatly dressed man and a dog with a bandaged paw.

Despite her obvious nausea, Frances gave a little squeal of delight to see the dog.

'This is Mr Bartholomew,' explained James. 'He will win us the war and take England to untold riches.'

Mr Bartholomew bowed. He was a doughty little man with a tight belly parting the gold buttons of his waistcoat. His white wig was grubby, sloping to one side to reveal a patch of pink scalp where his grey hair was thinning.

He bowed low, put a cautious hand to the slipping wig and gestured to the dog. The dog looked at Amesbury. It raised its wounded leg, as if petitioning him personally.

'If I may explain, Your Majesty,' said Bartholomew, addressing the King, 'perhaps you've already heard of my bold solution to navigation at sea.'

Amesbury felt despair wash over him.

Bartholomew gave a little cough and straightened his wig. 'As you gentlemen know,' he said, 'no man has solved the issue of keeping correct time aboard a ship. Until now.'

Amesbury looked on cynically. It was true that clocks couldn't keep time aboard ship. The rolling motion and changeable weather played havoc with their workings. But what had the dog to do with it?

'The dog is wounded,' explained Bartholomew. He reached in his coat and brought out a knife. 'This knife inflicted the wound.'

'Sympathetic magic,' agreed the Duke of York enthusiastically. 'Hurting the weapon will worsen the dog's wound.'

King Charles looked appalled. 'Why must a dog be hurt?' he asked, reaching down to pet the animal, sympathy shining in his brown eyes.

'And how does that help with navigation?' demanded Amesbury as the dog barked and licked the King's ringed fingers.

Bartholomew wagged a finger. 'We place the dog aboard a ship,' he said. 'Back on shore at exactly noon I burn the knife blade.' He paused for effect. 'The dog aboard the ship will feel the hurt on the knife and howl loudly.' Bartholomew grinned proudly. 'Those aboard ship will know it to be noon in England,' he concluded. 'And from this they can calculate their longitude. Their exact position at sea.'

Frances's little forehead was puckered. 'What does it mean?' she whispered to the King.

Charles, who'd been kneeling, patting the dog, stood, pleased to be able to impart his wisdom. 'Sailors cannot calculate longitude,' he explained. 'So they must sail in sight of a coast, in the path of pirates and enemy ships.'

'With my invention,' promised Bartholomew grandly, 'Your Majesty will plot a faster course to the New World. You will beat the Dutch and return with riches.'

'You mean to win a war against the greatest admiral of the age,' said Amesbury, his voice thick with contempt, 'by the use of an injured dog?'

Temporarily forgetting her seasickness, Frances had moved forward to pat the dog.

James turned to Amesbury. 'You see?' he said. 'There is no need for negotiation with the Dutch. With the riches we'll win from the colonies, we'll rebuild our navy in weeks.'

'Your Majesty,' said Amesbury, seeing doubt in the King's face, 'even if this scheme were viable, it takes months to reach the New World.'

'A ship has already been sent,' interjected James. 'The *Loyal London* set sail months ago, with its longitude dog aboard.' He smiled at Amesbury. 'I myself invested in the voyage. The *Loyal London* will return in days, laden with spoils.'

The Duke of York turned to Frances, inviting her approval.

'A dog is a jolly creature,' said Frances. 'I'm sure he would greatly cheer the sailors at sea.' She clamped her mouth shut suddenly. Her nausea seemed to be returning.

The King smiled at her. 'We are alike in our love of dogs,' he said, gazing at Frances.

'We don't need the stars or an injured dog to tell us,' protested Amesbury. 'We have no navy. The Dutch mean to invade and have the resources to take England. Sue for peace,' he advised, 'before the Dutch realise how great their advantage to be.'

Charles hesitated. Then his eyes dropped to Frances, her tiny frame swaying. She was now noticeably green.

'I will not sue for peace,' he announced loudly, his voice thickening with kingly grandeur. 'The intellectual might of the English will best the Dutch.'

Amesbury opened his mouth to protest, but Frances jackknifed suddenly. Wine-coloured vomit splashed heavily on the planked floor. Amesbury's monkey chattered in alarm and raced up the leg of the general.

'Frances!' Charles moved quickly to her side. 'The lady is unwell,' he said, his frown daring anyone to laugh at the growing wine-coloured puddle. He waved a hand. 'Someone see to this.'

The few servants were milling uncertainly. Amesbury reached forward, tugged a cloak free from the nearest, dropped it over the vomit and bowed.

The King nodded gratefully. 'We must return to Whitehall and see Frances cared for,' he decided, fitting an arm around Frances's wavering form. 'The chill air has upset her delicate constitution. James's longitude solution seems a sensible one,' he concluded distractedly.

'We'd better pray the dog works,' muttered Amesbury to his monkey as the King retreated, bearing Frances unsteadily on his arm. 'If De Ryker catches so much as a glimpse of our mothballed navy, we'll be hacking our vowels and drinking gin by Christmas. Those of us who aren't dead,' he added.

Chapter 29

Charlie and Lily were heading towards the illegal cockfighting arena near Whitehall. High on a pike was Cromwell's head, placed there by the King on his return to parliament. King Charles had dug up the Lord Protector's remains and given them a traitor's death as revenge for beheading his father.

'We'll set a mantrap in the cockpits,' Charlie explained. 'I do it all the time.'

'To catch thieves on the run,' said Lily, 'not a man following you.'

'The principle is the same,' said Charlie. 'Be where someone isn't expecting.'

Flying feathers could already be seen. Several pits were filled with men and fighting birds. A loose crowd obscured the cockerels, but the loud crowing rose above the male jeers and shouts.

'They forecast the future with fighting cocks?' asked Lily, catching the strains of shouted bets.

'Each pit is for a different bet,' Charlie confirmed with a nod. 'There they bet on wars.' He pointed. 'Over there is the King's affairs, and there are smaller ones for matters of the day. No one is allowed to bet openly on the death of the King or predict unpatriotic outcomes to wars,' added Charlie. 'This is a harmless outlet for such talk. It's illegal, but the authorities allow it.'

They were moving past a pit where two birds had been crudely dressed as Holland and England, each with a national flag neckerchief. Men cheered for England and shouted obscenities at the Dutch bird.

'You disappear into the crowd when I signal it,' said Charlie. 'I'll draw our pursuer into the little betting shack.' He nodded to a make-shift shed at the edge of the fighting ring, large enough to hold a few men and a bet taker. With the fight in progress it was currently deserted. A string of horseshoes to bring good luck to gamblers hung in the empty doorway.

'How will you get him inside?' Lily was eyeing the wooden out-house dubiously.

'Just be ready to make sure no one sees me lure him in,' said Charlie.

'What if he's stronger than you?'

'Good chance he is,' said Charlie, who was wiry rather than mus-cular. 'But the element of surprise is worth two men.'

'Better hope he's not strong enough for three,' muttered Lily as they drifted into the thick of the shouting gamblers.

Charlie gave the signal, and Lily vanished with impressive aplomb into the net of tankard-swilling men. He waited a moment to be sure. Then he caught a flash at the edge of his vision. A man with a Dutch pipe was moving into the crowd.

Charlie nodded to himself. Crowds always gave people a sense they couldn't be seen. He was hoping their Dutch tracker would let his guard down and come close enough for Charlie to catch a good look at him. But he was too clever for that, keeping his distance.

Charlie moved towards a pit where men waved almanacs and two ragged birds had been styled as planets. One wore a red hood for Mercury, another a green hat for Venus. As the birds fought, the astrolo-gers gabbled excitedly about the planetary outcomes and made notes.

Charlie moved to the edge of the crowd. A row of beggars was seated hopefully on the outskirts, waiting for any generous-spirited winners once the fight had ended.

Charlie sized up a large man, lurching drunkenly from foot to foot, cheering. He took out his eating knife and gave the gambler's side a sharp prod with the blade. The drunk man turned to the person standing next to him.

'You should have a care with your sword!' he accused.

The other man turned, taking a step back to assess his aggressor. As he moved, Charlie slipped behind, ducked low and threw himself down with the seated beggars.

Ignoring their looks of surprise, Charlie turned around his leather coat and put it on inside out, exposing the mouldering lining. He picked up a quick hand of mud and ran it over his face and hair. Then he waited.

For a moment he thought the Dutchman wouldn't take the bait. Then he saw a tall figure in a large hat, a smouldering pipe clutched in his fingers.

The Dutchman was clearly looking for him. But in all Charlie's experience, no one ever looked down at beggars. This man was no different.

His face was obscured by the hat, but Charlie could tell by his body language he was scanning the crowd. The Dutchman began slowly circling the cockpit, edging nearer the betting booth.

Back a little more, urged Charlie. *A few steps more.*

When he judged the peripheral vision to be right, Charlie pulled back his arm and hurled a stone in the direction of the entrance. It struck the edge of the hanging horseshoes in the doorway and they tinkled gently.

The Dutchman caught the sudden motion and turned sharply. Charlie saw him hesitate, then move towards the entrance.

He was taller than Charlie had hoped, but the plan had worked perfectly so far. Charlie raced quickly towards the betting shack. Behind him he saw Lily fall into place, ready to deter anyone about to come inside.

He stepped silently through the dark doorway. The Dutchman stood with his back to him, taking in the empty shack. There was a small covered table, and he moved forward as if to look behind.

Then he hesitated and began to turn.

Charlie darted forward, throwing his arms around the man's neck, but the element of surprise had been lost. He'd meant to pull the man bodily to the floor. Instead he pushed back, sending them both down.

Charlie twisted in the dirt, trying to gain the upper hand. The Dutchman turned and deployed a strangely familiar wrestling move.

In his surprise Charlie released both arms.

He was fighting a dead man.

The hat tilted back and the head came into view, a grin splitting the face.

Charlie's mouth dropped wide open as his assailant grabbed him in an affectionate bear hug.

'Charlie,' said a familiar voice. 'Good to see you, brother.'

Waves of relief shuddered through him, and a tight anguish he didn't realise he'd been holding slowly unwound.

'Hello, Rowan.'

Chapter 30

Judge Walters adjusted his pearly eyepatch and settled his black robes comfortably in the chair. The drowning was about to begin. His seat was drawn close to the window of a riverside tavern, a prime position to witness his justice carried out.

The view from the alehouse was of the wide Thames flowing past Deptford to Greenwich. It was known as Execution Dock. But the locals had come to call it Pirate's Wharf. Boats had gathered on the river to watch the unlucky convict meet his end.

A muffled roar went up from the river. The Judge craned his head slightly to see that his guard had arrived. They dragged between them the half-dead body of the convict. Walters watched the pirate, still choking from his half hanging, dragged to the edge of the docks.

The Judge raised his hand and called for wine. His vista from the opposite bank was perfect for viewing the rising tide. Surrounding him were empty seats. This half of the alehouse was always deserted when the Bloody Judge came to sit.

The tavern owner arrived at his side with a jug of sweet wine. Judge Walters gestured he should pour.

'Anything more?' asked the tavern owner uncomfortably.

The Judge knew he wasn't welcome in the alehouse, but the land-lord was too frightened to refuse him. The Judge leaned back slightly in his chair and removed a snowy lace handkerchief from deep in his black robes.

'The girl serving ale at the front of the house,' he said. 'Your daughter?'

The landlord paled. 'That she is. A good lass.'

'I'm sure she is.' Judge Walters wiped his mouth carefully on the white lace. 'Send her to join me.' He gave a mirthless smile. 'I should like some pretty company whilst I wait for the tide.'

The landlord visibly recoiled. 'Might you choose another girl?' he suggested. 'There's no shortage of willing women this side of the harbour.'

'I don't keep company with dockside whores,' snapped the Judge. 'You're fortunate I don't bring justice to this lawless part of the docks. Send me your daughter.'

The landlord cringed, his face pained. He vanished momentarily and seconds later his young daughter arrived. The Judge thought her to be around fifteen – the same age as Frances Stewart. Nowhere near as pretty in her plain wool dress and white cap, but her plump face and blonde hair were attractive enough.

'My father suggested you wanted some company.' She hovered uncertainly, as if she hoped the whole incident was a misunderstanding and he might send her away.

'Sit.' The Judge gestured impatiently.

The girl sat on the bench next to the Judge's chair, perching herself uncomfortably so her body was positioned as far as possible from his. Her eyes drifted to the window. The pirate was being chained to the dockside now. Water was lapping at his knees.

The girl was staring at the Judge's pearly eyepatch.

He tapped it. 'When I was a naval officer,' he said, 'pirates caught up with our boat whilst we sailed back from Antigua. Tortured us all.

They killed my brother right in front of my eyes. Hung him from his fingertips and gutted him.' The Judge paused, as if vividly picturing the scene. 'But I survived, as you see,' he concluded. 'And now I work to be sure no man will fear a pirate.'

The girl made no answer, chewing her lip uncertainly.

The Judge saw how the pirate sagged against his chains, and he smiled.

'Once the water reaches their chest, they often say all kinds of things,' he explained. 'Confessions, repentings. It's most entertaining. The sound carries, even from this distance.'

The girl swallowed. 'I've never seen it,' she said.

'Every Londoner should be made to see justice carried out,' opined the Judge firmly. 'It deters crime.' He turned to examine her face, white with repugnance at the dying pirate. 'What is your name?' he asked.

'Selena.'

Her voice sounded small.

'After the ancient Moon Goddess Diana,' observed the Judge. 'Do you know your stars?'

'My father says they are heathen things,' said the girl carefully, 'and I mind him.'

'You've heard of the Deptford murders?'

'Folk speak much of them,' said Selena, measuring every word.

The Judge nodded. The tide was lapping the man's torso now. The steady nature of the death was what pleased him best. Seeing the man's life slip away with each lap of the rising water.

He could tell that Selena was fascinated despite herself. Women were all the same. Death awed them. A ripple of power eddied through him.

'The same bodies came nineteen years ago,' he observed. 'You would be too young to remember.' He turned the tankard in his hands. 'Nineteen years,' he said, 'is the exact time it takes for the stars in the heavens to make a complete revolution and come back to how they once were.'

'You're very learned to know such things,' said Selena politely.

'I've made it my business to be educated in the stars,' agreed Judge Walters. 'A man can tell the future from the skies.' He broke off and fixed his single eye on hers. 'What do you hope your future might be?'

Selena swallowed. There was something menacing about his tone. 'A good husband.' She faltered. 'Healthy children.'

The Judge nodded slowly. 'Yet you have not acted wisely if you wish for such things.'

Selena felt a redness creep up her neck. What could he be talking about?

'You are friends,' continued the Judge, 'with a girl named Lily Boswell. A gypsy.' He spat the last words.

Selena's skin turned icy. Her hands prickled with sweat. 'I don't know who you mean, sir,' she said.

The Judge's gaze was fixed on the dock now. Selena found herself following it, watching the drowning man. She could almost feel the water lapping at her own chin.

'Yes, you do,' said the Judge. 'Lily Boswell has been in here.'

'Father doesn't allow gypsies.'

'But you do,' said the Judge. 'You've a soft spot for them.'

Selena felt panic rise up. 'I only served her food and drink,' she gabbled. 'There was no harm in it.'

The Judge nodded. 'But you saw her drunk,' he said. 'Drunk gypsies talk.' His eyes flashed. 'What did she say to you?'

'Nothing. I swear.'

The Judge turned to look at her. 'I would hate for your good father,' he said, 'to watch his daughter drown opposite his own tavern.'

Selena blanched. 'I think . . . I only remember she mentioned treasure. Lily had heard rumours. She was looking for Ishmael Boney. I don't know why.'

'What else?' demanded the Judge.

'She needed a thief taker,' said Selena. 'I remember now. She said a man called Charlie Tuesday would help her find the treasure.' She let out a breath. 'That's all I know. I swear it.'

The Judge turned the facts in his mind. Charlie Tuesday. He'd heard of the thief taker. But why was the gypsy looking for Ishmael Boney?

He stored this away with what he knew. The astrologer was under the King's protection. The Judge looked back at Selena. The stupid girl was close to fainting. He felt certain she'd told him everything she knew.

'Come closer to the window,' he said, his good eye glittering. 'I think it best you watch justice done. I want to be certain you understand what I am capable of.'

Chapter 31

'I've been trying to get you alone,' explained Rowan, tipping back beer at his usual breakneck speed.

They'd retreated to an intimate back room in the Seven Stars Tavern usually reserved for smuggler deals. Lily had given Rowan one long suspicious look, then announced she'd wait elsewhere whilst they talked. Charlie felt as though he could breathe again. That a lost part of him had been returned.

The two brothers bore an obvious resemblance, with large expressive eyes and eyebrows. Though where Charlie's nose was kinked and his lip scarred from a bucking horse, Rowan's handsome features were unscathed. They both had slightly curling hair, thick and unruly, though Rowan's was dark to Charlie's dusty blond, and worn longer to disguise half an ear missing from a knife fight.

'I'm a wanted man.' Rowan's eyes shuffled back and forth. 'Can't risk being seen in public.'

'Why didn't you find me before?' demanded Charlie. 'I thought you were dead.'

'I'm sorry,' said Rowan. 'Truly. I couldn't risk it.' His brown eyes had the same poetic quality as Charlie's, and it was unnerving to see his own charm played back at him. 'I couldn't take the chance,' Rowan continued, swigging more ale. 'I owe money to the Oracle.'

'The Oracle?' Charlie didn't bother to hide the horror in his voice. The Oracle was probably the most dangerous man in London. He was a smuggler king, living deep under Southwark in a secret black market known only to the city's deadliest felons. The Oracle's genius for discerning boat cargo and selling the information to smugglers had earned him his title and fame. He was also insane, vengeful and powerful. All in all, a bad man to owe money.

'Why did you borrow from the Oracle?' demanded Charlie.

'I sold false gunpowder to the wrong man,' admitted Rowan. 'Made and spent a pretty penny. Turns out he was a trader for the Oracle. How could I have known?'

Charlie groaned. 'I told you,' he said, 'black powder was a bad business.'

Rowan nodded. 'You did,' he conceded. 'But you have to admit I was good at it. No one knew my gunpowder to be false. I told you about that highwayman's face when he tried to shoot me down.'

'How much do you owe?' Charlie wasn't smiling.

'Too much.' Rowan gave a rakish grin.

'Why did you come back to London?' asked Charlie. 'The Oracle will find you.'

Rowan's eyes locked on his brother's. 'To warn you,' said Rowan. 'The Dutch plan to invade London. They have a fireship pilot named Janus. He is . . . unstoppable I think. He has no fear of death or consequences.'

Charlie tried to hide his reaction to the name, holding his tankard close to his face.

'Same as you then,' he replied casually.

Rowan wasn't fooled.

'Maybe worse,' admitted his brother with a smile. 'You've heard something of Janus?'

'Only a rumour,' said Charlie, eyeing Rowan's face. 'Janus is said to resent our family. Or perhaps me in particular.'

Rowan absorbed this slowly, drinking beer.

'There were stories Janus was English,' he said. 'Some even said a royal. I thought it part of his myth.' He sipped more beer thoughtfully. 'Some thief you found out?' he suggested. 'Some villain?'

'I don't know.'

'You hear things at sea,' continued Rowan. 'Stories mostly, but sometimes . . .' He stopped with a strange laugh. 'Do you ever wonder,' continued Rowan, 'why our mother gave you that key instead of me?' He pointed to the key bound at Charlie's neck.

Charlie didn't answer.

Rowan shook his head. He drew out a charm. 'Some of us sailors carry protectorates.'

It was a grubby copper coin showing Neptune holding a trident, with St Peter on the reverse.

'It got me to thinking,' continued Rowan, 'the key is the same for you. She gave it to keep you safe.'

Charlie was silent, uncertain as to how to reply. The implication was their mother had cared for him and not for Rowan.

'Doesn't matter,' said Rowan into his beer. 'I'm not used to the strong ale here. I've drunk too fast. Our mother is gone.'

His face had closed down in the expression Charlie was well used to. In the orphan home Rowan had barely spoken for two years. It had taken all Charlie's efforts to get enough food to keep him alive.

Rowan put a hand on Charlie's arm. 'The Dutch plan to sail up the Thames and take the capital. You have to get out of London.'

'How did you come by this intelligence?' asked Charlie.

'I went to sea to escape the Oracle,' said Rowan shiftily. 'Joined with the navy under a false name. But men came looking. So I defected to the Dutch.'

'You turned traitor?'

Charlie's stomach turned. This was getting worse and worse. He realised why Rowan couldn't risk being seen.

'It's hardly treachery,' said Rowan breezily. 'Half the King's navy are doing it. My Dutch has finally come in useful.'

This at least was true. Charlie and Rowan had both been orphaned speaking fluent Dutch. While they were growing up, it was their secret language between one another.

'Life at sea is not so bad,' added Rowan, seeing his expression. 'The Dutch are fair masters, and they pay us. I learned the skills of sailing in the navy. I can tie knots and tar a deck with the best of 'em.'

'If only you'd learned them in service of your own country,' sighed Charlie, whose lifelong dream had been for Rowan to learn a trade and cease his illegal schemes, sponging off women and accrual of debts.

'What if I came by some money?' suggested Charlie. 'Could I pay off the Oracle? Bring you back?'

'You wouldn't have enough,' said Rowan easily. 'I owe five hundred pounds.'

Charlie absorbed this. It was more than most men earned in a lifetime.

'I'm on to something,' said Charlie. 'It might bring money.'

Rowan laughed. 'I thought it was I who had the foolish schemes.'

'Before our mother died, I think she left clues,' continued Charlie. 'Clues that could unearth something valuable. If there was enough money,' said Charlie, looking intently at his brother, 'would the Oracle let you live?'

Rowan put out a hand calloused by rigging and saltwater. He patted Charlie on the shoulder.

'I didn't come here for you to rescue me like when we were boys,' he said. 'I came because I don't want you to die at the hands of a Dutch soldier.'

'What about your absence?' said Charlie, suddenly fearing for Rowan. 'Is that not mutiny?'

'I'm not crew on De Ryker's ship,' said Rowan. 'My part of the fleet is docked in Holland for a few days' whoring. But I must go quickly. If any of the Oracle's men find me here, they'll have my guts.'

'What if I could raise the money?' said Charlie.

Rowan shook his head. He stood and hugged his brother.

'It's too late for me, Charlie. Save yourself.'

Chapter 32

De Ryker's good eye was scouring the rolling sea. Below deck, men were still working on the fireship, hanging sailcloth soaked in tar and rehanging the cannon holes to fall down, coursing fresh air over the flames.

'There she is.' De Ryker pointed. 'England. Once we are on the Thames, Janus will sail out and meet us. With the Eye of Heaven we shall easily overcome England's tricksy waters.' The admiral looked out to sea.

'You're certain it's real? The Eye?' Cornelius was relieved to be back above deck. Next to De Ryker, his skinny frame was almost comically puppet-like.

De Ryker looked out to sea. 'Perhaps the Eye has the power Janus thinks. Perhaps it doesn't. Thorne twisted Janus. I've heard things. Children's bones were recovered after the astrologer was executed.'

Cornelius shuddered.

'Thorne was a mathematician,' said De Ryker. 'Legend has made him a sorcerer, but I think him a more practical man. Janus was only a boy when he was in Thorne's thrall. Likely he remembers with the imagination of a child. But if the Eye doesn't have the power of true

Sight,' concluded De Ryker, 'I know for certain it can lead us up the Thames and lead us safely through the shoals.'

'You think the Eye is a map?' asked Cornelius.

'Most likely a map or a compass of uncommon power,' said De Ryker. 'How else could Thorne have found that enemy ship?'

'And you trust Janus to return with it?'

'I know Janus better than he knows himself,' said De Ryker. 'I don't need to rely on his loyalty. He cannot stand the mundane or the ordinary. Janus's sense of adventure will ensure his return.'

De Ryker nodded out towards England. 'We shall take London by force,' he promised. 'The rest of the country will quickly follow. Think of the opportunity. She has steel, lumber, brass. The Dutch will rule the waves.'

De Ryker threw the log overboard and watched its path. 'Dead reckoning,' he said. 'That's what the English call it.'

The log picked up speed, and De Ryker frowned at it.

'Four knots,' he decided. He swung his attention to the compass. Then to the North Star. 'By my account,' De Ryker decided, 'we're seven miles from English waters. The King has not yet sued for peace,' he added. 'I imagine Amesbury tries for it, but he will be too late.'

'Do you think Amesbury suspects,' asked Cornelius, 'who Janus really is?'

'No,' said De Ryker. 'If he did, he would already be looking for the Eye himself.'

A rolling wave of acrid vapours rolled across the deck. Cornelius tried to hold down his nausea. His head ached. De Ryker thought for a moment.

'Our latest fireship needs a new name,' he decided. 'We shall call her the *Lucifer*,' he said. 'That is a fitting name, is it not? Lucifer can be either a flaming torch or the Devil himself.'

'Shall I arrange a ceremony?' suggested Cornelius uncertainly. 'Wine?'

De Ryker thought for a moment. 'Do you know why new ships are splashed with wine?' he asked.

Cornelius shook his head.

'It's from a tradition of blood,' said De Ryker. 'The old ships were launched with a sacrifice. Now we use red wine to represent human blood.' He looked at the prow. 'The *Lucifer*,' he said, 'is a ship of death. I think the old ways would be more fitting. Have we any prisoners of war?'

Cornelius swallowed, then nodded.

'Good,' said De Ryker. 'Bring me a prisoner.'

Chapter 33

'Where is it?' asked Lily. 'The Maze of Lost Souls?'

They were back in Charlie's lodgings, planning where to go next. He'd filled Lily in on Rowan's warning, but she'd expressed suspicion at his brother's motives.

'It's a tangle of buildings and passages,' explained Charlie. 'The Maze is part of the Palace of Whitehall's lesser-known outbuildings. It's a winding set of streets that were once shops and homes. Over the years they've become part of the palace.'

'The old streets have become a maze?'

'They were always difficult to navigate,' said Charlie, 'but now the fronts have been made to look the same, to better hide people. They're dark, close – a warren of tiny alleys with nothing to differentiate one part from the other.'

'Who hides inside?' asked Lily as they passed a bakehouse and a dairy.

'Unpopular folk,' explained Charlie. 'People who would be in danger to be publicly known. Executioners, informants,' he added, calling to mind the hotchpotch of strange people who dwelled in the meandering passages of the Maze.

'Guarded?'

'Yes.'

'Sounds perilous.'

'It is,' said Charlie. He looked at the darkening sky. 'You think the Eye could be worth money?' he said.

Lily looked surprised. 'I thought you only wanted to find your family.'

The sliver of scar on Charlie's upper lip twitched. 'I've found all the family I need.'

Lily raised her dark eyebrows. 'You think your debtor brother will return?'

'You must be the only woman in London who doesn't want to rescue him,' smiled Charlie.

'I know his type,' replied Lily darkly. 'I've done with it long ago.'

'You'd be a good partnership,' teased Charlie, who secretly feared Lily might fall for Rowan's charms. 'You're the only woman I know who's a match for him.'

Lily turned her dark eyes on him, and for a long moment he couldn't read her at all.

'What of your Maria?' she asked finally. 'Were you a good partnership?'

Charlie hesitated. The question had taken him by surprise.

'In some ways,' he said, 'we were.'

'That's what I thought,' said Lily after a moment. Her voice had gone strangely quiet. Then she frowned, sliding the ruby ring up and down her finger. 'If you want to pay your brother's debt, I think the Eye could be worth a great deal of money,' she said, changing the subject abruptly. 'The old King took a lot of pains to find it. And even if it has no actual worth as treasure, the Queen Mother pays huge prices for any memorabilia of her dead husband.'

Charlie nodded. 'I need five hundred pounds,' he said, 'to bring Rowan back. Do you think it could raise so much?'

'Maybe,' said Lily. 'It would have to be worth a thousand then. Five hundred each.'

They both considered this. It was a huge sum of money.

'It's too dark to reach the Maze now,' Charlie said. 'We need sunlight to stand a chance of navigating.'

He suddenly felt bone-tired.

'We should get some sleep,' said Lily.

Charlie moved to his bed, wondering if she might huddle in next to him. But Lily was sat turning the ring in her hand. And before he knew it, he'd fallen into a deep sleep.

On some level, Charlie knew he was only dreaming. His mother's tapestry swung in his thoughts, the angels with their cross. In his mind the rings moved, fitting together over the tapestry. Something was loosening. An old memory. And Charlie had a feeling it was a memory best left in the past.

Charlie was walking. He felt afraid, as though he'd been here before. There was something beneath his feet, and he stumbled. Charlie looked down to see the ground was strewn with broken weapons. There were swords and spears, twisted over and bent, shields split in two, blunted sickles. They were ancient and muddy, as though they'd been dragged from the depths of a river.

Then he was in a huge dark room. Fear rose in his throat. He thought something very bad had happened here. There were enormous black cogs, interconnected, but Charlie couldn't see what they controlled.

Partly visible behind them was a man in Royalist dress, his hair long to his shoulders. He sat in shadow, his hands moving fast over something Charlie couldn't see. He continued working steadily, tapping, turning, fitting small pieces.

Then he saw a woman. His mother, Sally Oakley.

'Husband.'

Sally stepped from the shadows and put a hand on the man's shoulder. The man didn't look at her.

'Tobias Oakley is your husband.'

A sacrifice needs blood . . .

It was a whisper on the air. Charlie felt a shudder go through him.

A light flared and a demonic face showed in the gloom. A bearded head with curling hair. Clutched in his arm was an upended boy, terror freezing his stricken features. Ranged around his feet were the remains of dead children.

'It's only a statue,' said a familiar voice.

He was aware of a warm presence at his side. Rowan. Relief washed through him.

'Don't fear, Charlie,' he whispered. 'I'll let no harm come to you.'

The horrors of the room seemed to fade at his older brother's reassurance.

. Then there was a loud rumble and the great cogs began turning. A shaft of light pierced the dark.

Charlie had the sudden sense that a dangerous presence had entered the room. Someone he had great reason to fear.

Janus.

Rowan vanished away, leaving a void of cold terror in his place. Charlie tried to turn, fear rising.

'Charlie!' his mother's voice came high and loud. 'He is coming for you!'

'Charlie!' a female voice sounded in his ear.

He felt rough hands shake him. Charlie awoke to find Lily's large brown eyes staring down at him.

'What is it?' he groaned, trying not to be disconcerted by her proximity.

'You were shouting in your sleep,' she explained. 'Something about a prophecy.'

Charlie sat up, attempting to remember. 'A bad dream,' he said. 'Or perhaps a memory.' He squeezed his eyes shut, trying to think. 'It must have been from a long time ago,' he decided. 'My mother was still alive. And Rowan was . . .' He struggled for the words. 'Rowan was like he was before we were orphaned. He hadn't given up.'

This part of the memory pained him more than anything else. Charlie had forgotten there'd been a time when Rowan had been his hero and protector. He suddenly burned to free his brother from the Dutch ship.

Lily's face set in sympathy. She knew about Charlie and Rowan's upbringing in the orphan house.

'Perhaps I underestimated my mother,' said Charlie. 'I thought of her as a servant in a household, stitching for her work. Perhaps she was more.'

Charlie got to his feet. 'Come on,' he said. 'Let's get to the Maze of Lost Souls. We need to find Ishmael Boney.'

Chapter 34

Amesbury was walking along Whitehall's luxurious corridors. De Ryker's ship had been sighted dangerously close to the English coast and he feared the worst. Was the admiral going to try to invade London whilst England was weak from fire and plague?

The treacherous waters of the Thames's shoals and mudflats should have made this unthinkable.

What does De Ryker have? wondered Amesbury. *What advantage does he have to make him so bold?*

It all hinged on the mysterious Janus. The fireship pilot believed he could find the Eye. And Amesbury had seen first-hand how powerful it was in battle, though he had never been able to puzzle out how the Eye had allowed Thorne to know his location. The astrologer had no experience of sailing and no understanding of navigation. How had he gained the information necessary to find Amesbury's ship?

As he drew close to the great doors, he could hear that the King was already speaking to someone. The familiar voice brought him up short.

The King was talking with his brother, the Duke of York.

'The Judge served with me aboard the *Swiftsure*,' the Duke was saying. 'Pirates murdered his brother. It warped his mind.'

Amesbury slowed his step deliberately to listen to the loud voices filtering through the door.

'At least three of the bodies were convicts from the Marshalsea,' continued the Duke. 'His prison.'

The footmen either side of the large door moved to open it. Amesbury's monkey caught sight of a piece of fruit in the pocket of one of the footmen and gave a high chatter of excitement. The voices on the other side of the door stopped.

'Amesbury,' he heard the King say. 'I must hear him.'

The door was opened, and Amesbury entered with a low bow. He righted and nearly took a step back in surprise. The room had been lined with star maps, charts of astrological movements and images of the planets and stars. Reclined in the centre were the King and his brother, surrounded by naked women. The Duke of York was dressed as Neptune and the King as Mars. A Roman-style meal of grapes, towering cakes and flagons of wine had been assembled.

The women lounged enticingly on red cushions. They held out fruit seductively or proffered glasses, their soft, bare limbs draped around the King and the Duke of York.

For a moment Amesbury thought the brothers had arranged a Roman orgy. He recognised several of the women from a bordello near Whitehall. One lay completely reclined, head tilted back on a cushion, legs parted very deliberately in the direction of the King. Another girl had manoeuvred herself to press her bare breasts against the Duke of York's exposed chest.

Then Amesbury realised. The King and the Duke were having a portrait painted. The King was the God of War, his brother God of the Sea. It was a statement of colonial power to decorate the King's court.

'Amesbury!' The Duke of York waved, his chest bare, a white toga barely covering his muscled midriff. He held an elaborate trident, and his biceps and ankles were encircled with gold cuffs. A tall half-crown rested atop his long brown hair.

'What do you think?' asked the Duke, gesturing to the nude women. 'I'm having a painting for my birthday.' The Duke tapped his nose knowingly. 'Not my actual birthday of course. You know how that could be misused by astrologers. My official birthday. I mean to gift it to Charles, for his public rooms.'

'A fine gift,' said Amesbury. 'And Your Royal Highness is wise to conceal the hour of his birth.'

'What news?' asked the King. He wore a red toga and shining gold breastplate with a Roman centurion's helmet over his curling black wig.

'The Dutch have been sighted off the coast,' said Amesbury. 'Your Majesty, it's such a bold move. I can only think they must be in possession of some great intelligence or weapon.'

The King righted himself, wincing as the breastplate dug in. 'What could De Ryker have?' he asked.

'A local pilot perhaps,' said Amesbury. 'Something has given him more courage than seems rational. And De Ryker is not the kind of man to attack rashly.'

Amesbury had a sudden memory of De Ryker, his skin deeply browned and thickened by years at sea. The admiral's right eye was clouded from navigating by the sun, and he had a presence on deck that could be felt across an entire fleet.

'The Eye?' suggested the King. 'Could Janus have located it? Brought it to him? My father thought it would win him the war.'

'It's possible,' agreed Amesbury.

The King was looking intently at Amesbury, and the old general wondered if Charles knew why he'd changed sides all those years ago.

'Your Majesty,' said Amesbury, 'might you reconsider bringing Buckingham back? He is an excellent commander, and we're in dire need of men.'

'Buckingham is banished,' snapped Charles.

Amesbury was silent. The naval commander was rumoured to have been sleeping with Barbara Castlemaine, but heartbreak was a poor reason to lose a country.

'I shall head the fleet,' said the Duke of York. His eyes twisted hopefully to his brother. 'You know I have a fine command aboard a ship.'

Charles's face was suddenly stricken. 'No,' he said. 'You were nearly beheaded by chain shot last year. You are impetuous, James. You throw yourself to the front line with no thoughts for your safety.'

The Duke swung around to importune Amesbury, who winced at the imminent prospect of the scanty toga dislodging. The Duke paused to better fasten it.

'The sailors respect James,' said Amesbury carefully.

Charles shook his head.

'There is another option,' said the Duke, still adjusting his Neptune toga. 'We wait for the longitude experiment.'

'Your Majesty . . .' began Amesbury, knowing what the Duke of York was about to suggest.

'The *Loyal London* is due back from Tobago any day,' continued the Duke. 'Think how Frances Stewart will enjoy a pretty new pearl necklace.'

'Your Majesty,' sighed Amesbury, 'a wounded dog cannot keep time at sea.'

The general was fighting to keep his annoyance in check. He'd seen hundreds of ridiculous attempts to find longitude. All had failed.

'James is learned in astrology,' said the King, warming to the idea of colonial wealth. 'He consults on every small thing and assures me this plan will succeed.'

'All England loves mapping the stars,' said Amesbury. 'Publishers sell more almanacs than Bibles. But predicting the future is not the same skill as charting a ship.' He held back a deep sigh. 'My advice is the same as it's been for the last year,' he said. 'Sue for peace now. You don't have the resources for war.'

'The Thames is the greatest sea barrier in the world,' said the King. 'The entrance is a maze of deadly shoals and hidden sandbanks. No navy has ever got through it.' He smiled at his brother. 'Great kings must take risks on occasion,' he decided. 'Let the ship return from Tobago.'

Chapter 35

Charlie was leading Lily into the tangled outskirts of Whitehall. The King's Palace was a jumble of brick buildings, bordered by clusters of outhouses. It was amongst this labyrinthine muddle of streets that the Maze was hidden.

'We follow the royal crest to the entrance,' Charlie explained. He felt beneath the underside of a windowsill. A Stuart ensign was burned into the wood.

'How do you know that?' Lily was peering at the symbol in disbelief. It was so small as to be virtually indiscernible from a knot in the wood.

'I notice things,' said Charlie. 'When the old King was in power, his spies used this maze to bring information to him. The mark helped them find the entrance in the dark.'

'Not a very subtle symbol,' observed Lily.

'The old King was notoriously bad at spy craft,' agreed Charlie.

'So the crests lead us to the maze entrance,' said Lily. 'But how do we get inside?'

'If the stars are with us,' said Charlie, 'Dave the Axe won't be at his post today. That leaves Big John, and he likes me. I got him his first bare-knuckle fight. He'll let us past for a few pence.'

Lily was looking ahead. 'Dave is an executioner?' she guessed.

Charlie nodded.

'Then the stars aren't with you,' said Lily. 'Because if that's the entrance' – she pointed at a dark conjunction of two brick buildings – 'there's a big man in a dark hood outside it. And I think he's stirring a cauldron of boiling heads.'

Charlie followed her gaze. Lily was right. Even from this distance he could make out the giant lumpy figure of the executioner and the ominous bobbing shapes in his steaming cauldron.

Charlie slowed. 'It is the executioner,' he said, thinking fast. 'We need a name of someone we're certain to be in the Maze,' he decided. 'We don't know yet if Ishmael is there.'

'Who?'

'I'll make a guess,' said Charlie. 'Keep behind me and be ready to run.'

Charlie forced himself to approach the brooding executioner with a casual step. Even so, the hooded head flicked up, yellowed eyes glaring in suspicion. The executioner held a long staff, with which he prodded a cauldron bubbling with oily liquid.

'Who're you?' he demanded.

They drew within sight of the cauldron's contents. Severed heads were rotating in the boil, sightless eyes turning upwards and back down again. A pungent blend of vinegar and spices designed to preserve the human remains mingled with the scent of boiled meat.

'Few more for the London Bridge pikes?' asked Charlie conversationally, addressing his remark to the pot.

The executioner, clearly unused to such interest in his work, swirled the contents self-importantly.

'I use cumin,' he said proudly. 'Keeps the features.' He dunked the long pole and turned over the nearest head in demonstration. 'Old Morris uses tar,' he added disapprovingly. 'You can't even see who they were once they're raised on pikes. Mine you see who they were. Even their last expression.'

The sides of the hood rose to suggest a grin was manifesting beneath. Then the executioner's eyes darkened suddenly as they settled on Lily.

'What business have you here?' he asked. 'Who's the gypsy?'

Behind him, Charlie heard the telltale rustle of Lily's hands closing on her knives.

'We're here to see the firework maker,' said Charlie easily.

The executioner slid a hand under the black hood and rubbed his jaw. 'Which one?' he asked after a moment.

Charlie inwardly swore. He'd not been prepared for this.

'The Dutch one,' he said, hoping the moment's hesitation hadn't been noticed.

The executioner's eyes narrowed. He spat into the cauldron. The phlegmy froth floated with the oily spices.

Behind him, Charlie felt Lily tense to run.

'Him!' roared the executioner. 'The Dutchie! He's lucky I don't turn him out myself. We don't like foreigners here. Nor heathen gypsies,' he added with an assessing glance at Lily. 'You'll not see a sensible man stir from his house this All Hallows' Eve,' he observed, giving the nearest boiling head a spiteful plunge with his stick. 'Nor attempt new business. Why do you not wait until after the eclipse to find your firework maker?'

Charlie thought quickly. 'Your heads,' he said, aiming for what seemed to be a point of pride for the executioner. 'I recognise the fine work. You did Cromwell?'

The executioner seemed to grow several inches.

'Cromwell was one of mine,' he agreed. 'The King asked for me especially,' he added, 'to properly avenge his father's killer.'

'A good thing for the country,' said Charlie. 'We'll be sure to take a better look on our way out of the Maze of Lost Souls.'

'Make sure you do,' said the executioner happily. 'Note how little damage the birds do.' He raised his dripping stick and stepped back to let them pass.

'Thank you.' Lily gave a dazzling smile as they moved past. 'And be a little careful with your gypsy heads. Or you'll bring a curse on yourself.'

Chapter 36

'You shouldn't have threatened him,' said Charlie as he and Lily entered the dark alley leading inside the labyrinthine streets.

'Who?' Lily was stepping carefully into the dark. The smell of boiling heads hung low on the air.

'The executioner guarding the Maze.' Charlie was appalled at how quickly she'd forgotten. 'He might come after us.'

'I'm allowed my pride,' said Lily. 'You don't know what it is to be persecuted every day in the city. Men like that shot my father and drowned my mother. I'd slit all their throats if I could,' she added, a malevolent look to her dark eyes. 'Every last one.'

'If you hate men like that so much,' said Charlie, 'why stay in the city, wearing your gypsy talismans?'

'London is where the money is,' said Lily in a tone that suggested this should be perfectly obvious. 'I only intend to stay as long as is necessary. And I can't conceal my dark skin or hair, so I may as well wear my talismans and charms openly. They'll know me for a gypsy whatever I wear, so why should I hide?'

'I think you like the danger,' said Charlie, who knew from experience that Lily couldn't resist a gamble.

Lily didn't contradict him.

The dark identical building fronts had closed around them. Jettied overhangs shut out most of the daylight, and the interchangeable doors and windows quickly became disorientating.

They drew to the end of the dark alley, and it split away in two directions.

'How do you know the firework maker?' asked Lily.

'I don't,' said Charlie. 'It was an educated guess. I assumed there would be a firework maker hiding in here. They were wanted men after the fire. Many fell to lynch mobs,' he added, remembering the angry crowds at some of the more spectacular explosions, 'and the King likes fireworks enough to protect his favourites. I didn't think there'd be more than one though,' he added. 'The Dutch are skilled at fireworks. It was the best I could think of at the time.'

Charlie hesitated, considering both directions.

'Which way?' asked Lily.

'It's a maze,' said Charlie. 'Stay on the right and it will always lead you out. So left,' he added, moving to press a hand to the left wall of the alley, 'will take you in. I learned that in St Giles,' he added. 'In a tenement slum you need to know how to get out fast.'

They were moving past a row of neat brick buildings now, more a narrow road than an alley.

'It's all deserted,' said Lily, looking at the darkened windows, the closed doors.

'Look at the chimneys,' said Charlie, pointing to the smoking stacks. 'There are people here. They just don't want to be found.'

'Then how do we find Ishmael?'

'If he's here,' said Charlie, 'he will be under protection of the King. Which means he'll still be stargazing.' He pointed to the buildings.

'Highest ground,' he said. 'They'll have put Ishmael on the highest ground. To best observe the heavens.'

'So how might we find high ground?' asked Lily. She was looking at the uneven dirt track, which gave no indication of heading consistently up or down.

'Drainage,' said Charlie. 'Lower ground is damper.' He pointed to the refuse channel, dug through the centre of the streets. It was loaded with filth thrown from the windows. Vegetable peelings, old bones and excrement floated in a pungent urine soup.

'We follow the gutters,' he said. 'That way.'

They traced the path of the sluiceway, keeping track of where the foul-smelling liquid dropped lowest. Charlie swung back a few times, accounting for where the angle of the sun would dry out sections of ground artificially. But alley by dark alley they wound higher, until they were in a dead end of eight houses.

'Here,' said Charlie. 'The water drops no lower. This is the highest part of the Maze.'

He looked up at the mix of thatch and slate roofs. There were no dormer windows or obvious attics.

'Thatch would be easier to cut,' he decided, 'for a stargazer. A slate roof would be an expensive thing to make a hole in. Astrologers favour the south side, do they not?' he added, shifting position to regard the buildings from a different angle. The roofs were shaded, and it was impossible to see from the street.

He turned his attention to the ground. Four houses with thatch. Two belonged to military men, he decided. They had flat-headed nails hammered into the door frames to signify the number of winning battles held by the occupants.

That left two. He stepped back and looked carefully, judging which might afford a better view to a stargazer. Then he studied the doors. They were both thick wood, with studded sections. One had a hanging bell, the other a door knocker in the shape of a goat's head.

Then he saw it.

'This one,' he decided, pointing to the goat's-head knocker.

'You're sure?'

'I'm certain it will tell us something,' said Charlie. 'This door knocker was hung recently. And there's a pentagram shape in the goat's mouth.'

Chapter 37

Janus was moving across the slippery mud of Dead Man's Curve, out of sight of the deathlarks. His small boat was hidden at the bank a little further upstream. Lying at his feet was a dead body. With difficulty he dragged it away from the banks and out of sight.

It was only then that he paused to make a proper assessment. This was his broken thing. His offering to the river.

Janus had floated the corpse near London Bridge and marked the moon and the tides exactly. But she had not come when he expected. Were his calculations wrong?

He felt frustration bubble up. He'd not been able to replicate his old master's workings. What was he missing?

Thorne was such a precise man. Was the weight of the body wrong? Had he underestimated the speed of the current?

He tried to remember Thorne's teachings. All he could call to mind was the astrologer's obsession with Roman civilisation and his preoccupation with giving his victims a dignified burial.

Janus balled his fists in frustration. Time was running out. Thorne had showed him nothing meaningful. He'd never meant to give him the Eye.

Janus knelt down in the boat and carefully removed the wool covering from the corpse. She stared back with white eyes. There was an expression of deep shock on her face.

Janus felt the familiar blackness well up. *The Bad Thing.* Suddenly he was back there, helpless and alone. He tried to focus his attention as De Ryker had shown him. But his imagination twisted instead to the terrible room of cogs and broken things. Janus fought to control his mind.

De Ryker floated back to him. He remembered the first time he'd seen the heavy boots descend into the prisoner's quarters. The terror as the admiral had named Janus the first sacrifice.

'The man of Saturn,' De Ryker had said. 'A cursed one. We'll stain the seas with his blood and quicken our path.'

Janus still didn't know how he'd managed to speak so quickly and convincingly. But he'd impressed De Ryker with his knowledge of the stars. The admiral had reconsidered his fate.

'I'm in need of a brave man,' he'd said. 'One gifted in death and destruction to pilot my fireships.' He'd cast a considering eye over Janus.

'Fetch a basket for the cursed one,' De Ryker had commanded. 'Lower him over the bow with a loaf of bread, a mug of ale and a knife. We'll see how brave he is.'

As they'd lowered the large fishing basket, with Janus quaking inside, De Ryker had leaned forward.

'Look to the stars,' he'd advised. 'There's peace there. Even for men such as we. If you survive without using the knife to cut yourself free, I may have a mission for you.'

Janus could still remember the endless days and nights in the basket, tossed by the stormy seas, terrified. Now, as then, he forced his gaze up to the endless carpet of stars twinkling brightly in the dark sky. Calmness descended. It was time to return the woman to Saturn as Thorne had shown him.

The body was unrecognisable from when she'd gone in the water. Only the markings identified her. Carefully he checked them. The carvings showed the exact time and place he'd floated the corpse.

Janus began making his ritual. Using rags he'd brought for the purpose, he washed and anointed the body with oil. After a moment's hesitation, Janus stared up at the stars, mapping the position of Venus's bright light. His hand closed on the copper-handled knife in his coat. It was time to make one last symbol on his broken thing.

Saturn was ready to take another child.

Chapter 38

Charlie raised the goat's-head door knocker and struck three times.

There was movement inside the house. Then a man with long silver hair opened the door a crack.

'What do you want?' His voice was wheezy, hesitant.

'Are you Ishmael Boney?' asked Charlie.

The fear in the man's face magnified.

'They took him already,' he whispered. 'Ishmael isn't here. Who are you?'

Charlie toyed with the right answer. 'We're . . . enthusiasts of his work,' he tried. 'We're trying to find him.'

The man's anxiety seemed to ease slightly.

'I'm very busy,' he said, 'preparing for the end of the world.'

Charlie and Lily hesitated.

'Just a moment of your time,' said Lily, batting her eyelashes.

The door opened wider. The man wore a white shirt, purple breeches ending at the knee, and his scrawny legs were stockingless, enclosed at the feet in black buckled shoes.

'I can tell you what I know,' he said. 'But I don't have much time. All Hallows' Eve approaches. I imagine you must be making arrangements for the apocalypse yourself.'

Behind the man was a narrow hallway of chaos. Possessions were stacked in a kind of frenzy. Open trunks were ranged around.

'I'm Gabriel Evans,' he said. 'Perhaps you've heard of my work,' he added hopefully.

'Your astrology?' said Charlie, taking a guess. 'It's well known in educated circles.'

Gabriel nodded happily, leading them further inside. His shambling walk made him seem made entirely of loosely joined bones.

'I'm not famed like some of the others,' he said, 'but I dedicate myself to understanding the stars, their movements.'

They were in a small parlour now, furnished only by a large desk and papers. Charlie guessed this room had been cleared in preparation for Doomsday. The cauldron on the fire had obviously not been used for a long time, and Charlie wondered how the old man ate. By the look of him, he didn't.

'You make predictions,' asked Charlie, 'based on the stars?'

'It is simply a matter of knowing the true nature of the stars at the time the question is asked,' nodded Gabriel.

'You're never wrong?' asked Lily sceptically.

'The planets never lie,' said Gabriel. 'If I am wrong,' he concluded grandly, 'it is because time by the Whitehall clock is never totally accurate.'

Gabriel pointed to a battered kettle. 'Will you take some nettle water? Excellent for the bowels.'

They both declined. The man poured his own cup, and settled himself at the desk with a number of alarming joint pops.

'Ishmael was taken by men who came in the night,' he said. 'A kidnap.'

Charlie and Lily exchanged glances.

'There are many people who might want Ishmael,' said Charlie grimly. 'People who think him guilty of murder. Maybe someone found him out.' He turned back to Gabriel. 'You were here with Ishmael?'

'No, I came after he was taken.' Gabriel crossed himself. 'His Majesty is kind to astrologers and has granted us sanctuary. With the coming eclipse, Londoners are unsettled. I've been threatened many times.'

'Ishmael would have made star charts and things of that nature, would he not?' suggested Charlie. 'Was nothing of his works left?'

'No,' said the astrologer. 'I drew several star charts to be sure.'

Charlie felt a glimmer of hope. Perhaps Gabriel had not properly searched, relying instead on his astrology.

'If Ishmael were kidnapped,' said Charlie carefully, 'he would hardly have had time to gather up his workings.'

'Clothes were left,' said Gabriel, 'and a little flour and milk. But nothing astrological. It was mostly as you see it now.'

He gestured to the neat fire and cauldron. Everything had its rightful place, Charlie noticed. A hook for every spoon, a lid for every pot. Ishmael was a methodical kind of man if his residence was anything to go by.

'Did it not strike you as strange,' asked Charlie, 'that he left no astrological workings of any kind?'

'Not at all,' said Gabriel. 'I've made powerful charts to discern where Ishmael's works could be. My calculations show his papers are aboard a carriage bound for the North of England. I am quite certain on the matter.'

'Ishmael did his stargazing from the attic?' suggested Charlie. 'Might we look there?'

'He did,' said Gabriel. 'But you won't find anything. I assure you my workings were perfect. The sun in Aquarius. A carriage headed north. There is no mistake.'

'Naturally,' said Charlie tactfully. 'We're both very interested in astrology,' he added. 'Do you study the stars from the attic also?'

Gabriel's thin chest inflated with pride. 'I have several devices of my own making up there,' he said. 'And I do most of my workings by starlight.'

'We should love to see them,' said Lily, catching on to Charlie's tactic. 'They sound most interesting.'

'Of course.' Gabriel stood with a gratified expression. 'It is a science, you understand. Not everyone gives astrology the credit it deserves. It is the fault of charlatans who forecast on cockfights and tea leaves, pretending at real science.' Gabriel beckoned them through the narrow hallways and the staircase beyond. 'No man can deny the influence of the stars on the earth,' continued Gabriel, moving towards the staircase. 'Men feel more angry and warlike when Mars is ascending. Women scheme their marriages to coincide with lusty Venus.'

They were ascending the rickety stair now, and beyond, Charlie saw a ladder leading to an attic.

'In day-to-day matters, astrology is also useful,' prattled Gabriel, moving towards the ladder. 'My own record for finding lost things is excellent. Only last week I found a man's spectacles.' He mounted the ladder with impressive dexterity for his age. 'This way,' he said. 'Have a care; it's steep.'

In the small entrance, Charlie could see a shaft of light where the roof had been partially cut away.

Taking hold of a rung, he followed Gabriel up into Ishmael Boney's attic.

Chapter 39

Lady Castlemaine's sumptuous apartments had welcomed an unexpected visitor. Amesbury's military clothing and muddy boots looked conspicuously out of place amongst her artfully amassed furnishings and trinkets.

'So you come for my help?' Lady Castlemaine had a spiteful look in her eyes. 'Why did you not help me before?'

Amesbury sighed. He'd been expecting this. He rested his bullish bulk heavily on a dainty chaise longue. It creaked under his weight.

'What could I have done,' he asked, 'about Frances?'

'You might have advised the King against it,' said Lady Castlemaine angrily. 'You might have told him how disgusting and debasing it is for a man of his years to chase a fifteen-year-old girl around the palace.'

Amesbury watched in dull amazement. He had never seen Lady Castlemaine display any kind of vulnerability. Yet here she was, voice quaking, hurt splayed across her beautiful face. He had a sudden terror that she might cry.

But Lady Castlemaine was made of sterner stuff. He watched in fascination as she pulled her feelings back into alignment. It was like watching a mask being put in place piece by piece.

'So why,' she concluded, 'should I help you?'

'It is not for myself I ask help,' said Amesbury, spreading his large hands. 'It is for England.'

'You suggest my loyalty needs prompting?' said Lady Castlemaine. 'You forget I was secretly toasting the banished King when you were fighting for Cromwell.'

Amesbury ignored the dig.

'Buckingham,' he said. 'Do you trust him?'

'What disgusting rumours—?'

Amesbury held up his hands to silence her. 'Save your acting for His Majesty,' he interrupted. 'I have no perturbation who shares your bed. But I do care,' he concluded, 'that someone close to the King could be working for the Dutch.'

Lady Castlemaine arched her high eyebrows. 'If you wish for my opinion, you must first tell me your suspicions against Buckingham,' she said.

Amesbury reached forward to help himself from a crystal decanter of sherry. The chaise longue beneath him gave an audible crack of distress. Lady Castlemaine winced, took hold of the decanter herself and poured the sweet wine into two exquisitely fluted crystal glasses. Amesbury took one in his bear-like hand, frowning at the tiny vessel.

'Very well,' he said, taking a sip. 'De Ryker has amassed a fleet at the mouth of the Thames. I think he means to invade. And he would only do so with good reason.'

Amesbury drained the sherry in a single further gulp and looked disappointedly at the tiny vessel.

'But the King doesn't see the danger,' concluded Lady Castlemaine, 'or you wouldn't come to me.'

Amesbury held up his empty glass in recognition of her perception. 'The Duke of York has persuaded the King that a foolish obsession with finding longitude can save them from the Dutch attack.'

'He hopes to find better navigation?' said Lady Castlemaine. 'Faster routes to the wealth of the New World?' Her eyes flashed with imaginary riches.

It hadn't escaped Amesbury's notice that Lady Castlemaine's apartments were replete with the spoils of conquest. Gold and jewels encrusted every lacquered piece of furniture. Dainty silverware for the preparation of chocolate was arranged with ceramics from China.

'It is a fantasy,' said Amesbury. 'We are decades away from such a navigational accomplishment – perhaps centuries – if longitude can even be solved at all. The Dutch are a day away.'

'What has Buckingham to do with this?' Lady Castlemaine moved forward to refill his dainty glass.

'You remember Thorne?' said Amesbury. 'You attended his wedding I believe.'

'They hoped a bride would temper his strange ways,' agreed Lady Castlemaine. 'I felt sorry for her. Didn't Thorne work alongside the Cipher?' She gave a shudder. 'Two mad cryptographers together, worshipping Roman gods, making sacrifices to the Thames. That was how I heard it.'

Amesbury smiled slightly. 'Thorne made a very powerful weapon,' he said. 'It was known as the Eye and thought lost. I believe the Dutch have sent a man to search for it in London.'

Lady Castlemaine looked interested. 'You think Buckingham seeks this weapon, meaning to give it to De Ryker?' She sipped sherry distractedly, her pretty face puckered in thought. 'A treason?'

'I think Buckingham may have been working for the Dutch as a fireship pilot,' said Amesbury, 'calling himself Janus. I think he's been murdering girls at Deptford, perhaps trying to replicate Thorne's work.'

Lady Castlemaine considered this. 'You have evidence for your suspicions?' she said eventually.

'Buckingham's disappearance coincided exactly with Janus's emergence on De Ryker's command,' said Amesbury, 'and he's been hiding his nationality. His mother is Dutch. Buckingham has also been sighted several times at Dead Man's Curve. At night.'

Lady Castlemaine nodded, thinking of her own discoveries. The lock of bloody hair, the almanac.

'Then you expect me to risk my safety at the hands of a killer?' she said.

Amesbury smiled broadly. 'You are much too clever for that.'

Lady Castlemaine drank sherry thoughtfully. Amesbury took her silence as acquiescence. But he knew better than to sigh in relief. Lady Castlemaine's help always came with caveats.

'Then you must do something for me,' she added.

Amesbury waved his hand. 'Name it.'

'Frances Stewart,' said Lady Castlemaine. 'I want her ruined. Banished from court.'

'I thought you were making headway there,' said Amesbury, surprised. 'From what I heard, she's your nightly bedfellow.'

Lady Castlemaine scowled. 'The girl is nauseatingly pious. She sleeps in my bed most nights. But God is a hard enemy to drive off.'

Amesbury nodded. He heaved his bulk up with a heavy sigh. Courtly politics was an unpleasant business. He was getting too soft-hearted in his old age.

'It shall be done,' he said wearily.

Chapter 40

Charlie followed Gabriel into the attic, with Lily behind him. They found themselves under a thatched roof, into which had been cut a neat hole. Daylight shone through.

Packed inside were provisions. Sacks of ships' biscuits, barrels of ale, pickles and a large side of salted beef. The rafters were ranged with hanging crucifixes, and pages from an old Bible had been torn out and fixed on the beams. They fluttered in the draught from the open roof.

'My arrangements,' explained Gabriel, gesturing to the stockpiled food, 'for the coming apocalypse. Enough food for half a year. I bought these protectorates from a Cheapside stall.'

A spyglass lay on the floor. Charlie picked it up.

'My own invention,' said Gabriel. 'You can see Venus crossing the moon on a clear night. I've tracked her pentagram for the last eight years.'

'Venus makes the shape of a pentagram?' Charlie was thinking of the corpse at Deptford.

'Of course,' said Gabriel. 'The five-pointed star. It's why the apple is the fruit of Venus.' He took in their blank expressions. 'The shape of the pips when you cut the fruit, you see?' He looked at Charlie, pleased to be explaining. 'Apple pips make the same shape as the Venus star, moving through the heavens.'

'I thought Devil worshippers used the pentagram,' said Lily.

'If they do, it is ill-used,' said Gabriel, sounding rather annoyed. 'The pentagram is Venus. The Love Goddess.'

'What about your goat door knocker?' said Charlie. 'That has a pentagram.'

'I presume it belonged to Ishmael,' said Gabriel vaguely. 'The goat is Capricorn of course – Saturn's sign. Venus and Saturn . . .' He trailed off. 'Perhaps some association more learned men than I know of.'

'Ishmael made the hole?' suggested Charlie, eyeing it from several vantage points.

Gabriel nodded. 'I believe so.'

'A precise man,' decided Charlie, taking in the way the thatch had been cut. Ishmael had taken the time to make careful strokes, minimising the fraying of the reed, where another man might have hacked and bludgeoned.

'Knows something about roofing too,' Charlie decided. 'The reeds have been slashed on an angle at the weakest point, as a thatcher would do it. Most people would cut horizontal, in line with the roof.'

Charlie let his gaze sweep the room. There was nowhere here to hide anything apart from the floor. And he could tell at a glance no floorboards had been disturbed.

He sat on his haunches and considered the scene. His thief taker's intuition told him Ishmael might have hidden something in the roof. The man obviously knew something about thatching. But the roof was large, and it would take them all day to search.

Charlie examined the problem. Where might an astrologer hide something if he wished to find it again? His scant knowledge of Ishmael suggested him to be a systematic man.

Charlie took off his coat.

'What are you doing?' asked Gabriel, alarmed, as Charlie fitted his long leather coat across the hole in the thatch.

The inside of the attic darkened. As his eyes adjusted, Charlie swept the thatched roof with his eyes, running systematically along the beams. Almost everywhere the thick reeds cut out the sun completely.

'Take away your coat!' demanded Gabriel. 'We can't see a thing.'

Charlie scanned carefully, tuning out the protests of the outraged astrologer.

There.

A suspiciously square patch where a glimmer of autumn sun lightened the thatch. The reed roof was thinner there, Charlie was certain. He removed his coat and walked towards it.

'What is the meaning of it?' asked Gabriel, less agitated now the attic was in daylight again.

Charlie raised his hand to where he'd seen that the thatch was thinner. At first he thought he'd been mistaken. Then he felt it. A tiny pocket had been cut into the roof, almost indiscernible to the naked eye. But enough to let a little extra sun through.

He pushed up his hand. Inside was a sheaf of papers. He pulled them free.

'My goodness,' said Gabriel. 'What have you there?'

'I think,' said Charlie, 'Ishmael Boney may have left something after all.'

Chapter 41

In the dark attic Charlie and Lily stared at the papers. There were tens of them, all made out in a neat crabbed hand. Most were star charts. Circles and squares were dotted with symbols of suns and star signs.

'I was certain,' Gabriel was saying, 'the moon was in Cancer. I am all amazement you found them here. I must go back to my charts and reassess.'

Charlie let his gaze hover over the papers. They looked disappointingly ordinary. Merely workings for what later made their way into Ishmael's almanacs.

Lily held up the star charts. 'These don't make sense,' she said sadly, 'unless you know astrology.'

'I don't think it matters,' said Charlie. 'From what I can remember, most of these have already been published in Ishmael's almanac.'

Then Charlie noticed something. A paper that looked different to the rest.

He picked it up. 'This is older,' said Charlie, seizing on it. 'See how the ink is faded? And the paper is rag mash, not wood pulp like the rest. We make finer stuff nowadays. The writing is different too,' he noted.

Charlie pulled it free and recognised it immediately.

'All Hallows' Eve,' read Lily, '1666.'

It was the four cherubims, headed by a heavenly interpretation, just as in Ishmael's almanac. And scrawled at the bottom was a signature.

'Thorne!' said Lily, reading over Charlie's shoulder. 'He's signed this chart as his own.'

Gabriel was on his feet at the mention of Thorne's name.

'This is his?' he said, touching the old paper reverently. 'The great master's?'

Lily frowned. 'You knew Thorne?' she said.

'All astrologers know of him,' said Gabriel.

'What do they know?' asked Charlie.

'He had great understanding of the stars,' said Gabriel. 'There are rumours of an apprentice boy of noble birth to whom Thorne entrusted his secrets. It's said he died or escaped to sea.'

Lily pushed a strand of black hair behind her ear. 'If Janus was the apprentice,' she said, 'what might his true identity be?' She considered. 'The Judge is high-born and a sailor. He would have been a boy back then. Or perhaps . . .' She gave a halting laugh.

'What is it?' asked Charlie.

'The Duke of York,' smiled Lily, 'would have been close to Thorne, the right age, and he escaped to sea. But it couldn't be.'

She met Charlie's eyes to confirm the ridiculousness of the idea.

'Not unless he has an identical twin,' agreed Charlie. 'The Duke of York's every move is noted.' He nodded to the chart. 'Let's consider what we have here.'

'So Ishmael has Thorne's *Chart of All Hallows' Eve*,' she said, 'and published it as his own.'

Charlie nodded. 'What we need to know,' he said, 'is how did Ishmael get this chart? Thorne died years ago. Were they friends? Or did Ishmael find it after Thorne's death?'

Something was stirring in his mind, making connections.

Thorne's interest in Roman gods.

Why was it suddenly nagging at him?

Gabriel was looking at the cherubims.

'What does it mean?' asked Lily.

'It's not so easy to decipher another man's workings,' admitted Gabriel. He frowned, his eyes sweeping the page. 'It's almost as though . . . the astrology is wrong,' he said slowly. 'The position of the stars and planets doesn't seem possible to me.' He scratched his chin. 'Perhaps a more learned man would know,' he said uncertainly.

Charlie matched this against what they knew of Thorne.

'Does anything else in the chart make sense to you?' Lily asked.

'That's the Eye of Heaven,' Gabriel said, pointing to a triangle with an eye radiating light inside. 'An emerald from Lucifer's forehead that symbolises the third eye. The knowing mankind has lost because of sin.' Gabriel scanned the flying cherubim. 'These angels here are a less usual way to depict Saturn,' he explained. 'Usually he is shown clutching a child or a scythe. The God of Death. This is a more ancient depiction. Saturn as God of Time.'

'But it isn't Saturn,' protested Lily. 'They're angels. Four angels. They have wings.'

'One god became four angels,' corrected Gabriel. 'Each head is an astrological season, to symbolise the unstoppable march of time,' he continued. 'Saturn comes from Cronus, the god who ate his children.'

Chapter 42

Lady Castlemaine let herself quietly into Frances Stewart's quarters. They were comfortably furnished for a lady-in-waiting, with a few telltale additions. A sumptuous rug and a lacquered cabinet that Lady Castlemaine recognised from the banqueting chambers. Two small beds showed that Frances shared the room with another girl. Lady Castlemaine wondered what her roommate thought of the royal attentions.

Her gaze drifted to a plate of little marzipan sweets – fantastically detailed sugar-work fruits with delicate leaves. A lump rose in her throat. Charles had sent her the same sweets when they'd arrived in Whitehall. She thought of her children. Each titled. Each safe. With the exception of her last little girl.

Lady Castlemaine took in the room. A long looking glass, with only a hairbrush. No powders or paint. Young girls had no need of such things. She caught her reflection in the glass and thought she looked good for twenty-eight. Her features still held the seductive shape that had first drawn the King. But unhappiness was ageing, and twenty-eight was a long way from fifteen. The mirror, she thought, was probably also a gift from Charles. He'd presented her with a similar ornament for her own apartments.

A sniffling sound drew Lady Castlemaine's attention to a door leading to a small chapel room. She walked towards it and found a youthful figure, head buried in her arms, prostrated on the short pew.

Frances was clad in her petticoats, and without the bulk of her dress she was tiny. Her soft, dark curls hid her face, pearl earrings hung from her dainty ears and a matching necklace spanned her chubby child-sized throat.

A mixture of rage and pity bloomed in Lady Castlemaine's chest. How could this little thing be causing her so much trouble? Setting her face to sympathy, she moved forward and tended a reassuring pat. Frances jerked upwards, terrified.

'I heard you crying from the hallway,' lied Lady Castlemaine. 'I could not help but see what was wrong.'

The devastation on Frances's young face deepened. She sat with her mouth hanging open stupidly, tears streaking her face.

'Something has happened,' discerned Lady Castlemaine. 'Has Charles been cruel?'

Frances hesitated, then erupted into fresh tears, shaking her head.

'There, there,' said Lady Castlemaine, snaking a perfumed arm around the younger girl. 'Tell me what happened. I told you I would protect you from him.'

Frances gave a giant sniff and rubbed at her red eyes. 'He's so kind,' she whispered, 'I truly think he loves me.'

Lady Castlemaine made her eyes wide. 'You poor girl,' she said. 'But I thought I'd taught you how to be careful of believing things like that.'

'I . . .' Frances hesitated. Her eyes drifted to the chapel cross, then back to Lady Castlemaine, desperate. 'I kissed him. Am I still . . . ?' began Frances, swallowing. 'Can I still marry?'

It took Lady Castlemaine a moment to realise what the younger girl was asking. Then it took every effort not to laugh.

'You're worried you're no longer a virgin?' she summarised.

Frances nodded rapidly.

Lady Castlemaine stroked her hair. 'What happened exactly?' she asked.

France swallowed with effort. 'It was . . . It's hard to remember. He's so good to me. He kissed me and then . . . it was much like you did.' Her face began reddening. 'In your bed when you showed me . . . what a man might do.'

'The caresses a girl might expect from her husband,' clarified Lady Castlemaine, 'if he truly loves her.'

Frances nodded, blushing scarlet. 'The other ladies have told me things,' she managed in a whisper. 'That the man has something between his legs that hurts you. It wasn't that,' she managed, her eyes beseeching Lady Castlemaine's understanding.

'Let me look for you,' Lady Castlemaine said. 'We can be sure you're still a virgin.'

'You could do that?' Frances's expression was dubious.

'Of course,' said Lady Castlemaine. 'An older woman knows such things.' She took Frances's unresisting hand and led her from the chapel to the bed. 'Lie there,' she instructed. 'Put up your petticoats as if we were readying for bed in my chamber.'

'Will it hurt?' Frances was aligning herself on the sheets.

'No,' promised Lady Castlemaine, sliding in next to her. The younger girl's legs were trembling.

Frances broke into a strange gasping sob. 'It's impossible to resist him,' she blurted. 'He's the King. He has ways of getting you alone that the other men . . . It wouldn't be allowed.'

'There's nothing to be frightened of,' soothed Lady Castlemaine, sliding a hand between Frances's small thighs. 'You should have come to me. I won't let any harm befall you.'

Frances nodded, relaxing into Lady Castlemaine's arms.

'You're certain this isn't sinful?' she asked as the older woman probed.

'Quite the opposite. There,' breathed Lady Castlemaine. 'You mustn't fear. You are still a virgin. Any husband you choose will know it.'

Frances let out a long breath. Tears welled up in her eyes.

'I was so frightened,' she admitted.

Lady Castlemaine pulled her closer.

'He told me,' Frances whispered, 'he would make me a duchess. But I don't want it. I only want to be married. To be a good wife.'

'Shh,' Lady Castlemaine soothed. 'I will help you. I'll find you a good marriage.'

Frances's blue eyes were pleading. 'You will?' she managed.

'Yes,' Lady Castlemaine nodded. 'You can always rely on my kindness.'

Frances nodded.

'But you must help yourself,' continued Lady Castlemaine. 'You have a cousin. Buckingham.'

Frances's pretty features clouded slightly.

'You know him?' asked Lady Castlemaine.

'He's a very distant cousin,' said Frances. 'I've never met him. But Buckingham is dangerous. There's a . . . a story about him. It's a secret in our family. I don't know if I should tell you.'

Lady Castlemaine stroked her cheek. 'There is nothing you can't tell me.'

Frances swallowed. 'They say he killed a girl during the Civil War,' she whispered, her eyes wide. 'Her mutilated body washed up near Deptford.'

'The family covered it up,' guessed Lady Castlemaine.

Frances nodded, looking as if she might have said too much.

'I fear Buckingham is involved with treason,' said Lady Castlemaine. 'I want you to meet with him. Find out what you can.'

The younger girl's face was a mask of shock.

'If you do this thing,' said Lady Castlemaine smoothly, 'I will make all the business with the King go away and find you a handsome husband to protect you.'

At this temptation, Frances's terror seemed to waver slightly.

'I will arrange for you to meet with him,' continued Lady Castlemaine. 'He has a locked drawer in his room. I will give you a key that will open it. You must find a reason to get him out of the room, look inside and report back what you see.'

Frances was shaking her head. 'I cannot,' she protested. 'How could I be alone with him? In his own rooms?' Her face darkened. 'He's a killer!'

Lady Castlemaine drew her face into a sad frown. 'I have made great efforts to be a friend to you,' she said. 'I meant to find you a husband. Protect you from the King. But now I find you are false, I am less inclined.'

Frances shook her head. 'I am grateful for all your attentions,' she said.

'Then be my friend,' said Lady Castlemaine. 'I would never put you at risk.' She pulled Frances closer and planted a kiss on her forehead. 'I'm the only person in court who truly cares for you. I'll see to it you're protected.'

Frances hesitated.

'You don't have to answer now,' said Lady Castlemaine kindly. 'Think about it.'

She drew the younger girl tighter in her arms and kissed her.

'Whilst we're in bed together,' she added, 'there's something else I should show you.'

Chapter 43

Charlie and Lily were sat on the floor of Gabriel's attic, astrological papers scattered around. The old astrologer had opened a barrel of pickled cucumbers and was crunching one loudly.

'I'm sorry I can't tell you anything much,' said Gabriel between bites. 'Astrology is a complicated science.' He tapped the cherubim. 'But these angels certainly represent Saturn.'

Lily gave Charlie an uneasy glance.

'You know of Father Time,' added Gabriel patiently, 'with his hourglass, scythe and a young child on his lap? That is Saturn, eating time and youth. In olden times he was shown as a four-headed winged god.'

'But the cherubim are Christian,' said Lily. 'How can that be?'

'Christian stories retell the paths of the stars,' said Gabriel. 'Things are mixed in the telling. The birth of Jesus is a star story,' he added. 'Jesus is the sun. He is born between Capricorn and Sagittarius, you see? Born in a stable. Between horses and goats. The sun dies at winter solstice – Christmas. Then rises again, just as Jesus was reborn.'

'So you're telling us,' said Charlie, struggling to understand, 'that this *Chart of All Hallows' Eve* shows Saturn as God of Time. But other astrologers see him as God of Death.'

'Yes,' said Gabriel, 'the end of time, the death of the world. What difference does it make?' He shrugged. 'The *Chart of All Hallows' Eve* is showing what astrologers already know.' He added, 'Tomorrow night Saturn will destroy the world.'

Lily had begun scratching distractedly at the attic floor with a knife. Gabriel looked on nervously.

'The *Chart of All Hallows' Eve* tells us no more than Ishmael's almanac,' she concluded.

'Maybe not,' said Charlie. 'But remember Macock's print house. We know Thorne and the Cipher likely worked together, hidden in a forest near the city.'

He picked up the old document. 'Rag mash paper,' he explained, 'uses a handful of finely chipped wood to strengthen the mix. Acorn is the preference, but they tend to use whatever they have to hand. Cryptographers make their own paper,' he continued, 'so this rag mash could tell us about the woods where Thorne and the Cipher were sited.'

'Walnut and birch for Hampstead Heath,' said Lily, catching on, 'oak and elm for Southwark.'

'Exactly.' Charlie was tearing a corner of the page. 'Dark flecks,' he said. 'Some kind of nutshell. Too dark for acorn, but not walnut either.'

He rubbed his scarred lip, considering the unfamiliar additive.

Lily took the corner of paper, chewed it, then spat out flecks.

'Weeping beechnut,' she concluded.

Charlie shook his head. 'It can't be,' he said.

'I'm certain of it,' said Lily.

'No weeping beeches grow in London,' said Charlie. 'They grow by water, and the Thames is brackish. Unless . . .' Then the answer came to him. 'The Upside-down Tree,' said Charlie slowly. 'It was planted especially for royalty in Hyde Woods. No one's been allowed near it since the time of the old King, when the woods were sealed.'

He was fitting things together in his head, building a picture of Thorne. A man with an interest in Roman gods.

'Hyde Woods is still owned by the Crown,' said Charlie. 'And I've heard stories,' he added slowly, 'there are catacombs underneath.'

'Catacombs?' asked Lily. 'Old Roman tunnels?'

'They were used to bury bodies hundreds of years ago,' confirmed Charlie. 'Now they are abandoned. There are a few scattered around the city,' he added. 'People use them for wine cellars or crypts. But London is boggy ground. Hard to tunnel beneath. Hyde Woods is higher.'

Lily toyed with the charms at her neck. 'The catacombs,' she said. 'You think they could be the Temple of Death?'

'It's possible. Romans are known for temples,' reasoned Charlie. 'We know Thorne liked Roman things. Hyde Woods is difficult to navigate and was heavily guarded in the old King's time. It would be a good place to hide a cryptographer.'

'That was twenty years ago,' said Lily. 'Surely anything of Thorne will be long gone now.'

'Most likely,' agreed Charlie. 'But Thorne wasn't the only cryptographer in Hyde Woods, was he?'

'You think the Cipher could be hiding in Hyde Woods still?'

'People still talk of the Temple of Death.' The more Charlie thought about it, the more certain he felt it was worth investigating. Hyde Woods was the perfect place to conceal the Cipher. 'The woods are dangerous,' he added. 'The King keeps a garrison there. Between the thieves and the armed men, the Cipher will be well protected if he's there at all. But I know an old poacher who can chart the woods. A good friend of mine. He'll get us into the catacombs.'

He grinned at Lily.

'A man called Bitey.'

Chapter 44

Janus was leaning on the door frame of the small half-timbered house, trying to focus. The door drew open, and a familiar woman appeared.

'You're back.' Bess's face couldn't decide on an expression. 'You're drunk,' she added.

'I missed you,' he managed.

The blood and horrors of the riverbank kept flashing before him. Janus settled his gaze on Bess. Her familiar pale skin and dark lashes. She had the thickset body of a woman who worked harder than she should, but there was something Janus found very comfortable in that. As though nothing could ever be truly terrible with Bess.

'That's the drink talking,' she replied more kindly. Her broad shoulders heaved up a little sigh, as if she knew she was to regret her next action. 'Come in,' she said. 'Better not let anyone see you.'

He followed her inside the little house. It was more neatly appointed than he remembered it. Then he saw the crib.

'I've got responsibilities now,' she said, nodding towards it. 'I keep no strong beer for callers.'

Janus found there was a lump in his throat. He moved towards the basket. Behind him he thought he felt Bess flinch, as though she didn't quite trust him.

Inside was a tiny swaddled baby. Its eyes were shut and the little mouth twitched in repose. The sleeping face seemed to draw him in. He wondered if he'd ever looked so peaceful, even as a baby.

Janus lowered a fascinated hand into the crib.

'He's asleep,' said Bess with more force than necessary.

Janus turned. 'Is he mine?'

'I don't know,' said Bess with a shrug. 'What does it matter?'

Janus felt suddenly very sober.

'It's my birthday today,' he said.

Bess's face fell. 'I'm sorry.'

Janus rubbed his dark hair. 'Born under a dark star,' he said bitterly. 'Child of Saturn. Evil.'

'Don't say it,' said Bess, moving to his side. She put a comforting arm around him.

Janus nodded to the sleeping child. 'What of him?' he asked. 'Do you know his stars?'

Bess patted his arm. 'He's a Leo. Well favoured.'

Janus closed his eyes, feeling relieved. He managed a smile.

'I meant to come sooner,' he said.

Bess gave a strange kind of snort. 'Of course you did.'

Janus strode over to where she stood, lifted her easily and swung them both to sit on a large rocking chair. Bess shrieked as the chair pivoted beneath them. Her long dark hair fell in a curtain over his arm.

'Let me go,' she laughed half-heartedly.

Janus wrapped her tighter in his arms, and she giggled. Bess never could stay angry at him for long.

'Why did you not write?' she accused.

He smiled at her. 'I was captured by De Ryker as a prisoner of war.'

C.S. Quinn

There was a pause as she examined his face. He'd always liked how she did that, her dark eyes raking his for the truth.

Just for a moment Janus wanted to tell her everything. How he'd killed to discover Thorne's Eye. But he knew he'd lose her, and he couldn't bear this last tiny pocket of ordinary existence to be gone.

'What's he like?' asked Bess, apparently deciding to believe him. 'De Ryker. Is he the devil they say?'

'He is and worse,' confirmed Janus. 'I'll never forget the sight of his huge leather boots descending into the prison quarters. De Ryker looks like an old sea god,' Janus continued. 'Craggy, like he's been preserved in sun and saltwater since the dawn of time. But wise too. One of his eyes is bleached to near blindness from navigating by the sun. The other is brown, deep brown, and it seems to look into your soul.'

Bess gave a gratifying shudder. 'Why didn't De Ryker kill you?' she asked.

Janus's face suddenly fell. 'He did,' he said. 'He did kill part of me.'

'What did he do?' asked Bess, touching his face with her fingers.

'He made us fight each other for entertainment,' whispered Janus. Suddenly he couldn't meet her eye. 'I killed men of my own crew.' Janus had a desperate memory of himself, ragged and blood-smeared.

Bess swallowed. 'You did what you had to do,' she said uncertainly, 'to survive. Men do worse in war.'

'Thorne twisted me,' said Janus. 'But it was De Ryker who made me a killer.'

'Shh,' said Bess. 'You're not a bad man.'

'You only say that,' said Janus, 'because you don't know what I've done.'

Bess flinched.

'De Ryker very nearly had me thrown overboard,' continued Janus. 'But I told him about the weapon.'

'The weapon from your boyhood?' asked Bess uncertainly.

'The Eye,' confirmed Janus. 'It's somewhere in London. Now the stars turn in my favour, I can find it.'

Bess looked at him for a long time. 'Then what?' she demanded. 'All your life you have looked for one adventure, then the next,' said Bess. 'I thought you would change. But you never did.'

Janus sat up a little. 'The Eye is all I've ever wanted. Since I was a boy. It's my birthright. Stolen from me.'

She was shaking her head emphatically.

'I'll make sure you're provided for,' said Janus, confused. 'Once I have the Eye, I can lay it all to rest. All the horrors.'

'I never wanted your money,' said Bess sadly. 'I'd have married you for your handsome ways.'

'Marriage was never so easy for me.'

She buried her hands in his dark hair. 'My noble prince,' she smiled, 'banished from all he loves most.'

'I'll get it back,' he said, 'no matter what it takes.'

'It doesn't matter.' She sounded much older suddenly. 'There'll be no end. Not until you have destroyed the world or died in the trying.'

He touched her face, unable to bear her disapproval.

'You're the only feeling I have left,' he said helplessly. 'You're my one weakness, Bess.'

As Janus said the words, he realised. Charlie Oakley had a weakness too. All he need do was exploit it.

Chapter 45

Lily and Charlie were waiting at the dark edges of Hyde Woods. Stars twinkled above. All around them were encampments. People who had been made homeless by the Great Fire two months earlier.

'The King had plans to make this a park for Londoners,' Charlie explained, 'but since the Great Fire he can't risk it being overrun.'

He gestured to the hundreds of makeshift tents crammed cheek by jowl around the outskirts of the woods.

'They don't let the refugees any further into the woods?' asked Lily, peering into the gloomy trees. The twinkling campfires stopped abruptly where the woods proper began.

'It's royal land,' said Charlie. 'The old King kept it for the deer and the wild boar. Gamekeepers have been brought back to protect it, and they're a harsh lot.'

He pointed high up in the trees, where several bloody shapes hung.

'What are they?' asked Lily, squinting for a better look. 'Deer?'

Dangling hooves could just be seen in the moonlight.

Charlie shook his head. 'They're men caught inside the royal boundaries of Hyde Woods. The gamekeepers sewed them into deerskins and hunted them down with dogs for sport. They're hung there as a warning.'

Lily swallowed. 'Then how are we to find the catacombs? I don't wish to be hunted down.'

'Bitey's an old friend. He's been poaching the woods for years,' Charlie reassured her. 'He'll have a way.'

There was a familiar clanking sound, and they turned to see Bitey shamble into view. He was dressed in his usual thickly grimed coat but had slung a cumbersome-looking bow and arrow over his squat frame.

'Evenin',' he grinned, exposing his trademark dark patch of wooden teeth in the night gloom. His gaze settled on Lily.

'You remember Lily Boswell,' said Charlie. 'She's an associate.'

He suppressed a smile at the slight surprise on Lily's face. Bitey's eyes flicked between them.

'Not a good night for poaching,' he said after a moment, nodding to the bright stars. 'Could do with some cloud.'

'We're not here to poach,' said Charlie. 'We're looking for the Cipher. We think he might be hidden in the old catacombs.'

'The Cipher,' said Bitey thoughtfully. 'He could be down there I suppose. The man is said to be a ghost.'

A sudden grunting sound emanated from Bitey's coat. Lily stared in alarm as a striped nose peeked indignantly from his filthy collar. A small badger was trying to wriggle free.

'A new friend?' asked Charlie, who was used to Bitey's fondness for baby animals. Though he usually reserved his guardianship for creatures that would grow large enough to eat.

'He's a decoy,' said Bitey, 'in case we encounter some authority. Don't go near the head end,' he added. 'He bites. Alright then,' continued Bitey amiably. 'I think I can remember the old entrance to the tunnels.'

He looked up to the moon. His gaze shifted to the North Star, and he held up two raddled fingers, closed one eye and squinted at the sky.

Then he lowered his hands, apparently pleased with his deductions.

'Old sailor trick,' he said with a wink, 'to locate things at night. Served me better as a poacher than it ever did at sea,' he added. 'Follow me.'

Bitey set off at a faster pace than his short legs might have suggested. Lily and Charlie followed behind, the edges of the dark woods casting deep shadows.

The spaced trees of the outskirts had quickly thickened to woodland, and they found themselves amongst black tree trunks and uneven ground.

'Can he see anything?' whispered Lily as they followed Bitey's dark form through the woods.

'He's got poacher's eyes,' said Charlie. 'Years of tracking in the darkness.'

A muffled thump alerted them to Bitey making heavy contact with a tree. He swore and retrieved his tricorn hat from where it had been jolted to the ground.

'Sometimes you need to find the trees,' he said good-naturedly, wedging the hat back down, 'to see the wood.'

Lily, whose gypsy childhood steered her expertly through darkened groves, looked unconvinced.

The old man drew to a sudden halt at a patch of overgrown hedgerow.

'P'raps here,' he decided, removing his hat.

He dropped to his knees and vanished beneath the thicket. For a moment the foliage waved wildly. Then Bitey emerged with thorns and brambles clinging to his shaggy head.

'Over here then,' he muttered to himself, vanishing for a second time.

'If he can't get us in,' whispered Lily, 'do you have another plan?'

They heard several deep thumps from inside the hedgerow, then a rush of soil dislodging.

Bitey re-emerged, smiling proudly. 'Still here,' he announced. 'After all these years. Overgrown, mind, but will still fit a man if he's brave enough.'

'What's still here?' asked Charlie.

'Poacher's hole,' said Bitey. 'Come with me.'

And once again he disappeared under the hedgerow.

Charlie lifted the thicket uncertainly. By the light of the moon he could make out a darker patch amongst the roots and thorns – a hole just large enough for a man.

Bitey's thick boots were vanishing through it.

'Are you mad?' hissed Lily as Charlie poked his head into the hole. 'He says himself he's not been here for years. You could be crawling to your death.'

'Bitey's survived civil war, plague and fire,' said Charlie, sounding braver than he felt. 'It'll take more than a poaching expedition to finish him off.'

He pushed forward and found the hole was bigger than it looked. Charlie crawled awkwardly through, then dropped down into a wide, round tunnel. Behind him he heard Lily follow him through the rabbit hole.

Chapter 46

The Dowager Queen, Henrietta Maria of France, sat straight-backed on a huge carved throne. The Queen Mother's tiny frame was festooned in grey lace and black silk, fashions from a time when kings had been gods. Her eyes were her son's, brown and drooping at the edge, but without the warmth. They were currently fastened in annoyance on an unexpected visitor.

'You mean to tell me,' she accused in the hard French intonation she'd never quite lost, 'you came to my house in Greenwich without an escort?'

The Queen Mother's gnarled old hands were worrying a bloodied pair of riding gloves, a memento from the execution of her husband.

'Yes, Your Majesty,' admitted Frances Stewart, her voice trembling. Up until this moment she'd been proud of braving the Whitehall-to-Greenwich ferry in a plain dress with her head down. Now all she could think about was the origin of the bloody keepsakes in the old Queen's liver-spotted hands.

In an effort not to stare, Frances moved her gaze to the wall behind the Queen Mother. Crowding every inch were pictures of the old, dead

King. He stared down imperiously, the curled moustache and little beard giving his neat features a pointed quality. In one picture he rode on horseback in full armour, an ermine robe falling to the floor. In another his hand rested on a large astrological chart, showing the twelve constellations.

Queen Henrietta fixed Frances in her stony gaze. 'You're interested in my paintings?' she enquired coldly.

'I . . .' Frances struggled for the right words. 'I am glad for Your Majesty. I thought such paintings were destroyed by Cromwell.'

The Queen's face tightened. 'They were,' she said, settling her eyes on the image of herself and the old King. 'I had painters remake them.'

Frances realised now what she found odd about the pictures. There were no family portraits. Queen Henrietta had only those of her husband alone.

'He was a god,' said the Queen, following Frances's gaze. 'A god they killed.' The gloves turned, then turned again. 'I chose you to attend my son,' she added. 'I *hope* you have not disappointed me.'

Frances felt herself flush. She had a sudden horror that perhaps the old woman knew every licence she'd allowed Charles to take.

'I came to ask . . . I hoped . . .' Frances stumbled. 'I thought you might know of a suitable marriage prospect.'

'For you?' Henrietta's voice rose to a kind of shriek.

Frances gave a shaking nod.

'And why might you need a husband?' demanded Henrietta. 'Have you done something you shouldn't?'

Frances dissolved into tears.

Henrietta's face turned icy. 'I'll have you thrown from court,' she said in a low voice.

'No, I haven't,' pleaded Frances. 'I never let him . . . It's just' – she paused to take a great sobbing breath – 'he's so charming. And I fear I might. I truly fear it.'

She looked up at Henrietta, her eyes brimming with naive hope.

'A husband does not always keep a woman safe,' said the Queen Mother. 'I should know.'

Queen Henrietta closed her eyes. She was tired. And dogged by memories. Since she'd returned to Greenwich, dead girls had been washing up at Deptford again.

It was the work of the man who had lost them the war. What was his name? Thorne.

She had a sudden memory so physical it made her stomach turn even now. The old King drawing her inside the darkness of Thorne's secret workshop. Stumbling on broken things.

'What is this place?' she whispered. 'Surely Thorne has run mad.'

'Peace.' The old King smiled at her. 'Thorne has his ways of working. A man of his talent mustn't be questioned.'

'I don't trust the commoner,' she said, insinuating herself close to her husband. 'How can you be sure he won't betray us?'

'Amesbury is useful,' reassured the King. 'He is strong. The men like him. And he is loyal to the Crown. My gold makes sure of that.'

They entered a massive room filled with giant cogs. Henrietta backed away in horror, but the King tightened his grip on her arm. She turned to him in shock and saw a familiar expression – the maniacal glint in his dark eyes that had grown steadily since the war began.

Thorne was hunched over a tiny object and barely looked up. But it was the wider room that was most disturbing. Henrietta was certain these were pagan things. Tools of Devil worship.

'You see,' he whispered gleefully, 'what power I hold?' His fingers fastened on her arm. He pointed to Thorne. 'We must not interrupt the sorcerer in his rituals.'

There was an unexpected movement in the corner. The Queen's gaze flicked to see a pale-faced boy watching Thorne. His eyes glowed in admiration.

For a terrible moment she thought it one of her own sons. Then the child stepped back into the shadows and she lost sight of him. She reassured herself her boys were safely back in the palace.

'Behold the power of the Eye,' whispered the King gleefully. 'We will see as God sees. We cannot lose this war!'

Henrietta's attention fixed on Thorne's little table, covered in jewels and precious metals. Her eyes widened.

The Eye.

This must be it. The weapon her husband had told her about. The Eye was so much smaller than she'd expected – and more beautiful than she'd ever imagined.

The Queen Mother opened her eyes and was faintly surprised to see Frances still cowering meekly before her. This stupid weak girl with her whole life ahead of her. How dare she complain? What did she know of suffering?

The Queen sat slightly forward on her throne. The hard wood must have been uncomfortable, Frances thought.

'I cannot help you,' said the Queen Mother. 'You must pray to God.'

Frances swallowed back her tears. Henrietta had been her last hope.

Her only option now was to spy for Lady Castlemaine. To put herself alone with Buckingham. The thought terrified her. But it was the last path left.

Chapter 47

Charlie and Lily followed Bitey through the dank earth tunnel. They shuffled in the dark on their hands and knees, Hyde Woods vanishing behind them. Charlie could hear the swish of Lily's silk dress and smell the damp soil.

Ahead of him he could see Bitey's square frame illuminated by the flare of a tinderbox. Then unexpectedly the earth opened up. Charlie dropped down, landing on his hands and knees in a dank pool of water.

Bitey was lighting a rudimentary torch.

'Catacombs,' he confirmed, patting the slim curving bricks. 'Been under Hyde Woods for hundreds of years. Poachers been using 'em for the past twenty.'

'What does this mean?' Lily's slim fingers were tracing Roman letters, chiselled neatly into the wall. They made a single word.

'*Ostium.*'

'Means "mouth" in the old Roman tongue,' explained Bitey. 'There's a few marked around London. Mostly old sewers still in use.'

'Mouth?' Lily was looking uneasily into the dark throat of the tunnel.

'We have a few hours until the torch goes out,' added Bitey. 'Plenty of time to make a search.'

The tunnel was the height of a man, round and neatly bricked. It smelt of long-forgotten damp places. Charlie touched the arc of the low ceiling. The amber bricks felt cool and dry.

'I can't imagine someone hiding down here,' said Lily, who'd brought up the rear quickly once she'd seen the torchlight. 'It's like a sewer.'

Charlie agreed with her. Disappointment bloomed. The narrow corridors seemed much too small for anyone to live and sleep in.

Lily was looking around. The ceiling was curved over, and bricked corridors snaked away in different directions like open mouths.

Bitey waved the torch. 'That way leads to under the gamekeeper's hut,' he said. 'We'll not take that path unless we wish to be hunted and gutted for sport.' He squinted around. 'Never been too sure about every path,' he admitted. ''S like a labyrinth. But that one,' he said, pointing, 'leads to a safe place. Comes out by the edge of a small lake, near the Upside-down Tree. The big beech tree,' he added, catching Lily's face. 'Where Londoners used to make wishes.'

'How do we find it again,' asked Charlie, 'if we lose our way?'

He was trying not to let the shadowy dark spook him. The damp tunnels brought back strange memories from his childhood.

In answer Bitey lowered his calloused hand to the ground. 'Running water,' he explained. 'Not much, but you can feel it at your feet. It flows to the lake. We need only feel the direction the water runs and follow it out.'

Bitey splashed over the watery floor, then stopped suddenly. He raised a warning hand. Then he knelt and drew a stout stick from some-where in the depths of his coat.

'Mantrap,' he said, extending the stick into the dark.

A metallic crack followed, and two steel jaws leapt forth from the water-soaked floor.

'Nasty things,' added Bitey.

'What would it be doing here?' asked Charlie. His instincts were on high alert now. Someone expected unwanted people in the tunnel.

Bitey straightened. 'Most likely an old one,' he said, but he sounded uncertain.

Charlie looked at the trap. Someone had rigged this tunnel for intruders. It gave him a bad feeling.

They went deeper, with Bitey leading the way. The catacombs widened slightly, and now something yellow glimmered in the torchlight.

Bitey paused, shining his torch.

'What is it?' asked Lily.

'Well I never,' said the old man. 'Haven't saw that before. This must be a path I missed.'

A thick swathe of tree roots cascaded down one side of the tunnel, covering the Roman brick in a knotty curtain effect.

'We must be near the river,' said Charlie. 'Willow trees.'

Bitey brought the torch lower, revealing lighter-coloured shapes dotted between the roots. This part of the tunnel had been lined with something.

'Is it . . . stone?' asked Lily after a moment. Then her gaze tracked up and she saw the empty eye sockets.

'No,' said Charlie grimly. 'It's bones.' He looked further along the tunnel to where the tree roots stopped. 'There's more here,' he added. 'A lot more.'

They all stared. Countless human bones had been meticulously arranged. Shallow stone shelves held grinning skulls, arranged in neat rows. Femurs and ribcages had been stacked to make patterns.

'There must be hundreds of them,' said Lily, moving to look closer.

'The Temple of Death?' Charlie suggested. 'Though no one could live in this tunnel,' he admitted, looking at the cramped passage.

'I don't like it,' said Lily. 'There's something bad down here. I can feel it.'

'Hyde Woods is a haunted place,' agreed Bitey. 'Ghosts of druids and monks.' He gestured vaguely upwards.

Charlie reached in his coat and removed a flat nail. Then he etched a careful cross on the nearest skull.

'We'll mark as we go,' he said uneasily. 'Let's keep moving.'

Chapter 48

The prison boat swayed in the Thames waters. Deep below deck Ishmael Boney sat chained to the floor. On the way to his confinement he'd caught glimpses of the shore and judged them to be anchored near Greenwich or Deptford. Ishmael had made out the tumbledown remains of Greenwich Palace and the old astronomical clock.

The trapdoor overhead creaked open and a darkly cloaked man descended the narrow steps. Ishmael tried to make out the man's face in the gloom. But all he could see was a pearly cross where one of the eyes should have been. The figure drew into view. It was an eyepatch. Ishmael could see it now. Pearly and glinting darkly next to a single cold blue eye. The man wore the white collar of a judge, with long black robes, giving him a crow-like appearance. Ishmael drew back instinctively. He was a brave man, but there was something truly evil about his captor.

'I've never met a Moor before,' observed the Judge, taking in Ishmael's dark skin and thick curling hair flecked with white.

He let his good eye roam disapprovingly over Ishmael's scholarly outfit, a long, loose brown silk coat tied with a fashionable white cravat.

'Perhaps your ancestors were transported on a boat like this.' The Judge swept an explanatory hand around the dank quarters. 'This is an old slave ship,' he explained. 'Already fitted out to hold prisoners. I find it extremely useful for detaining some of my more . . . *interesting* convicts.'

'I'm of Arabic origin,' said Ishmael. 'No one in my family was ever held a slave. And I am under the King's protection. You break the law in detaining me.'

The Judge smiled thinly at the mention of the law. 'I am Judge Walters,' he said. 'Perhaps you have heard of me.'

'The Bloody Judge,' said Ishmael. 'Your brutality is legendary.'

'So you can be sure I break no law,' said the Judge, seeming pleased at Ishmael's description.

Ishmael felt a knot of fear tighten in his stomach.

The Judge dropped down to be level with his face. He drew out a familiar almanac from inside his coat.

'What I would like to know,' he said, 'is where is the gypsy girl who came to see you?'

Ishmael frowned in complete confusion. 'What gypsy girl?'

'Her name is Lily Boswell. She is a spy and a thief.' The Judge was twisting a patch of skin on his ring finger. 'I know she came looking for you.'

'If she did, she never found me,' said Ishmael calmly.

The Judge stepped back, considering. 'We shall see how true that is,' he decided, 'when you hear the charges against you.'

This time Ishmael's dark eyebrows twitched ever so slightly.

'You are accused of murder,' continued the Judge. 'The girls at Deptford.'

Ishmael shook his head. He looked tired rather than frightened.

'I have nothing to do with those girls,' he said.

'Then how do you explain this image,' demanded the Judge, pointing at the cherubims, 'carved into the backs of dead girls?'

'You don't understand astrology,' said Ishmael.

'Don't patronise me,' spat the Judge. 'I am a seafaring man. I understand the stars and their workings.'

Ishmael hid a smile.

'This prediction for the Halloween eclipse,' continued the Judge. 'It is different to your other charts in the almanac. I might even say it had been made by another man.'

Ishmael rubbed his temples. 'Good astrologers use the work of others,' he said. 'There is nothing unusual in it. This depicts a prophecy made a long time ago by a man named Thorne.'

'And how did you chance upon Thorne's papers?' he demanded. 'The turncoat astrologer who the old King wanted dead.'

For the first time Ishmael's eyes widened slightly, as if he hadn't expected the Judge to know about Thorne.

'That,' said Ishmael evenly, 'is something I will never tell a man like you.' Ishmael looked the Judge up and down. 'You're looking for the Eye,' he decided. 'Thorne hid it so undeserving men like you would never find it.'

'You will help me locate it,' said the Judge icily. 'I mean to reorder things. The Eye will allow me to root out blackamoors and heathens and put them where they belong.'

'You mean to grow your slaving business,' said Ishmael disgustedly. 'I will tell you nothing.'

The Judge's face had grown pale with anger. He waved the almanac.

'You are a heretic. You arrogantly attempt to interpret God's will.'

'Ask the King if astrology is heresy,' countered Ishmael. 'His Majesty spent two thousand pounds last year having Isaac Newton build tools to chart the stars.'

'For navigation at sea!' said the Judge, outraged. 'A different science to prediction. Do you deny your almanac predicts the future?'

'I don't,' said Ishmael calmly, 'but can you explain why I would have predicted my own involvement in the Deptford murders?'

There was a sound above them, and the Judge heard footsteps. He turned sharply. A thickset sailor was moving down the narrow ladder.

'I was not to be disturbed,' said the Judge.

'The gypsy,' said the sailor, slightly red-faced from the exertion of his descent. 'She's been seen at Hyde Woods.'

The Judge's annoyance melted away.

'Hyde Woods? You're sure?'

The sailor nodded. 'The old executioner from the Maze of Lost Souls recognised her,' he said. 'Realised she was the one you were looking for and followed her. Saw her and the thief taker disappear near the entrance to the woods.'

The Judge's smile vanished. 'How could she have disappeared?' he demanded.

The Judge turned to Ishmael without waiting for an answer.

'She was looking for you,' he decided, 'in the Maze. What could she have discovered to lead her to Hyde Woods?'

Ishmael said nothing.

The Judge stared at him thoughtfully. 'Catacombs,' he said. 'There are catacombs below Hyde Woods. Old Roman things. Abandoned.' His cold smile widened. 'A perfect place,' he decided, 'for an astrologer to hide the Eye.' The Judge turned to his sailor. 'Tell the executioner he's earned my next ten heads,' he said. 'Who do we have in Hyde Woods?'

'The gamekeepers,' said the sailor.

The Judge considered this. 'Send them in,' he said. 'Tell them they may do what they like with the gypsy. Only return my ring. Come January, every ship on the high seas will be stuffed with my slaves,' he decided, savouring the thought.

Walters turned to Ishmael. 'You have a day to decide to tell me everything,' he said. 'After which you will join those pirates drowned at Deptford.'

Chapter 49

After several hours in the dark catacombs, Charlie had to admit defeat. The tunnels snaked away, turning in on themselves, and it was hard to get bearings. The catacombs were dark and airless, with an oppressive smell of damp earth. When Charlie's markings finally told him they'd searched every part of the underground network, the shadowy blackness had begun to throw up strange shapes and tricks of the torchlight.

They found themselves back in the ghoulish corridor of bones. Hundreds of ancient skeletons seemed to close around them, the neatly stacked skulls gaping in mockery.

Charlie's eyes searched the ordered remains and found the cross he'd etched.

'We've searched it all,' he said. 'There's nothing here.'

Lily twisted her mouth in disappointment. 'No cryptographer could have hidden down here,' she agreed. 'It's not habitable.'

They turned to leave. But as Bitey lowered the torch to light the uneven ground, Charlie noticed something.

Was it his imagination? Or had the torch in Bitey's hand flickered?

'Bitey,' he said, 'pass me the torch.'

Bitey handed him the flame, and Charlie held it close to the skulls.

'What are you doing?' asked Lily as the torch licked the ancient remains.

'This is the only part of the tunnel where something more could be hidden,' reasoned Charlie. 'The skulls could disguise something. I think the fire might reveal an air pocket.'

He moved slowly, keeping the flame level. The fire burned merrily as he moved it past the skulls, revealing no air current. Perhaps he'd imagined it after all.

His eyes fell on the tangle of thick tree roots further down the tunnel.

'Perhaps they weren't here twenty years ago,' he decided, moving towards them.

As Charlie approached the mass of roots, the flame flickered. Carefully he moved the torch up, then around. Now there was a distinct bowing of the flame. There was no mistaking it. There was air entering the tunnel from somewhere behind where the willow trees had burrowed.

'Strongest here,' said Charlie. 'The tree roots might be covering something,' he decided. 'Perhaps that's why they grew here. Maybe an underground spring or inlet behind them.'

Charlie peered past the torchlight. He thought he could make out the faintest of differences in the texture of the light.

'Here,' he said, ducking low and pulling out his eating knife. 'I think there's a crawl space.'

Lily moved closer. 'An entrance?' she said.

Charlie was hacking at the roots with his blade. They were thinner towards the ground and easier to cut. He grasped the severed ends and pulled. Dry soil and dead insects showered on to the earth floor.

'I think it leads somewhere,' he said, pointing to the space behind. 'The tree roots grew over the way in. I think it's an old burial chamber off the main catacombs or something like it.'

The opening was just small enough to stoop through. Beyond was gloomy but not quite darkness. Something like distant moonlight glimmered deep behind where the bones had been.

'It looks like a small room,' said Charlie. 'I don't think anyone is inside,' he added, listening in the dark.

'Perhaps it's only some old Roman thing,' suggested Lily. 'Part of the catacombs.'

'Most likely,' agreed Charlie, his eyes dropping to the decomposed insects at their feet. 'I don't think anyone has been inside for years.'

Suddenly a strange noise echoed through the tunnels. Metallic, like a gate shutting.

'What was that?' Lily's face was pale.

They stood for several tense moments, listening carefully. All was silent.

'Maybe some animal set off a trap deeper in the tunnel,' suggested Bitey.

But they all knew it hadn't sounded that way.

'Best you keep guard, Bitey,' decided Charlie, 'whilst we investigate. If you hear anything or sense even the slightest danger, wave the torch.'

Bitey nodded gratefully and straightened in the attitude of an earnest guard.

'I'll listen like a hawk,' he promised. 'Me and the badger.'

Charlie stooped and moved inside. Lily followed.

The room beyond was tiny, barely large enough for them both to enter. In the centre of the room seemed to be a kind of stone plinth. But the small chamber was totally dark, with the exception of one muted ray of light.

It took a moment for their eyes to adjust. Then Lily and Charlie drew back in amazement. Something on the plinth was moving.

Lily crossed herself. 'It's haunted,' she breathed. 'Charlie, there are spirits here.'

'No.' Charlie shook his head. 'I think those people are real.'

Chapter 50

Charlie and Lily stared in disbelief.

'Ghosts?' breathed Lily.

The bones in the corridor behind them had suddenly taken on a new meaning. To Charlie's surprise, she took his hand.

The secret room behind the skulls was small, dug out of the earth and lacking the Roman brickwork that had lined the old catacombs. In the centre was a small raised stone block. And shining on to it was a ghostly image of London, like a mirage, shimmering in the moonlight.

The picture was moving. Tiny figures were walking about.

Charlie stepped forward to investigate, his heart in his mouth.

'Charlie, no!' hissed Lily. 'You mustn't wake the dead.'

Her face was stricken; her free hand clutched at the talismans around her neck.

Charlie tried to remind himself that gypsies were superstitious. But the ghostly picture looked so ethereal, as though beamed there from another dimension. He reached out a tentative hand to touch it and a portion of the picture vanished, reflected instead on his sun-browned hand.

'Is it a haunting?' asked Lily. Her terror seemed to have abated slightly.

Charlie shook his head. 'I don't think so,' he said. 'I think it's . . . a trick of some kind.'

The glowing image was of London brought low by fire. Blackened stumps of buildings were interspersed with attempts to rebuild. The waterfront near Deptford could just be seen in the middle distance. Tiny figures went about their business.

'I've seen something like this before,' said Charlie. 'At the Finchley Circus.'

'It's a circus trick?' Lily was looking warily at the moving image reflected on the stone block. A ghostly picture of London twitching in miniature.

'It's called a camera obscura,' said Charlie. 'You set up a mirror above a darkened room. If you get the angle right, it reflects something light from outside into the dark part inside.'

Charlie looked up. Now his eyes had adjusted to the darker room, he could see that a patch of the ceiling above them was cut away. Dim light was beaming thinly through it. He stepped up on to the stone block to investigate. He pushed his hands up into the gap and felt the flat, cold surface of glass.

It had been set at an angle. Charlie pushed it up experimentally and found himself looking up into the night stars over Hyde Woods.

'Someone's set a mirror above us and another high in the trees,' said Charlie. 'It reflects light down into the room.' He jumped down from the stone block.

'Why would someone make a circus trick down here?' asked Lily.

'Astrologers use them too,' said Charlie. 'I think they're useful to avoid staring directly at the sun. Though this one is particularly clever,' he added, 'because it reflects an image from so far away. Perhaps another mirror is set high in the trees.' He thought for a moment. 'It feels like something Thorne would make,' he said. 'The cleverness of it.'

He turned in the semi-gloom, to see something had been etched on the wall.

'The path of the sun,' said Charlie, moving to touch where a sun symbol had been made many times in a distinct arc. 'Look,' he said. 'There's a picture here.'

The shape of four rings had been joined, each linking to a few words.

Lily moved forward to look. 'The ring bearers,' she breathed. 'Each is named here.' Lily read aloud. 'Oakley,' she read. 'Aquarius the sailor.'

Charlie felt for the ring, deep in his coat. 'It was my father's then,' he said. He was remembering Janus, searching for the ring, resenting Charlie or his family. Could this be where it started? With Tobias Oakley being appointed a ring bearer?

'Leo,' Lily continued reading aloud, 'the royal blood.' She twisted her own ring on her finger.

'Royal blood,' she said, wondering, 'but no name. My ring was lost at sea.'

They were both thinking of the King and his dangerous escape to Holland as a young man.

'Those are the two rings we have,' said Charlie. 'What's left?'

Lily's gaze travelled back to the wall. 'The Cipher,' she said. 'Scorpio, the shape-shifter.'

'One of the missing rings belonged to the Cipher?' said Charlie.

'It looks that way,' agreed Lily.

'But the Cipher isn't down in the catacombs,' said Charlie, trying to stem his mounting frustration. 'We searched them all. There's no part habitable.'

He was looking around the dank little camera obscura. The tiny chamber had barely space for both of them to stand.

'But if Thorne was here,' Lily pointed out, 'the Cipher might be somewhere else in the woods.'

They reflected on the huge dark forest.

'If the catacombs aren't the Temple of Death,' said Charlie, 'I don't know where else we should look.'

Lily nodded her agreement, turning back to the wall. 'The last ring is named for Thorne,' she said. 'He is marked as Taurus, the Temple of Venus.'

There was a long pause.

'The Temple of Venus,' said Lily. 'A clue to where Thorne's ring might be found?'

'I've never heard of any temples in London,' said Charlie, searching his expansive knowledge of the city.

'What about Temple Bar?' suggested Lily.

'That comes from the Knights Templar,' said Charlie. 'It's nothing to do with old Roman gods.' He thought carefully. 'Some of the brothels call themselves Temples of Venus,' he said doubtfully.

Then Charlie noticed something about the dark room.

'If this was Thorne's camera obscura,' he said, 'he changed its purpose.' Charlie pointed at the walls. 'The camera no longer shows the sky,' he pointed out. 'Now it shows the city.'

'So Thorne was watching something in the city?'

They both looked at the reflected image.

'The fire,' said Lily sadly, looking at the flattened prospect. 'Whatever Thorne was looking at burned down.'

Charlie tried to imagine the relative heights of the old buildings and what Thorne might have been able to see. He could make out the blackened stumpy walls of St Paul's, tiny in the reflected portion of the picture, and the grey remains of Baynard's Castle.

There was something here, Charlie was sure of it, but for the moment at least the facts weren't coming together.

Then another thought occurred to him.

'If Thorne used the camera to look on the city,' he said, 'we could use it too.'

'To look on the city?' asked Lily.

'To look on Hyde Woods.' Charlie stepped up on to the block. 'If we turn it,' he said, 'it can give us an overview. Something we can't see on foot. Perhaps we'll see some clue to the Cipher that way.'

Charlie began twisting the mirror, checking the reflection at his feet as he did so. Slowly a panorama of Hyde Woods came into view. Now the stone block showed a vista of treetops.

'That's the lake,' said Lily, pointing to a patch of open water. 'That's the barracks.'

'What about that?' asked Charlie, pointing to a small building on the periphery.

'An old church?' suggested Lily.

They looked at the small building set deep in the woods, far removed from the barracks. The roof seemed to be tiled, but in a way that Charlie was unfamiliar with. And there was no spire to identify the steeple of a church or chapel.

There was a sudden flickering of light at the entrance to the room. Bitey was waving the torch in desperate warning.

Chapter 51

Buckingham poured Frances a glass of wine.

'You've never been inside a tavern before,' he guessed.

He'd had a cosy fire lit in his comfortable rooms and had the table set with several fine wines. No harm in charming her, he'd reasoned.

Nervously she shook her head. Buckingham smiled. He hadn't expected to like Frances. But something about her innocence delighted him. Too many port-side whores, he supposed, had left him jaded.

She was dressed in an unassuming navy dress that did the exact opposite of what he supposed she hoped. Instead of making her plain, it highlighted her youth and beauty. She could make dark wool look expensive, where other women cheapened enormous silks.

In contrast, Buckingham had dressed deliberately to seduce. He wore his shirt slightly open and his long dark hair tied loosely with a black ribbon.

'You're sure you won't take meat?' he suggested.

She shook her head shyly.

'Some bread then,' he decided, cutting a slice. 'I cannot eat alone.' A sailor's quirk. He smiled at her.

Frances tried to stop her gaze flicking to the door. She'd bribed a stable boy to distract Buckingham. Where was he?

'Is it very awful,' she asked, taking a slice of bread, 'out at sea?'

'It can be very terrible,' he agreed. 'Cold hammocks at night, with only rum to warm you. Fear of your life from pirates.'

Frances's dark eyes softened in pity.

'But glory too,' he said. 'Many sailors speak of lost treasure. Buried Aztec gold. A lost Eye to show a man the world as God sees it.'

He didn't know why he was telling her this. Only that she seemed to listen so intently.

There was a knock at the door. Frances tried not to let her relief show.

Buckingham frowned, rose and opened it. The stable boy Frances had bribed earlier was standing on the other side. She looked away, ashamed at her subterfuge.

'Your horse,' said the stable boy. 'She seems lame in one leg. We can find you another mount for tomorrow,' he added.

'She's a favourite of mine,' said Buckingham, concerned. 'I'll see to her myself. I shouldn't be a moment,' he added to Frances as he stood to leave. On his way to the door, Buckingham was unable to resist a final glance at her, sitting so prettily by the fireside.

The moment he was out of the room, Frances stood. She slipped a hand in her pocket and drew free a small key.

This key will open any lock.

So Lady Castlemaine had told her.

She stepped quietly across the room and seized on the first of the two drawers. To her surprise it opened. Inside were letters. All, so far as she could see, from women. Curious despite herself, Frances picked one up. It was from a woman named Sally Oakley.

For some reason she found her eyes following the writing down the page. And hardly realising she was doing it, Frances began skimming the contents.

206

Sally Oakley had been a sixteen-year-old Royalist girl when the Civil War began. Her family policed her every move. She'd been married in arrangement to a man named Thorne.

Frances identified with the young Sally, controlled and instructed, with no rights of her own. She knew she should be searching Buckingham's desk, but something about Sally's story intrigued her.

Frances frowned at the next part. There was no suggestion of consummation or children. It seemed to be a marriage of minds. Sally went on to describe how she'd worked for the Royalist cause, attempting to reinstate the King. She and Thorne lived separate lives. Then she'd fallen in love with a commoner named Tobias Oakley and they'd made their own wedding. The letter finished saying she was pregnant and happy.

Realising she'd wasted time, Frances bundled the letters back. She pulled at the second drawer. It was locked. Her heart skipped. She fingered the key, her palms sweating. So far she'd only been sneaking where she shouldn't. This was actual burglary. Frances heard a noise on the stairs and turned a quick glance to the door. She waited a tense moment. Nothing. Her ears must have deceived her.

Frances thought of the King in his court. The growing daily pressure to retain her virtue. Trembling, she turned the key in the lock and slid open the drawer.

Frances drew back with a gasp, her hands covering her mouth. A copper-handled knife caked in old blood rolled to the front of the drawer. Beneath it were papers drawn with grotesque bloody pentagrams.

Frances stared in horror.

Buckingham was a killer. And a worshipper of Satan.

There was a noise behind her, and she started. Buckingham was standing in the doorway, his face grim.

'Well, well,' he said slowly. 'Have you heard the story of little girls who look where they shouldn't?'

Chapter 52

Charlie and Lily emerged from the camera obscura to a stricken-looking Bitey.

Back in the tunnel there was a distinct sound of footsteps somewhere deeper in the catacombs. Charlie's heart lurched.

'Perhaps gamekeepers,' said Bitey, his face pale. 'Though I don't know how they heard us. Best make a run for it.'

Bitey hesitated, then dipped his hand in the flow to choose the direction.

'This way,' he decided.

They dashed down the tunnel, their feet splashing in the water. They could hear voices now, along with the ominous sound of heavy boots.

As they rounded a dark corner, the air was filled with a sudden terrible smell.

'What's that?' asked Lily, covering her mouth.

'It's the badger,' said Bitey apologetically. 'They're sympathetic creatures. He must know we're afraid and has let off a little bad air.'

'A little?' Lily was covering her face with her sleeve.

Bitey's torch suddenly died, plunging them into darkness.

'Do not fear!' came Bitey's voice. 'I see moonlight.'

They heard the old man stop and give a sudden grunt of surprise.

'Strange,' he muttered. 'I can see the Upside-down Tree and the lake clear by the moonlight.' His hand banged against something metallic sounding.

'Someone's sealed this place,' said Bitey uneasily, 'since last I was here.'

Charlie found his way in the dark to Bitey's side. The exit from the tunnel led, as expected, to the muddy side of a little lake. But it was no longer open. Someone had sealed the exit with a thick metal grid.

His stomach pitched. They were trapped. Charlie felt an unexpected contact in the dark. Lily had grabbed his hand.

Footsteps were splashing closer through the tunnel.

'The gamekeepers,' breathed Lily, gripping his hand tighter. 'They'll hang us.'

'They'll do worse than that,' said Bitey grimly.

Charlie forced his mind to calm and considered their options. The tunnel was wide, brick-lined, with nowhere to hide. The first flash of a torch would expose them all.

They could hear muffled voices now. At least two men, Charlie calculated.

He let his hands wander across the metal grille. It was half a foot thick in places, bolted securely into the tunnel exit. His fingers felt the joins, searching for somewhere the brick might be loose, but all was firm. He found what he thought could be hinges, but they were too thick to work free.

In desperation Lily grasped the thick bars and pulled as hard as she could.

'Even if we could loosen it,' said Charlie, 'we'd have to work free every post. It would take all night.'

They could hear their pursuers nearing. In a moment, Charlie judged, they would turn the corner and catch them here.

They had twenty seconds at most. Charlie closed his eyes.

Think. He wouldn't accept there wasn't a way out of this. Rowan was still trapped at sea, and Charlie refused to die at the hands of Hyde Woods gamekeepers.

A possible answer came to him suddenly.

'There are hinges,' he said, feeling in the dark. 'Perhaps there's a door built in to allow people to open and shut the grate.' His fingertips found out an edge on the lines of metal. 'There's a gate built into it,' he confirmed. 'Maybe it has a lock.'

'What good will that do us?' demanded Lily, panic-stricken.

'I can pick locks,' said Charlie, feeling methodically in the dark for the keyhole.

His fingers worked systematically, feeling along the hinges to where a lock might be.

There. A depression in the metal alerted him to a keyhole.

'I've found it,' he said. He tugged his lock-picking earring free from his coat and fitted it into the lock.

A glimmer of torchlight shone from the direction they'd come in. For a moment the exact shape of the keyhole was revealed. It was larger than he'd thought. Charlie lifted the earring, feeling for tumblers.

There . . .

The curved earring caught the first tumbler. For a long moment it held, then gave a shriek as the keyhole partially yielded. There would be three tumblers, Charlie thought, for this size of lock. His earring found the second tumbler, and it thudded free.

Footsteps splashed loudly behind them, and an unfamiliar man's voice rang out in the tunnel.

'Well, well,' it said. 'What have we here? Three little thieves for Judge Walters's prison.'

Charlie swivelled the earring, but the third tumbler held. Carefully he leaned back, trying to exert pressure without unbending the earring. For a moment he looked to lose his grip. Then with a heavy clang the third tumbler shot and the bolt turned. The grille swung open, and Charlie pulled his earring free.

'Quickly.' Charlie grabbed Lily and Bitey, flinging them through the open gate into the wet mud of the lake shore beyond.

He heard shouts and running feet behind and dived through after them. Charlie's feet slid on the mudbank, but he managed to right himself. Using all his strength, he began heaving the grille back shut.

He felt two large bodies fling themselves against it from the other side. The gamekeepers were trying to follow them through the door.

'Quickly!' gasped Charlie as Bitey and Lily scrabbled to help. 'Push it shut!'

They heaved, sliding on the mud shore. The strong gamekeepers had the advantage of firmer ground. Inch by inch they began opening the grille. Lily slipped in the mud and lost a handhold.

Charlie grabbed the bow on Bitey's back and jabbed blindly through the gaps in the grating. He heard a grunt of pain as a gamekeeper fell back.

'Now!' Charlie shouted, putting his shoulder against the gate.

Lily managed to regain her hold. They heaved, and with a loud clank the door closed and the lock shot home.

From inside the tunnel the gamekeepers began shouting.

'We must hide, and quickly,' said Charlie, seeing a torch flare in the near distance. 'There are others nearby.'

Then they saw it. The magnificent weeping beech.

'Over there,' decided Charlie. 'We'll hide under the Upside-down Tree.'

Chapter 53

Frances's hand was on the drawer where the bloody knife and papers daubed with pentagrams lay. Buckingham looked so furious that she found herself mute with terror.

'I assume,' said he, staring at the terrified Frances, 'that the King put you up to this.'

She managed to shake her head. Buckingham hesitated.

'Who then?' he demanded.

'It was Lady Castlemaine.'

Buckingham strode towards her and grabbed her slim wrists. 'You had no right,' he hissed.

Frances looked up into his dark eyes and, for some reason she couldn't explain, was not afraid.

'I know,' she said calmly, 'and I'm sorry for it. My situation with the King is intolerable, and Lady Castlemaine promised to help me escape.' Her wrists were still held tightly in his hands. Frances eyed the bloody knife and pictures. 'What are these?' she asked. 'Why do you have them?'

'What do you think they are?'

'Some Devil worship,' she suggested.

'You're not afraid? You must have heard the stories about me.'

She looked into his face. 'Should I be?'

Buckingham released her wrists and sighed. 'No,' he admitted. 'You need not be afraid.' He raised a hand and brushed a strand of curling hair from her face. 'There is something about you,' he said, 'that makes me want to be honest. Perhaps because you're so young.'

Frances said nothing.

'Come sit,' said Buckingham, leading her to his small bed.

Frances felt her legs move beneath her. They both sat down. He passed her a cup of wine and poured one for himself. She took it in shaking hands but didn't drink.

'It's a sacrificial knife,' said Buckingham, 'used in Roman times. To make offerings to the gods.'

'Animal sacrifice?' asked Frances, horrified.

Buckingham smiled grimly. 'The knife is not for animals.'

Frances's limbs felt liquid and weak. 'You kill people?' she whispered.

Buckingham shook his head. 'That knife belonged to a man named Thorne. He was a very clever man. Many said wicked. He was banished from the Church for some heinous crime his family concealed.'

'What crime is great enough to forfeit heaven?' Frances's young face was stricken.

Buckingham smiled slightly. 'You're too young to know.' He drank some wine. 'Thorne's wealthy family couldn't spare him from excommunication, but they paid bribes to prevent justice. His conspirator wasn't so fortunate. They burned him. A young man of eighteen.'

Frances had a sudden image of the burnings that took place at Tyburn. The hideous screams and stink of rendered flesh.

'Afterwards Thorne became greatly interested in Roman gods,' continued Buckingham. 'By his own twisted morality they were more merciful and broad-minded than the Christians who had refused him.' Buckingham's gaze dropped to the knife. 'Thorne began conducting experiments. I don't fully understand the practice. But they involved

213

sacrifice to the Thames. Convicts were used. I believe this was how Thorne justified killing. A Roman afterlife was preferable to a Christian hell.' Buckingham's eyes had a faraway look now. 'But Thorne's first victim was not a convict,' he said. 'She was a girl I loved deeply. We were engaged when they recovered her corpse at Dead Man's Curve.' He shook his head at the memory. 'She'd been marked . . .' His voice shook a little. 'Her body was cut with symbols.'

Frances swallowed, remembering that a similar thing had happened recently.

'Many thought me her murderer,' continued Buckingham. 'Jealous or jilted.' He let out a long sigh. 'I was too heartbroken to stop the things being said of me,' he concluded. 'I went to sea. Only came back for the new King.'

'Why were you banished?' asked Frances.

'I was trying to discover more about Thorne,' said Buckingham. He frowned. 'I was obsessed with finding the why. There were some documents belonging to Thorne in the old King's library. The papers you found. Mostly they only provoked more questions.'

'What kind of questions?' Frances was intrigued despite herself.

'Something about birth charts,' said Buckingham. 'Thorne had left a false birthday as a message of some kind. I discovered the hour of the King's birth and was banished, so I returned to sea,' he continued. 'But then someone began repeating Thorne's wicked work. And I mean to discover him.'

Frances sipped wine and stared at the knife. 'It's your way of making amends,' she said after a moment, 'to the girl who died.'

Buckingham nodded. 'But to find the killer, I must get close to the King again.'

'To what purpose?'

'You've heard of the Dutch pilot Janus?'

Frances nodded.

'Janus is English. English and perhaps in the King's court.'

Frances gasped. 'Surely not? A traitor so close?'

Buckingham nodded slowly.

'Why are you telling me all this?'

Buckingham smiled his best charming smile. 'Someone must get close to the King to find this traitor out. I had thought it should be me. But now I've met you . . .'

Frances shook her head. 'I won't do it. I won't spy on the men at court.'

'You will,' he said. 'You must learn to play courtly games if you wish to succeed under a Stuart monarchy.'

His dark eyes flashed, and Frances felt the doors of another cage begin to close around her. Then something deep in her soul recoiled, and anger flashed. From the time she'd arrived in court, Frances had been nothing but a pawn, clamoured after by the King, manipulated by Lady Castlemaine. Now Buckingham thought to use her too.

She remembered Sally Oakley's letters. Her bravery was inspiring.

Frances's little jaw set firm. Lady Castlemaine was right. No one would help her. She must help herself.

Frances looked into Buckingham's dark eyes.

'I will help you,' she lied. 'Look for my letter. You must come in secret to my rooms in Whitehall. I will spy for you and tell you what I discover.'

Chapter 54

Under the low branches of the Upside-down Tree, Charlie, Lily and Bitey breathed sighs of relief.

The magnificent tree took up a long section of the Serpentine River bank. The birch was ancient and enormous, the birch's supple branches falling downwards in a large curtain, screening off a dark interior large enough for a house. Soft moonlight fell in dappled patches through the branches.

'Look at that,' breathed Lily.

The bark of the tree was carved with writing. It covered every spare inch from the ground to the branches.

'They're wishes,' said Charlie. 'This was a wishing tree for common folk. They came here to ask for wisdom.'

Lily's eyes trailed the winding writing. 'It's all about the war,' she said sadly. 'People ask wisdom for their brothers and sons, to keep them safe.'

'We should search for the building we saw from the camera obscura,' decided Charlie, 'before it gets light. We might still find the Cipher.' He turned to Bitey. 'You should get back to safety.'

Bitey visibly sagged with relief. 'I've been a help then,' he said earnestly.

'Come find me in the Bucket of Blood,' promised Charlie. 'You'll not want for a drink for the next week. Take the torch,' he added.

'You'll need it,' said Bitey.

Charlie shook his head.

'Best you use it. Be careful of gamekeepers,' he added.

'Always have been.' Bitey vanished through the thick branches of the Upside-down Tree.

Charlie and Lily moved deeper into the trees of Hyde Woods as Bitey retreated. The bright moon lit their way as they tracked towards the building they'd identified from Thorne's camera obscura.

'It can't be much further,' said Charlie, charting their path through the dense trees. 'The foliage turns thicker here, the same as we saw around the building.'

They passed more dark trees, alert to the sound of gamekeepers. Then in the middle distance a stumpy shape loomed.

'It's a broken Roman pillar,' said Lily, touching the top of the squat shape with her fingertips.

'There's more,' said Charlie. 'I think they once marked a path.'

He pointed to a parade of white stone stumps, lining what might have once been a wide road. The severed Roman columns were over-grown and disguised with moss, with none having survived to higher than a few feet. But the route they delineated was not as inaccessible as it would have been, Charlie thought, if no one ever came here.

'This way,' he said, following the path the columns had once made into the trees.

After a few yards they came to a halt. The pillars ended in a squat stone building, ancient and covered in creepers. The thick stone construction was reminiscent of an old church. But there was no steeple, and the thick wooden door was topped by a stone triangle. It looked completely abandoned.

They hesitated, taking it in.

'It must have been beautiful,' said Lily, looking at the overgrown building. 'What do you think it was? A temple?'

'I think a Roman temple,' agreed Charlie, 'long deserted. It's not far from the catacombs, where the dead were buried.' His eyes roved around the lumps of carved stone. 'I think it was probably a temple to Saturn,' he said, 'the God of Death.'

'The Temple of Death,' breathed Lily. 'The Cipher.' The excitement in her eyes was shadowed with wariness.

'It feels wrong,' she said. 'If the Cipher is imprisoned here, where are the guards? And the locks?'

'I don't know,' admitted Charlie, feeling uneasy. 'They would have to bring him food,' he said. 'Water for washing. The way here has been trodden recently,' he said, pointing to the ground at their feet. 'And the door is new. The original would have long rotted away.'

They moved closer. There seemed to be no lock or bolt. Only a simple latch.

'Should we open it?' asked Lily. Reflexively, she took out a knife.

Charlie hesitated. He had a feeling that something very bad was on the other side.

'Be careful,' said Lily as he moved to open the door. 'It could be a trap.'

But as Charlie pushed the latch down, the door opened with surprising ease.

Chapter 55

Charlie opened the door to the strange old temple. Outside, the trees of Hyde Woods rustled in the breeze. Inside was gloomy, with a low ceiling and thick white walls. The floor was a faded mosaic, the tiles missing in places, and four thick square pillars supported the ceiling. To the sides were stone shelves. Some were filled with the same macabre arrangements of skulls and bones they'd seen in the catacombs. But others had been cleared and were stuffed full of scrolls. Rolls of paper that Charlie guessed ran to thousands. It was like a ghoulish library of the underworld.

Charlie could see tiny symbols and letters scratched in chalk all over the walls in impossibly neat squares. He felt a thrill of nervous excitement.

'Look,' he whispered. 'Codebreaking.'

Shafts of moonlight dropped down from patches of missing ceiling, and at first glance the stone chamber seemed empty. Then Charlie saw a shape, sitting almost motionless towards the back of the room. He froze. Lily took a tighter hold of her knife.

It was a woman, her body sat perfectly still on a small wooden stall. Her hands were sewing in the automated way women have as they get older. She looked incredibly ordinary, like a washerwoman or a pie seller. Her body had the comfortable bulk of old age and was clad in well-worn green wool. She had thick greying hair gathered beneath a white linen cap, soft rounded features and a double chin with a prominent wart.

Beside him, Charlie felt Lily relax slightly.

'She must be a servant or a cook,' she whispered.

The immediate area surrounding the woman had been decorated like a neat cottage. There was a functional table and stool, with a wooden plate and plain cutlery laid out in readiness for a meal.

'Do you think the Cipher is hiding somewhere?' Lily whispered to Charlie. Her eyes were roving the dark space, testing for hiding places.

Charlie walked closer to the woman. Her pale green eyes followed him as he drew nearer. But this was the only acknowledgement her face gave of an intruder. She watched him calmly as he approached. Her fingers pulled and dived at her sewing.

Charlie sized her up. He guessed her to be around forty, and despite her simple clothing, her hands and face showed no obvious signs that she worked for a living. The chubby hands looked soft. Charlie noted they were dusted with something white, like flour.

Not a servant, Charlie decided. *A wife? A sister?*

But surely a relative of the Cipher's would be better dressed and cared for.

'We're looking for the Cipher,' tried Charlie.

The woman's pale eyes hovered over him. He saw something then, beneath the homely features. There was a cleverness. But something missing too. Some facet of human emotion. The way she regarded them was almost bird-like.

'He isn't here,' she said simply. Then her eyes dropped back to her work.

'Do you know where he is?' Charlie moved closer to her.

The woman's concentration was on the knotted threads. 'He won't be back,' she said, pulling and tying. 'Not until the snows come.'

Charlie and Lily looked at each other. Charlie's mind was working, taking in the room. He looked back at the chalk symbols and letters scratched on the walls. Then his eyes drifted back to the woman's pale fingers pulling at threads. Where her forearms emerged from the wool dress, the skin was blue with cold. Her sewing was dusted white, like her fingertips, he noticed, as though frost was forming. She reminded him of Thorne's camera obscura. A distant view into another world.

'Do you know where he is now?' pressed Lily.

'He won't be back,' the woman repeated in identical monotone. 'Not until the snows come.'

'You've said that,' said Lily, growing frustrated. 'But it isn't what I asked.'

The woman didn't look up. Her hands moved steadily.

'He won't be back—' she began.

But Charlie interrupted her. 'It's you,' he said slowly, looking at the woman. 'You're the Cipher.'

Chapter 56

Janus slid carefully down the mudbank and towards the little cluster of fires. It was dark by the river, and the secret route had taken him to a little inlet where the Thames flowed inwards. Janus's heart quickened. This was smuggler territory, behind the Marshalsea prison. The most dangerous place in London.

Janus made the secret whistle, high and clear.

'Who goes there?' growled a voice. 'Speak, before I dash out your brains.'

'Surely,' said Janus, stepping into the firelight, 'you remember me?'

The dark face managed a half smile. His features could be seen more clearly now. The guard was an ex-slave. Enormous and finely muscled with jet-black skin. He wore a mixture of seafaring clothes, most too small for him, with a torn officer's jacket stretched tightly across his broad back and failing to meet at the front.

'I remember,' he said.

'I saved your life,' Janus reminded him. 'They would have cast you from the ship in a barrel with the other slaves.'

The guard shrugged non-committally. 'Perhaps you did,' he said. 'Or perhaps you saved your own skin.' He jerked a thumb towards the group. 'They'll not bring you more Marshalsea women,' he said. 'They know you pilot for the Dutch.'

'I'm not here for a prisoner,' said Janus. 'Let me by.'

The guard stood aside, his expression unreadable.

Janus walked carefully over the mud. Three men sat by the fire, passing around a bottle of rum and cleaning their weapons. The nearest, a bandana tied around his head, stood quickly as Janus approached.

'Well, well,' he grinned, 'what have we here?'

'I need information,' said Janus, not bothering with pleasantries. 'You told me the thief taker is looking for the Eye. What do you know of Charlie Tuesday's brother?'

'Rowan Tuesday?' The smuggler looked surprised at the question. 'He sold false black powder for a while, then fled to sea, owing money.' The smuggler wiped his nose and looked thoughtfully at Janus. 'Some say Rowan Tuesday joined the Dutch.'

'What does the thief taker know of his brother's whereabouts?' asked Janus.

'Likely he knows Rowan is a traitor,' said the smuggler, leaning closer so his scarred face drew level with Janus's. 'A traitor, same as you,' he accused.

'You're a smuggler,' said Janus. 'You have no loyalty to the Crown.'

'Well now, funny you should mention that,' said the smuggler. 'A little bird has told me what you're looking for.'

'Is that so?' replied Janus evenly.

The smuggler nodded slowly. 'We hear Charlie Tuesday is also looking for the Eye,' continued the smuggler, 'and the thief taker knows London,' he taunted. 'He might not be noble like you. But Charlie Tuesday is famed for his cleverness.'

'We'll see how clever he is,' said Janus, 'in fear for his brother's life.'

'You'll never capture Rowan,' opined the smuggler. 'He's as wily as the thief taker.'

'We'll see,' said Janus with a smile.

'You were foolish to come back here,' said the smuggler. He was reaching for his knife.

Janus frowned. 'You think because I wear a fine coat I am not dangerous?' he said. 'I have known horrors you cannot even imagine. The children who you think sleep safely? I've seen them bloody and screaming, cast into the dark depths of a cold river.'

The smuggler's smile dropped away. 'Sorcery and such talk,' he said, his voice shifting uncertainly, 'holds no terrors for us. We fear only the Almighty.'

'I answer to greater gods,' said Janus. 'True magic is but a trick. Looking here,' he added, holding up a ringed hand, 'when you should be looking there. And you should have been paying attention to your men.'

The smuggler turned in shock to see his colleagues standing, their guns aimed towards him.

Janus smiled apologetically. 'A smuggler's loyalty is easily bought,' he said. 'You should know that by now.'

With a cry of fury the smuggler launched himself at Janus. Janus stepped slightly aside, catching him with an outstretched arm. The smuggler's eyes widened; then he gave a choking gasp of pain.

'Better this way,' said Janus, holding the knife firm between the smuggler's ribs. 'I couldn't have you telling Charlie Tuesday what you know. Not before he realises what could happen to his brother.'

Chapter 57

'You're the Cipher,' repeated Charlie, staring at the strange woman. He was sure of it now. Something in her expression confirmed it.

Her pale eyes settled on his face. She stopped sewing.

'I?' she said. 'I am but a woman.'

'You have chalk dust on your sewing,' said Charlie. 'And the code-breaking' – he pointed to the letter-strewn wall – 'stops at around your highest reach.'

She tilted her head and muttered something quickly in a foreign language.

'Jij bent van de Koning?'

She was testing him, Charlie realised, on the assumption that a fellow codebreaker or spy would speak Dutch.

Charlie translated without thinking: *You're from the King?*

She had the accent of someone who'd only ever read Dutch. Years of decoding, Charlie guessed, had given her a kind of working fluency, but there was no harmony to her speech.

'We are,' he lied in Dutch.

He had a sudden strange feeling, as though they'd been lured here. Flies in a spider's web.

'Where are your guard?' he asked in English. 'Why are you not better protected?'

She smiled, and this time a glimmer of something more like real amusement was in her eyes.

'This' – she gestured to her rounded body – 'is all the protection I need. In all the years I've been here,' she continued, 'you're the only one who has ever guessed who I am.'

Lily, who could now understand what was being said, had the tense expression of someone piecing things together fast in her mind.

'No one knows?' asked Charlie. 'Not even the men who bring food?'

'They think him a ghost or a spectre,' said the woman. 'Able to vanish at will. They leave codes and I deliver them back. Perhaps they think me his companion or servant. No one cares enough about a plain old spinster to ask.' Her eyes levelled on his face. 'Except for you,' she said. She was taking Charlie in now, and her expression was cool.

'And what about you?' asked Lily. 'Why don't you leave?'

The Cipher's eyes lifted to Lily, as if seeing her for the first time. She took in Lily's open-shouldered red dress, the charms at her neck, glossy black hair, caramel skin and beautiful features.

'A gypsy,' she said in her strangely monotone voice. 'They used to hang them.'

Lily's face darkened.

'I cannot leave,' continued the Cipher, making no indication she realised she'd given affront, 'until I've completed the work.'

There was a definite edge to her flat tone now. As though speaking about this particular subject made her anxious.

'What work?' asked Charlie.

Her eyes shifted to the back of the room. 'The scrolls,' she said. 'They must be read. All of them.'

'Codebreaking?' guessed Charlie. 'The encrypted papers intercepted from Dutch spies?'

The woman frowned. Her hand began twitching uncertainly. 'That's only part of it,' she said. 'The ancient wisdom must be deciphered.'

She was passing her sewing agitatedly back and forth in her hands now.

Charlie looked at the great library of scrolls. It would take a lifetime to read them all, even for a genius.

So this was how they'd trapped the great Cipher, thought Charlie. She was clever enough to escape any prison. But something in her nature couldn't let the scrolls go unread.

Lily's face suggested she was making the same deductions.

'Did you try and escape?' asked Charlie softly. 'Years ago? With Thorne?'

'They must be completed,' said the Cipher. Her voice had risen in volume now. Her hands made claws that clenched and unclenched. 'But every day they bring more.'

Charlie didn't know whether to feel angry or sad. The Cipher had been tricked into staying in this strange old library. But he couldn't imagine her in the outside world either.

The Cipher flicked a glance at Lily. 'She doesn't speak it?' she guessed, reverting to heavily accented Dutch.

'No,' said Charlie.

The Cipher assessed him carefully. 'You're a clever man,' said the Cipher, again in Dutch. 'I like cleverness. But perhaps your skills end with her.' The Cipher eyed Lily coolly. 'She,' she concluded, 'is not to be trusted.'

Charlie stared at the Cipher in confusion. He couldn't be sure if she knew Lily or had simply taken an irrational dislike to her. It wasn't uncommon for women to take issue with Lily's courtesan appearance.

Opting for loyalty to his friend, Charlie switched to English.

'We have a . . . a riddle you might help solve.'

Charlie took out his ring. The Cipher's eyes opened a little wider.

'Why, this was his invention,' she said. 'Thorne's. It's one of the codebreaker rings.'

Chapter 58

The Cipher was turning the ruby ring in her hand. It looked as though the memory of the old ring pleased her.

'You know it's a codebreaker,' said Charlie. 'Do you know how it works?'

Her eyes gave nothing away. Even Charlie's practised card sharping could glean no clue from her expression.

'You have the others?' she said after a moment.

Lily hesitated. Charlie nodded, and she reached into her dress and handed the second ring over.

The woman fitted them together with a satisfied smile. 'Only two?' she asked.

Charlie nodded. 'We want to know,' he said, choosing his words carefully, 'what code they might break.'

The Cipher pursed her lips. 'They were Royalist things,' she murmured. 'We don't use them now. I cannot tell you what they solve.'

Charlie's heart sunk. There was a long silence.

'Might you take a guess,' he suggested eventually, 'at what code they might have been used for?'

She frowned. 'I don't make guesses.' She hesitated, turning the rings, apparently reluctant to relinquish the puzzle.

'What about this paper?' asked Charlie, tugging free Thorne's *Chart of All Hallows' Eve*. 'Might you know anything of this?'

Her pale eyes flared suddenly. She took the paper carefully in her hands.

'Thorne's work,' she breathed. Her eyes roved the workings delightedly. 'He never came back,' she added. 'He was the only one who was ever kind to me. He told me about the Roman ways. How they had different ideas to Christians. There was a Goddess of Wisdom. Unmarried, yet men respected her.'

The Cipher's face darkened as if at some black memory.

'You and Thorne were lovers?' suggested Charlie, but as soon as the words left his mouth he knew it wasn't the right assumption.

To his surprise the Cipher gave an eerie laugh.

'Oh no,' she said, 'not Thorne. He took no *woman* for a lover. It was said not even his own wife.' Her eyes dropped to the key at Charlie's neck and twitched away again.

Charlie had a sudden picture of the man in his dream. Thorne, with his mother standing at his side.

'Thorne took an apprentice,' added the Cipher, 'to inherit his wisdom. The two-faced boy.'

'Janus?' said Charlie, his mind whirring. 'Did Thorne call the boy Janus?'

The Cipher gave a slight nod.

'What was the boy's real name?' asked Charlie.

'I only know he was of great bloodline,' said the Cipher. 'Thorne hid him away, close and secret. Not even I could break the code of where. Though they tried to make me.'

Her eyes had a haunted look.

Charlie felt sorry for her then. He saw the Cipher as a pawn of war. A woman too intensely clever for her own good, trapped in this strange temple by her own compulsions.

230

'Thorne was so very clever,' said the Cipher. 'He discovered things in his secret workshop. Things that could win the war.'

'It's real then?' breathed Charlie. 'The Eye?'

The Cipher smiled coolly. Charlie realised suddenly that she'd told them nothing whilst seeming to tell them what they wanted to know. She was tricky. And he had a bad feeling she didn't really want to help them.

'It is real and it isn't,' she said enigmatically. 'The Eye of Heaven is what men make it. But it is powerful. And if the Dutch find it, London will fall.'

'I think Thorne's old apprentice is looking for the Eye,' said Charlie, trying to appeal to her patriotism. 'If Janus finds it, he means to give it to the Dutch.'

The Cipher blinked in amusement. 'Janus may play at helping the Dutch. But that isn't why he truly seeks the Eye.'

'Then why does he look for it?' asked Charlie, confused.

'I think to destroy you,' said the Cipher, 'Tobias Oakley's son.'

Charlie felt icy fear in the pit of his stomach. Was she raving?

'Janus is always one step ahead of the spymasters,' she added, glancing at the codebreaking on the wall. 'But they try to catch him and cut off his head,' she added without emotion, 'as they did to Thorne.' She was watching Charlie's face with interest. 'As they will do to both of you,' she concluded. 'You have broken the rules by coming here,' continued the Cipher. 'My temple is under royal protection and it is treason to enter uninvited.'

The Cipher gave a satisfied nod. 'You will both bleed on the executioner's block, just as Thorne did.'

Chapter 59

Cornelius knocked carefully on De Ryker's cabin door. The night was dark, but a soft glow shone from the thick windows. He waited as the ship creaked beneath him, wishing he was back in his swaying hammock with the men below.

'Come,' De Ryker's gravelly voice sounded.

Cornelius opened the door. Inside, De Ryker was poring over ship's charts. Maps and compasses covered every corner of his great desk. A half-drunk glass of wine was by his elbow, but no empty plate.

De Ryker never ate in the nights before a battle.

'How goes it?' De Ryker looked up.

'Calm,' said Cornelius. 'England is in our sights.'

De Ryker gave a twisted kind of smile. 'All Hallows' Eve tomorrow. When dawn breaks on All Saints' Day, they'll know something is awry,' he said. 'But Janus will bring us the Eye, and then it will be too late for them.'

'You really have so much faith in him?'

'No,' said De Ryker, 'but I've a talent for spotting wounded men. I know how they work and how they can be manipulated.'

'Janus is wounded?' Cornelius was momentarily confused.

'Something very bad happened to Janus,' said De Ryker, 'when he was a boy. I asked him of it; he pretended there was nothing to tell. But I have heard him shouting in his sleep about "the Bad Thing". And always he speaks in perfect English.'

Cornelius knew better than to try and deduce what this might mean.

'Janus claims to have been Thorne's apprentice,' said De Ryker, 'so he must have been important. Noble. But I know what kind of apprentices Thorne took. The boy was likely subjected to horrors.' De Ryker paused. 'The English are dread brutes,' he decided. 'Throwing children into the Thames is part of their history. I should not be surprised if the old King revived such a practice to avoid his fate on the executioner's block.' His eyes dropped back to the charts.

Cornelius saw the famous Thames river, wide at the mouth, where it flowed into the sea.

'No one has ever conquered her,' said De Ryker, following Cornelius's gaze. 'We shall be the first.' His salt-scabbed finger followed the winding path and stopped at London. 'We shall be the first,' he repeated. 'And the English shall bow to a Dutch king.'

Chapter 60

The Cipher snaked out a hand and pulled at a cord that had been hidden in the darkness. Above them a loud bell clanged in the rooftop.

She was sounding the alarm.

The clang of the bell must be echoing across all of Hyde Woods, Charlie realised. Whatever guard was assigned to her protection would be here in moments.

Lily drew a knife and in a single snake-like movement had the Cipher pinned to a wall.

'Tell me,' she demanded, 'what code the rings solve. I know you know.'

The Cipher shook her head defiantly. 'He is the son of Tobias Oakley,' she whispered. 'I recognise his key. His father was a traitor, and I'll not give Thorne's treasure to Oakley's son.'

Lily leaned close. 'I've four more knives in my skirts,' she threatened. 'And I've time enough to use them all. So tell me what you know, or you'll be trying to solve codes with no fingers.'

The Cipher's face was flat, devoid of expression. Her mouth stayed shut.

'It won't work,' said Charlie, reading her emotionless features. 'She doesn't fear knives.'

'Then what does she fear?' demanded Lily. 'We have only moments.'

Charlie's attention swung to the library of scrolls. He ran towards them.

Instantly the Cipher's calm demeanour shifted.

'Stop!' she demanded, her voice strangely high. 'You must not touch the work!'

Charlie pulled free a scroll, and the Cipher gave a terrible shriek.

'Tell us!' he demanded. 'What do the rings solve?'

The Cipher's eyes were fixated on the scroll, her body twitching agitatedly. 'You already have it,' she babbled. 'You already carry the code.'

It took Charlie a split second to work out what she meant.

'Thorne's *Chart of All Hallows' Eve*?' he said. 'The rings solve it?'

The Cipher nodded.

'How?' asked Charlie.

She shook her head. 'I don't know, I swear it. Only Thorne and the other ring bearers knew. Return the scroll!' The Cipher's eyes were twitching back and forth.

'Where are the other rings?' demanded Lily.

'No,' said the Cipher. 'I won't betray Thorne.'

Charlie took out a tinderbox from his coat and sparked the flame. The Cipher jerked bodily.

'Tell me,' he said, 'or I'll burn it.'

'You would not,' whispered the Cipher. 'You couldn't. Not the old wisdom.' Charlie moved the flame higher.

'Wait!' shrilled the Cipher. 'Wait!'

'Then tell me now,' he said.

The Cipher was looking upwards, as if remembering. For a moment it seemed she wouldn't answer. Then she spoke.

'Thorne gave me a ring,' she said finally. 'He made me a ring bearer. But the ring wasn't safe here and I couldn't leave. So he hid it for me.'

'Where?' urged Lily.

'The sign of the goddess,' she blurted. 'The Goddess of London at Custom House. Take away the flame.'

Charlie ignored her.

'What London goddess?' he asked. He'd been to Custom House and never seen anything approximating it. He pictured the large building. It was a vast space in which to hunt a little ring.

Lily turned to the Cipher. 'What sign of the goddess?' she pressed. 'What goddess is there at Custom House?'

'I never went there,' said the Cipher. 'I only decoded pictures and maps. All I know is there's a secret passage at Little Bear Steps.' Her eyes shifted to Charlie. 'I've told you everything,' she pleaded. 'Please. Return the scroll.'

In answer Charlie pushed the roll of paper back into its previous place on the shelf.

Lily was still holding the Cipher firm.

'Let her go,' said Charlie. 'We need to leave. Now.'

With some reluctance Lily released her hold. The old woman fell to a sitting position and backed away from them. As they raced for the door, she put her head in her hands and rocked.

'They'll catch you,' she muttered as Charlie and Lily sped from the strange temple. 'They'll cut off your heads.'

Chapter 61

Janus dropped easily into the old tunnel under Custom House. There was a long-lost ancient entrance here. Only a few knew of it.

Little Bear Steps.

The steps hid the original Roman gateway into London. The door of the goddess. Janus took in the muddy ground with satisfaction.

The thief taker hadn't been here. But Janus thought it possible he'd hunt the third ring here. Time to remind Charlie Tuesday what he was risking.

His beloved brother.

Janus found himself at the old stream, past the broken things. There was Roman road beneath him now. A lost section buried long ago deep beneath the city.

Then he stopped by an old mosaic on the wall. The tide was coming in. Water ran over Janus's feet.

Carefully he placed his warning. If Charlie Oakley made it here, he would see it. If the thief taker was as soft-hearted as Janus hoped, a threat to his brother would be enough to stop him searching.

Or would it?

Janus realised he couldn't truly be certain of the thief taker's love for his brother. Best be sure. He regarded the map.

The mosaic was of London as it had been as Londinium, hundreds of years ago. It was faded, made in thick tiles. Each little building and temple was drawn in two dimensions, surrounded by the thick London Wall.

Thorne had loved this old map. It had survived hundreds of years. It seemed such a shame to destroy it, but he couldn't take the risk. The map showed the Temple of Venus – hidden, but a clever man might still discern it. The smuggler's words drifted back.

Charlie Tuesday is famed for his cleverness.

Janus picked up a large cobble from the old road. Then he swung his hand, smashing it into the mosaic. The ancient tiles splintered and fell. He swung again, smashing apart the image.

Coloured fragments dropped to the floor and were washed away in the tidal flow.

He looked at the destruction. Dusty plaster and crumbled ancient stone.

For a moment a pain seared through him. He could imagine Thorne's face. But it was better this way. Safer.

A strange emotion surged. Fear, Janus realised. He dreaded Thorne, even now after all these years. The memories of being kept in the dark had a power over him manhood hadn't shaken.

A sudden possibility came to him. He hadn't yet been to all of Thorne's old places. There were demons yet to be faced.

Hyde Woods. The Cipher.

Could she still be there? In her old hiding place? If she was alive, Janus thought the Cipher would stay in the strange prison of her own making forever.

She was a ring bearer. She may even know where Thorne hid the Eye.

Janus hadn't seen the Cipher for nineteen years. But something told him she'd want to help Thorne's old apprentice.

Chapter 62

Amesbury's face was tight with horror as the *Loyal London* limped into the dock. Even from this distance he could see that the vessel was less than half manned. The sails hung slack, the deck rotten; a secondary mast was broken.

She floated painfully slowly into the harbour. Amesbury saw the toothless red-eyed sailors. Their lips were misshapen, soft with scurvy, and they were covered in bloody ulcers. Many could barely walk the gangplank as the dockers secured the ship.

A man in ragged, filthy officer's clothing was helped on to shore. Amesbury moved forward. The officer's legs buckled on dry land, and Amesbury caught him before he fell.

'Here.' Amesbury urged a tankard of wine into his hand, manoeuvring him to an upturned barrel to act as a seat. The man grasped it gratefully and sat, his legs shaking uncontrollably.

'Your captain?' asked Amesbury gently.

The man only shook his head and drank more wine.

Amesbury shifted his gaze back to the deck. Rotting bodies lay all over it. He guessed the men hadn't the energy in the final days to throw the corpses overboard.

A strange memory of Thorne filtered back, days before he met his end. Amesbury could still vividly picture the devastation on the astrologer's face as he explained that the Church had refused to bury his condemned lover. The executioner had hung what was left of the burned man in chains for the mice and rats to gnaw on.

Amesbury reflected on the things that changed men's natures. A beloved's corpse subjected to indignity and horrors. Thorne hadn't the resilience to bear such barbarity.

Amesbury returned his attention to the bodies piled aboard the ship. There were so many, he thought sadly, who had died in sight of land. And many more, he thought, looking at the crew, who wouldn't survive landing.

'Tobago?' asked Amesbury.

The officer's face twisted at the memory. 'A hellhole,' he said. 'The Spanish were there before us and the Dutch heavily armed.'

'The injured dog failed to mark the time?' said Amesbury. His eyes were resting on the deck, where a limping dog was being led down the gangplank.

'The dog didn't howl as planned,' admitted the officer. 'Though he became beloved of the crew. He's a good-natured creature. Pirates drove us off the coastal route into open sea.'

His bloodshot eyes met Amesbury's.

'You couldn't gauge your position?' guessed the old general.

The officer nodded bitterly. 'The days became weeks,' he said. 'The humidity got into all our equipment. Rotted and rusted. By the time we found Tobago, the men were starving.'

Amesbury patted his shoulder sympathetically, knowing all too well the horror of being lost in the open sea.

'You are home now,' he said. 'Rest and restore your health.' He pointed away from the docks.

'There's a flophouse,' he said, 'and a tavern. The King has seen to it you and your men will be well cared for. Enjoy some good food and women,' he concluded. 'In time you may tell His Majesty of your adventures.'

The officer smiled weakly, showing a few remaining teeth. His mouth was soft and dark, like a rotting plum.

'I might not last long enough,' he said, 'to tell the King how we suffered.'

'I've seen worse than you land at Deptford,' lied Amesbury.

The rotting-fruit mouth wavered.

Amesbury helped the officer to his feet and on to the burly shoulder of a dock worker.

'See this officer has a good hammock and plenty to eat and drink,' Amesbury ordered.

The dock worker nodded, helping the officer on to a cart with the stumbling contingent of half-dead men.

Amesbury had a sudden memory. Another man staggering to an uncertain future twenty years ago.

Thorne was shaking, unable to hide his horror.

'You mean to lead men to their deaths!' he protested. 'I gave you the Eye to heal England. To gift you the power of the old gods.'

The old King's expression changed. He was a small man, and since he'd begun to lose the war, his bundle of nervous tics had flowered into unpredictable outbursts.

'I am appointed by God!' he barked. 'I am a god on earth!'

Thorne shook his head. 'I will not tell you,' he said, 'where the Eye is.'

'I've heard enough treachery,' said the old King. 'Amesbury, take the astrologer away.' His pale fingers began clenching and unclenching convulsively. 'You will make him tell us, Amesbury,' he concluded, 'where this Eye is hidden. Use any means necessary.'

Amesbury had stepped forward and grasped Thorne roughly by the coat.

Torches on the docks were flickering. Amesbury realised men were still coming from the scurvy-struck ship. He shook himself back to attention. The men were pitiful, limping on ulcerated legs. Their faces bore a strange mixture of hope and resignation.

'Journey's end, lads!' bellowed Amesbury. 'The cart will take you to wine and women!'

The general's rallying tone was something he'd perfected in war. His words brought a weak cheer from the sailors.

The little longitude dog lay breathing weakly on the dockyard floor, a snarl of furry ribs and bones. Amesbury eyed it sympathetically.

'Find a meal for the dog,' he said. 'If he doesn't upset my monkey, I shall give him a home.' Amesbury sighed. 'That ship was our last hope. Without Tobago the King is bankrupt. He must barter with Holland or be invaded.'

The dock worker watched the men being transported away. 'The Crown paid for a flophouse and whores?' he said.

'A deal was struck,' said Amesbury. 'Let's just say Scarlet Molly has a finer horse than she did this morning, and I will walk back to London.'

'That was kind,' said the dock worker.

'It's tactical,' said Amesbury. 'The King will need all the good feeling he can get if the Dutch try to invade.'

'I doubt those men will last the week,' opined the docker. 'Dead men don't tell tales.'

'Dockside whores do,' said Amesbury. 'One thing I've learned from civil war' – he patted the docker's shoulder – 'keep your men close and the women closer.'

Chapter 63

Charlie and Lily slept for a few hours on the edges of Hyde Woods before making their way to Custom House. They walked the few miles west to east in silence, Charlie still assailed by memories of vivid dreams. He'd seen Thorne, an eye daubed on his forehead, working on a small table with tiny tools. Rowan had been there, a warm comforting presence. Then his brother had been dragged away and the dark man had come. Janus. *Unmask him,* a voice whispered, *and you discover his weakness.*

'I've been thinking about the goddess at Little Bear Steps,' said Lily as they walked. 'Diana is the Moon Goddess. Chaste and pure. She's also the Bear Goddess,' she added. 'There's a story that she put a bear in the stars.'

'There's bear legacies all over London,' said Charlie. 'Bear Lane, Bear Street. Perhaps that means something.'

The approach to Custom House was a riot of noise and colour as Charlie and Lily neared. The adjoining harbour was thick with all kinds of ships, laden with bounty from the New and Old Worlds.

They passed a clutch of almanac sellers, who made a particularly good trade from suspicious sailors.

'The foul Dutch will lose their war on England's seas!' bellowed a scrawny man waving a clutch of pamphlets. 'The stars tell it!'

'If only we could find Ishmael Boney,' said Lily as pamphlets from rival astrologers were waved at them. 'He could interpret the *Chart of All Hallows' Eve* for us.'

'Not without the rings,' said Charlie. 'I've been thinking,' he added, 'about the fact Ishmael Boney was never seen at Mother Mitchell's house. The more I think on it, the more I find it strange. He wasn't married, and he'd recently come into money. There aren't many men who wouldn't find their way to Mother Mitchell's in those circumstances. There's no taste her house doesn't cater to. Apart from one.'

Lily regarded him with interest.

'If Ishmael was a molly,' he explained, 'he'd have no interest in Mother Mitchell's house. She only keeps women.'

'You think Ishmael Boney likes men?'

'The Cipher alluded that Thorne was that way inclined,' said Charlie. 'What if that's how Ishmael learned his astrology? If they were both mollys, maybe they were lovers.' He turned the possibility around in his mind. 'Thorne dies and his lover takes his papers and workings,' he suggested.

They could see the cluster of arriving ships now.

'You've been to Custom House before?' asked Charlie, noticing Lily's face had adopted the considered blank expression she assumed when she was hiding her emotions.

'I was here a long time ago,' said Lily, looking at the sails. 'I've never been back.'

'How old were you?'

'Too young.' She was looking at the children, aged ten or eleven, making their way off the ship with frightened expressions. They were Northerners by their clothing – dark woollens, old-fashioned linen caps and makeshift shoes. Likely they'd worked for their passage and hoped to seek their fortune in the city.

'London pounces the moment they land,' added Lily sadly, scanning a collection of ill-intentioned-looking adults making their way to the youngsters.

Her gaze settled sadly on a pretty little girl. A fat woman dressed in silks was already waddling up to her, a false smile plastered on her chubby face.

'Emily Green!' Lily's voice sailed over the dock.

The fat woman turned, confused.

'Remember me?' Lily gave her a dazzling smile, took a knife from her skirts and waved it in casual greeting.

The fat woman's acted smile faltered.

'She'll do better without your kind of help,' said Lily, nodding to the small girl. 'Leave her to find honest work.'

The woman was glowering now, torn between the temptation of the young prize and Lily's threat. She hesitated, then spat in the dust and walked away.

Lily holstered her knife and turned to Charlie. 'The Judge is behind this,' she said. 'He makes a business from slaves. Employs women like her.' Lily's eyes narrowed. 'We need to find this ring.'

But as they neared the steps, a bloody roar could be heard. Charlie slowed, then stopped.

'We can't get to Little Bear Steps,' he said. 'Look.'

Lily's face fell. 'Who are they?' she asked.

'Sailors' wives,' said Charlie grimly. 'And they want their husbands' pay.'

A mob of scrawny women had the Custom House entrance and the nearby steps to the river surrounded. They were screeching at the top of their lungs, waving their fists and throwing rocks at the building. A handful of guards were keeping them back, but it looked as though the women could riot at any moment.

'Give us what we're owed!' shouted one particularly loud woman. 'Our children starve!'

'The sailors haven't been paid in months, maybe years,' said Charlie. 'It's a national scandal.'

'Why haven't I heard of it?'

'The King keeps it under wraps,' said Charlie. 'Would you want your city to know your navy was on the brink of collapse?'

'So we can't get in?' asked Lily, angling for a better look at the steps.

'Not that way,' said Charlie. He rubbed the scar on his lip thoughtfully. 'There's another way around,' he decided. 'We'll walk down by the river. But it'll take longer.' He looked up at the sun. 'All Hallows' Eve tonight,' he said. 'We'd best hurry.'

Chapter 64

It took Charlie and Lily several hours to get to Little Bear Steps along the Thames mudbank. The steps formed a thick wooden jetty jutting out into the river, with slippery stone stairs to the side leading down to the water.

The Thames was blocked with ships trying to complete their business before All Hallows' Eve. The streets teemed with dispossessed sailors and frightened Londoners arming themselves with protectorates and charms.

'We've lost almost half a day,' said Lily.

She was looking at the sun, which now signalled noon.

'Only six hours until dusk,' noted Charlie, thinking of the approaching eclipse.

They moved back downriver, passing a clutch of sailors buying coins at a little minting house.

Charlie hesitated for a moment. Something was tugging at his intuition, like an itch in his brain. For some reason his memory kept drifting back to the bloated body of the dead girl, her poached-fish eyes, the silver coin in her mouth.

'The coin,' said Charlie, 'in the dead girl's mouth. It was minted near here.'

'You said by St Ursula's Church,' said Lily, casting her mind back.

'St Ursula's Church,' agreed Charlie. 'Lily, give me your almanac.'

She passed it to him. Charlie flicked through the pages. Then he stopped at a familiar star constellation. The shape of two bears.

'Here,' he said, 'read this part.'

Lily shot him a look of confusion, then settled her gaze down on the open almanac.

'It's the constellations,' she said. 'Great Bear and Little Bear.'

'But how are they called? What is the astrologer's name?'

'Ursa Major,' she read. 'Ursa Minor. It's Latin I think,' she added. 'Roman for "big bear" and "little bear".'

Charlie nodded. 'Ursa,' he said. 'St Ursula's Church. I think there could be a connection. If Custom House was once a temple to Diana, the Bear Goddess, then perhaps St Ursula's Church is some legacy.'

'That doesn't help us find the entrance the Cipher talked about,' Lily pointed out.

'No,' said Charlie. 'But there's something else I remember about Little Bear Steps. Locals call it "Oyster Gate", but now I think on it, no oysters are landed there.' Charlie was calling to mind the trundling oyster carts with their large barrels, supplying cheap taverns in the east. 'Oyster ropes are strung further upriver and landed at Barking. So,' he continued, 'what if oyster was once *ostium*?'

'*Ostium*,' said Lily slowly. 'Your friend Bitey said that was the Roman word for mouth.'

'An old translation,' agreed Charlie. 'I was thinking the same thing. If Little Bear Steps was once an *ostium*,' said Charlie, 'it's most likely something to do with water supply or sewage, so it would be low. Under the steps. And there's an old inlet,' he continued, 'set into the side of the river on Little Bear Quay. A few mudlarks live there, but no one assumed it leads anywhere.' He laughed. 'Sly little bastards have probably been raiding Custom House at night.'

Chapter 65

The King turned the gold door handle. His fingers shook a little. Behind him the Duke of York brought up the rear. A musty smell greeted them. Old paper and books.

'I had the rest of the palace refitted,' explained the King as they moved inside. 'I left this until last. On my return I made a visit to the old library. I haven't been back since. I couldn't bear to see it . . . as it is now.'

They both stepped into the room. Carved wooden bookshelves covered one large wall. But they'd been mostly stripped bare, with only a few volumes and manuscripts remaining.

'It was Father's favourite room,' explained Charles. 'There was a large chair there.' He pointed to where a plain wooden chair faced a functional desk. 'A great table here,' continued Charles, gesturing wide with his ringed fingers. 'I remember he had lacquered cabinets, bright like butterflies. I hid in them as a boy.'

'Father let you play in here?' asked the Duke of York, surprised.

Charles smiled. 'No. He didn't let me play anywhere. I was the future King. But one of the nursemaids let me inside once.'

The Duke of York's face darkened. He was growing a curling moustache, Charles noted, in the style of the late King.

'I hardly knew our father,' said the Duke of York. 'He wasn't as you are with your children.'

'No,' agreed Charles. He liked his small children to play at his feet in the royal bedchamber.

'I always thought how ashamed Father would have been,' said the Duke of York, 'to see me as a grubby urchin running around Dutch taverns whilst Cromwell ruled.'

Charles put a hand on his brother's sturdy shoulder. 'We fled as boys,' he said, 'but we came back together.'

Charles examined his brother's face, so like his own, but younger and less weighed with duty. The King felt a sudden flash of envy. What he would give to return to those carefree days in Holland. He was so tired of wars and plots. His mind turned to the fresh-faced Frances, so amenable, so simple. She was like a draught of cool water on a hot day.

'You know the same thing is happening again at Deptford?' said James quietly. 'The dead girls? As in Thorne's time.'

Charles nodded.

'I stayed in Thorne's workshop for a time,' added the Duke of York. 'They hid me away there in the dark, waiting for a time to safely escape to Holland. It gave me nightmares. Thorne gave me a ring,' he added. 'It was how I was able to buy passage to Holland.'

'I'm sorry,' said the King. 'We should have fled together. I had to try for one last battle.'

'Have you ever wondered what the Eye could be?' asked the Duke of York. 'To allow Thorne to find that ship?'

The King pondered. 'There are stories it is an emerald. Perhaps a jewel of great value. Something to bribe an informer for details of the enemy.'

'Or a fearsome device to torture it out of them,' said the Duke of York. 'It could be a powerful spyglass,' he suggested. 'Thorne might have seen the enemy from afar.'

The King shook his head. 'Isaac Newton is working on such a thing now. If he succeeds, his invention will see all the way to the stars. But no spyglass can see through fog and storm or over the curve of the earth.'

There was a pause.

'I still see our father,' said the Duke of York, 'walking up to the executioner's block. I see myself charging out, freeing him before the sword falls. You should let me go to sea,' he said, 'and defend us from this Dutch threat.'

They were both silent for a moment.

'It's not as when we were young men,' said Charles. 'You cannot charge fearlessly into battle. I will have no sons with my Queen. You will inherit the throne.'

James made a strange shudder, as is physically shrugging off his stately restrictions.

'You're a fool to think it,' he said. 'Parliament thinks me too like our father. They will take off my head before the crown touches it.'

'What if I were to remarry?' suggested Charles. 'Frances Stewart is young. Healthy.'

'You'd start a war with Portugal,' said James. 'They'd never forgive the affront of your passing their barren princess over.'

The Duke of York gave a sad smile. 'You're as trapped as I, Brother,' he said.

Chapter 66

Charlie and Lily dropped down into the thick mud at the base of Little Bear Steps. Ahead of them was the old inlet. It was circular. An old Roman bricked sewer that had disgorged refuse into the Thames.

'Look at the construction,' said Charlie. 'The same style as the catacombs.'

Lily nodded.

They pulled themselves into the old entrance. The ground beneath their feet was intricate brickwork, working into the curve of the large old pipe, wide enough to walk through.

They passed a few sad dwellings. Bits of sacking and cloth that made shelters of sorts for mudlarks. But the occupants were absent – out on the river, trawling for whatever they could find.

Piled up in mounds were their findings. It was mostly detritus from the Great Fire. Melted tankards, half-burned household goods and scorched leather had been tossed into the giant waste disposal of the Thames. Luckier mudlarks had recovered water-damaged possessions accidentally pitched overboard as Londoners scrabbled to escape the flames by river. There were bundles of part-rotted cloth and furniture swollen and cracked by the waters.

As Charlie and Lily tracked deeper into the tunnel, evidence of the mudlark's occupation ran out abruptly. The ground was slick with slippery tidal mud, and as the light grew dimmer, something clanked beneath their feet.

'Look,' said Charlie. 'Things have been thrown down here. This wasn't the mudlarks.' He peered into the darkness. 'Looks like . . . weapons,' he decided. 'Swords and spears.'

'They're bent over,' said Lily, following his gaze. 'Broken.' She met his gaze. 'Why haven't the mudlarks taken them?' she whispered. 'Those little urchins will take an old stick if it floats past.'

'They must think them cursed or holy,' said Charlie uncertainly. Though it was a strange sentiment to imagine in a mudlark.

The swords had been deliberately twisted over backwards or snapped in two, and the spears shattered.

'It's like old Norris at Dead Man's Curve said,' said Charlie. 'Broken things to appease the river.'

There was a shaft of light striking through the gloom. Charlie looked upwards. Above them was a wide bricked shaft. Judging by the quality of daylight coming through, it opened inside a building.

'I think there was some kind of well up there,' he said, 'linking to the Thames. People must have thrown things down it.'

They moved further into the tunnel. The road beneath them smoothed out now, and Charlie could tell by his bare feet they were on a neatly cobbled path.

'It's an old Roman road,' he said. 'Hidden away all these years.' He peered up at the ceiling, trying to get his bearings. 'We're a good few feet below the city,' he decided. 'The whole of London must have been on lower ground back then, nearer the river.' Up ahead the tunnel seemed to run out. 'Looks like it's a dead end,' said Charlie disappointedly.

'Maybe the Cipher lied,' said Lily.

But something just before the passage's conclusion caught Charlie's attention. Markings in the gloom. He stopped.

'Look,' he said. 'There was something here. Some sign or . . . picture.'

'A sign of the goddess?' suggested Lily hopefully. She moved closer to examine the part of the wall where Charlie was looking.

'It's an old mosaic,' she said. 'Or was. There are still some words in Latin at the top.' She frowned. 'Londinium Ursa,' she read. 'London Bear?'

'Someone's been here before us,' said Charlie. 'It's all been smashed away.'

He knelt, searching with his fingers. A shallow stream flowed over his hand.

'The tide going out,' he said, questing in the dark waters. His fingers closed on a few fragments still holding on in the little eddy.

Charlie straightened, examining them. 'They're mostly washed away,' he said, looking at the pieces. 'But this damage was done recently. See how the tile edges are still clean where they were broken. Even a single tide would have darkened these with silt.' Charlie stood up, turning a fragment of mosaic thoughtfully. 'So someone came here today,' he said. 'Someone who doesn't want us to know what was here. Janus?'

Lily bent down and fished in the little stream, her hands casting around. 'It must have taken force to smash it,' she reasoned. 'Perhaps some pieces fell further than intended. Here!' she added, her hands closing on a tiny pile that had fallen to the edge of the tunnel, free of the rising tide. 'There are a few pieces here.' She gathered them up. 'Nothing much,' she said, turning them. 'They're all the same. A greenish colour.'

She showed them to Charlie.

He was examining the fractured remains of the mosaic. It was difficult to see in the dark, but he thought he could make out the remnants of a thick ring around the edge, and tiles of the same colour Lily held at the bottom.

'It could have been a map,' he said eventually. 'Look at the bottom edge. Those pieces look the same greenish colour as yours. They could represent the river.'

'An old map of London,' said Lily, moving closer, 'from Roman times?'

Charlie nodded, standing back from the shattered image. 'The thick outline could show the London Wall,' he said. 'See how it breaks here to fit the old gates? Lud Gate, here,' he said, stabbing a finger. 'Ald Gate, Bishop's Gate, Moor Gate . . . The Tower. I'm sure of it,' he concluded. 'So what about the old Roman city would someone not want us to know?'

'There's not much left,' said Lily doubtfully. She pointed to a figure. 'That looks like . . . it could be a building with a double roof,' she decided.

Charlie nodded. 'Then these lines might be single roofs. So this would be a large building.' He thought for a moment. 'It's where St Martin's Church would be.'

'But there were no churches in Roman times,' said Lily.

'No,' agreed Charlie, 'but there was something there. Something larger than a usual house.'

He stared at the mosaic. A pattern was emerging.

'All the large rooftops,' decided Charlie, 'are now churches.' He stabbed a finger. 'This is where All Hallows is now. And this . . . this was once St Ursula's, before it burned down in the fire.'

'Why would a Roman map have modern churches?'

'Perhaps it's not Roman,' suggested Charlie, though the map seemed old.

'What's that there?' Lily asked, pointing to the door of the double-roofed building. 'It looks like part of a fork.'

'That's the site of St Olave's church,' said Charlie. 'The fisherman's saint.'

'The fork could be a trident,' suggested Lily.

'For Neptune,' agreed Charlie. 'Neptune, God of Fishermen, became St Olave's church.'

He remembered what Maria had said about the religions mixing.

'What if the churches,' said Charlie suddenly, 'mark where the old Roman temples are? The Christian and Roman religions combined,' he said. 'What if they merged the buildings too?' He considered the map. 'There's a St Ursula's Church next to Custom House. Perhaps Custom House was originally the Temple of the Bear – Diana's Temple.'

Then his eyes caught something wedged tightly into the side of the map.

Lily was peering closer at the mosaic fragments. 'Pity it's so badly smashed,' she said. 'We could have found where Venus's Temple was. The writing in Thorne's camera obscura suggests there's a ring there.'

'I think that's why it was broken,' said Charlie. 'Janus was here.' He was reaching towards the object jammed into the side of the stone map. Even before he pulled it free, he felt icy fingers of fear close around his throat.

'This map showed something he didn't want us to see,' said Charlie in a cold voice. 'And he means for us to stop looking.'

At his strange tone of voice, Lily turned questioningly. Then she saw the bunch of fabric in his hand.

'It's Rowan's,' said Charlie. 'I don't know how. But Janus has my brother.'

Chapter 67

Janus looked up. He'd found his way to the old temple without realising it. Saturn's Temple in Hyde Woods. The catacombs and temple were the remains of Roman death worship in London.

Janus bowed his head in reverence to the powerful god. Thorne's words floated back to him.

We are no murderers. We only take offerings to the Thames and reassign the dead.

He wondered if perhaps the Cipher had died, and after all these years some other codebreaker had replaced her.

For a few seconds Janus waited, tense, wondering on the best course of action. Then he decided. The warning knock. He drummed the complicated tattoo from boyhood. The one he'd overheard and learned so carefully when Thorne thought he wasn't listening.

When there was no answer, he carefully pushed the door. Janus waited a fraction of a second, and having assured himself no trap was set, he walked into the room.

The Cipher was sitting on her usual stool, straight-backed, in the same plain dress she'd always worn. Her rounded face had hardly seemed to age in its ordinariness, and the pale eyes were the same, deadly clever and whirring.

'Who are you?' she said. Her voice was lower than he remembered but still with the same cold monotone. 'How did you know his knock?'

There was deep fear in her eyes. Janus realised he had frightened her using Thorne's secret knock. Not knowing unsettled her.

'You don't remember me?' he said, pulling down his mask.

Her face fluttered in confusion. She stared for a long moment. Then something like recognition set into place.

'Thorne's apprentice,' she said quietly. 'You were Thorne's apprentice.' Janus nodded.

'Thorne's apprentice,' she said again. 'But you died.'

'I only hid for a time,' said Janus. He wondered suddenly if she knew of the Bad Thing. It was possible, he supposed. Much information passed through her hands. 'I've come back for the Eye,' he concluded.

Her face darkened. 'Thorne is dead,' she said.

'I was there,' said Janus. 'I saw him die.' He hesitated. 'Thorne wanted the Eye to be found,' he explained. 'This year. At this time. During the lunar eclipse. I've tried to locate it,' Janus added, 'using Thorne's old methods. Dead reckoning. The tides.'

'That is clever,' she said, though her expression didn't match the words.

Janus nodded. 'I've calculated nothing exact,' he admitted. 'I'm not the mathematician Thorne was. I only know the Eye is east of the city.'

Something flickered in the Cipher's eyes. 'Your shadow,' she said. 'Your shadow was here.'

Janus's breathing tightened.

'Charlie Tuesday,' she said. 'He goes to the temple at Custom House. If he finds the ring, he may find the Eye before you.'

The Cipher was moving towards the back of the temple, towards the scrolls.

Janus stayed taut, ready for a false move. He knew never to trust the Cipher.

'Thorne's camera obscura,' she said, turning to him.

'I remember it,' said Janus, wondering on the significance of this.

'Thorne changed where the mirror was pointing,' said the Cipher. 'Just before he was captured.'

'He'd had it trained on the stars,' agreed Janus uncertainly. 'Then he shifted the focus to watch for intruders.'

Even as he spoke the words, Janus realised something wasn't quite right. The story he'd been told as a child didn't fit with his adult understanding.

'But there would be no reason,' said Janus slowly, 'to watch for intruders in Hyde Woods.'

The Cipher nodded. 'Perhaps he set the camera obscura to keep safe watch on something valuable,' she concluded.

And just like that Janus knew. It all came together in a rush of realisation. How Thorne loved illusions.

Looking here when you should be looking there.

Suddenly Janus was certain he knew where the Eye was hidden.

Chapter 68

'It's a piece of Rowan's shirt,' repeated Charlie, holding it tightly. 'Irish linen. I bought it back from the pawnshop just before Rowan vanished. He was wearing it the last time I saw him.'

The realisation was so painful he closed his eyes for a moment.

'Let me see.' Lily took the piece of shirt. She unravelled it. Inside was a copper coin.

'His?' she asked, holding it.

Charlie recognised the amulet immediately. He managed to nod. Thick despair was gripping him. It was a worn copper coin of Neptune, with St Peter on the reverse side. The same charm his brother had pulled out to show him back in the Seven Stars Tavern. But he'd assumed Rowan had made it back to his ship and was safely concealed amongst the Dutch sailors.

'I've only just got Rowan back,' he said. 'Now I've put him at risk. If he's still alive.'

'He's still alive,' said Lily. She moved to Charlie's side and took both his hands in hers. 'Janus is a fireship pilot,' she said, holding his fingers tightly. 'A tactician. The threat of a fireship is often terrible enough to make the enemy surrender. He knows this. Janus only threatens. At least for now,' she concluded with her usual honesty.

Charlie felt his fear ebb slightly. 'We need to stop searching,' he said. 'Whoever Janus is, he knows about me. He knows my family.' He let his hands drop from Lily's and rubbed his temples. 'Janus even knew we'd come here,' he added. 'Whatever his means of intelligence, it's too good to risk Rowan.'

Lily's mouth set. 'We can't stop now,' she said. 'We've still got the London Goddess sign to find. If we uncover the third ring, perhaps it will lead us to the fourth.'

Charlie was shaking his head. 'You don't understand. I won't lose Rowan again.'

'I do understand.' Lily looked suddenly angry. 'Think you I've not lost brothers and more? My whole family died at the hands of men like Judge Walters. Thousands will follow on his slave ships.'

'I can't—' began Charlie.

But Lily interrupted him. 'Do you imagine Janus will set your brother free if you stop hunting the Eye? Charlie, Janus burns men alive.' She was staring fiercely at him. 'All you'll succeed in doing is letting Janus bring the Eye to the Dutch. They'll invade England and kill us all. And they won't spare an English traitor like Rowan just because you've been fool enough to help them.'

Charlie felt the coil of unease in his stomach grow. He knew she was right.

'I could find Rowan,' he said, 'whilst Janus is distracted hunting the Eye.'

'Where would you hunt?' she challenged. 'The whole of London, where he was last seen, or all of the English seas, where he was next headed? Charlie, think,' she urged him. 'There is only one way to be sure of getting your brother back. The Eye.'

'The Eye finds things,' said Charlie, following her train of thought. 'You think we could use it to discover Rowan's whereabouts?'

'Even if the Eye proves false,' said Lily, 'you could still use it to barter.'

'Janus would likely not harm my brother if he thought the Eye in jeopardy,' said Charlie. 'He's taken great risks to find it.'

Charlie had the strangest feeling, as though he knew Janus's mind, the tactics he would deploy.

'You're right,' Charlie admitted. 'Finding the Eye is the best chance of getting Rowan to safety. Wherever he is.' He studied the empty space where the tiles had been. 'But we're at a dead end,' he added. 'Without the pieces there's no way to deduce anything else from the map. The tide has washed everything away.'

'Yet we know we're in a place linked with Diana,' said Lily, frustration lining her features. 'And St Ursula's Church is nearby. It feels as though we must be close.'

Charlie let his mind track around the vicinity. Then it hit on something.

'The well,' he said. 'Back in the tunnel was an old well. The light coming through was too subdued to be direct daylight. I'm sure it opened into some kind of building.'

Charlie set his mind to getting their bearings, deep under the city. His mind kept forking back to Rowan, held captive, perhaps even underground somewhere damp and old like this. He forced himself to focus.

'It could open into something that was a Roman temple,' he suggested. 'The well might have been part of the original structure.'

They tracked back to where the wide circle of light fell on the damp stone floor. The well shaft was just above their heads.

'The bricks in the higher part are uneven enough to climb,' said Charlie, pointing to where the plaster had crumbled free, leaving step-like troughs in the brickwork. 'But this part is too smooth.'

He ran a hand over the well shaft immediately above their heads, surprisingly well preserved through the centuries.

Lily was rummaging in her skirts. 'Perhaps not,' she said, taking out her knives. 'The plaster is old and loose.'

Lily prodded with the blade of a knife experimentally. It pushed between the bricks with relative ease, sending a shower of sandy rubble to the ground. She reached up, inserted a second knife and hauled herself up.

'Just one more blade,' she said, her voice tight with effort, 'and we can use the knives as steps.'

Charlie watched as she plunged a third knife into the side of the well, then pulled herself up to tiptoe gingerly on the bottom blade.

'There,' she gasped, reaching upwards. 'I've made it up to where I can climb.'

Charlie took hold of the first knife as Lily's little foot left it, pulling himself into the well shaft. He swung his body, heaved and righted himself, using the knife as a foothold. Then he began to climb.

'Leave the knives!' called Lily from above. 'We might need them to get back out. I've got more.'

Charlie could hear her panting with exertion above him.

'I hope we find this ring,' she managed through gritted teeth. 'It's a great risk you take for your debtor brother.'

'Rowan is all I have left,' said Charlie. 'He hides his good nature, but it's there.'

'Is that why you save so many thieves from the noose?' asked Lily. 'And take work for food and favours when you could be employed for gold? Everyone says it,' she added, pausing for breath. 'Charlie Tuesday always finds the goods. But the thief slips away. Is it because of your brother?'

'If you saw the kind of men who steal and why they do it, you wouldn't send them to the noose either,' replied Charlie, heaving himself up. 'And Rowan came here to warn me,' he added defensively. 'Risked his life. We look out for each other. Always have, always will.'

Charlie couldn't explain to her what Rowan was like before the orphanage. How underneath it all his brother was the same hero who had protected him, even if others didn't see it.

'I don't care about your brother,' said Lily sharply, 'I only care about . . .' She stopped climbing suddenly. 'I can hear voices,' she whispered.

Charlie pulled himself level with Lily and listened carefully. Then his face opened in recognition.

'I've been here before,' he said. 'We've come to the right place.'

Chapter 69

Filtering down the old well was the undoubted shouting and bargaining of Custom House.

'Docking sailors,' said Charlie, 'arguing their taxes.'

Carefully he raised his head a few inches over the precipice and looked out.

The well shaft was tucked towards one side of Custom House, attracting no interest from anyone. Further beyond were tax collectors sat at long tables, with sacks of money and jewels ranged near their feet. Captains and sailors jostled in untidy queues, waiting to state their case.

A number of guards stood on duty, but they were either watching the queuing men or policing the doors, where the shouts of angry sailors' wives could be heard from outside.

'It's safe,' whispered Charlie. 'Come on.'

He pushed up and climbed out. Lily came behind him, dusting down her skirts.

Inside, Custom House was organised chaos. The half-built structure was filled with long tables and disorderly lines of seamen. It was now mid-afternoon, and the atmosphere had turned desperate. Everyone wanted business settled before the ill-fated All Hallows' Eve fell. Suntanned colonial traders haggled for tax breaks on bundles of tobacco and sacks of spices. Fat merchants from the Baltic and Sweden imported lumber and iron, their thick woollen clothes white with sea salt. Wealthy British captains in thick frock coats shipped wool and copper from England's North. Outlandishly dressed adventurers wore bright feathers and spoils of the New World.

Above them the old crest of London, with its proud lion, looked down on the assembled sailors, its jewels and gilding twinkling in the morning sun.

Charlie and Lily slipped quietly away from the well and mingled in with the queuing crowd.

A man barred their way.

'Good morrow!' he announced, opening his coat to display an array of navigational wares. 'Might I interest you in the latest seafaring equipment?' He removed a complicated-looking device. 'Chart your place at sea,' he enticed. 'Find new lands. This quadrant was used by the captain who discovered Barbados.'

Charlie tried not to let his troubled mind overwhelm him. Conning new sailors into buying miraculous tools was exactly the insalubrious kind of activity Rowan would be engaged in. He was about to issue a friendly decline when the salesman's face switched in recognition.

'Charlie Tuesday!' he said. 'You helped my brother-in-law recover his carpentry tools.' His eyes shifted to Lily and widened. 'You!' the salesman accused.

Lily eyed him distractedly; then her eyes narrowed. The man was backing away now, pulling his wares closer to his body and crossing himself.

'What did you do to him?' Charlie asked as the salesman vanished into the crowd.

'He put his hand where he shouldn't,' said Lily distractedly, looking around Custom House. 'Why is everyone shouting?' she added.

'Custom House is all about negotiation,' said Charlie. 'The captains take the worst of their stock and pretend it accounts for the whole. The customs men know it and make their calculations of tax accordingly.'

'If this place has been here since Roman times,' said Lily, glancing towards the well, 'I don't see any evidence of a temple.'

'Perhaps it was an old entrance to the city,' suggested Charlie. 'Diana is the Moon Goddess. The moon rules the tides, water. Arrivals by river all come this way.'

'We just need to work out where the goddess would be,' said Lily. She glanced around. 'There's nothing Roman left,' she concluded.

'The goddess could also be symbolised by a bear,' Charlie pointed out. 'Maybe carved into some old stonework.'

'The only animal I see is the lion in the crest,' said Lily.

Charlie looked up to the Custom House crest. Something about it had nagged at him since they'd entered the building. Suddenly the answer came to him.

'I've found it,' he said.

Lily followed his gaze. 'The English crest?' she said. 'The lion?'

'Look more closely,' said Charlie. 'Does the snout not look rather snub? The mane has been added later,' he decided, 'but the form is still there. It was once a bear.'

'The sign of Diana,' said Lily wonderingly.

'The London Goddess,' agreed Charlie. 'If her temple was once the entrance to the city, it would fit.'

'It would explain all the streets and lanes dedicated to bears,' agreed Lily. 'And all the St Ursula's Churches.'

They both stared at the large Custom House crest. It was of ancient carved wood, decorated with jewels and gold leaf that had been added over the years.

'That crest is old,' said Charlie. 'Perhaps it was even Roman. Rather than make a new one, they just adapted it.'

'I see the bear now,' said Lily. 'But I don't see the ring.'

'Look at the mouth,' said Charlie.

Lily looked. And there, glistening red between the bear's grinning teeth, was a shining ruby.

'That's it,' she said excitedly. 'I can see gold at the edges where the band begins.' She turned to Charlie. 'How do we get to it?' she said. 'It's high on the wall.'

'We can't come back at night,' said Charlie. 'There's no time. Halloween is less than twelve hours away.'

Lily chewed a fingernail.

The great crest stared down at them, tantalisingly close. With the guard presence at Custom House, Charlie judged they'd be dead or arrested within ten seconds of attempting to rob the crest.

His mind roamed possible routes to the ring. There was a pile of thick ship's netting on one of the customs tables. Charlie calculated it could be thrown to hook the crest, making a kind of ladder to climb up to the ring.

'What if I create a disturbance?' suggested Lily. 'These men are already halfway pitched for a riot. I need only distract them for a few moments.'

'There are too many guards expecting it,' said Charlie. 'The last robbery at Custom House was over ten years ago. They've heavily guarded it since. Each official has a gun and a sword.'

He moved thoughtfully to the window. 'They're well protected against an internal attack,' he said slowly, 'but they won't be expecting one from outside.' He pointed to the band of furious sailors' wives, shrieking and hurling rocks at the windows.

'So what do you suggest?' asked Lily, eyeing the medley of women. 'We let those harpies inside?'

'Exactly that.'

Chapter 70

The sailors' wives were clustered thickly around Charlie, shouting and jabbing their fingers at Custom House.

They'd lost more time than Charlie realised getting inside Custom's House. By the angle of the sun it was now late afternoon, and he tried to dismiss the thought of Rowan and time slipping away.

He looked anxiously to the doorway, hoping Lily would accomplish her part of the plan. Charlie had managed to persuade the women to draw back from the entrance to make Lily's plan more likely to succeed. But the atmosphere was quickly turning ugly.

'He tricks us!' accused one woman with meaty forearms and a broken pitchfork. 'He only wants to draw us away from Custom House.'

'I support your cause,' reassured Charlie. 'You must only wait a few moments. Then you might make your case inside.'

A few younger women looked mollified, but the older stalwarts were spoiling for a fight.

'We go back!' shrieked a snaggle-toothed woman with a broken nose. 'Demand our rights!'

'A moment.' Charlie kept his voice soothing, holding his hands out in a placating gesture. He glanced again at the huge door.

Where was Lily? Distracting men was one of her greatest abilities.

Suddenly the entrance opened a crack. The guards outside turned in surprise, a few words were muttered, then they vanished into Custom House.

'There,' said Charlie, not bothering to hide his relief. 'The guards are gone. You have a few minutes to get inside.'

The woman with the thick forearms raised her pitchfork. 'We will have our men's wages!' she roared.

The women took up the cry, and the mob moved as one thundering force towards Custom House.

Charlie saw the scarred and weathered faces glare at the semi-open doorway. The women meant business. He ducked amongst their midst as they flocked towards Custom House in one deafening movement.

The heavy door was thrown back. The protestors poured through, screaming for justice. On the other side, Charlie caught a glimpse of Lily talking animatedly, with a seductive expression, to a group of guards. He sensed her alarm wasn't forced as she turned to see the mob tunnelling through the now open doorway.

The guards were taken completely by surprise. Many were resting on their guns, waiting for the day to end. The sudden pack of furious women was so unexpected that a few men dropped their weapons in shock.

Now inside, the sailors' wives had no problem matching their political agenda to physical action.

'Justice!' bellowed the pitchfork woman. 'We mean to take what our husbands are owed!'

They fell on the merchant sailors, pulling at stock samples, looting any valuables they could see. Their leader quickly found the stash of confiscated contraband, stacked untidily behind the end table. She shouted to her colleagues, and they rushed as one to seize the goods.

An unfortunate customs man stood and tried to bar their way. When the leader pushed him aside, he grabbed at her thin dress. There was an audible rip, and the woman screamed in outrage.

'This is our dues!' she screamed, kicking him square in the groin. 'Move aside!'

The customs man doubled over in pain. A guard moved quickly to his side, punching randomly into the pack of women. He caught the leader square on the jaw and she twisted, spitting blood.

An outraged howl echoed up from the women, and the guard's face turned from grim duty to surprised terror. Charlie saw his wig flying aside as he went down, and twenty women landed on him, tearing fist-fuls of hair and clothing.

Charlie's attention turned to Lily, but she'd already managed to slip away from the male guard. She caught his eye and beckoned to the back of Custom House, where the crest hung.

Charlie raced towards the netting he'd seen earlier and scooped it up. But as his fingers grasped the tough rope, he felt someone fall on him from behind, clutching at the net.

'The property is ours!' shouted a sailor's wife, brandishing a kitchen knife.

Charlie reached back to hold her scrawny wrists, but the woman let out a banshee shriek, and several heads turned towards the tussling pair. Women raced to help their friend, teeth bared, rudimentary weapons waving.

Suddenly a flash of red silk stood between them.

'Get away from him!' shouted Lily, knives held out. She twisted to Charlie, who had worked the net free from the woman and managed to extricate himself from her grip. 'Go!' Lily shouted.

Charlie hesitated, seeing her outnumbered.

'Quickly,' she added, her eyes desperately taking in the odds.

He stepped towards the wall and flung the net, trying to drown out the hissed insults of 'gypsy' and 'whore' sounding behind him.

The netting fell awkwardly, only half catching on the crest. But he didn't have time for a more secure hit. Charlie dug his foot into the net, feeling it jerk downwards, then hold. He put one hand over the other, climbing carefully to avoid dislodging the makeshift ladder, then risked a glance at Lily. She was backed against the wall, a growing mob of women surrounding her. He moved faster, scaling the rigging, ignoring the uncertain footholds as he climbed higher.

His hand landed on the lion's snub snout, but his position was too precarious to get a firm hold. He managed to snag his fingertips on the mouth, where the ring was lodged. Then inch by painful inch he got a grip on the ring. It was wedged too tight to pull free.

'Charlie!'

He heard Lily's cry of terror. He looked down to see one of the sailors' wives lunge at her throat with a broken poker. Forgetting the ring, Charlie moved higher on to the crest, securing his footing. He unhitched the netting and threw it downwards. The heavy rope landed on the women nearest to Lily, dropping them to the ground in a tangle of shouts and screams. The surrounding sailors' wives fell on to the netting, trying to free their colleagues. In the confusion their attack on Lily was temporarily forgotten.

With his extra weight now completely on the wooden crest, Charlie heard the shriek of ancient nails pulling free from the wall. The lion jerked back a few inches, and Charlie strained to hold on as the wooden mount began to lever free from the wall.

Lily looked up gratefully. Then she saw Charlie was trapped high above the hard ground. The split in the wall showered plaster dust, and the crest creaked free another inch. Charlie dropped downwards with it, desperately hanging on.

'The wool sacks!' Charlie was looking towards a consignment of yarn, shipped down from sheep farmers in Newcastle.

Lily understood immediately and ran to the cargo. She dodged a guard who grabbed at her and shouldered aside a sailor's wife headed for the same booty. Then she grasped the wool sacks and began hurling them beneath the crest. She'd landed three when Charlie felt his hold give way completely. The wooden decoration levered free and plummeted to the ground, taking him with it. Charlie felt himself fall heavily on the wool sacking and rolled quickly to avoid the crest. It smashed apart next to him, causing every head in Custom House to turn in his direction.

Lily was at his side, pulling him up. Her eyes lighted on a flash of shining red, buried in the shattered remains of the crest.

'The ring!' She scooped it up and pocketed it. 'This way!'

'Halt!' shouted a guard. 'That woman steals a jewel from the crest!'

'The well!' said Lily, pulling a dazed Charlie behind her.

He heard the crack of a gunshot and saw a haze of burning powder. Then the entrance to the old well was in front of them. They swung inside as more gunshots rained over their heads and were climbing back down towards Little Bear Steps, leaving the mayhem of Custom House behind.

Chapter 71

Amesbury approached the dark double doors. He risked his life coming here. The Queen Mother had tried to bring about his death for twenty years.

The footman outside moved forward to bar his way. 'It is the time of Her Royal Highness's ceremonies,' he said. 'She cannot be disturbed.'

Amesbury dropped a warning hand to his sword. The footman sized up the general's expression and stepped back.

Inside the room the Queen Mother was on her feet, her hard wooden throne sitting behind her. Her old-fashioned black dress did little to bulk out her bird-like frame, and Amesbury thought she looked like a mean little crow, peering agitatedly in his direction.

Pictures of the old King in all his autocratic delusion glared down at Amesbury. The general almost felt sorry for the Queen Mother. She'd made her own giant mausoleum to her tyrant husband and was living inside it.

At her feet was a wardrobe of the old King's black clothes and white collars, laid out carefully as though a person were still inside them. Towards the edge of the clothing display was a range of disparate artefacts, some bloodstained. There were coins bearing the dead King's head, a locket with his portrait and a scrap of curling brown blood-soaked hair.

A footman had been in the act of laying more objects neatly in the array. But he'd stopped as the unexpected guest entered the Queen's chambers.

Amesbury made the briefest possible of bows. 'I see you kept the astronomical clock,' he observed, nodding to outside, where the distant tick of the mighty clock could be faintly heard. 'I might have thought it brought bad memories.' He hesitated. 'Greenwich,' he said pointedly, 'seems a strange choice for the mother of our King. Just downriver of Deptford dockyards. Particularly when this is where you and your husband were residing when he lost his kingdom.'

The Queen Mother's lips drew even thinner. 'Leave us,' she said, gesturing to the footman, who'd come in after Amesbury. 'The turncoat won't stay long.' She regarded Amesbury icily. 'You're still alive,' Henrietta said. 'My husband should have had you killed when he had the chance.'

Amesbury smiled slightly. 'The old King certainly took every opportunity. Perhaps the chance was not so opportune as you imagine.'

'Yes.' Henrietta's black beady eyes were fixed on Amesbury. 'Men like you are difficult to kill.'

'Quite so,' agreed Amesbury. 'But I come on another matter.'

'I have nothing to say to you, turncoat,' spat Queen Henrietta. 'Nor do you have any power to induce me to talk. When I tell my son, the King, you were here . . .'

Amesbury reached in his leather purse and pulled out a bloody handkerchief.

Henrietta's eyes fell on it greedily. Her thin lips parted.

'His?' she said quietly.

Amesbury nodded. 'I can bring you many such things,' he said, tossing it into the array. 'Hundreds of loyal subjects dipped their handkerchiefs in your dead husband's blood or kept his likeness as tribute.'

'What do you want?' she said after a moment.

'I want you to tell me,' he said, 'about Thorne's apprentice.'

She blinked her little hard eyes fast. 'You don't know?' she said finally. 'Yet it was you . . .'

'Yes,' agreed Amesbury, 'it was I who last saw Thorne.'

Amesbury wondered how much Henrietta knew. She was sharp in a blinkered way. Did she know what he'd done all those years ago? He remembered it all too well.

Amesbury was taking in the high brick walls, the piles of books and papers.

'So this,' he said to Thorne, 'is where you have been hiding.'

Amesbury's gaze had settled on a pile of jeweller's tools.

Thorne smiled thinly. 'I'd tell you more,' he said, 'but I fear you have more pressing matters to discuss with me. The King wants you to torture me. But I will not tell you where I hid the Eye.'

Amesbury shut the door behind them. 'What about the girls?' he said. 'Will you tell me of them? Seven corpses washed up dead at Deptford.' Amesbury moved closer. 'Did a man of your great bloodline think,' he said, 'a few commoners wouldn't be missed?'

Thorne put his head in his hands. 'It's not what you think,' he whispered.

'Then tell me what to think,' said Amesbury. 'The court is alive with rumours about you. Your tastes. The friend who was burned.'

Thorne's eyes blazed suddenly.

'I heard,' said Amesbury gently, 'you never recovered from the death. Your interests turned to Roman gods. Sacrifice.'

Thorne tensed as the general picked up a wicked-looking awl.

'I would guess,' said Amesbury slowly, 'that you used these tools to make the Eye.'

Thorne said nothing.

'I would also assume,' continued Amesbury, 'that a man so skilled would use the same apparatus to hide his creations. Not in this room, however,'

Amesbury decided, watching Thorne's face. 'A man like you, a man of such genius, a stargazer, he would choose somewhere . . . symbolic.'

Amesbury's hand grazed a few more tools. A chisel of exquisite precision, tiny pliers, a jeweller's hammer.

'I think,' he said, walking towards Thorne, 'that the tools that hid the Eye might also be able to reveal its location.'

Thorne breathed out, his face pale.

Amesbury loomed closer. He was so large, Thorne found himself shrinking back. Amesbury eyed the door, then lowered his voice.

'We are brothers, you and I,' he said quietly. 'Bound by blood oath to protect England.' He paused. 'But I do not believe,' he continued, 'that the old King still holds England in his heart.' He pushed tools into Thorne's hands. 'You will need these,' he said, 'to destroy the Eye.'

Thorne shook his head. 'I cannot,' he said. 'My apprentice—'

'Will be better without such a legacy,' interrupted Amesbury. 'If you try to leave your apprentice the Eye, you will be captured and killed.'

Thorne was silent.

'What about you?' he said. 'When the King discovers your betrayal . . .'

Amesbury gave him a good-natured thump on the shoulder, jolting Thorne's thin frame.

'My allegiances have changed,' he said. 'I mean to seek my fortune with Cromwell.'

Amesbury was the only man Thorne knew able to say something so ludicrous convincingly. He spoke as though he would simply stroll on to the battlefield and take off his Royalist sash.

'They will call you a turncoat,' said Thorne.

Amesbury shrugged. 'They have called me worse,' he said. 'I have already undertaken secret naval missions for Cromwell. I mean to defend England.' He considered for a moment. 'The old King's son. He could have promise. Brave lad. Full of feelings. But he has a lot of growing up to do. Perhaps one day he'll be fit to rule with his head, not his heart.'

Amesbury glanced at the door again. 'I'll see you're not disturbed,' he said. 'Go now. Get to Deptford Docks and don't look back.'

Amesbury realised Henrietta's dark eyes were narrowed at him.

'You expect me to believe you know nothing?' she said.

'No,' said Amesbury, 'I thought I knew who Thorne's apprentice was. But I was wrong.' He paused, choosing his words. 'The apprentice would have been young at the time,' he said. 'Barely a man. Perhaps a sheltered boy with an interest in astrology.'

Henrietta caught the implication, and her whole body tightened. Her narrow face seemed to retract in on itself, as though she were vanishing into her chair.

'I'll have you gutted,' she whispered. 'Your head will be paraded on a pike.' She closed her eyes tight.

'I made no accusation,' said Amesbury calmly. 'Named no name.'

'The Dutch seem to think they can find the Eye,' continued Amesbury.

Henrietta gave a little start in her chair.

'If you tell the truth,' she decided, 'my sons are in great danger.'

Amesbury nodded.

The old woman pursed her lips. 'Very well,' she said. 'I'll tell you.'

Chapter 72

Charlie and Lily had climbed back down into the secret tunnel under Custom House, leaving the attacking mob behind them. They reached the smashed map of the city, breathing hard.

'The last ring,' said Lily. 'We need to find the Temple of Venus. Quickly,' she added. 'It's only hours until sunset.'

Charlie closed his eyes, willing himself to think. Rowan's life depended on it.

Lily was looking at the broken mosaic of London.

'Much of the map is missing,' decided Charlie, 'but there are only seven Roman gods in astrology. Maybe we could find Venus by elimination.'

'We're assuming Venus's Temple is now a church?' asked Lily.

'An old church,' agreed Charlie. 'One of London's originals. We can discount St Olave's as Neptune,' he added, 'symbolised by a trident. And St Ursula's is the Bear Goddess. Diana, the Moon.' Charlie studied the rest of the smashed mosaic. 'I think this was an upturned arrow here,' he said, pointing, 'joined to part of a circle. Mars?' he added, calling to mind the symbol from Lily's almanac.

Lily nodded.

'It's on the site of St Martin's Church,' said Charlie. 'And something like it is also near Clerken Well and Aldgate. That's where St Martin's the Great and St Martin's on the Wall are today.'

'Mars became St Martin,' said Lily. 'Four remaining.'

Charlie scrutinised the wall. There were no clues left. He racked his mind for what he knew of Roman gods.

'What's missing?' said Lily. 'Which churches aren't on this map?'

'Many,' admitted Charlie. He scanned the broken pieces. 'All,' he admitted. 'And even if we knew which saint was Venus, she probably had several temples, like Mars and Jupiter. He pointed at the remains of the trident. 'There are at least three St Olave's churches inside the city too,' he added.

Something else occurred to Charlie. 'All Hallows' is the old festival of Venus,' he said. 'It's her season. Libra is ruled by Venus. Halloween is when people bob for apples and make marriage games.'

'Which means?'

'I think Venus,' said Charlie, 'is All Hallows church.'

Lily's eyes widened as she considered the possibility of this. 'But there are many All Hallows,' she said finally.

'Yes,' agreed Charlie. 'All Hallows by the Tower. All Hallows on the Wall.'

'It would take us a day to search them all,' said Lily. 'All Hallows' Eve is tonight.'

'There's something else,' said Charlie. 'My mother's sampler mentions sunset.'

'When the sun goes down, you shall return your pledge to Him,' said Lily, remembering.

'There is an All Hallows famed for sunsets,' said Charlie. 'All Hallows by the Tower. It's the oldest church in London. People used to come from outside the city to see the sunsets through the stained glass. It's one of the few windows not smashed by reformers in Cromwell's time.'

'Sounds like a long shot,' said Lily.

'Maybe not,' said Charlie. 'There are also Roman remains there. Thorne was fascinated with the old gods. Perhaps the tapestry was my mother's clue to find the last ring.' He thought for a moment. 'Although that does leave us with a problem,' he concluded, his thoughts drifting anxiously back to Rowan.

Lily rolled her eyes. 'Another one?'

'The last sunset before All Hallows' Eve is less than an hour from now,' said Charlie. 'And All Hallows by the Tower will be filled with smugglers tonight.'

'Smugglers go to church?'

'Not generally,' he said, 'but they do on All Hallows' Eve. Sailors are the most superstitious men you'll ever meet,' he added, 'and smugglers have a lot of dead friends.'

Chapter 73

The Judge stood over Ishmael Boney. He held the almanac.

'I've heard stories,' he said, 'from my pirate prisoners. They tell me of an Eye of Lucifer. A Temple of Venus hidden in London.'

Ishmael sighed. He didn't seem unduly frightened.

'You say you're a man of the stars,' he said. 'Surely you recognise the pentagram of Venus.' When the Judge didn't reply, he continued. 'Lucifer,' said Ishmael, 'means "light" in ancient Latin. It's another name for Venus. The Morning Star. The brightest star in the sky.' He spanned his hands. 'A long time ago,' he said, 'Christians decided the Roman goddesses were unholy. Venus and her pentagram became Lucifer, the fallen angel with his apple of temptation. And since Venus is Goddess of Love, Lucifer became associated with lust and sin.'

Ishmael held two hands apart. 'Lucifer,' he said, waving one, 'fallen angel of lust. Satan, the angel of death. They're two different gods. But we've interwoven them.' He knitted his hands together. 'The two old gods became intermingled and confused. One Devil representing death and darkness, lust and sin. Venus's apple became forbidden fruit, the temptation of Eve and reason for the Fall of Man.'

'You're telling me,' said the Judge, 'that this pentagram isn't a sign of Devil worship.'

'To astrologers it's a sign of heavenly love,' said Ishmael.

'And the Eye of Lucifer?'

'The third eye.' Ishmael touched his forehead. 'The higher understanding man forgoes to enjoy Venus's apple and pleasures of the flesh. It can gift men the power to see as no other sees. Venus's season is now,' he continued. 'Have you never wondered why we make marriage rituals and eat apples on All Hallows' Eve? Even our old churches celebrate the Love Goddess.'

The Judge managed a thin smile. 'All Hallows by the Tower,' he said slowly. 'The stained glass . . .' He paused, picturing the windows. 'Then you have just told me where I might find my errant gypsy.'

Chapter 74

The sun was already setting as Charlie and Lily neared All Hallows by the Tower.

All around were Londoners celebrating Halloween. Beggars and actors went from door to door, their faces painted ghoulishly, offering to chase away evil spirits for a few scraps of food. The scent of soul cakes was heavy on the air as poor children trooped to each house, offering prayers to the dead in return for fruited bread.

Apples hung on strings along the backstreets, and young people jostled to try and bite them or threw the peel over their shoulders to discover the initial of who they would marry.

'Many fear the eclipse,' said Lily, noting the hanging charms. 'Those people read Armageddon from the Bible.'

A trembling group of ragged Londoners lay on their backs looking up at the stars, praying fervently. Play-acting mummers had dressed in ghoulish masks and were casting their reflections to scare away evil spirits. Elsewhere people had barricaded their homes.

'You were right,' said Lily as they came close to the church. 'Smugglers.'

She was eyeing a couple of burly men sat tending a little fire. Locals were keeping a wide berth. The smugglers were standing next to the small carved bust of a woman.

'They've placed a ship's figurehead,' said Charlie, 'to show they've claimed All Hallows church for Halloween.'

The wooden figurehead was tiny by the standards of King Charles's grand warships. It stood a foot high, carved with a large ruff at her neck and a golden crown stretching over her wavy hair.

'Queen Elizabeth,' said Charlie. 'Sailors think her lucky.'

Charlie took in the lingering shafts of sunlight, racking his brains for a way to get inside the church. His eyes rested on a west-facing stained-glass window.

'Look,' he said.

Lily followed his line of sight. 'The four cherubims are pictured in the window,' said Lily, 'just like in the almanac.'

'And on my mother's tapestry,' said Charlie.

He breathed out, praying for Rowan's sake they'd found the right place. Thorne's Temple of Venus.

'Now all we need do is oust an entire crew of murderous smugglers,' said Lily sardonically. 'And the sun is nearly set.'

Charlie let his gaze track around the outside of the church, looking for opportunities. A patch of the roof was missing. Either tiles had been raided or weather had damaged it. But whatever had happened left Charlie with an idea of how to clear the church. If they could get up on the roof, the plan just might work.

Charlie considered the angle of the sun, assessing where light would fall.

'I have a plan,' Charlie assured her, 'to get those smugglers out. Do you think you can charm those mummers out of their mirror for a few minutes?' He nodded to an enthusiastic group of play-actors casting masked faces into a mirror to scare away the dead.

Lily assessed the troupe. 'Easy enough,' she decided. 'They're all men.'

'Good. We need to get the guards away from that figurehead.'

'How do we do that?' asked Lily, looking at the burly men with dismay.

Charlie grinned at her. 'On All Hallows' Eve,' he assured her, 'that's the easy part.' He picked up a handful of stones. 'All we need is a few restless spirits,' Charlie explained, 'and those two guards will scatter straight for the church. The hard part,' he added, 'will be getting them out again.'

Chapter 75

'You're sure this will work?' asked Lily as they climbed on to the roof of the church. 'I thought a camera obscura need to be dark inside.'

'I'm no astrologer,' admitted Charlie. 'It might not work. But we can't wait until after sunset. It will be too late. If it's not dark enough now, it never will be.'

They'd surmounted the roof of the church, Lily carrying a piece of broken mirror borrowed from the Halloween mummers and Charlie bearing the small ship's figurehead tucked under his arm. The hole in the tiles loomed beneath them, giving Charlie and Lily a bird's-eye view of the interior.

Ranged everywhere inside were smugglers. Some held crosses or offerings to dead friends. Others sipped rum and waved amulets against evil spirits whilst they talked and played cards.

'If it works,' said Charlie, looking down at the smugglers, 'it will cast a ghostly image of Queen Elizabeth on to the ground. On All Hallows' Eve I think that will be enough to scare a group of superstitious sailors out of the church.'

Lily nodded. The sound of smugglers drinking and carousing drifted up.

'Where shall I put the mirror?' she whispered, manoeuvring it.

Charlie called to mind the camera obscura they'd seen in Ishmael Boney's residence.

'Angle it that way,' he said, gesturing under the roof tiles, 'so the outside light falls on it.'

Charlie pulled the figurehead so she was reflected in the glass. Then he manipulated the mirror so it cast a beam of light on to the floor of the church.

A few smugglers eyed the flash of unexpected light. At first Charlie thought the effect hadn't worked, that the image couldn't be seen. Then he heard a hubbub of uncertainty drift up.

The gloomy church was dark enough to show a faint outline of Queen Elizabeth, transparent and ethereal. But it wasn't the full ghostly effect that Charlie had hoped for.

The smugglers were gathered around the pale image. Several were clutching their amulets or pointing and gesticulating. But they weren't leaving. Then an unearthly noise echoed through the night sky. Charlie's blood turned to ice. It was a shriek like the waking dead. Beneath him the smugglers scattered.

Charlie turned to see Lily, a fist twisted strangely over her mouth. She drew breath, and he suddenly realised the dreadful sound had come from her.

Lily dropped her hand. 'Did it work?' she asked. 'Are the smugglers gone?'

Charlie nodded. 'How did you do that?'

'It's an owl call,' said Lily proudly. 'I learned it as a girl.'

'Come on,' said Charlie. 'We can climb down and get into the church through the back window. We'd better hurry,' he added. 'It might not be long until the smugglers realise they were tricked.'

~

Charlie and Lily slipped into All Hallows by the Tower. It was bigger than it looked from outside, with rows of long pews. The remains of a large altar stood at one end, large in the Tudor style.

Lily looked to the west side of the church, where the four cherubims were immortalised in the stained glass, flying around the red cross. The stained glass cast long bands of coloured light in the setting sun. They dappled the stone floor in a beautiful kaleidoscope.

Charlie moved away from the window, taking out his mother's sampler.

'You think the answer in the window?' said Lily. 'But how are we supposed to decipher it?'

Charlie held up the sampler. The scenes didn't match perfectly. But the cherubims were unmistakably the same, their animal heads staring out.

'The window has been here a long time,' he said. 'My mother must have stitched this later. Perhaps the differences in the scenes are significant.'

But so far as he could tell it was just an ordinary window, installed years ago with the others when the church was built.

'Sunset,' he said, thinking aloud. 'What changes at sunset?'

He followed the pattern of the light. It formed a long finger on the floor, with the arched tip pointing to the centre of the church.

'The light makes a kind of arrow shape,' he suggested. 'The light from the window is stretched further at sunset.'

'It points to the nave,' said Lily, turning to look. 'But there's nothing there.'

They stared into the empty space, shadowed in the dwindling evening light.

'Something astrological?' pondered Charlie. 'A constellation reflected somewhere else in the church?'

Lily looked around. 'Taurus, Leo, Aquarius and Scorpio,' she said. 'I can only see ordinary saints and images from the Bible.'

'Thorne wasn't religious,' said Charlie. 'At sunset make your pledge. Perhaps there's a deeper meaning.'

Outside the church the sky was growing dark.

'The light will soon be gone,' said Charlie. He was looking at the evening sun flooding through the church window, painting the floor with coloured light.

Leading in the stained glass cut the tinted light into distinct shapes – rectangles, squares and diamonds. It was like a magnificent painting on the plain floor.

Something occurred to Charlie. Slowly he unfurled his mother's tapestry, holding it taut.

'The stained glass makes a pattern on the floor,' he observed. 'What if the sampler fits into that somehow? Reveals something?'

Lily turned to the vast pool of coloured light. 'Perhaps there,' she suggested. 'It makes a rectangle around the right size.'

Charlie laid the tapestry carefully on the floor, allowing the rainbow of refracted light to fall on his mother's sewing. Beams of red, green and blue cascaded on to the stitched cherubims. It fitted perfectly, the edges of the tapestry squaring off with where the thick leading of the large window broke the light.

They both stared at the tapestry. But no obvious answer appeared in the cloth.

'Can you see anything?' asked Lily, looking at the light.

'No,' said Charlie. He assessed the dappled colours. 'The light from the window blends in places,' he pointed out uncertainly.

Lily looked up at the window. 'Maybe we're too late,' she said. 'The sunset time is almost gone.'

Charlie thought for a moment. Then he twisted the sampler around. 'Perhaps if we align it,' he said, 'so the picture on the sampler is in the same direction as the window . . .'

'There!' Lily pointed excitedly. 'The colours make a shape! Look!'

Chapter 76

'My marriage was not like modern marriages,' said Queen Henrietta. 'My King was God's appointee on earth.'

She eyed Amesbury, daring him to disagree. He said nothing.

'My husband confided in me,' continued Henrietta. 'Thorne was building him a very powerful weapon. But in order to build it, certain practices were carried out.' She hesitated.

'What practices?' pressed Amesbury.

'Dead reckoning,' said Henrietta. 'Thorne was studying dead reckoning.'

'Dropping a weight from a ship to gauge the speed of the current?' confirmed Amesbury, surprised that the Queen was familiar with the term.

'Thorne was using floats to gather information on the movements of the moon,' she explained. 'The tides and currents give valuable information.'

'Floats?' asked Amesbury uncomfortably.

'Thorne wanted access to Dead Man's Curve,' continued Henrietta, 'to observe the moon's influence on the tides. He tried all kinds of ways to chart the flow of the Thames. But all were frustrated. Anything he put in at London Bridge was fished out and stolen by mudlarks.'

She was silent, leaving the general to infer the rest.

'The only things that made it downriver,' Amesbury supplied in a tired voice, 'were corpses.'

'My husband never told me . . . exactly,' said Henrietta. 'But I know convicts were taken from the prisons. I saw the King's face when he returned from his meetings with Thorne. And I was at his side when he kneeled in chapel every spare moment, praying for forgiveness.'

'The old King thought he had offended God?'

'Thorne insisted on returning the bodies to the river as some kind of offering,' said Henrietta. 'Some heathen practice.' She shuddered again. 'Their souls were damned in any case.'

Amesbury considered this. 'Someone is copying Thorne's work,' he said. 'Bodies are washing up once more.'

'No,' said Henrietta. 'That cannot be.'

Amesbury blinked. 'Why not?'

Henrietta fixed Amesbury with her mean little eyes. 'Thorne realised he'd been mistaken. Charting the stars was only part of what he needed to develop the power of the Eye.'

'Then what did he need?'

'He asked for jewels, exotic woods and gold,' said Henrietta, 'Thorne locked himself away with many tools. My husband never forgave himself. Those dead girls had been for nothing. So as you see,' she continued, 'it was a mistake that my husband spent the rest of his life trying to atone for.'

Chapter 77

Inside All Hallows church the sun had almost set.

Charlie stared at his mother's tapestry. A large portion now matched the light from the window exactly – red to red, blue to blue, green to green.

'The tapestry was made to reveal something when placed under this window,' said Charlie. 'Some kind of shape.' He pointed to the stitching.

Standing out against the matching colours was a dark patch. It made the shape of a cross, with a distinct spot of red light in the corner.

'A cross with a red dot?' said Lily. 'What does it mean?'

Charlie's mind addressed the problem logically, forcing down the growing panic that finding no answer could forfeit his brother Rowan's life. His finger followed the shape of the cross. Then the answer presented itself from the tapestry in front of him.

'It's a map,' said Charlie. 'This church is a cross shape. It's a plan of the interior.'

He stabbed a finger at the red spot of light. 'So this must be the ruby ring.'

Charlie sprung to his feet, staring around All Hallows.

'If the tapestry makes a floor plan for the church,' he said, 'the ring would be over there. In that far corner.'

They both turned, assessing the direction the stained glass revealed. At the back of the building was a large stone statue, exactly matching the red dot of light on their map.

'There's something there,' said Lily. 'A saint statue.'

They raced over to it.

'St Lucia,' said Charlie as they reached the statue. 'Saint of Light.'

The statue was a grey stone girl dressed in a flowing dress and holding a torch. She had a crown bearing a five-pointed star.

'Lucifer to Lucia,' said Charlie. 'She even wears the Morning Star.' He touched the pentagram at her crown.

'We're in All Hallows church,' Lily pointed out. 'The name represents the season of Venus.'

Charlie's trained eye was moving carefully over the stonework. 'Lucia wears a ring,' he said. 'Unusual for a saint.' He raised a finger and tapped it. 'Clay,' he said. 'Not stone. This was added later.' He took out his knife and scraped at the stone ring. Dusty clay showered down. A glint of red shone out.

'The ruby!' said Lily excitedly, moving to help pick away the pieces of clay.

'It must have been here all these years,' said Charlie. 'Hidden in plain sight. And no one noticed their saint had a new ring.'

Charlie had a sudden surge of hope. Midnight was hours away. Perhaps they could find where Thorne had hidden the Eye and use it to gain Rowan's freedom.

Lily was pulling off the ring. 'There's something wedged inside,' she said. 'A roll of paper.' She uncurled it. 'It looks like . . .' She frowned. 'A list of ingredients.'

Lily read them aloud.

3 pints vinegar
4 oz. alum
1 oz. gum Arabic
4 oz. finely rasped Brazil wood
She turned to Charlie in puzzlement.

'What does it mean?' she asked.

Charlie contemplated.

'Brazil wood is used to make fine furniture and instruments,' he said. 'A highly smuggled commodity. Pirates are always on the lookout for it. It's worth a fortune.'

'Queen Catherine's dowry came with Brazil wood furniture,' said Lily uncertainly. 'It's displayed in Whitehall.' She frowned. 'Why would anyone want to shave it down and mix it with vinegar?' asked Lily, looking at the recipe.

'Perhaps it has some exotic purpose,' said Charlie. 'Some Aztec medicine. Alchemy. Though I've never heard of Brazil wood used that way.'

'The recipe was put there deliberately,' said Lily. 'A clue to finding the Eye?'

'Could be,' said Charlie. 'We now have all four rings. Let's fit them together and see what happens.'

They took out the other three rings and joined them. The jewellery clicked seamlessly into place to make a large ruby cross, banded by gold, with the circular bands hanging down on the underside.

Charlie turned them in his hands, hoping for clues as to how they might solve a code. But there was nothing.

'The rings don't seem to make any shapes or signs,' said Charlie disappointedly, turning them in his hand. He passed the rings to Lily and took out Thorne's *Chart of All Hallows' Eve*.

'Nothing I can see,' said Lily, looking at the rings. 'Is there something on the chart that could solve it?'

Charlie scanned the *Chart of All Hallows' Eve*, shaking his head. He looked over to where his mother's tapestry lay on the floor, under the dappled light of the stained glass, thinking it might help them.

Charlie froze. The tapestry was gone. Instinctively his gaze spun to the door. A dark figure stood blocking entrance.

'Well, well,' said a cold voice. 'Looks like the little gypsy thief and her thief taker have found us some treasure.'

Chapter 78

Janus was sailing east to Deptford, where he was certain the Eye was concealed.

With the wind behind him, Janus felt calmer. On passing Custom House he'd learned of a fracas from the local boatmen. This could only mean one thing – Charlie Oakley was still hunting the Eye.

This realisation had initially disconcerted Janus. The thief taker wasn't as sentimental as Janus had expected. He'd underestimated his opponent – perhaps Tobias Oakley's son was a worthy adversary after all. But even if Charlie Oakley found all the rings, Janus would easily beat him to where the Eye was hidden.

He smiled bitterly. Who'd have thought a simple man of no rank or birth could challenge Janus, with his fine name, his legacy?

He turned the little ship, catching the wind, and let the breeze carry him downriver. Janus still had enough time to get to Thorne's lost treasure before it was destroyed at midnight.

The Thames was beginning to curve now, churning the river to a fast-moving eddy. Janus dropped the sail and prepared to let the water take him.

He saw a dark shape on the water. The bloated body of a dead calf had been carried downriver. Something about it tugged at his mind.

The sacrificial remains in Thorne's cellar.

Janus closed his eyes, trying to chase away the helpless boy inside. He saw himself dangling from the grip of the dark god, his flesh torn by the bared teeth. Then he was back in the familiar nightmare, where the silence of the dark Thames closed over his screams, cold water rushing into his ears, his mouth.

But now Janus considered, he had never seen Thorne bring the children back. Only seen the bones mount up and known the master meant to kill him next. His eyes settled on the stinking corpse on the river. How long did it take for flesh to strip away from bone? Months? Years?

Janus felt suddenly as though Thorne's godlike status was peeling away, and his own self with it. He put a hand on the undulating prow, trying to draw stability from the hard wood.

It's no evil thing I did, he reminded himself. *Those people were condemned to hell. I only mark them with the star of Venus, the Love Goddess. They go to a better afterlife than the church offers. The silver coin pays their way.*

Janus fixed his concentration on the sails of the tiny ship. He negotiated the bulging waters expertly, letting his sails bloom again in the wind and righting his course east to Deptford. But his hands were shaking.

Suddenly he couldn't be certain what about his past was real and what wasn't.

Thorne had made a great revelation before Janus fled to Holland. The stars didn't hold all the answers. The Broken Things and star charts were important. But ultimately Thorne's attention had been elsewhere in those last few months in England.

Had Thorne taught him everything and nothing at all?

Chapter 79

Charlie looked towards the door.

There stood Judge Walters, a pistol directed at them. He was flanked on both sides by two burly men. Prison guards from Marshalsea by the look of them, Charlie decided. Not men he wanted to cross.

'You.' The Judge was pointing at Lily, his pale face tight with fury. 'You stole something belonging to me. I will have it back and watch you drown for your crime.'

Charlie felt Lily's hand drop to where her knives were.

'Perhaps Ishmael Boney was right after all,' added the Judge. 'The legendary Eye is real and you may lead me to it.'

Charlie logged this. So the Judge knew where Ishmael was.

The Judge moved closer to Charlie. He pointed to the rings and *Chart of All Hallows' Eve*.

'Throw down the jewellery,' he said, 'and the paper. Or you'll watch the gypsy die slowly.'

'Don't,' whispered Lily.

Charlie shook his head. 'I've already endangered my brother,' he said. 'I won't risk you.'

He threw down the rings and the chart. The Judge darted forward and scooped them up.

'The map to the Eye of Heaven,' he breathed. 'And the rings to read it. This is some treasure indeed.' A nasty expression of triumph crossed his features. 'My trade shall rule the oceans,' he said. 'Every heathen and gypsy shall be shipped back to their rightful servitude.'

'I am in the King's employ,' announced Lily.

'You're a thief,' spat Walters, 'like all gypsies. You'll die without your spymasters even knowing we met.'

Lily opened her mouth and shut it again.

'Where is it?' demanded the Judge. 'Where is the Eye of Heaven?'

'We don't know,' said Charlie.

'Take a knife,' hissed Walters to the nearest guard, 'and cut off the gypsy's fingers.'

'Wait!' shouted Charlie as the man grabbed Lily roughly. 'I'm telling you the truth. It's a mystery we can't solve.'

'So London's famed thief taker is finally bested,' said Walters with a humourless smile. 'Somehow I can't believe that.' He considered them both for a moment.

'You can't make us talk,' said Charlie.

'What are you doing?' hissed Lily. 'This isn't a man to be baited . . .'

Charlie touched her arm. 'Trust me,' he whispered.

'Very well,' said Judge Walters. 'If you think yourselves so brave, a spell on my prison hulk will afford us some entertainment.' He turned to the guards. 'Take them to the ship. We'll see how tight-lipped you are,' he added, 'when you see what tools I have for my convicts.'

'I hope you know what you're doing,' said Lily as burly men grabbed them and pushed them from the church.

'So do I,' said Charlie. 'We can't solve the code without Ishmael Boney. And I think we'll find him on the Judge's ship.'

Chapter 80

The guards led Charlie and Lily up the gangplank of the dark prison hulk. Up close it was even more mouldering and dank than it looked from the water. The huge round-bellied hull had been extended upwards with several rambling roofed structures. They shuttered off most of the open decks, making the ship dark and enclosed.

'We need to solve Thorne's code before midnight,' explained Charlie. 'This is the fastest way I could think of.'

Lily's eyes widened. 'Are you insane?'

They'd entered a warren of rotting wooden corridors shambolically erected on deck. Over their heads they could hear the squawks of nesting seagulls, who had made the meandering rooftops their home.

A smoky fire had been lit and a vast cauldron of indiscernible slops bubbled. The Judge and his guards led Charlie and Lily downwards through a narrow set of stairs and then down again. Now the only daylight visible was from tiny portholes, over which had been hammered heavy bars.

'I think Ishmael Boney is down there,' said Charlie. 'Think about it. We face a painful death if we don't discover where the Eye is hidden. Ishmael Boney could be our chance.'

'That's your plan?' said Lily. 'To give the location to Judge Walters?' Her face bore an expression of deep betrayal.

'The Dutch are coming,' said Charlie. 'All will be chaos by All Saints' Day tomorrow. If the Judge finds it at all, he'll likely be too late, and the extra time might give us a chance to escape.'

They passed by a thick stench that told Charlie deceased prisoners were housed in an adjoining room, before the ship sailed downriver to offload on Dead Man's Island.

'What about Rowan?' asked Lily quietly as the smell was gradually replaced by rank odours of close human occupancy. 'You'd risk your brother for me?'

'I have to be realistic,' said Charlie, not meeting her gaze. 'Besides,' he added, 'I thought you didn't care about Rowan.'

'I don't,' said Lily, 'or Judge Walters.'

'Then who do you care about?'

'Isn't it obvious?'

A guard was opening a large gridded trapdoor, and the Judge turned to address them.

'You're fortunate,' he said. 'Most died of cholera this week, so it's not so crowded. We're waiting on another consignment from the Marshalsea.'

The guard led them down steep wooden steps into a dark prison deck. Bolted to the planked floor at every half yard was a set of cruel-looking leg irons. Lying around were a handful of morose prisoners, pale and thin. Charlie scanned the prisoners, looking for someone who could be Ishmael Boney. But all the men looked too long in residence and poorly dressed.

Lily was looking around in horror. 'It's an old slave quarters,' she said. 'You must have packed them in like cattle.'

'This old hulk was my first slave carrier,' confirmed the Judge, seeming pleased at her reaction. 'The cargo decks are still very useful. Very *secure*.' His single eye settled on Lily. 'A great deal of your kind were once sold from this ship, along with the negroes. We trade with faster craft now, and when I have the Eye I'll buy an entire fleet.'

Charlie was thinking of Rowan, held captive somewhere. He tried not to imagine the hundreds of desolate people who'd been chained here, sailing to terror and servitude.

Judge Walters's pearly eyepatch twitched. 'My prison guards always enjoy a keelhauling,' he added. 'A gypsy will make particularly good entertainment for them. They're making the arrangements for you now.' He smiled coldly. 'You've never seen a keelhauling?' he guessed. 'It's a trick I learned from pirates. String a rope from stern to bow, attach your prisoner to one end and pull him underwater the full length of the ship.'

The Judge gestured to indicate the great size of the hulk, watching Lily's face closely for a reaction. She was staring at him, eyes burning with hatred.

'I've made some improvements to the practice,' he continued. 'You'll see them soon. Unless,' he added, 'you tell me how to find the Eye.'

Lily was about to spit a retort when Charlie stopped her.

'We told you the truth,' he said, 'about the rings and the paper. But we know more than you. If you leave them with us, we can tell you where the Eye is hidden. We only need time.'

Walters considered this. 'Very well,' he said, pulling them from his coat. 'I'll grant you one last request.' He eyed the dwindling twilight cast from the open trapdoor. 'You have an hour,' he said. 'If you don't reveal it, I'll have an answer out of you by force.'

The Judge turned, and they watched his silver-buckled shoes ascend the narrow ladder. Guards followed behind and the trapdoor slammed shut. They heard a heavy bolt sliding into place.

'He's a monster,' said Lily, looking around. 'Charlie, we can't give him the Eye. I'd rather drown.' Her eyes burned fiercely.

'It might not come to that,' said Charlie. He took in the dark quarters, his eyes landing methodically on each prisoner. Then he saw a small man with his arms wrapped around his knees, sitting as far away as possible from the other prisoners.

He had dark skin, thick curling hair and his clothes were scholarly – a black robe finished with a neat collar.

Charlie approached. 'Ishmael Boney?' he asked.

Two brown eyes looked up. They scanned Charlie and rested on the key at his neck.

'It's you,' he said. 'Charlie Oakley.'

Chapter 81

Charlie and Lily stared at Ishmael. The dark prison brig rolled underfoot.

'You know me?' said Charlie finally.

'No,' he said, 'but I recognise your key. Thorne told me about you.'

'Did you know Thorne?' asked Charlie.

Ishmael pressed his lips together and looked away sadly.

'We hoped,' pressed Lily, 'you might be able to help us.'

The astrologer stayed silent.

'We found a chart,' said Charlie, 'with your papers. A *Chart of All Hallows' Eve* once belonging to a man named Thorne. I think you knew him well.' He paused, watching Ishmael's face. 'I think you were his lover.'

Ishmael's eyes flicked up sharply. 'What do you know of Thorne?' he said after a moment.

'He knew my mother,' said Charlie. 'Sally Oakley.'

'Sally.' Ishmael gave a faint smile. 'The wife.'

'They were married?' said Charlie.

'A marriage of convenience,' said Ishmael. 'Arranged by the families. I don't know if they ever saw one another for more than a few hours after the wedding day. Thorne was not inclined to a bride.' His eyes met Charlie's. 'As you seem to know.'

'It's true then,' said Charlie. 'You were his lover?'

Ishmael nodded. He looked very sad.

'I was Thorne's apothecary for a short time, just before his imprisonment. He had nightmares of being burned, and I prescribed him sleep tinctures. We were both interested in astrology and our friendship became something more.'

'Did Thorne have an apprentice?' asked Charlie. 'A boy named Janus?'

'There was a boy,' agreed Ishmael slowly. 'Under Thorne's protection. I think his identity must have been important. He was kept confined for his own safety.'

'Confined?' asked Charlie. 'Thorne was cruel to his apprentice?'

Ishmael shook his head. 'Thorne was strict with the boy from necessity. It was a terrible war and important children were in danger. Thorne was a genius,' he added. 'He was never recognised for it. People spoke of him as evil. But he was a good man, tortured in his soul. He loved that child.'

'You never knew who the boy apprentice was?' pressed Charlie.

'All I know is Janus's identity was a close secret,' said Ishmael. 'If you knew who he was, you could likely defeat him.'

'I don't want to defeat him,' said Charlie. 'I only want for us to escape here and free my brother.'

Ishmael nodded. 'Thorne spoke of passing on wisdom,' he said. 'He left me a letter, requesting I publish his *Chart of All Hallows' Eve* a few weeks before tonight's eclipse. He never told me what the Eye was, and I respected his wishes and didn't ask. But he did tell me that if the Eye wasn't found before midnight it would be destroyed. Lost forever.'

Charlie felt hopes for his brother slipping away. Midnight was only a few hours away. Unless Charlie was able to use the Eye to bargain, Janus would have no reason to keep Rowan alive.

'The Dutch know about the Eye,' said Charlie. 'They're set to find it tonight. Thorne's apprentice has turned traitor.'

Ishmael's eyes widened. 'That cannot be,' he said. 'The Eye is powerful. If it falls into the wrong hands . . .'

'Help us,' said Charlie, tapping the paper. 'Help us discover it.'

Ishmael's eyes dropped to the chart.

'I can't solve this,' he said.

Lily moved forward. 'Please,' she said, taking his dark hand in hers. 'You must try.'

But Ishmael only shook his head sadly. 'I can't,' he said. 'This chart is not true astrology. It's a nonsense.'

'What?' Charlie shouted the word in his surprise.

'Thorne's *Chart of All Hallows' Eve*,' said Ishmael, 'maps no future planetary movements. As an astrological chart it's completely meaningless. He must have made it for some other purpose.'

Chapter 82

The rings and *Chart of All Hallows' Eve* were laid out on the swaying floor of the prison brig. Charlie and Lily were staring at Ishmael.

'The star signs on the rings symbolise only the ring bearers,' said Ishmael eventually. 'One for each. Nothing more that I can see.'

He was turning the cross of rubies carefully in his hands.

'But they must read the chart!' Lily's voice had risen in frustration.

Ishmael tapped the markings on the *Chart of All Hallows' Eve*.

'Thorne was a far greater astrologer than I,' he said, 'but his *Chart of All Hallows' Eve* doesn't show the planets as they move. Even I can tell you that. Saturn is high, but it will not collide with Jupiter. Such a thing isn't possible.'

'Why would Thorne do that?' asked Lily. 'Why would he make a false chart?'

'We know the *Chart of All Hallows' Eve* is coded,' said Charlie. 'Perhaps it's part of the code. The rings must tell us more,' he added. 'They must give the exact location. But how?'

They were all silent. The clues seemed to have run out.

'What of the recipe?' said Charlie, pulling out the slip of paper they'd found inside the ring.

Ishmael regarded the list, scanning it. 'Vinegar, alum, gum Arabic,' he read, 'and powdered Brazil wood.'

'Perhaps Brazil wood is used in astrology,' said Charlie hopefully, 'to make some astrological tool.'

'I've only seen Brazil wood used for its good red colour,' said Ishmael, 'to make furniture, violins and the like. It's not used in astrology.'

'Some metals are signified by planets,' suggested Charlie. 'Wood also?'

Ishmael spread his dark hands. 'Iron for Mars, lead for Saturn,' he agreed. 'But not wood. That is something of druids and pagans. And Brazil wood wasn't known in those times,' he concluded.

They examined the rings again.

'Is there nothing?' said Lily desperately, 'nothing else in the pattern of the astrology symbols?'

Ishmael shook his head. 'I'm sorry,' he said. 'Nothing that I can see. Thorne had a chance to flee with me to Holland,' he added, closing his eyes tight at the memory, 'but he insisted on returning to a secret workshop to hide the Eye. That was when they captured him.' His dark eyes looked up at Charlie. 'If you knew where his workshop was,' he said, 'that's likely where the Eye is hidden.'

Above them they heard the trapdoor creak and open. Dark shoes descended the wooden ladder. And then Judge Walters was down with them.

'Your time is up,' he said. 'Do you have an answer for me?'

'You promised us an hour . . .' began Lily.

Walters raised a hand. 'My guards are anxious for their entertainment. I am not of a mind to afford a thief any more courtesies. I have been more than generous. It's time for justice.'

Chapter 83

As the prison guards pulled Charlie up on deck, the piece of paper he'd found in the last ring fluttered to the ground. One of the guards swooped down triumphantly and snatched it up.

'What is it?' demanded Judge Walters impatiently.

'Perhaps a clue to the Eye,' said the guard, passing the paper.

The Judge grabbed it in his pale fingers. 'It's nothing,' said Walters dismissively. 'Only an old ink recipe.'

He held it up, letting the breeze take it fluttering over the side of the ship and into the dark waters below. Charlie watched it fall helplessly, realising it might have been their last chance to solve Thorne's code.

An ink recipe.

Things were matching up in Charlie's head. But he couldn't quite bring them together.

'Keelhaul the gypsy,' said the Judge. He gave an evil smile. 'We have a different style of torture here,' he said, watching her face for a reaction. 'Pirates duck men lengthways to drown, but we don't do that.' He waited for Lily to respond, and when his victim's answer was unforthcoming continued speaking. 'We keelhaul side to side. That way you drag across the hull, where the barnacles are. This old hulk hasn't had her undersides scraped in ten years,' he concluded. 'You won't drown on the first ducking and my men take bets on whether the lacerations kill you before you breathe water.'

'I would never give you the satisfaction.' Lily's face was set in cold defiance.

The Judge smiled. 'We'll see.'

Two guards grabbed Lily by her small shoulders.

'Wait!' Charlie stepped forward.

The Judge glared. 'Your turn will come,' he said.

'She can help you find the Eye,' said Charlie desperately. 'If you kill her, it will be lost forever.'

The Judge's face twisted into a smile. 'How pathetic,' he said. 'London's famed thief taker has been seduced by a gypsy whore.'

Lily writhed against her captors, trying to strike at the Judge. He paused, taking in her face.

'I remember the night you stole my ring,' he said. 'You had the same rage in your eyes when I told you about my gypsy slave ships,' he added, 'but the fight in you won't last long underwater.'

Lily struck back against the guards holding her and this time she managed to get a hand free. Her nails raked across the Judge's face, leaving a trail of bloody claw marks. He gave a hiss of pain and stepped back, holding his scratched face in rage.

The Judge gestured to his men, clicking his fingers irritably.

'Duck the thief taker first. Bring the gypsy to the side of the ship. Let her watch the life bleed out of her friend.'

'No!' The colour had dropped from Lily's face. 'Please,' she whispered.

Charlie felt rough hands take hold of him. Two large guards were pushing him to the edge of the deck.

He glanced at Lily, trying to signal she should attempt an escape. But her face was a mask of devastation, her lips moving silently.

The guards slammed Charlie against the side of the ship. A dripping rope was brought up from the deep. He felt strangely detached as the guards pulled it tight around his waist, as though it was happening to someone else. Below him the swirling Thames mirrored Charlie's churning thoughts.

An ink recipe. The rings. Thorne's Chart of All Hallows' Eve.

Lily was looking down, her lips moving in silent prayer. The Judge grabbed her long dark hair and forced her head towards the side of the ship.

'I want to be sure you watch,' he said. 'We'll see if you're so defiant when you know what awaits.'

One of the guards holding Charlie leaned in close.

'Wait!' Lily had found her voice and was screaming.

Charlie thought she sounded far away. Pieces of Thorne's code were coming together, but too slowly. Charlie was certain he knew the answer. But it refused to be dredged from his mind.

'He knows how to solve the paper!' said Lily. 'Look at his face. Charlie is the cleverest thief taker in London. If you send him to his death, you'll lose any chance to find the Eye.'

'Enough talking,' commanded the Judge. 'Throw him overboard.'

Charlie felt himself raised up to the edge of the ship. A guard leaned close.

'We reckon there's colonies of sharp things tall enough to take off your head,' he grinned. 'Least that's what happened to the last man we dragged fore and aft. Enjoy your dip.' And he shoved Charlie forward hard.

Even as he tumbled overboard, Charlie's buzzing thoughts were trained on the problem. It was only when he hit the waves that he remembered to breathe in before the water closed over him.

The Thames struck him like a punch to the face and he felt his head fling back at the impact. The rope tightened around his middle, and he was wrenched under, away from the sunlight and down to the deep.

Charlie's first awareness was the cold seizing his limbs. Then a huge shape loomed. The hull of the ship, impossibly large, appeared before him. It was clustered with mysterious protrusions, misshapen, some several feet in length like enormous fingers. Colonies of razor-sharp barnacles had swelled to outrageously sized groupings from years in mild tropical waters.

Charlie saw the first overgrowth come directly for him at head height. On the ship above guards had begun heaving on his rope, pulling him fast towards the hull. Desperately Charlie made an ungainly underwater roll, missing the towering structure but sending his prone body crashing against the hull.

He put out his hands and felt barnacles lacerate his palms. Then the rope dragged him backwards, grinding his shoulder blades against the rough hull. Charlie gritted his teeth. He swivelled into a ball, pushed out with his feet and managed to clear the next protrusion unharmed.

He could make out the beam of the hull now. There was another half of barnacle-wreathed ship to endure, and he could see blood from his injured hands eddying into the water. As his lungs began to constrict, a muddled image floated up.

Charlie saw the rubies flashing, imagined himself looking deep into their red depths.

The rings are an illusion. Thorne's secret is in the rubies.

He drove away the floating pictures, refusing to give up. The sharp barnacles came towards him again and Charlie thought desperately for a way to protect his hands. He pulled at the thick rope, but the knot was impossible to budge and the hemp cord too sturdy to be cut by the sharp hull.

Then it occurred to him that the strong bindings could be an advantage.

Pulling hard, he tugged back a portion of rope and wrapped it around his bleeding fists. This time, as the barnacles loomed, he extended a ball of tough hemp and bounced off harmlessly.

Now he needed to build a rhythm, letting his protected hands strike the sharp hull at intervals, pushing away with his feet.

The technique almost worked. At one point the rope yanked him hard sideways and he lurched, feeling his arm snare. But for the most part he kept his body and head free. His lungs were bursting now and he looked up. A faraway pinpoint of light could be seen, and he had to prevent himself from gasping in relief.

Moonlight! But it seemed so far away.

The lack of air was blurring his vision now, his hands and feet growing clumsy. They slipped from the hull, bouncing him and opening a long cut on his side.

Don't breathe in.

A red light was shining through the water. Moonlight, stained from the eclipse. And just like that, Charlie saw it. He saw how the rings solved the code.

Then air broke across his face and he gasped. He felt himself lifted up and out, dangling like a fish on a hook. The hard deck slammed against his back, knocking the air out of him.

He turned on his side, coughing and spluttering, choking out salty Thames water. Through the daze he saw Lily. Warmth oozed from a cut in his side and his palms were on fire, but the relief on her face told him his injuries weren't severe.

'He's barely hurt,' said the rough voice of a guard. He sounded disappointed. 'Those barnacles should have cut him all over.'

'Give him another dip.' It was the Judge's voice. 'We'll see more blood when he drops unconscious.'

'Wait,' said Charlie, the words coming thickly. 'Wait.'

But before he could get the words out his chest went into spasm, hacking water from deep in his lungs.

The guards began hauling him to his feet, pushing him back to the edge of the ship.

'The Eye,' gasped Charlie.

Walters hesitated.

'I can solve Thorne's code,' Charlie breathed. 'I know how to locate the Eye.'

Chapter 84

King Charles raised his hand to knock on Frances Stewart's door. He hesitated, hardly able to believe his luck. Completely unprompted, she'd coyly suggested she might welcome a king's visit to her room.

For a moment he thought he heard voices inside and wondered if Barbara was here with her. He wished suddenly he'd not drunk quite so much wine.

Charles lowered his fist and knocked loudly. Almost immediately he heard Frances's girlish voice sail forth.

'Come in!' she called.

Charles pushed open the door. To his delight, Frances was in bed, half dressed, the covers pulled up high. For a full few seconds he was in complete bliss. The object of his desires was finally within reach. He decided then and there he would try to make her his Queen.

Then his slightly blurred vision made out another figure sitting by her bed.

He could hardly believe it.

Buckingham.

Lady Castlemaine's old lover was perched on the white coverlet, his dark hair tied in a ponytail, long leather boots crossed casually.

Buckingham was horrified to see the King. He stood uncertainly, stumbling slightly on Frances's rug.

'Your Majesty,' he stammered, bowing clumsily.

'Buckingham.' Charles's voice was icy. 'What are you doing in a lady-of-waiting's bedchamber?'

'I . . .' Buckingham couldn't answer.

'You are aware,' thundered Charles furiously, 'this girl is but fifteen and unmarried. How dare you!'

'Your Majesty,' began Buckingham again, his eyes on Frances.

'I'll have you hanged,' raged Charles, 'for offending this lady's honour!'

'Your Majesty.' Frances was speaking now, letting the cover fall a little. 'Did your Queen not tell you?'

Charles twisted towards her drunkenly. 'My Queen? Catherine?'

Frances nodded demurely. 'Her Majesty Queen Catherine has granted permission for us to be married,' said Frances smoothly. Her brown eyes settled on Buckingham, whose face was aghast. 'Buckingham is my fiancé,' she added, 'and means to remove me from court to his country seat.'

Deep hurt flashed on Charles's face. For a moment it looked as though he might erupt in fury again.

'Your Majesty,' said Frances, speaking quickly, 'you know how sensible I am of the great honours you have done me. But if I might not receive my own fiancé into my chamber, I am no better than a prisoner.'

There was a tense silence.

Charles hung his head suddenly. 'I didn't know,' he mumbled, 'how you felt.' He swung uncertainly, not sure which way the door was. Tears pricked his eyes and he raised a hand to hide them. 'I must speak with the Queen,' he mumbled finally, more to himself than anyone else. He forced himself to stand tall and marched straight-backed from the room.

As the door thudded shut, Buckingham turned to Frances in horror.

'Your fiancé?' he said. 'Have you any idea what kind of trouble you've gotten me into?'

'Yes,' said Frances, 'I do. The King will be furious with you, and you'll never be allowed back at court. But I think His Majesty loves me well enough to spare your life. I'll petition for us to be granted use of your family seat and lands outside London.'

'You wish to be my bride?' said Buckingham. He looked to be seriously considering the idea now.

'I wish to leave court,' said Frances. 'You have your faults, but I think you a good man deep down. I believe I could learn to love you.' She gave a small smile. 'You told me,' she said, 'to learn to play the courtly games. Well, now I have.'

'We could never come to court,' said Buckingham. 'The King would be too angry.'

'I never want to come back to court,' said Frances. 'I am tired of the intrigues and the rules. At Whitehall an unmarried girl is a pawn for people like you and Lady Castlemaine to shuffle around. I want to be queen of my own simple life. Married and honest. And you are to be my rescuer,' she added firmly, 'whether you like it or not.'

Chapter 85

Charlie pulled himself upright, his clothes dripping with Thames water. The deck of Judge Walters's prison ship felt reassuringly solid beneath him.

Lily broke free from the guards holding her and rushed to Charlie's side. She wrapped her arms around him, staring into his face in concern.

'I can solve the paper,' said Charlie as Lily helped him into a seated position.

Walters's eyes widened in distrust. 'Then do it,' he said after a moment. The Judge flung the *Chart of All Hallows' Eve* towards him.

Charlie knelt and spread the paper on the floor. 'I think parts of the chart,' he said, 'are written in a different colour ink.'

Lily stared. 'The recipe,' she said. 'The Judge said it was for ink.'

'I assumed it must be some exotic alchemy or medicine,' said Charlie. 'When Walters dismissed it as an ink recipe, I thought more simply. Shavings of rich red wood can also make a scarlet dye.' Charlie took the cross of rings and held them over the chart, praying he was right. 'An ink recipe,' he continued, 'for a very subtle shade. This ink is very slightly pigmented red. It's such a small difference,' he explained, 'that the eye doesn't see it. Only the colour of a certain ruby brings it out.'

'The *Chart of All Hallows' Eve* is drawn part in black ink, part in coded ink?' said Lily.

Charlie nodded. 'That's why the astrology is meaningless,' he said. 'Thorne's chart doesn't make sense because it's only a conduit to hide coded letters.'

Charlie held up the cross of rings so the ship's lantern light shone through the rubies.

'These rings aren't marked with symbols to solve a code,' he said. 'The red jewels make a kind of spyglass, to read the different colour ink.'

Carefully he slid the cross shape over the paper. From the dense scrawl of black writing, letters leapt into clear relief through the shaded colour of the rubies.

'The configuration of the rings joined together,' Charlie continued, 'reads the coded letters in order. It's extremely clever,' he concluded.

He drew the rubies slowly across the page, revealing Thorne's lost code. Bit by bit the words took shape.

'It's . . . a poem,' said Lily. She began reading aloud. 'When tide and time a circle make,' she began, 'and dread Saturn seals Jupiter's fate . . .' She paused as Charlie shifted the rings along, revealing more words. 'Then luck will break and time will end,' she continued, 'And mighty Heavens the world will bend.' She stopped as the rings came to the edge of the page.

'Tide and time a circle make?' Charlie frowned.

'Time will end,' added Lily uneasily. 'What can it mean?'

Judge Walters was hovering hawklike over the chart.

'It's the apocalypse he forecasts,' said the Judge grimly. 'Time will end at midnight tonight.' He turned to Charlie and Lily. 'It appears you have outlived your usefulness,' he announced.

'Wait,' said Charlie. 'It's not the apocalypse Thorne forecasts.' He thought quickly. 'It's . . . a location,' he said.

The Judge eyed him coolly. 'You attempt a trick,' he accused.

'Tide and time form a circle,' improvised Charlie. 'It means the Island of the Dead. It forms a circle at high tide. The Eye is hidden on an island downriver.'

Charlie waited, silently willing the Judge to believe his deception. Beside him he could feel Lily tense.

'The Island of the Dead,' said Judge Walters thoughtfully. Then he smiled. 'Where the cholera victims and prisoners are buried. We can be there in less than an hour.' He paused. 'What of the rest of the code?' he asked. 'Saturn seals Jupiter's fate?'

'An exact place on the island,' said Charlie. 'We need Ishmael Boney. He can read the stars to show the place the Eye is hidden.'

The Judge nodded. 'Get Boney,' he growled to a guard. 'Give him a spyglass or whatever he needs. Set the sails and take us downriver.' He smiled to himself. 'By midnight the Eye will be mine and all the slave bounty of the oceans.'

There was shouting on deck as the guards opened the sails. Then Charlie saw Ishmael Boney, his eyes wide with terror, being led up on deck.

'The Eye,' Charlie told him as he was manhandled next to them. 'It's on the Island of the Dead.'

Ishmael looked confused.

'The locals call it the Isle of Dogs,' added Charlie meaningfully, hoping Ishmael had lived long enough in Deptford to have knowledge of the local waters. 'The high tides form a circle.'

Something like understanding flashed on Ishmael's face. The Isle of Dogs was a marshy no man's land.

Charlie handed Ishmael the *Chart of All Hallows' Eve*.

'Take us here,' he said, stabbing a random star sign, 'where Jupiter meets Saturn.'

Ishmael nodded slowly. He raised his eyes to the sky and pointed upriver.

'Where is it?' growled the Judge, growing agitated in his excitement to find the Eye. 'Tell me quickly.'

'Sail towards Greenwich,' said Ishmael quietly. 'I can tell you more when we get closer to the Island of the Dead.'

'What are you doing?' Lily had crept close to Charlie. 'You're leading the Judge straight to the Eye.'

'No,' whispered Charlie. 'The Eye isn't on the island. Ishmael knows that. It's mostly marshland that way.'

'Then why are we going there?'

'We're going to beach the ship.'

Chapter 86

Janus was making his arrangements in Deptford. The Eye was tantalisingly close, but he knew it was better to secure his plans.

No more failures, he promised himself. *This time I will succeed.*

With the dockyards all but deserted, it had been easy to steal aboard a small ship and lay out a few flammables on deck. Not a true fireship to be sure, but the flames would rise high enough to cause alarm and ensure his own little craft could sail out of the docks unmolested.

Magic, he thought to himself, remembering Thorne's words, *is nothing more than distraction.*

Janus observed that the same was true of Charlie Oakley. His attention would be fixed on rescuing his brother when he should be looking for the Eye.

Janus felt almost sad about it. For all his skills and bravery, the thief taker was so easily beaten. Janus had suffered from such weaknesses for family once. But his time at sea had divested him of such attachments.

Or had it?

It occurred to Janus that he'd built an unlikely kinship with De Ryker. The admiral had seen his cleverness and nurtured it. Against all the odds Janus realised he'd grown to feel a kind of love for the old man.

He could still remember the bloody cage on board ship, the strange feeling of comfort he drew from it when all the other prisoners were quaking with terror.

'De Ryker means us to beat one another to death for the sport of his crew,' whispered a fellow captive. 'They make bets on the sole survivor.'

Janus looked away. 'Then you will all die,' he said, staring at the sea.

As a boy, Janus had lain awake waiting for the dark god to claim him. After countless nights, waiting for death was familiar, and terror had become a part of him. He knew the other captives, paralysed with fear, would be no match.

'You pretend you are not frightened?' De Ryker had asked Janus when he'd returned to the cage, soaked in the blood of other prisoners.

'I'm always afraid,' Janus replied, 'but I've made fear a friend. He lives quietly enough.'

De Ryker hesitated. Then he threw back his head and laughed.

'Perhaps,' he decided, 'another trial. Since you fight so well and thrive on terror. You will pilot my fireship. See those cannons?' De Ryker had explained. 'They will be aimed at you. Steer your fireship right, and you'll live. Fail, and I'll blow you from the waters.'

He'd studied Janus's face for a reaction. 'I've seen the bluff and bravado of hundreds of men,' said De Ryker. 'There's something different about you.'

Janus settled back against the bloody bars of the cage. 'I have lived in the shadow of the dark god,' he'd said. 'You are nothing to him.'

Janus had learned fast, and by the time De Ryker had put him at the helm of his third fireship, with instructions to fix it to the enemy or die trying, Janus's expertise had bested any other pilot's.

He had come to love the tense power of the fireship, engineering the fuses and the combustibles to make a floating bomb. He remembered the day De Ryker had come to trust his expertise.

'We should use faster ships,' said Janus, 'and English gunpowder. Their serpentine powder has a better saltpetre concentration. It flares better and will combust a steadier fuse. Then,' he concluded, 'we attack at night.'

De Ryker's eyes bulged slightly. 'Such a thing cannot be done.'

'With your permission,' said Janus, 'I think we could flame the Queen Catherine.*'*

'If you manage to do what you say,' said De Ryker, 'you will have earned the title of Fireship Commander. You will no longer be caged and may fit out the next fireship as you see fit.'

Janus bowed his head in thanks.

'Don't thank me yet,' said De Ryker. 'You haven't succeeded in the thing you promise.'

But Janus had succeeded. And after the sinking of the *Queen Catherine*, he'd been given licence to fit his ships with serpentine powder and travel to England to find the Eye.

Janus reflected on how his desire to escape De Ryker had ebbed. Already, he knew, De Ryker was overseeing the manufacture of his latest and deadliest fireship. The guided missile that would explode England's navy as she floated in harbour.

But it suddenly occurred to Janus that he'd replaced one tyrannical, bloodthirsty master with another. And he'd done it gladly.

Chapter 87

The first fingers of eclipse had begun as Judge Walters's prison ship sailed towards the Isle of Dogs. They cast a blood-red crescent on the side of the shining moon. Charlie guessed that midnight could only be hours away.

If they didn't find the Eye by then, the only thing likely to free his brother would be lost forever.

As they sailed east, a few guards began making noises of protest. Those with more sailing experience were baulking at the marshland around Greenwich and the Isle of Dogs.

'They say the ship could run aground,' said Judge Walters, speaking to Charlie. 'You're certain this is the correct route?'

'Ishmael uses Thorne's astrology to steer us a safer course,' said Charlie. 'It's a higher kind of navigation not known to most sailors,' he improvised.

'Head towards Greenwich,' said Ishmael. 'There's a safe landing place there. You'll need to take a smaller boat to the Island of the Dead.'

The Judge was staring downriver uncertainly. The ship was gathering speed now, heading towards Greenwich.

'The Eye is said to grant the sight of the angels,' added Charlie. 'Thorne hid it well so no ordinary man might find it.'

The Judge smiled at this. 'Yes,' he said, 'it will take determination and courage to find. But the rewards will be great.'

A few sailors were murmuring discontentedly.

'I am your captain,' growled the Judge. 'Follow my orders or you'll go the way of the prisoners below.' He clicked his fingers impatiently at Ishmael. 'Which way now?'

'The same course,' assured Ismael.

The Judge nodded. 'Find a craft large enough for a few men,' he ordered. 'I'll steer out to find the Eye with the astrologer and the thief taker.'

He was grinning at the prospect of his prize, oblivious to the tell-tale heads of reeds that had begun poking up from the waters around Greenwich.

Charlie was scanning the river, looking for the firmest marsh hiding beneath.

'Get ready,' he muttered to Lily and Ishmael. 'The ship will lurch this way.' He indicated. 'We can jump.'

'Into the water?'

'It's only a few feet deep,' Charlie assured her. 'It's marshland underneath.'

'You're sure about that?'

Charlie nodded. 'Bunch your legs as you fall,' he added, 'to lessen the impact.'

He could see a patch of thick marsh ahead.

'Brace yourselves,' he said. 'Get a good grip on the side of the ship.'

The Judge turned in confusion as they moved to take a hold. Understanding dawned in his single cold eye, but too slowly. He made a lunge towards them, just as the ship gave a great shudder beneath them.

The Judge was jolted to the side, away from a firm handhold. Men in the rigging were desperately swinging to the sails, trying to alter their course, but with an ominous grinding sound the ship slowed to a halt. Then she began to tip.

Judge Walters's face was a picture of shocked rage as he slid uncontrollably across the deck. His shouted orders were drowned out as guards fell this way and that, tumbling down the angled deck.

A few crashed into rigging. Others clutched helplessly at barrels and falling objects. The ship's tilt intensified, and now men were slammed hard to port.

'Hold on and climb over!' shouted Charlie as the floor slanted under them. They pulled themselves up the side of the ship. The marshy Thames was beneath them.

Charlie turned to see a dazed Ishmael and a determined-looking Lily.

They heard Judge Walters's furious voice from somewhere on deck.

'Get hold of the prisoners!'

'Now!' said Charlie. 'Over the side!'

Black water loomed beneath them. Charlie saw Lily hesitate and remembered she couldn't swim.

'You'll land on marsh,' he promised her. 'The tide isn't risen high yet.'

'How can you know that?'

'I don't for certain,' he admitted, 'but it's a better chance than at his hands.'

He nodded to Judge Walters, who was scrambling up the deck towards them.

Charlie jumped, throwing himself over the edge. He heard Ishmael and Lily splash into the Thames beside him. Water enclosed his head, and he sunk deep into the river. Then his feet hit soft mud and he righted himself.

They landed with the fields of Greenwich on the dark horizon.

Ishmael was face down in the water, and Charlie heaved the old astrologer to his feet with difficulty.

'This way,' said Charlie, scanning for Lily. 'Head towards the mainland.'

'It's boggy,' gasped Lily, splashing upright.

Charlie was at her side, helping her free her waterlogged skirts.

Above them the huge ship was teetering in the mud.

'Get up quickly,' urged Charlie. 'It's going to tilt again and crush us.'

They stumbled to their feet and waded fast through the shallow waters. Above them they heard the creaking of the huge hull as it tipped towards them. The shouts of the sailors and the Judge on the deck above rent the night sky.

As they splashed through the boggy marsh, the prison boat seemed to come after them, backlit by the blood-red moon. They dashed free as the beached ship sent a wave of water crashing against their backs. Up ahead was drier land.

'Where now?' asked Lily as they made for it.

'I know where the Eye is,' said Charlie. 'It's not far, but we don't have long.'

He was looking at the moon, over two-thirds shaded red.

'Wait!' Ishmael was gasping, limping with difficulty.

Now free of the water, Charlie could see the old astrologer's foot was bent at a strange angle.

'I'll distract the Judge,' said Ishmael. 'Make sure his men don't follow you.'

'It's too dangerous,' said Charlie. 'Come with us.'

Ishmael shook his head. 'If what you say is true, it's more important to stop Janus getting the Eye,' he said. 'I'm an old man. Let me have this last adventure.'

He managed a lopsided smile. 'I'll head back to Deptford,' he promised, 'making enough noise to draw any pursuers. I'll only slow you down in any case.'

Lily's hand was on Charlie's shoulder. 'He's right,' she said. 'If you want a chance of saving your brother, we need every second on our side.'

'We're already there,' said Charlie, pointing to the large buildings up ahead. 'I think the Eye is in Greenwich.'

Chapter 88

'It's a trick,' growled Amesbury. 'De Ryker has no intention of suing for peace.'

King Charles put his head in his hands. All he could think of was Frances. Things seemed so simple with her. He could forget about the pressing weight of kingship and feel like a young man again.

'De Ryker raised the white flag at Dover,' said Charles. 'We must honour the terms of warfare.'

'I fear he makes so bold,' said Amesbury carefully, 'because he has the Eye.'

'It's a nonsense,' muttered Charles. 'The Eye doesn't exist. It's a . . . a fable dreamt up by Civil War propagandists to blacken my father. If the Dutch are fool enough to hunt for it, let them squander their resources.'

Amesbury was silent, remembering a conversation with Thorne all those years ago.

'You're hard on the boy,' said Amesbury.

Thorne nodded. 'He must learn discretion if he is to survive Republican rule.'

'But to keep him here.' Amesbury gestured to Thorne's ghoulish decorations.

'*The workshop is the safest place for him,*' *said Thorne sharply.* '*Cromwell hunts nobles.*'

'*The boy is too young,*' *said Amesbury.* '*He fears you.*'

Thorne closed his eyes. '*It can't be helped. The deaths are . . . necessary. He'll understand when he's older.*'

Amesbury shook his head. '*He won't. You'll twist his mind. Make him a killer.*'

Had his predictions come true? Had Thorne's apprentice turned murderer and traitor?

'De Ryker will lure us into talks whilst his fleet invades,' insisted Amesbury. 'Why else would he have a legion of men-of-war floating off English waters?'

Charles sighed. 'The Duke of York says it's better to go into negotiations with your sword held high,' he said. 'He thinks De Ryker simply wants to enter negotiations in a strong position. The Dutch know we would see their ships.'

Amesbury had heard this argument before. The Duke of York was an excellent sailor, but he tended to favour situations of bravado rather than strategy.

'Where is James?' asked the King. 'Why is he not here?'

'I sent a message for the Duke of York, but I fear it wasn't received,' said Amesbury. He decided to opt for honesty. 'I think he's been going out to sea,' he added, 'in secret.'

Charles looked less surprised than Amesbury might have imagined.

'James likes to disguise himself and take the little yacht out,' admitted the King, 'the *Fan Fan*. You know how he misses sailing. He only cruises the Thames. I'm sure he'll be back soon.'

'We need him safe,' said Amesbury. 'If De Ryker meant to negotiate, he'd force us to meet him in Breda. Make clear his position of strength. A man of his experience does not come seeking a truce, cap in hand.'

They both considered the truth of this.

'Even so,' said Charles slowly, his large mouth downturned, 'we can't refuse the terms of warfare. If he comes to negotiate peace, we must play along. Publicly at least.' His eyes swung to the general's. 'Amesbury, you must mount a protection for the coast,' he decided. 'If De Ryker is trying for some trick, we'll be ready for it as best we can.' He rubbed his temples. 'Find James,' he decided. 'Send him to Chatham. Make sure De Ryker sails nowhere near Chatham.' His mouth set into a tight line. 'If the admiral sees our mothballed navy, we'll lose England.'

'Twice would be careless,' muttered Amesbury. 'You've only just got England back.'

Chapter 89

'The location of the Eye came to me straight away,' explained Charlie as they put distance between them and the beached ship. 'Tide and time a circle make. It's not an island. Thorne is referring to a clock. An astronomical clock.'

'Astronomical?' asked Lily.

'An astronomical clock shows star signs and tidal times,' explained Charlie. 'There are two in London,' he added. 'One in Hampton Court and another in Greenwich. The Tudor rulers used to reach their riverside palaces by barge, and they used the clocks to chart the moon and navigate the tidal changes of the Thames.'

'When tide and time a circle make,' said Lily, understanding. 'The clock is a circle showing the Thames's movements. But it could equally be at Hampton Court,' she pointed out.

'Greenwich is the best place in London for stargazing,' said Charlie. 'High land. And the carved bodies washed up at Deptford, less than a mile away. Then there was Thorne's camera obscura,' he concluded, 'facing east. It occurred to me Thorne might have meant for it to sight the river near Deptford, where his Eye was hidden.'

'So you had Judge Walters sail you directly here,' said Lily. 'Clever. But the Queen lives in Greenwich now. Surely the clock will be guarded?'

The marshy land became firmer as they reached Greenwich's wooded outskirts.

Charlie shook his head. 'The Queen's House is new,' he explained. 'During the Civil War the royals stayed at old Greenwich Palace. It's deserted now.'

He was looking through the trees for where the old palace began.

A strange noise stopped them in their tracks.

'What was that?' asked Lily. 'It sounds like . . . bells. Death knells,' she added uneasily, thinking of the bells rung in church when the dead were brought out.

An uneasy feeling crept through both of them. The pealing of bells had long been associated with restless spirits. The strange noises grew louder as they neared Greenwich Park.

Charlie pointed up into the trees. 'It is bells,' he said. 'Look. Brass bells. Someone has hung them here to deter evil spirits.'

'Brass to ward away evil,' said Lily, looking up.

Decaying apples had been hung from the branches, and the trunk bore a carved pentagram.

'All Hallows' Eve,' said Charlie grimly. 'Locals must have put this here to ward off evil.'

'What does it mean?' asked Lily.

'Nothing,' said Charlie uneasily. 'Local superstition. We need to get to the palace.'

Chapter 90

Janus regarded Thorne's workshop silently. It was completely unchanged. The same as he remembered it from all those years ago. The broken weapons, bent swords and broken shields were still here, silted in a layer of ancient mud.

This had been one of Thorne's obsessions. Collecting the broken things sacrificed to the river gods.

Things were shifting in Janus's mind now. Certainties from his childhood were taking on a different shape. The once-frightening room was no more than the hoarding place of an obsessive inventor. The dark gods and shadowy spectres had fled.

The Eye, Janus wondered. Was the Eye really what he thought it was?

'I was only a boy,' he said aloud. 'I couldn't have known those children had died long ago. I thought them your sacrifices. I thought you meant for me to die along with them.'

His accusation was greeted with silence. Then he remembered Thorne's voice.

'The old gods,' his master had explained, 'are wild and savage. But they can be tolerant and kind. They do not judge. You cannot save a life once

Saturn has claimed it. But you can make the passing sacred. You can gift it to Lucifer.'

Janus moved towards the door leading to the clock tower mechanism. He grasped a large handle, hidden to the side of the entrance. Another of Thorne's little secrets, concealed in the shadows. As the crank shifted, the door to the clock opened.

The dank smell of disuse greeted Janus, but the astronomical workings were still moving, turning the hands, charting the Thames's tides.

Inside the old tower was a rickety set of wooden steps. Janus climbed them quickly. Behind him the large mechanism whirred and clicked. Interlocking cogs turned relentlessly around.

Janus had almost ascended the stairs when he saw a flash of gold.

A box. A small metal box had been set high up into the workings of the clock.

Breath catching in his throat, Janus climbed the last few stairs.

At the top was a wooden platform, jettied out above the clock mechanism. Behind it the back of the enormous clock face turned slowly, marking the seconds. There were fewer than twenty minutes until midnight.

His eyes settled on the metal box. It was barely a hand high, thick brass and crafted so expertly it was impossible to see the joins.

The unmistakable perfection of Thorne's work.

On the front was a set of concentric circles cut into the brass plate. They were dotted with metal pegs and jewels. Tiny sapphires, rubies and emeralds winked out.

Janus felt a sudden flush of emotions, remembering his old master. The care he dedicated to his craft. Janus was so taken with the beauty of the box that it took him a long moment to realise its purpose.

Then he realised Thorne's last trick.

Chapter 91

The wood thinned and the ruins of Greenwich Palace came into view through the trees. It was vast, sprawling out across the waterfront.

Charlie and Lily stared at the rambling building.

'It must have been a great palace once,' said Lily, taking in the many fallen roofs, the dilapidated red brick and the stone Tudor roses.

'It's big,' agreed Charlie, considering the enormous building.

'There's no clock,' said Lily, 'and it seems like midnight is nearly here.'

She was looking up at the moon. The eclipse had almost covered it now. Charlie judged they had around fifteen minutes until the moon turned entirely red and the Eye was destroyed.

Charlie thought for a moment. 'At Hampton Court the clock is at the front gatehouse. We're at the back of the palace. The fastest way is through the building.'

They stared at the crumbling edifice. For some reason neither wanted to go inside.

There was a rustle in the bushes and they both started. A rabbit raced away. Charlie drove down a shudder. All Hallows' Eve was getting to him.

'This way,' he said, starting uneasily towards a broken old door. 'It's overgrown but we can get inside there.'

They climbed through the battered entrance, pushing aside creepers and foliage, and were greeted by a damp smell of disuse. Inside was gloomy, barely lit. Desecration lay all around.

'Look at it,' whispered Lily. 'It's all been gutted.'

All that remained of Greenwich Palace was an empty shell. The huge internal doors were long gone, and the frames had been wrenched free. Faded patches on the painted walls showed where grand pictures had been taken down. Broken remains of several enormous mirrors lay shattered. Even the Tudor floor of elaborate black-and-white tiles had been smashed up in places and looted for scrap.

Charlie and Lily moved through the abandoned palace into a second large room.

'Someone's been here recently,' said Charlie. He pointed to the remains of a smoking fire, still smouldering on the tile floor, and a rudimentary palette bed.

There was a blanket fixed at an angle across a corner of the room. Charlie's eyes zeroed in on it as he wondered what was hidden behind it.

'Look.' Lily was pointing to a vast pentagram on the floor. It was drawn in blood. She swallowed. 'This is where Janus did it,' she said. 'This is where he killed the girls.'

Charlie moved towards the blanket.

'Don't.' Lily's eyes were round with fear.

He pulled away the curtain and stepped back, stomach churning. The familiar statue was smaller than Charlie remembered it. It was a man with Roman-style curling hair and a beard. The sightless eyes stared coldly outwards. The muscular chest was tensed and a sinewy arm crooked. Gripped in the white fist was the leg of a child, upended and dangling, arms waving in distress and fear.

Saturn. The god who ate his children. Charlie looked to the statue's feet, but he already knew what he would see, and his stomach tightened in anticipation.

A jawbone, barely longer than his little finger, a broken femur the size of his hand. Pints of blood, now old and caked, had been splashed over them.

Charlie's gaze lifted to the child's tiny stone face, twisted in pain and horror.

He felt Lily at his side.

'The Deptford women,' said Lily. 'They were brought here first. A sacrifice to the old gods?'

Her eyes were moving over the old statue. The god's free arm cupped the writhing child's back. His bearded head was lowered. The lips and teeth were bared in the attitude of tearing flesh from the child's exposed chest.

Charlie's mind felt liquid and jarring. He forced himself to focus.

'Tidal times,' he murmured, looking at numbers chalked on the stone floor. 'Janus made calculations of the tides here.' He frowned, then a possible reason for the dead girls at Deptford came to him.

'Corpses,' he said. 'Dead bodies are the only things that float all the way downriver. Everything else is taken by the mudlarks. He used them to measure tides. Perhaps he hoped to recreate some calculation of Thorne's. Find his old master's hiding place.'

'Then why not raid a graveyard?' said Lily, looking at the pile of tiny bones. 'Hunt the slums? London is not low on corpses.'

Charlie was calling to mind the body at Deptford. A convict with a silver coin in her mouth.

'Perhaps,' he said, 'Janus thinks he does no wrong. He kills only those condemned to die. Places a silver coin for an underworld that will deal with them more mercifully.'

'A Roman afterlife?' said Lily.

'Better than a Christian hell,' said Charlie.

Lily hesitated, eyeing the statue. 'You remember it,' she said, 'don't you?'

Charlie nodded. 'It wasn't here,' he said, trying to collect himself. 'It's been moved.' He was looking at the bones piled at Saturn's bare feet. 'The river silt preserves things,' he added. 'These bones could be hundreds of years old. Centuries. Remember what Norris said,' he added. 'In ancient times people made sacrifices to the Thames.'

'Thorne had an obsession with Roman gods,' said Lily. 'Perhaps he dragged these from the mud at low tide. A clever man's interest in the stars that turned dark.'

'But if Janus was Thorne's young apprentice,' said Charlie, 'he may not have realised how long corpses take to decompose. Perhaps he thought his master killed children. Even feared himself next in line for sacrifice.'

Charlie forced himself to drive away the strange memories, the eerie thoughts assailing him.

Then he heard it. A faint ticking sound.

'I think I hear the clock,' he said. 'Towards the front of the palace.' He eyed the reddening moon through a broken windowpane.

'We don't have long,' he decided. 'Let's go.'

Chapter 92

Janus stared at the box in the clock tower. The little brass square dotted with jewels. A circle to symbolise the heavens, he realised. Rings revolving out from a central sun.

It was a star chart. Tiny crystals etched into the solid brass showed constellations. The pegs marked the planets with their differing colours. But their positions were wrong.

Janus stared for a long time.

It was a puzzle of course. Thorne had always loved puzzles. Put the star chart right and open the box.

The solution was simple to a man who knew Thorne and his workings.

After a few moments' consideration Janus began moving the pegs.

Neptune to here. Saturn to here.

Carefully Janus entered the planetary positions of the eclipse. But as he reached the right configuration of the stars, moving the moon into position, nothing happened.

Anger boiled up.

It must be right. His planetary placements were perfect.

Frantically he moved the pegs again, checking his workings. Still nothing. Janus slammed his fist into the front of the box. The sturdy brass shell barely moved.

Then he realised. There was only one man in London who carried the code.

Janus had a sudden terrible premonition.

Charlie Tuesday. What if he's found the rings and solved Thorne's clues? *He might track the Eye here and steal my birthright after all.*

Desperately Janus took out his knife, determined to prize apart the box by force. It was only then he saw how expertly Thorne had protected the Eye.

The box had been integrated into the workings of the clock. Janus's fingers followed the mechanism to be sure. Attempt to open the box by force and a spring-loaded mechanism would shunt it forwards. The huge hands of the astronomical clock would pass through a narrow aperture skilfully banding the centre of the box. Anything inside would be crushed. The precious Eye would be destroyed forever.

Janus pondered for a moment. He was certain only Charlie Tuesday could enter Thorne's code. He wondered if the thief taker even understood what he knew.

Charlie Oakley. The golden boy.

His mind turned the problem around, thinking of ways to trick the information out of Charlie Tuesday. Then a possible solution presented itself.

The answer was so obvious he almost laughed out loud. Saturn was not a god of action and movement. He was passive, acquisitive. Janus must sit back and let his enemy gather the spoils, then move in and take them from him.

Use the thief taker. His lucky stars will lead you to the prize.

The more Janus thought about it, the more sense it made. Perhaps this was what the prophecy meant all along. Jupiter and Saturn. Life and Death. And death always triumphed in the end.

Chapter 93

Charlie and Lily were standing outside the clock tower at Greenwich Palace. Above them the huge clock ticked the minutes away.

It was seven minutes until midnight struck.

'The clock shows planetary movements,' said Lily. She was pointing to a moving circle of spheres on the clock face. The gold hands and circles made an intricate dance around one another, shifting planets and tidal times as the year went on.

'It's the rest of the prophecy,' said Charlie, referring to the shapes of Saturn and Jupiter heading towards one another in a gold orbit.

When tide and time a circle make
And dread Saturn seals Jupiter's fate
Then luck will break and time will end
And mighty Heavens the world will bend

'When Saturn meets Jupiter,' explained Charlie. 'At midnight on All Hallows' Eve,' he said, pointing, 'those planets will collide on the face of the clock. Look at the angles. The clock will break at midnight. Time will stop. Thorne altered this whole clock to be one giant countdown.'

'The eclipse,' said Lily. 'Thorne must have plotted the star charts nineteen years ago.'

Instinctively they looked up. The full moon was now painted almost entirely blood red.

'The Eye is destroyed at midnight,' said Charlie. 'It must be somewhere inside the mechanism for Thorne's hiding place to work. A place that will change when the clock strikes twelve. That only really leaves the mechanism.'

'Then we must hurry,' said Lily.

Charlie and Lily moved around the edge of the tower. There was a large door, which appeared to be locked. But when Charlie reached for the handle, it turned easily.

He hesitated. 'This doesn't feel right,' he said. 'It's too easy.'

'There's no time,' said Lily. 'We have minutes.'

A black corridor opened ahead of them. It was littered with broken swords and shields.

'Come on,' said Charlie grimly. 'I recognise this place. It's this way.'

They moved through the corridor into the large room of Charlie's dreams.

Lily pointed to a small door set at the back, adjoining where the clock tower would rise. To the side was a lever, and unthinkingly Charlie reached towards it and pulled.

The heavily bolted door clicked and rumbled from somewhere deep in its depths.

'How did you know to do that?' asked Lily as the door swung open.

'I don't know,' admitted Charlie. Something else came into his mind, but he resisted saying it out loud.

If I know how to get in the tower, so does Janus.

Inside, the narrow clock tower was crammed with spinning cogs and whirling movements. Charlie scanned the dark confines for something that didn't seem part of the working movement. It didn't take him long to find, perched high at the top of the tower.

'Up there!' he pointed triumphantly, where they could see the outside clock face reversed. 'There's something set high up.'

'Let's go,' said Lily, looking at the clock face. The hands were nearly at midnight.

They raced up a narrow wooden staircase that took them to the very top of the clock tower. And as they reached the summit, Charlie's heart sunk at the sight of another puzzle.

'It's a box,' he said.

Etched on the front was the Eye of Providence, set in a triangle with beams of light spilling forth.

'This must be where Thorne hid the Eye,' said Lily.

The brass cube was etched with circles, like planetary orbits. Set inside were round metal pegs, some bearing a coloured jewel, others etched with a symbol.

'Star signs,' said Lily, touching one. 'The jewels mean something else.'

'The planets,' said Charlie. 'Each planet has a different colour. Green for Venus, red for Mars.' He tapped them, taking in the wider construction.

'The box is part of the mechanism,' he said. 'Thorne must have planned this years in advance. Look at how the clock hands are placed.'

Lily eyed the turning shafts of metal. 'The clock hands will pass through the centre of the box,' she said.

'But only at midnight tonight,' Charlie pointed out. 'Look how the astrological configurations add a tilt to the hands. They only move into the box when the planets and the time are both right.'

Charlie frowned at the circular map of heaven. 'Unless this chart shows a particular planetary configuration at midnight, whatever's inside this box will be crushed.'

'The Eye will be destroyed,' said Lily.

Above them the giant clock ticked away the seconds to midnight. There was a minute left.

Charlie took out Thorne's *Chart of All Hallows' Eve*.

'The answer must be here,' he decided. 'Thorne left this star map to find the Eye.'

His eyes lifted to the brass orbits and then dropped back to the star map.

'What is it?' demanded Lily, looking to the ticking seconds.

'The pegs have already been set according to this chart,' he said. 'Someone has tried and failed.'

Charlie felt hope drain away. He was no astrologer. Thorne's *Chart of All Hallows' Eve* was the only answer he could think of. Unless . . .

The patterns of circles and planets rearranged themselves in his mind. A strange idea bubbled up.

'I think I know how to solve it,' he said. 'It's a birth chart. But you have to know whose birthday it belongs to.'

'Whose?'

But Charlie barely heard her. His hands were moving the pegs, positioning and repositioning.

'Blue is Neptune's colour,' he muttered. 'Purple for Jupiter.' His hands began moving faster, aligning the pegs to where he thought they would fit.

The clock ticked away their final seconds.

'That's it,' muttered Charlie, moving the final planet. He stood back. Nothing happened. Behind them the massive hands completed their circuit.

'We're too late,' said Lily as the minute hand moved to strike the hour. 'It's midnight.'

There was a deafening chiming of bells, and they both put their hands to their ears. Charlie waited for the crunching sound of the Eye being destroyed.

Then there was an unexpected click. The metal box shot forward and the hands passed harmlessly around the back. Its front fell open to reveal the contents.

Lily and Charlie moved forward. Inside, a jewelled sphere glittered. The Eye had not been what Charlie was expecting. It was the size of his spanned hand, round and exquisitely made.

'It's beautiful,' said Lily, staring at the gold- and diamond-encrusted object, 'but I don't understand. That's the Eye?'

Charlie nodded.

Locked inside the box for all these years was nothing more than an elaborately decorated clock.

Chapter 94

Amesbury was looking helplessly out to the old fort.

'I sent clear instructions,' he said. 'Landguard was to fortify its defences.'

Captain Naseby spread his hands in a *don't blame me* gesture.

'Funds were sent,' he said. 'The men on the fort were half starved. The money—'

'I can see where the money went!' raged Amesbury. 'There's a *brewery* on that fort!'

He pointed at a tall chimney, merrily puffing out hop-scented steam.

'No navy has attempted a raid on the Thames,' countered Naseby helplessly. 'The fort hasn't been used in over two hundred years.'

'You didn't notice the Dutch ships amassing on the English coast?' shouted Amesbury. 'You didn't receive my orders to fortify?'

'We did, but . . .'

Amesbury forced himself to calm.

'Could De Ryker have a local pilot?' suggested Naseby. 'Someone to steer them through the shoals and sandbanks.'

'No,' said Amesbury. 'I keep every pilot capable of such skill under close watch.'

'Then we have nothing to fear,' said Naseby. 'The Thames can't be negotiated by a foreign invader. It's a labyrinth of hidden dangers lurking just below the surface. Even locals run aground.'

'Maps have been drawn,' said Amesbury.

'Fantastical things,' said Naseby. 'The river is too broad. A map is useless unless a ship could chart an exact location.'

'That,' said Amesbury, 'is what concerns me most.'

He balled his fists. 'The next part of the coast is Chatham docks,' he said. 'If De Ryker gets that far upriver, he'll see our mothballed ships.'

Naseby paled. 'There are no defences,' he conceded. 'If De Ryker has enough luck and bravado, he could sail right in and burn our entire navy.'

'Such as it is,' agreed Amesbury. 'I fear De Ryker has access to something very powerful. Something men killed to create.'

He was remembering Thorne telling him how the bodies had come to be.

'The first girl was the hardest to kill,' Thorne explained. 'Her family had refused her marriage to Buckingham. She'd taken deadly nightshade when I found her. The poor girl was screaming in agony.'

Thorne took a juddering breath. 'Suicides are damned to hell,' he said. 'Refused a dignified burial.'

His eyes had a faraway look, and Amesbury knew Thorne was remembering his young lover, burned at the stake and hung out for the crows.

Thorne swallowed. 'I cut her throat and gave her body to the river,' he said, 'marked for Venus with a silver coin. When she washed up at Dead Man's Curve, I realised the old gods had given me a sign. I'd been trying to chart the tides for months, but mudlarks plundered anything I floated downriver.'

'You used bodies,' said Amesbury grimly, 'to measure the moon's influence on the tides. But you were wrong.'

'*The moon and stars were not the tools I ultimately needed to perfect the Eye,*' admitted Thorne. '*But they were part of the learning. I spared those girls,*' he added, seeing Amesbury's face. '*I sent their souls to a better place. You've killed more than I, in the name of war. Yet my work will change the world. Can you say the same?*'

'*We may not know in my lifetime,*' said Amesbury. '*You're convinced the Eye works as you hope?*'

'*I am,*' said Thorne. '*But we won't know for certain for another nineteen years.*'

Chapter 95

'It's small,' said Charlie, gazing at the Eye. 'Smaller than almost any clock I've seen. Thorne must have been a master at his craft.'

'But what's valuable about a clock?' asked Lily. 'Why would the Dutch want it so badly? They can plunder more jewels and gold than this in the colonies.'

'Perhaps nineteen years ago this was more of a miracle of construction than it is now,' suggested Charlie, 'and the Dutch were misled.'

But even as he said it, Charlie knew that must be wrong. Nineteen years. What was so significant about nineteen years? He weighed what Lily had said about the great wealth of the colonies.

Charlie reached inside. The Eye was attached to part of the larger astronomical clock. He gently pulled it free.

'That's interesting,' said Charlie. 'There's a fitment at the back. The Eye has been regularly wound by the movements of the larger clock. Thorne wanted his invention to keep time.'

Then the answer came to him.

'This little timepiece,' he said slowly, 'has been inside the astrological clock for nineteen years. It's been tossed and jolted with the mechanism. It's endured nineteen hard frosts and hot summers.'

'It's metal,' said Lily. 'Why wouldn't it endure?'

'Lily,' said Charlie, 'look at the time.'

Lily looked at the little clock. Its jewelled face was showing nine minutes past midnight.

'In all this time,' said Charlie, 'it's only slipped by nine minutes. Less than thirty seconds a year. And that in conditions similar to on a ship.' He pointed to the metal box. 'I think Thorne set this all up,' he said, 'to test his clock. He couldn't risk it aboard a ship, so he invented the next best option. Thorne made a box with a mechanism to ensure the clock stayed wound, and hid it exposed to the elements for nearly two decades.'

Lily's eyes widened as she realised the implications of this. 'This clock would work aboard a ship,' she said, 'but no clock can do that. Conditions are too intemperate.'

'This one has,' said Charlie, 'for nineteen years.'

Carefully he opened the back of the clock. The insides whirred and spun. Charlie recognised brass cogs and intricately wrought springs, but other parts he'd never seen in a clock before.

'He's used wood as well as metal,' said Lily, peering over Charlie's shoulder.

She was staring at a few tiny parts, pieces of wood crafted so small it was incredible to think they'd been made with human hands.

'It's darker than any wood I recognise,' said Charlie. 'Perhaps some dense oily tree from the colonies. It would explain how the Eye kept time,' he added. 'The biggest problem clock makers have is lubricating the works. The oil thins in hot weather, sticks in frost.'

'In which case,' said Lily, 'it could tell longitude. Keep time in different climates. Men could know their position, even in uncharted ocean.'

They paused for a moment, taking in the magnitude of this possibility. The notion was nothing short of miraculous.

'To see as the angels see,' said Charlie. 'That's why Thorne was so interested in Saturn. We thought of him as the God of the Dead. But he's also the God of Time.'

'If this clock can truly keep time at sea,' said Lily, 'there's no limit to what it's worth. They could sail faster routes direct to colonies. Discover new ones. Whichever country owned it would rule the seas.'

'They also could navigate the Thames,' said Charlie. 'Dutch spies have drawn maps of the shoals, but they're useless without an exact position. With this clock an enemy could sail all the way to London.'

'We need to get it to the King,' said Lily, 'before Janus finds us.'

'Wait.' Charlie raised a warning finger.

'What?' Lily looked around them.

'Do you hear that?'

Lily listened for a moment. 'I don't hear anything.'

'Exactly,' said Charlie. 'The astronomical clock. It's stopped ticking.'

Suddenly the wooden platform beneath them shook. Charlie stumbled. Then a great crack sounded and they both dropped several feet. Lily skidded, tried to right herself and fell back towards the high drop.

Instinctively Charlie grabbed for her dress. The Eye fell from his hands into the tangle of wooden beams and moving wheels far below.

Chapter 96

Charlie pulled Lily back to safety, eyes darting around the narrow tower. Thorne's Eye had fallen somewhere deep below them, into the huge workings of the astronomical clock.

'What happened?' asked Lily, breathing hard. 'Did Thorne design the tower to fall if the clock was found?'

'I think someone's in here with us,' said Charlie, adjusting his footing. 'And they've jammed the mechanism of the astronomical clock.'

He pointed to where the mighty cogs were now juddering with pressure. Small cracks were opening like rivulets up and down the structural beams.

'The Eye!' said Lily. She was pointing at a collection of cogs halfway down the tower. Thorne's clock rested on a beam just beneath them.

Charlie's eyes followed the moving cogs. 'We need to be careful,' he said, watching the huge grinding metalwork. 'The whole mechanism is under huge pressure. It could break apart any minute.'

Then out of the corner of his eye, Charlie spotted something. There was a dark shape at the bottom of the tower, moving easily up the beams.

'You were right!' shouted Lily. 'There's someone down there! We need to get to the Eye!'

Charlie swung and landed on the next timber. Then he stopped. The shadowy figure was examining a lower part of the mechanism. He made some adjustment, then the cogs shuddered again.

'He's trying to dislodge the Eye,' said Charlie, slipping faster through the beams and weaving parts. He placed a foot on a moving dial and launched himself free just as another turned in on him.

Below them, Thorne's longitude clock shook towards the edge of the beam. It dropped on to a turning cog and began revolving downwards. Lily raised her knife arm just as the Eye was about to drop out of sight and the blade hit metal. The cog reverberated, then stopped turning, Lily's knife twanging between its teeth. Thorne's clock was balanced precariously on top.

'Go!' Lily shouted. 'You can still get it.'

Splinters of wood were raining freely from the structure now, and a terrible shrieking sounded from the shaking cogs. The pressure of the breaking mechanism was splitting the tower apart. Lily's knife blade was already buckling.

Charlie dodged moving parts and leapt across beams as fast as he dared. For a moment it seemed the dark man had vanished. Then Charlie saw him in a different part of the tower. Automatically he followed the path of the cogs from the man to the Eye.

It was only a few feet beneath him now. But as the pieces connected in his mind, Charlie realised with a sinking feeling what the man was engineering. The dark figure made an expert adjustment, and the cog on which the Eye lay began turning in the opposite direction. Lily's bent knife dropped free, and Thorne's clock began moving away.

Charlie lunged, narrowly missing a fragment of sharp metal firing out from a disintegrating cog. His fingers brushed the Eye, but he was too late. Thorne's longitude clock dropped from sight. Then a gloved hand reached out in the dark below and caught it.

Charlie saw the clock disappear into the figure's shadowy grip. A masked face came into view, wearing a black handkerchief, like a highwayman. But before Charlie could identify who he was seeing, the man vanished.

Charlie knew in a moment it was him.

'It's Janus!' he shouted to Lily. 'He has the Eye!'

'Deptford Docks is the nearest harbour,' said Charlie. 'It's less than a mile away.'

Lily's face was grim. 'If he escapes the city by water, he can take the Eye direct to the Dutch navy.'

Charlie was trying not to dwell on the birthday he'd entered into Thorne's box. The planetary positions that had unlocked the Eye. It could only mean one thing.

His brother was in greater danger than he'd ever imagined.

Chapter 97

Charlie and Lily were running full pelt for Deptford Docks. They rounded the bend in the river, where the blood-red moon cast an eerie light on the moored ships.

'We're too late,' panted Lily as they slowed to take in the scene. 'Janus came by horseback,' she said, pointing to a sweating steed tied to a nearby post. 'He must already be on a ship.'

Charlie's eyes were trained on something further out in the harbour. It looked like a naked flame gliding towards them. It was only when he smelt the fumes that Charlie's brain adjusted to what his eyes were telling him.

'There's a flaming ship,' he said, 'heading for the dockyards.'

Shouts sounded. A few half-awake dock guards had noticed the blaze and were pointing uncertainly towards it. Smoke curled from its prow, and as they watched, flames burst upwards from the deck.

The dockers were moving into action now, racing to protect ships and secure the harbour.

'A fireship,' said Lily. 'It must be Janus's doing. Why does he not escape with the Eye?'

'It's a diversion,' said Charlie. 'Look how slowly the ship moves. She is drifting. There's no pilot.'

Something about the strategy was so obvious to him. Charlie tuned out the shouts of the panicked dockers moving to protect the harbour. What was it someone had told him long ago?

All magic is a trick. Looking here when you should be looking there.

Charlie forced his attention away from the burning ship, out to where Janus didn't want to draw attention. He saw it immediately. A small ship was sailing straight out of Deptford Docks, and no one had even noticed.

He's always been there, whispered a voice. *He's always been just a few steps away.*

'Janus fired that ship,' said Charlie with surety, 'but he was on another vessel when he did it.'

Lily followed his gaze. 'Janus diverts the dock guards,' she said, understanding, 'so he can get out of Deptford with the Eye.'

She was looking at the triple gates that guarded the docks. They stood empty and unmanned. Janus's ship was sailing towards them. Charlie made a quick calculation. The gates were several hundred feet away. He set off at a run.

'We can get to the gates,' he shouted. 'Close in on Janus before he leaves the docks.'

In a moment Lily was running beside him.

His eye suddenly caught something fluttering high on the fireship. A flag. Charlie slowed to be sure. Then he knew.

'What is it?' asked Lily, seeing his ashen face.

'The flag,' said Charlie. 'It's a prisoner-of-war flag.'

'There are men on that ship?' Lily's eyes widened in horror.

'I think Janus signals that Rowan is on the fireship,' said Charlie grimly. 'His final trick to be sure of escaping.'

Lily's mouth dropped open in horror. 'He means to burn your brother?'

Charlie nodded. 'Janus wants me to choose,' he said, 'between my brother and England.'

Lily was silent.

'And he thinks he knows,' continued Charlie, 'which I'll choose.'

'Your brother,' said Lily, a flat expression on her face. 'He knows you'll choose your brother.'

Charlie uncurled his clenched fist. Inside was Rowan's copper talisman. The face of Neptune glittered up at him.

He hadn't been sure before. Now he was certain. The birth chart to open Thorne's box. It all made sense.

He let out a breath.

'What will you do?' asked Lily.

'I'm going to surprise Janus,' said Charlie. 'Because I know who he is.'

Chapter 98

Amesbury's horse was charging down the uneven dirt track to Chatham. The Thames was out of sight, and he knew he must still be miles away.

How could De Ryker have attacked so boldly? The possibilities lurched in Amesbury's mind. He'd assumed Thorne's Eye would never be found. Had his apprentice lived after all?

'A false birthday?' said Amesbury. 'That is how you mean to hide the Eye?'

Thorne nodded. 'I've taught him the stars and the old gods. When he discovers his birthday was my last gift to him, he'll understand.'

'His birth chart will open the box,' said Amesbury. 'Saturn to represent time. It is ingenious,' he conceded, 'but carries great risk.'

'It is the only way to keep him safe,' said Thorne. 'No one will ever suspect my apprentice carries a code to unlock the Eye. Not even him.'

'And if he never discovers his birthday is false,' pushed Amesbury, 'he'll believe his disposition evil.'

'I've made a contingency,' said Thorne. 'Nineteen years from now a prophecy will be published in a public almanac. I must hope I've taught him enough to understand it.'

'You rely on too many uncertain factors,' said Amesbury.

'It's the only choice I have,' said Thorne. 'The King wants me killed. He may succeed. Better the Eye is destroyed than falls into unworthy hands.'

Amesbury cursed his mistake. He should have expected Thorne's apprentice could turn traitor. Now he was faced with defending England from the greatest navigational power known to man.

Naseby's horse drew up beside Amesbury, matching his pace.

'I've ordered as many soldiers as I could from nearby towns,' Naseby was saying as the horses bolted along the dirt track. 'They've been instructed to bring two pounds of shot and a yard of match cord a piece.'

'Matchlock musketeers can't touch De Ryker's ships from land,' growled Amesbury. 'We need cannons. And there isn't time.'

'Where is the Duke of York?' asked Naseby. 'I'd hoped to see him at Landguard, fortifying the defences. Without a royal presence it's more difficult to rally the men.'

Amesbury rubbed the sweat from his brow. He'd wondered the same thing.

'It makes no difference,' he said, evading the question. 'De Ryker will sail right past our pathetic excuse for a fort,' he predicted, 'before we have time to arm ourselves. Our only hope is to get to Chatham docks before De Ryker sends in a fireship.'

'We'll never get the ships out of harbour in time,' said Naseby.

'We won't,' agreed Amesbury, 'but our fleet has better cannons than the Dutch. If we can rig the sails in time, we might make a stand.'

Chapter 99

'If Janus is who I think he is,' said Charlie, 'he wouldn't risk my brother on that ship. He couldn't.'

'Which means?'

'Which means my brother is somewhere else,' said Charlie. 'And we can still get the Eye back. Come on!'

They raced towards the triple gates as Janus's boat neared the edge of the docks. There was an iron lever to release the wheels to turn the gate. Charlie grabbed it and pumped. Slowly the gates began to close.

Janus's ship was gliding towards them, so close they could almost touch the towering sides.

'They're not closing fast enough!' said Lily, running to help Charlie at the lever. 'He's getting away.'

The escaping ship was at the gates now, fair wind driving her through.

Charlie pumped harder. Slowly the wheels gathered speed. The prow of the ship was level with the gates now, but the huge wooden barriers were closing painfully slowly.

They pushed and pulled the lever with all their might, arms burning with the strain. The wheels were turning faster now, the momentum building. Suddenly there was an enormous crack of wood on wood.

'It's working,' said Lily, pumping furiously. 'The gates have trapped him.'

But Charlie had stopped.

'No,' he said. 'He's got away.' Janus had expertly piloted the ship through the narrow gap, the gates scraping at the side. 'I doubt one in a thousand pilots could have done it,' added Charlie with begrudging admiration. He was taking off his coat.

'What are you doing?' asked Lily.

'There's netting hanging at the side of his ship,' said Charlie, judging his distance from Janus's escaping craft. 'I can still get aboard and stop him.'

The bow was only a few yards away from where they stood.

'Wait!' Lily grabbed his arm. 'If you die out there,' she said, 'I want you to know I think of you as more than an associate.'

He smiled at her. 'What do you think of me of?'

'Just don't die.' She bit her lip. 'The birth chart – the one you entered to open Thorne's box. It was yours, wasn't it? Is that why you think you can stop Janus? Because Thorne left you the Eye?'

But Charlie had already dived into the dark dock waters.

Climbing the side of the ship was harder than Charlie had anticipated. After his long swim out, his waterlogged clothes pulled him down, making every clambering movement twice as difficult. There was a swathe of thick rope netting overhanging one side, and he aimed for it.

Charlie gritted his teeth, shot out a hand and grasped the thick net. For a moment he held fast, breathing heavily. A sudden gust of wind blew out the sails of the ship. Charlie lost his hold and slipped. Then a wave crashed against the netting and Charlie twisted up into it. He had just enough time to realise he was caught fast when another wave crashed. It smashed his head against the side of the ship, wrapping the net tight around him.

As he slipped into unconsciousness, Charlie's thoughts scattered. The dark man was there again, a few steps behind him.

He is your fatal flaw, he heard a voice whisper. *You are his.*

Chapter 100

'Put more flammables down near the stern,' commanded De Ryker. 'That's where the main flame should catch. The serpentine gunpowder is very good,' added the admiral.

They'd finished laying barrels of pitch and brimstone across a honeycombed network below deck. Now the men were strewing brush and straw across the top. De Ryker took an armful of tinder and began laying it.

'Janus will be here soon,' said De Ryker, looking approvingly to the sails, painted with tar so flames would race up them. 'Ready to sail his fireship into the heart of England.'

He looked out at Landguard Fort, retreating in the distance.

'Who would have imagined,' said De Ryker, 'the English defences would be so poor? The very entrance to their country has hardly a cannon.'

'Their attempt at fire didn't come anywhere near our ships,' agreed Cornelius, 'but they rely on their tricky river to deter us.'

De Ryker smiled.

'I see a light!' shouted Cornelius. 'It's a sloop, rigged with the colours Janus promised.'

'He has the Eye.' De Ryker could hardly contain his excitement.

'Janus did well,' admitted Cornelius, 'navigating out of Deptford.'

'The English had no reason to suspect a boat leaving their waters,' said De Ryker dismissively. 'That was the simple part of the plan.'

He looked out to the small ship bobbing on the Thames.

'All my life,' said De Ryker, 'it's been near misses. We are the same in that, Janus and I. Not this time. This time we take England or die trying.'

De Ryker's eyes moved to the last barrel of serpentine gunpowder. Then he took out his pistols, emptied them one by one and filled them with the superior gunpowder.

Weapons loaded, he raised his spyglass again, and in the growing dawn light De Ryker suddenly noticed something amiss.

He strained his good eye to see. There was something tangled in a fishing net slung over the side of Janus's small ship. As he looked closer, he saw it was a man. Dead or at least unmoving.

Does Janus know he has someone tangled in his net?

'Get Janus aboard the *Lucifer*,' growled De Ryker, dropping his spyglass. 'Along with whatever's in his net.'

Chapter 101

Amesbury and Naseby had paused a few miles from Chatham and were looking out to sea. The general heard hoof beats behind him and turned.

A familiar horse was making fast towards him, the muscular body powering across the dockyard. Amesbury's mouth lifted.

It was the Duke of York.

'Amesbury!'

The Duke of York reined in his speeding horse moments from the mounted general. Behind him a small retinue of soldiers took the rear.

'I've been at the local towns,' he said, 'requisitioning cannons and shot. They're not built for taking down ships,' he added apologetically, 'but they're something.'

Amesbury nodded, though deep down he knew such measures would be nowhere near enough to deter a Dutch invasion.

'It's too late to defend the Thames mouth,' he said. 'De Ryker is coming straight for us with everything he's got. Have your men send arms upriver. Fortify the approach to London.'

The Duke of York nodded. 'Thorne's apprentice,' he said. 'You think he turned traitor?'

Amesbury nodded. 'I fear Janus has turned traitor and successfully found the Eye,' he said. 'We should have done more to keep him loyal. He is clever. Just like his father.'

Chapter 102

Charlie awoke to a mouth full of sea salt and an ache in his head. Strong fumes rolled over him. He could barely breathe, he realised. The reek of sulphur and pitch was choking.

Two eyes were looking down at him. They weren't kindly.

'Well, well,' said a man speaking in Dutch. 'Janus has brought an unexpected gift.'

Charlie tried to stand and realised his hands were bound in front of him. With difficulty he shuffled to a sitting position.

The man had a brace of pistols slung over his chest. He removed one and trained it on Charlie.

'Lucky I saw you there, knotted up in the netting,' continued the man. 'Who knows what you might have been planning?' He frowned.

Charlie was putting things together now. The man wore a ragged-looking wide-brimmed black hat ornamented with sun-bleached feathers. His face was sun-lined, and one of his eyes was almost opaque.

'You speak Dutch?' continued the man. 'You know me? I am Admiral De Ryker.'

Charlie tried to swallow, but his mouth was parched. 'I've heard of you,' he managed. 'I never wanted to meet you in person.'

De Ryker smiled at this. 'I'm not as bad as your English propaganda tells it,' he said. 'I only execute prisoners if absolutely necessary.' He smiled, revealing surprisingly white teeth. 'And not,' he said, 'if I decide they're useful.'

Charlie was silent.

'You came to retrieve the Eye,' decided De Ryker.

Charlie said nothing.

'There was a prophecy,' continued De Ryker. 'Saturn would eclipse Jupiter. London will fall.'

'No,' said Charlie, managing to pull himself a little more upright. 'That wasn't the prophecy. Saturn and Jupiter don't represent planets. Thorne meant them to symbolise the old gods. The purpose became muddled.'

'Oh?' De Ryker cocked his head, intrigued.

'Saturn is the God of Time,' said Charlie. 'Jupiter is the God of Luck. What Thorne meant was that if the Eye worked as he hoped, time would beat luck. The Eye would navigate the waves rather than hope and fortune.'

'Tell me,' said De Ryker, 'do you think Janus will be pleased to see you? Particularly when you look so much like one another.'

'I don't know,' said Charlie truthfully.

'What is your relation to him?' asked De Ryker.

'We grew up together,' said Charlie. 'The man you call Janus is my brother, Rowan.'

Chapter 103

'Janus was trying to keep his identity a secret from you,' guessed De Ryker.

'Yes,' said Charlie. 'Perhaps he thought I might have the power to change his mind.'

De Ryker smiled. 'Then I knew your father,' he said. 'Tobias Oakley. He was a seafaring man and an excellent shipbuilder.' De Ryker's eyes settled on Charlie's key. 'I hear,' he said, 'your father made all kinds of things for the English before his untimely death. But he made the mistake of coming to Holland to try and restore your worthless King to the throne.' De Ryker gave a brief smile. 'I tried to buy Tobias Oakley for the Dutch,' he continued. 'He had great talent. But his loyalty was misplaced. When I heard he'd been captured and killed by pirates, I felt truly sorry.'

De Ryker eyed Charlie. 'Janus is like a son to me,' said De Ryker. 'He is part of my crew. My men are his brothers. You hope he'll betray me? He won't.'

'His name is Rowan,' said Charlie.

'We'll see,' said De Ryker. He put his fingers to his lips and made a high whistle.

Charlie heard footsteps and then saw a familiar face.

'Rowan!' Charlie couldn't keep the relief from his voice.

His brother's face bore the same blank expression Charlie remembered from the orphan home. He felt hope drain away.

'Janus is of my mind,' said De Ryker. He clapped Rowan on the back. 'A son of my heart. I mean to protect him and make him great.'

Rowan was looking at Charlie. There was a long silence.

'How did you know it was me?' he asked finally.

'A few things,' said Charlie. 'When I discovered Thorne had an apprentice, it occurred to me he might have a son. Since Thorne preferred men to women, the only likely mother would be his legal wife. And my key.' Charlie touched it. 'Why should our mother leave it to the youngest? It made no sense unless we had different fathers. The key belonged to my father, not yours.'

Charlie reached into his coat and brought out a closed fist. He uncurled his fingers. Rowan's Neptune amulet glittered inside.

'This was the final part of the mystery,' he said. 'A coin to pay the dead.' He threw the dark-coloured coin, and Janus caught it. 'It was Thorne's,' said Charlie. 'You kept it since boyhood. I thought it copper, but it isn't. It's silver, stained red–brown with blood. Did you take it from the executioner's block?'

Rowan nodded. 'I grew up in your shadow,' he replied, 'fighting to be someone I wasn't. Now I've made my own path. De Ryker has shown me how to embrace my dark stars.'

Charlie didn't know what reaction he'd expected. But it wasn't this.

'Rowan,' Charlie said, shaking his head, 'don't do this. We can go back to England with the clock. I'll talk to the Oracle. There'll easily be enough money to free you.'

Rowan's face tightened. 'Always in your debt, little brother,' he said. 'I'm a child of Holland now. After we invade, I'll be a rich man in my own right.'

'And what of me and your fellow Englishmen?' asked Charlie.

'You'll join the Dutch cause or die,' said Rowan. His eyes flicked to the sea captain. 'Don't underestimate De Ryker,' he added. 'His methods can be very persuasive.'

De Ryker was staring at the two brothers, apparently enjoying the drama.

Charlie closed his eyes, trying to calm the tumult in his mind.

'It's not too late for you, Rowan,' he said, though he knew in his heart it was.

His brother's face flashed a sudden fury. 'Do you have any idea what it was like growing up the least-favoured child?' demanded Rowan. '*Charlie Oakley*,' he said, sneering the name, 'the golden boy. Tobias Oakley's son. My own mother left you the key and all the secrets, and me nothing. Me!' he added, striking his heart with his fist, 'the legitimate firstborn son.'

'She didn't.' Charlie was shaking his head.

'You must think me a fool,' said Rowan. 'How else did you open Thorne's box and retrieve the Eye? Our mother left you a star chart to open my birthright.'

'You think she told me how to open Thorne's box?' asked Charlie. 'She didn't. But she did love you,' added Charlie quietly. 'She left you something better than a key. Your birthday.'

For the first time Rowan seemed to flinch.

'I didn't know how to open the box,' said Charlie. 'So I entered a star chart I remembered from when we were boys. The planets from the hour of your birth, Rowan, unlocked the Eye.'

Something like dawning realisation figured on Rowan's face. The bitterness in his brow lifted slightly.

'Did it never seem strange to you,' continued Charlie, 'that your birthday made such an unusual chart? All Saturn?' Charlie saw something in Rowan's face and pressed his advantage. 'Our mother died before she could tell you the truth,' he said. 'You were left the greatest gift of all. The key to unlock Thorne's Eye. But she died, and you grew up thinking your birthday real.'

Rowan's face was twisted in confusion.

'Why must you always risk your life for mine?' he demanded. 'We're not even true brothers. You know that now.'

'We're not brothers because of blood,' said Charlie. 'We're brothers because of what we survived together.'

Rowan shook his head. 'Little Charlie Oakley,' he sighed, 'always doing good. This is the real world, Brother. Some battles can't be won.'

Rowan moved towards Charlie, grasped his younger brother's bound hands and helped him to his feet. He hugged Charlie tightly, then backed away, his brown eyes empty.

'I'm sorry, Charlie,' he said, 'but De Ryker is right. Your faith in me is misguided. It always has been.'

Rowan handed the clock to De Ryker, and the admiral bellowed a great laugh of triumph. He turned it wonderingly in his hands.

'One of us had to win,' said Rowan. 'Don't take it so hard, Charlie. It could have been you. Loyalty always was your downfall.'

De Ryker was examining the clock. 'Such treasure!' he gloated. 'After we take England, Holland will rule the waves. We shall own every colony in the New World.' His eyes settled on Janus. 'You shall be my first hand,' he said, 'and be well rewarded for your loyalty.' De Ryker turned to Janus. 'Your brother will face the same trial you did. Perhaps you'll see him again.'

Rowan had a distant look now. Like a practised general ready for battle.

'Time to ready your fireship, Janus,' De Ryker grinned, gesturing to below deck. 'After the *Lucifer* is deployed, you will have bought your freedom and will enter London at my side.'

'You've loaded the serpentine gunpowder?' Rowan asked.

'The finest black powder is in all our weaponry,' promised De Ryker. He patted the guns slung across his body. 'Your fuses will burn steady.'

As Rowan vanished from sight, De Ryker studied the dark sky.

'I don't like misplaced loyalty,' he said quietly, more to himself than Charlie. 'You are a distraction. A danger. Janus's allegiances cannot be risked. But you are fortunate,' De Ryker concluded. 'I will give you a seaman's execution in recognition of your brother's loyalty.'

Chapter 104

Charlie stood on the deck of the *Lucifer*, his hands bound helplessly in front of him. De Ryker was pointing a pistol steadily at Charlie's chest, Thorne's Eye gripped tightly in his other hand.

'It's just us here,' said De Ryker conversationally. 'Janus is below deck. A small crew will join him shortly, but for the moment it's just you, me and this pistol.'

For a moment Charlie thought he meant to kill him on the spot. Then the old admiral paused.

'A living son of Tobias Oakley,' he said slowly. 'What do you know of your father?'

Charlie hesitated. 'Nothing,' he admitted. 'I don't remember him.'

'Your father was a great seafarer,' said De Ryker. 'He was killed by a brutal pirate. A man called the Phoenix.' He paused, watching for a reaction. 'Still thinking of your brother?' guessed De Ryker. 'He has no loyalty to you.'

He sounded almost sorry.

'So people keep telling me.'

Charlie assessed the distance between him and De Ryker. He thought them to be ten feet apart. The longitude clock was still clutched protectively in the admiral's hand.

'But what you should know,' continued Charlie, 'is my brother has no loyalty to you either.'

De Ryker smiled. 'Janus couldn't betray me even if he wanted to.'

'My guess,' continued Charlie, 'is Rowan means to steal your fireship.'

'I have cannons trained on every fireship he pilots,' said De Ryker. 'Janus knows I don't trust him.'

'I imagine,' continued Charlie, 'Rowan suggested some bold new measure to make the *Lucifer* more flammable. Perhaps serpentine gunpowder? Rowan's always been gifted at sourcing fake black powder.'

De Ryker called to mind how Janus had sourced the gunpowder.

'It was no false gunpowder,' he growled. 'I saw it flame.'

Taking advantage of the admiral's uncertainty, Charlie stepped forward.

'A little slight of hand,' said Charlie. 'A small sample of good gunpowder hidden in a pocket is an old trick. I doubt you would have fallen for it had you not trusted Rowan.'

'No man would be so foolish,' said De Ryker. But he sounded less sure. He gripped his gun more tightly, training it on his captive.

Charlie moved closer. 'My brother would,' he said, stepping slowly as he spoke. 'Believe me. I've spent my whole life trying to talk Rowan out of foolish schemes. Likely he targeted you for the very reason no one else would dare. I expect he was gauging the best time to disarm you and escape with a good ship from the start.'

Charlie hesitated. He'd halved the distance between them now. Only a few steps remained.

'And if your gunpowder isn't real,' said Charlie, 'your pistol is useless.'

At De Ryker's shocked expression, Charlie pounced. With his wrists bound in front of him, his movements were restricted. But he managed to close the last few feet to the admiral.

Instinctively the admiral fired his gun. The mechanism clicked harmlessly against the false gunpowder. Charlie moved in and managed to snatch the Eye with his bound hands.

De Ryker threw his whole weight forward and sent Charlie crashing to the deck. He grabbed Charlie's bound wrists and reached for his knife. Charlie twisted, but the admiral was too strong. De Ryker delivered a blow to the side of his head that left his ears ringing and snatched at the Eye.

The ship tilted slightly and Charlie took advantage of the movement, flinging his body weight sideways. He rolled free and struggled to his feet, racing with his bound hands in front to the edge of the *Lucifer*. But De Ryker was an experienced sailor, adjusting easily for the swell and springing up to pursue Charlie.

Charlie turned. Then he held Thorne's clock over the side of the ship, above the Thames waters.

De Ryker stopped dead, his eyes fixed on the longitude clock.

'Come any closer,' Charlie threatened, 'and I'll drop the Eye.'

'Wait,' said De Ryker. 'I can help you. At sea you hear stories,' he continued. 'Don't you want to know about your father?'

Charlie watched De Ryker carefully for signs of a trick.

'Some say Tobias Oakley could never have been bested at sea and escaped in disguise,' said De Ryker softly. 'You look a lot like him. If he still lives, we might find him together.'

Charlie said nothing. He was thinking of Rowan, somewhere below deck.

'If you joined me,' said De Ryker, 'you could take Janus's place. A great seafarer such as Tobias Oakley. His blood is in your veins.'

De Ryker was moving forward now. Charlie shook his head.

'Keep back,' he said. 'I would never betray Rowan.'

De Ryker smiled. 'Perhaps I believe you,' he said, 'yet I don't believe the son of such a sailor could destroy the longitude clock.'

He lunged, and in his surprise Charlie moved his hands forward to defend himself. De Ryker was on him in moments, his fingers closing on the clock.

Charlie launched his hands upwards. Thorne's Eye went sailing towards the edge of the ship. De Ryker leapt forward to catch it, but Charlie lowered his head and charged. The two men went sprawling on the deck.

Behind them the Eye dropped out of sight over the side of the *Lucifer*.

De Ryker's mouth dropped open in horror.

'The Eye,' he whispered. 'No!'

The admiral raced to where the clock had fallen. But the Thames showed only an expanding pool of ripples. The Eye had sunk out of sight, down to the muddy depths.

'No!' De Ryker's face was tight with rage. He turned to Charlie, bound and lying prone on the deck of the ship.

'You have cost me the world,' he hissed, advancing on his captive with his knife drawn. 'And you shall suffer accordingly.'

Chapter 105

Charlie saw De Ryker close in, knife held aloft. But the blow to his body never came.

From the side of his vision he saw a dark shape tackle De Ryker. The captain was thrown from view. Charlie got to his feet with difficulty. The admiral was grappling another man, both fighting brutally.

De Ryker's knife dropped to the ground only a few feet away from Charlie. The blade was bloody. Charlie made for it on all fours and grasped the handle in both hands.

He glanced at the fighting men. They had shifted to the side of the ship, raining blows on one another.

With difficulty Charlie turned the knife, resting the handle on the deck, angling the sharp point upwards to cut his ropes.

There was a guttural cry. Charlie's eyes flicked up in time to see a man fall overboard.

The other man leaned on the prow, blood pumping from his side.

It was Rowan.

As Charlie cut the last of his ropes, he saw his brother collapse in a wide pool of his own blood.

Charlie raced to his side. Rowan had a jagged knife wound between his ribs. His breathing was fast and ragged. Charlie fell to his knees, tore away part of his shirt and bunched the wad of fabric to stem the blood. But Rowan shook his head.

'It's too late for me,' he managed. He coughed, and blood appeared in his mouth.

'No,' said Charlie. 'I can get you back to London. Find a surgeon.'

'You never did know when to give up, little brother.'

'You saved me,' said Charlie. 'I was right about you.'

Rowan gave the faintest of smiles. 'After you told me my birthday was false, I realised my stars might not be so dark after all.'

'You were to steal the *Lucifer*,' said Charlie, eyeing the huge deck where his brother lay. 'You could have escaped, left me to my fate.'

Rowan nodded. 'She's a good, fast ship,' he said wistfully. 'I've been working on getting her for months.' He frowned. 'Was it true what you said? My father left me my birthday so I might find the Eye?'

Charlie nodded.

Rowan considered this. 'All this time I thought my father hadn't trusted me enough,' he said. 'I thought he died without telling me where the Eye was hidden. I didn't realise he'd left me the means all along. My birthday.'

Rowan reached into his pocket and took out the silver coin with Neptune on one side, St Peter on the reverse.

'I saw him die,' he said. 'Thorne. My father. Mother wanted me to stay away, but I slipped out. He put this in his mouth at the end,' Rowan continued, 'so his soul would go to Roman gods.' He was turning it thoughtfully. 'I should have returned the coin to the Thames, but I could never forgive him for betraying me.' He pushed the coin into Charlie's hand. 'My father was not a good man,' he said. 'You can decide his fate.' His brown eyes looked up at Charlie. 'I hated you when you were born,' he admitted. 'I thought our mother loved you best.'

'She loved you too,' said Charlie.

'I know,' said Rowan. He patted Charlie on the shoulder. 'By the time you were two you were right enough. I never told you that. Then our mother died . . .'

Charlie remembered Rowan's tiny pale face and hooded eyes. The face of a child who'd seen their mother murdered.

Rowan's eyes were clouding over now. He was looking at Charlie. 'Bess,' he said. 'Bess in Covent Garden.'

Charlie searched his memory for Rowan's many girls and settled on one with dark hair who Rowan had seemed particularly fond of.

'The actress?' said Charlie.

Rowan nodded. 'She has a boy . . . I think . . . my son,' he managed. Rowan was silent, his eyes far away. He managed to swallow. 'Take the *Lucifer*,' he said. 'Sail back to London. Pine resin and pitch sell for a pretty penny. There'll be enough money to see Bess and the boy are well cared for.'

'I can't sail,' said Charlie.

'I already set the sails for you,' said Rowan. 'Whilst you were on deck with De Ryker. The wind blows west. If you pull anchor, she should drift that way. Hail some sailors at Greenwich and have them crew you back. They'll work for pennies.'

The effort of speaking had exhausted him now. Rowan sunk back, his breath coming in short gasps. Then his eyes stilled and his lips stopped moving.

Charlie looked at his face for a long time. He closed his brother's eyes and stood staring out into the Thames. Then he drew his hand back and launched Thorne's silver coin into the river depths.

Chapter 106

A crew of shouting Dutch sailors pulled De Ryker from the water. He emerged on the deck of the *Eendracht* dripping wet, a determined glint in his eye.

'Janus is dead,' he said. 'The Eye is gone. Pass me the spyglass.'

A terrified sailor handed the spyglass to his captain. De Ryker moved to the prow of the massive man-of-war, spyglass glued to his good eye. He saw the *Lucifer*, now far on the horizon, the wind blowing her west with Charlie Oakley still on board. Angrily he swung the spyglass.

'We approach Chatham,' he observed.

His quartermaster, Cornelius, moved forward, the only man brave enough to approach the half-drowned admiral.

'We've made it this far without the Eye,' ventured Cornelius, 'and Chatham seems unmanned. Perhaps something can be salvaged from the situation.'

De Ryker made no answer, surveying the scene, picking out ships he recognised. The *Royal Charles*, the *Loyal London*, the *Royal Oak*. They were all here. England's greatest ships. But there was something strange about them.

The admiral gripped the spyglass tighter, trying to work out what was amiss. Then he realised. The masts were down. England's greatest ships weren't set to sail.

King Charles has mothballed his navy.

De Ryker's mouth dropped open in astonishment. England had nothing with which to defend her waters. It was all shored up at Chatham. The country must be even more destitute than he'd imagined.

De Ryker's mind whirled over this incredible advantage, deciding what terms he would negotiate, which colonies Holland would demand.

Then a terrible juddering sound echoed out from under his feet. He knew instantly what it meant.

'Aground!' shouted a terrified Cornelius. 'We've run aground!'

De Ryker roared with frustration. He could see England's navy, so very close, so undefended. And here they were, beached on a mudbank, with King Charles's greatest ships less than a hundred yards away.

De Ryker knew reinforcements must be on the way. Amesbury was clever and would be heading for Chatham. If the general arrived to find the Dutch flagship beached in Chatham docks, he'd use the docked ships to blow them out of the water.

'Can we fire on the English?' suggested Cornelius. 'Destroy their cannons?'

De Ryker shook his head. 'We can't turn our ship,' he said. 'We're sitting ducks.'

'The tide is rising,' said Cornelius. 'We'll be free in under an hour.'

De Ryker's mind was whirring. If Amesbury caught them here, they were dead men. But an hour . . . De Ryker scanned the tides.

'It could be enough time,' he decided, 'to make our escape.'

'You mean us to retreat?' asked the shocked Cornelius.

'Charlie Oakley destroyed the Eye,' said De Ryker. 'We have no means to navigate these waters.' He looked across the wide Thames. She seemed so calm, so inviting.

'A ribbon of water leading straight to London,' said De Ryker with a sigh.

His quartermaster knew better than to answer.

De Ryker's attention was now fixed on Chatham docks, thick with expensive ships.

'They make better men-of-war than us,' he observed. 'England has deeper ports to make low hulls. Good for stability. See all the guns?'

He pointed to the nearest, sitting low in the water with the weight of her cannons.

'The *Royal Charles*,' he said, eyeing England's magnificent flagship. 'She chased us back to Holland last time we engaged. They've repaired her scars.'

The deck gave a sudden lurch. The tide was rising faster than they'd predicted. It swirled around the banked ship and she began righting.

An idea occurred to De Ryker.

'How many grappling hooks do we have?' he asked.

Cornelius looked surprised. 'Perhaps twenty,' he estimated.

'Long ones? Enough to tow a man-of-war?'

'It's possible,' said the quartermaster. 'We keep enough to pull a second rate, in case one of our ships becomes unseaworthy in combat.'

De Ryker turned his face to the sun. The breeze was picking up.

'There's a good wind,' he said. 'As soon as we lift from this mud-bank, throw the grapples at that ship.' He pointed.

'You want to take England's flagship?' confirmed Cornelius.

'The *Royal Charles*,' stated De Ryker. 'We'll carry her from England's own waters and serve King Charles a humiliation he won't forget.'

Chapter 107

Amesbury rounded the curve in the river. The old general spurred his steed, panting. The clustered masts of Chatham dockyard were ahead, and Amesbury saw with surprise he was not too late.

De Ryker's ship had not yet reached the dockyards. The remaining force of England's beleaguered navy floated peaceably. Amesbury could hardly believe it.

Then he saw De Ryker's ship in the far distance. He held the spyglass closer against his eye, his heart lifting.

The *Eendracht* was sailing away.

Then Amesbury saw what she was sailing with. De Ryker had captured England's flagship. The King's magnificent *Royal Charles* was being towed back to Holland.

Amesbury's mind flashed with variations on how to present this mortification to the King. He heard the faint sound of boisterous singing drift towards the dockyard and guessed De Ryker's men had struck up a mocking chorus as they passed the English towns and villages along the Thames.

Naseby's horse drew level with Amesbury's.

'De Ryker withdraws,' he said, sounding amazed. 'Why now?'

Amesbury dropped his spyglass and saw a great wash of mud floating in the water a little way from the dockyard.

'Perhaps,' he decided, 'De Ryker didn't have the means of navigation I feared. It seems as though his attempt on the Thames was made of bravado and some good fortune. But it ran out at Chatham.'

'They were here?' said Naseby, taking the spyglass. 'Beached?'

'From the height of the water, the rising tide only just saved them,' said Amesbury regretfully. 'If we'd been here an hour earlier, they would have been helpless.'

'De Ryker must have tried his luck after all,' said Naseby. 'You have to admire the bravery of the Dutch,' he added begrudgingly.

'I'm of the same mind,' agreed Amesbury. 'Though it doesn't seem a strategy a man of De Ryker's experience would employ.'

They both watched as the pride of England's navy disappeared slowly downriver, the catcalls and hoots of De Ryker's men drifting away on the breeze.

'A good day for England,' decided Naseby. 'They'll have bonfires in London when we announce the foiled attack.'

'Better they save their wood for the coming winter,' said Amesbury. 'De Ryker knows our weakness. He'll be back to take England.'

Chapter 108

King Charles had been silent for a long time.

The huge throne room seemed to loom around them. Amesbury wondered for a moment if the monarch had actually heard him.

'I returned from Holland on the *Royal Charles*,' said the King finally. 'To reclaim England.'

'I remember,' said Amesbury.

'We laughed at the doubters. Those who said England would stay a republic.' He let out a long sigh. 'Now she's with De Ryker. It's a humiliation.'

Amesbury left a tactful silence before speaking.

'The loss of a first rate from our own waters is mortifying,' he agreed, 'but more disturbing is De Ryker now knows the extent of our weakness. He'll be back to invade,' he said. 'Soon.'

Charles hardly seemed to hear him. There was a long pause, then he spoke.

'She's gone, Amesbury,' said the King, raising his brown eyes sadly.

C.S. Quinn

It took Amesbury a moment to realise Charles was talking about Frances Stewart rather than his first-rate ship.

'She wants to marry Buckingham.' Charles was fiddling with one of the heavy rings on his fingers. 'Queen Catherine says I should give them my blessing.'

Amesbury was temporarily struck dumb. He was trying and failing to understand how a thirty-six-year-old man could be infatuated with a fifteen-year-old girl when his country was about to fall.

'I would have married her,' concluded Charles morosely.

'Such talk is foolish,' tutted Amesbury. 'Your Majesty, for a king to marry his lady-in-waiting – a man might as well take a shit in his hat and clap it on his head.'

This raised a ghost of a smile from the King.

'Your Majesty,' said Amesbury, a thought occurring to him. 'Frances's beauty is her youth. Have her painted. Then you might always keep a piece of her, just as you love her now. Let Buckingham have the hard reality of a wife.'

For the first time in weeks, Charles seemed to lighten a little.

'Yes,' he said, sitting up a little. 'Yes, that is a very good idea. The Royal Mint is looking for an image for our coins. I was thinking Britannia in her armour would very well represent the English spirit. Frances will model for it.'

'A Roman emblem?' said Amesbury.

'Such things are very fashionable,' said Charles. 'We'll give her a helmet like Athena, and she can hold Neptune's trident to show we rule the waves.'

'Very good,' said Amesbury. 'Frances as Britannia will be on every silver coin in the land.'

'Buckingham may marry her,' said Charles, 'but every time he spends his money he'll see his wife and I. Two sides of the same coin.'

There was a glint of malice in his eyes. 'Perhaps Frances's beauty will grace English coins long after my reign is over,' Charles added.

The thought seemed to please him. Then his face darkened.

'My children,' he said, 'I swore they would have a safe and comfortable home, never fleeing to safety, never fearing for anything.' The King turned to Amesbury. 'So now,' Charles decided, 'we must address matters of war.'

Chapter 109

The Bucket of Blood tavern was hosting a puppet show. Above its large barrels, homespun marionettes caroused and waved wands. Below, the puppeteers squeaked songs of foolish astrologers and false eclipses. A saucepan to symbolise the moon had been covered in red cloth.

Charlie watched as the marionettes bounded away from it, wooden arms waving in terror. The assembled drinkers cheered and banged their tankards.

'You decided to stay then?' said Charlie to Lily. 'No sea voyages?'

She smiled into her tankard of foaming ale. 'For now. London hasn't yet lost all her charms.'

She gave Charlie a careful glance, then looked away again. He smiled to himself. Then he noticed a familiar face. Bitey had entered the tavern. Charlie called for the tap boy and gestured he should bring another pint of beer.

When it arrived, he handed it to Bitey. The old poacher toasted him enthusiastically and took a long sip.

'The Eye was real then?' asked Bitey, wiping foam from his beard. 'Everyone is saying you found it and it might have guided ships in longitude.'

'Might have,' agreed Charlie. 'We'll never know. It's at the bottom of the Thames.'

'A pity,' said Bitey.

Charlie thought for a moment, choosing his words carefully. 'Thorne wanted the clock for a better time,' said Charlie. 'I don't think nineteen years was long enough.'

He was remembering the slave brig, where he and Lily had been held. The sad chains to hold people to be sold as cattle.

'Perhaps not,' said Bitey. He turned his gaze to the cavorting puppets. 'Someone else might invent something just as clever one day.'

A meaty bellow of joy echoed around the pub. Charlie glanced at the puppet show. A wooden ship bearing a satanic effigy of De Ryker popped up from behind the beer barrels. Another, waving an English flag, was chasing it away.

'We've seen off the Dutch right enough,' said Bitey, raising his tankard in toast. 'You can smell the bonfires all over London.'

Charlie nodded. The air was thick with woodsmoke. After plague and fire, Londoners were desperate for something to celebrate, though rumour was fast spreading that their victory was more hollow than had been reported.

'The Dutch will be back,' said Charlie. 'They've seen how weak we are and have taken a prize ship.'

'The *Royal Charles* should satisfy De Ryker for a time at least,' suggested Bitey.

'I don't think so,' said Charlie. He was remembering De Ryker's sun-worn face, the determination etched in his old features. 'Another man perhaps. But I think it will only make De Ryker more hell-bent on taking London.'

'He'll have to find a way to navigate the Thames,' said Bitey, 'and it sounds as if that one chance was lost to him.' He chinked Charlie's tankard. 'Shame you came away with nothing valuable.'

'I wouldn't say that,' said Charlie, looking at Lily.

She was entranced by the puppet show, following the weaving and bobbing.

A woman with a tray of pies had entered the pub, and Charlie signalled her over. He bought three meat pies and handed one to Bitey and one to Lily. She took the food absent-mindedly and beamed him a smile.

'Perhaps you're right,' said Bitey, taking a grateful chomp with his wooden teeth. 'Some victories are less obvious than others. And it seems to me,' added Bitey carefully, 'there's more to know about that key of yours.' He nodded to the double-sided key around Charlie's neck.

'De Ryker claimed he knew my father,' agreed Charlie thoughtfully.

'What do you make of that?' asked Bitey.

'I don't know,' admitted Charlie. 'Perhaps his secrets are best buried with him.'

'Perhaps,' agreed Bitey good-naturedly. 'Bit of quiet might do you good in any case.'

Charlie drained his beer. 'Maybe,' he said, looking at Lily, 'but I've a feeling London won't stay quiet for long.'

Truth is stranger than fiction.
One of the below events is fictional.
Can you guess which?

1. The Dutch tried to invade England in 1666, getting as far as Chatham, where they stole the *Royal Charles*, England's flagship man-of-war.
2. Barbara Castlemaine engaged in seductive warfare on Frances Stewart, including a theatrical same-sex wedding.
3. London streets were still smoking several months after the Great Fire.
4. Longitude experiments included using an injured dog and sympathetic magic to tell the time.
5. An image of Frances Stewart as Britannia now adorns the English fifty-pence piece.

Answer correctly to unlock a free secret history of *Dark Stars*. You'll discover more about Barbara Castlemaine's shocking sexual proclivities and the truth about Frances Stewart's marriage and the Dutch attack on London. Go to www.thethieftaker.com/darkstars

About the Author

C.S. Quinn is the bestselling author of *The Thief Taker* and *Fire Catcher*. Prior to writing fiction she was a travel and lifestyle journalist for *The Times*, the *Guardian* and the *Mirror*, alongside many magazines.

In her early academic career, Quinn's background in historical research won prestigious postgraduate funding from the British Arts Council. Quinn pooled these resources, combining historical research with first-hand experiences in far-flung places to create Charlie Tuesday's London.